The Imati

C T Hillin

This is a work of fiction. Names, characters, places and incidents are the product of the author's imagination or are used fictitiously.

Benetone Hillin Entertainment
1323 15th Street
Santa Monica, Ca 90404

To my mother, Luana Hillin
Without her, this would not be possible

Acknowledgements

SPECIAL THANKS TO Matt Heller for finding both me and this manuscript, my manager Brett Etre for always believing this book would be a reality, my brother Daemon Hillin for his unwavering support, Rachvin Narula, Kulthep Narula, Karen Moreland and her TVHS creative writing students, Ronnie Goyal, Michael Cendejas, Michelle Wolfson, Sarah Kolb-Williams, Karen Jean Olds, Drew Rissman, Mina Joukar, Joshua Wells, and Carrie Vasios.

And of course, a million thanks to my mother, Luana, who for years was the best editor, sounding board and storyline supervisor any author could ask for.

The Book of Alastrina Byrne

Do not stand at my grave and weep,
I am not there; I do not sleep.
I am a thousand winds that blow,
I am the diamond glints on snow,
I am the sun on ripened grain,
I am the gentle autumn rain.
When you awaken in the morning's hush
I am the swift uplifting rush
Of quiet birds in circling flight.
I am the soft starlight at night.
Do not stand at my grave and cry,
I am not there; I did not die.

—Mary Frye

Los Angeles, California – April – Present Day

Awake

I'M NOT SURE what tipped me off first—the blaring smoke alarm above my bedroom door, or the intense smell of campfire seeping through my walls—but whichever it was, I opened my eyes with the innate feeling that something was definitely wrong.

The deep-noted *beep—beep—beep* echoed around the room, so I did what any normal person would do: I ripped the damn smoke detector from the wall. *That's better*, I thought. *Me: one; irritating noise: zero.*

Only, with the commotion of the alarm it had momentarily slipped my mind that I had a much bigger problem on my hands, exemplified by the grayish-white smoke snaking its way through the crack between my doorway and the wooden floorboards. Sirens blared from a few blocks away. It occurred to me, then, that my house was on fire.

I ran to my bedroom door and reached for the doorknob, but it immediately singed my palm. "Ahh," I yelled as I snapped my hand backward. *Should have seen that coming. Not that it matters; it'll heal quickly.*

I glanced around the room, unsure of the best way to flee from the scene. I was trying not to panic. Fire can't kill me—I know that from experience—but it still hurts like hell.

Suddenly, my bedroom door burst open and a large man dressed in bright orange, his face covered by an alien-looking mask, stood in front of me, silhouetted by the blazing flames behind him. He was quite the picture of heroism.

He rushed toward me, trying to pull me from what he believed was my inevitable doom. He was trying to save my life, but I pushed him off of me, screaming, "Wait—no! Let me go!" The force of my shove sent him tumbling backward; I was stronger than him, after all.

Instead of fleeing to safety as the fire raged in the rest of the house, I ran to my closet. People always ask themselves what they would save, if they could only save one thing from a burning building. I already knew my answer. It's something I've had for hundreds of years, and it's the only connection to my real life. It's priceless.

I lifted up a floorboard in the back of my closet and grabbed the tiny metal box hidden beneath it. I quickly stuffed it in a small purple backpack. Then I saw Cat just sitting there, sleeping on my towels. *Okay, I guess I'd save two things,* I thought. I grabbed the orange and white cat that had started out a stray but had somehow wriggled into my life, wrapped him in a towel, and headed for the now-broken door. *Best to just make a run for it.*

I burst out of my one-story LA home, my clothes singed, burns on my arms and legs. Cat immediately jumped out my arms, fearing for his own life, and scampered off. The night air felt cold compared to the dark inferno I had just been immersed in. Paramedics were already standing by. *Oh, crap,* I thought to myself. *How will I explain the already-healing burns to the hospital doctors? "Hi, I'm an Imati" won't exactly fly as an excuse . . .*

They were all rushing toward me, the paramedics; they wanted to help, they wanted to make sure I didn't pass out and die on them . . . but little did they know, I've been dead before.

Los Angeles, California – April – Present Day

The Escape

THE THING ABOUT interrogations is that they're always the same. They have been for thousands of years. I myself have been through one or two. The main take-away is: *less* is always more.

I was sitting in a grey and black room staring at the one-way mirror. You've got to love the one-way mirror—as if I don't know that standing on the other side are a bunch of cops in suits listening in. Unfortunately for me, police stations are not a good place for my kind: too many questions, with all the wrong answers.

My mirror trance was broken when a woman, about thirty-five, slowly walked in wearing a grey suit, her hair tied up in a bun. She had black-rimmed glasses and carried a thin file folder. She sat down calmly and I stared back at her. Time to play the I'm-only-seventeen-and-totally-innocent card.

Of course, I *am* innocent; *I* didn't light my house on fire. But then again, I'm not exactly seventeen.

"Mackenzie Jones, correct?" The suit-lady asked me.

"Yes, that's correct." *As in, that's alias number five hundred and sixty in a long list of fake lives, but who's counting?*

"Hello, Mackenzie. I am Dr. Paula Anderson. Do you know what I do?" She was speaking to me like I was a child.

"No," I said, and I really didn't. I'd already been questioned a dozen times that night, and I assumed she was just another person eager to take my statement.

"I'm a board-certified psychologist. I work for the Los Angeles Police Department as a profiler. They sent me in to help you." She cracked open the file she'd walked in with.

Oh no. This is not good.

"Okay." I mean, what else do you say when someone says they're about to dissect your life—a life that is, by any definition, totally made up?

"Mackenzie, have you ever had thoughts of ending your life?"

"What?" I asked, surprised by the question. It was a curveball, for sure.

She rephrased the inquiry off my surprised reaction. "Do you ever suffer from depression, insomnia, or an inability to connect to those around you?"

Well, suit-lady, yes, yes, and yes . . . but that's because I'm immortal and torn between, you know, trying to stay alive and coping with the fact that I won't die. It's a mixed bag of emotions, to say the least.

I decided the safest bet was to just play dumb. "Please—I don't understand what's going on. I did nothing wrong. I mean, aren't *I* the victim here? I just want to go home."

"We know, Mackenzie, but unfortunately, we can't release you right now. Your house was burned down, and when the rescue team came in, you pushed them away. Do you think this might have been an attempt to end your own life?"

"Oh my God, no. I pushed them away to save Cat," I explained. *That ought to clear things up.*

Suit-lady looked confused. "Cat? Is that your friend, or . . . your roommate, possibly?"

"No," I said. "It's my cat." *Duh.*

"You stayed in a burning house, risking your life . . . to save a cat?" she said dubiously.

"Yes." *What's so hard to believe?* Again, it's not like I was going to die.

"Mackenzie, I checked into your file, and it's pretty thin. You have transcripts from Beverly Hills High School for this year, and a high school in Las Vegas, but there's no mention of your parents. Where are your parents, Mackenzie?"

These questions were getting out of hand. Like I said, law enforcement is the worst. It used to be simpler, back when there were no computers or social security numbers. In the old days, all it took to make a new identity was, "Hi, I'm Jane Doe, nice to meet you," and boom: mission accomplished. In fact, the last time I was in California, I used a .45 caliber and some moonshine to get around. But not anymore—now there are records, paperwork, and DMVs, and people always wanted to know where my parents were. *I've been Mackenzie Jones, simple high school student, for nine months now, and Mackenzie's parents are dead, just like mine. How's that for an answer, suit-lady?*

"My parents are dead," I said curtly. *I'm thinking an escape is definitely going to be necessary, which is a bummer, because Mackenzie could have lasted five years—but now she'll have "arson" and "suicidal" on her record, which is not something I need.*

"Mackenzie, you've been through a traumatic event tonight, but you have to understand, the fire department has determined there was ample evidence of arson. Do you know what that means?"

"That someone tried to kill me," I muttered. Then, suit-lady's words began to sink in, and I realized: *Someone tried to kill me.* Not exactly happy news.

"Well, I wouldn't go that far. Perhaps the culprit is closer to home. Perhaps you can think of a reason why *you* might try to hurt yourself?" *Ugh—psychobabble.*

There was a faint knock on the door. *Thank God,* I thought, as a new man entered. He was wearing a black suit. He whispered in suit-lady's ear and she got up to leave. "I'll be back, Mackenzie. This is Special Agent Winchester, and he's going to ask you a few more questions."

Special Agent Winchester sat down. He closed the file in front of him without looking at it and slid it to his left. Apparently, he didn't believe in psychology.

Agent Winchester motioned to the one-way mirror, signaling for the concealed officers to stop recording. *That's never a good sign.*

"Hello, Alastrina." Those two simple words instantly sent shock waves through my body. "It is Alastrina, right? Alastrina Byrne?" He continued, "I'll have to admit, I like Mackenzie a lot better, as far as names go." His cocky grin reached across his entire face as he spoke. Of course, he had every reason to be cocky; he knew my real name.

"Well, that's not fair," I began, trying to stay calm when all I really wanted to do was shove his face into the table. "You know my real name, but I don't know yours."

"*Lux et Veritas*—ring a bell?" He said it like it should, but it didn't.

"Um, no . . ." I said with well-placed sass. "What is that, like, your little secret society sent here to kill me by setting my house on fire?" The look on his face said *jackpot,* so I continued. "Well, news flash, buddy: fire won't kill me."

"I wasn't sure you were one of them, so I informed my colleagues to smoke you out—literally." He let out a slight chuckle. I usually find people laughing at their own jokes rather charming, but when Agent Winchester did it, it was just plain irritating. He continued, "Then, I let the LAPD do a little digging into a suspicious background, and now here you are, served up on a silver platter."

"What do you think you're going to do?" I asked. "Chop off my head right here in the police station? I don't think so." Obviously, this man was an assassin. I'm definitely way off the reservation, so I was more concerned how he found me than what he was going to do to me. This night was not going well, to say the least.

"Not at all, Alastrina," he began, and then he leaned in very close to my face and dropped his voice to a whisper. "I'll take you into custody, transport you to another station—you know how these places are, always shuffling people around—you'll sadly go missing, and *then* I'm going to chop off that pretty little blonde head of yours."

"Gee, sounds fun, can't wait to see how it plays out," I said. This guy was really starting to bug me. *First he burns down my house, almost killing Cat—my cat—and now he's trying to kidnap me? Well, I'm not going to take this sitting down, that's for sure.*

At that moment, Dr. Anderson walked back in the room. *Maybe I can use her to help me*, I thought. But she said, "Mackenzie, you're being transferred to a juvenile facility. You'll spend twenty-four hours on suicide watch, and then we'll reevaluate your mental capacity. Understand?" Agent Winchester immediately shot off a sinister-looking grin.

Then, Dr. Anderson added, "Special Agent Winchester will be your police escort."

Well, isn't that just icing on my crap-cake.

"Here are your belongings," she said as she handed me the purple backpack I'd come in with.

"What about my cat?" I asked.

"I'm sorry, we didn't find him."

Poor Cat. Suddenly a stray again, just like me. Kind of makes me wish I'd tried a little harder on his name.

I walked out with Agent Winchester, who was forcefully holding me by the arm as he led me through a deserted parking lot toward a black town car. *This doesn't seem right*, I thought. There were no other cops, no paperwork to check me out; something was definitely wrong, and I had a sneaking suspicion Agent

Winchester had someone on the inside. This was it, I decided. *Now or never. It's time to run.*

As soon as we reached the car, Agent Winchester revealed a pair of shiny, restrictive handcuffs. As soon as he placed the first metal ring around my wrist, I yanked my right arm backward and elbowed him straight in the nose. I turned around quickly and stuck a right roundhouse kick into his left shin. His knee buckled and he fell to the ground.

Then, he grabbed a small knife, hidden in his right ankle holster, and took a swipe at my torso. I jumped back, dodging the blade. *I gotta get out of here.* He threw the knife down, broke open his rear car window, and grabbed a long sword from the backseat. *Wow, really—a sword in the backseat? I hate assassins.*

Since we were in the back parking lot no one was around: just me, the crazy assassin, and the long blade he meant to chop off my head with. He swung; I ducked and tackled him to the ground, knocking the sword from his hands. It made a *pinging* noise as it slid across the pavement.

I managed to pin Agent Winchester down and grab his car keys from his left pants pocket. People always keep their keys in their left pocket.

"How did you find me?" I screamed at him.

He smiled, mocking my question. I put my right hand around his throat. "How did you find me?" I asked again.

He laughed and choked out, "It was an accident. You were in the wrong place at the wrong time, and I read you . . . but you were blank. Kind of tipped me off." I realized suddenly that Agent Winchester wasn't just any assassin—he was a Seeker.

"You're lucky I don't kill people anymore," I said, and then slammed his head into the pavement so he conked out. I grabbed my pack, which had fallen to the ground, jumped in the town car, and sped away. A cell phone was sitting inside his center console. *Finally, some good luck.*

I dialed as fast as I could to reach the one person who could help me. *Come on . . . pick up. Pick up!*

"Hello," a voice said on the other line.

"Delilah, it's me, Alastrina. I need your help."

"Ally, what's wrong? Where are you?"

"Oh, you know, making a high-speed getaway from a police station where a Seeker tried to kill me . . . the usual."

"What?" she yelped back.

"Look, I'm making a quick stop, but then I need you to meet me at the storage yard so I can grab some gear, and Delilah—I have no idea why you sent me to Los Angeles, but that plan backfired, so I *really, really* need to find a new city, ASAP."

"Okay, okay," she said, sounding a little stressed. "I'm about thirty minutes from the storage yard, I'll meet you there. And Ally . . ." She paused. "I swear, I didn't see this coming."

"And here I thought you saw *everything*, Delilah," I laughed. "Don't beat yourself up about it. I've been through worse."

Burbank, California – April – Present Day

Road to Belfast

I PULLED UP to Pete's Storage Yard in the stolen black town car. By this time, Cat—who I'd picked up from my ash-filled yard—was safely riding in my passenger seat, and it was almost two a.m. Delilah was waiting for me by the front gate. She was wearing jeans, tennis shoes, and a simple blue T-shirt. She hardly looked like a member of the Order of Ajna—the greatest mystics in the world— but here she was in Burbank, with ripped jeans and my spare storage key.

"Nice ride," she quipped as I got out of the car. Cat stayed behind for the moment.

"Not for long—it's your job to get rid of it for me," I said.

Delilah pouted at the thought of this. "Hey, you're the Jason Bourne type, not me," she fired back.

"Well, you're the one with the third eye, so you should know *exactly* where to dump it right?"

"You're hilarious!" She shoved me lightly, kind of like a big sister would. It was nice to have a friend, especially one as powerful as Delilah.

Dee was older than me, in the external sense. She was twenty-five compared to my seventeen. Of course, I trumped her in the literal sense, but people usually forgot that when they looked at my face—but not her. She was trying to help me find my path in life. In fact, it had become a mission of hers, like I was a pet project. She had led me to LA, and now it was her job to get me out of it.

"Okay, unit number 427, come on down," Delilah said as we reached the metal and concrete container. I always set up storage units, spare lockers, or safety deposit boxes when I came to new city. I never knew when I would have to flee.

"Well, I'm glad this stuff is here, ya know, since my house was burned down tonight."

"Oh, come on, you hated LA anyway."

"That's only because it's not really a city—more like a giant strip mall. Plus, there's nowhere to park, and come on, what's with all the blonde people? This"—I pointed to my own golden-hued hair—"is natural."

"Well, we're not all full of Imati blood to make us look so gorgeous and shiny, Ally."

"I'm not shiny," I said, almost offended. Delilah always remarked on my looks, and I always tried to ignore her. The standards of beauty constantly changed, but my face—it stayed the same.

"Remind me to buy you more mirrors . . . and then remind yourself to use them."

"Whatever, just open the container," I replied.

Delilah unlocked the container and I walked inside. It was mainly boxes filled with journals, books, IDs, a spare car, cash, and weapons. Standard seventeen-year-old stuff. I went to the crate full of fake IDs . . . but everything was out of date. I had only been in LA nine months, so I wasn't as prepared as I should have been.

"I can't use any of these passports," I said, defeated.

"It's not a big deal. You'll get new ones." Delilah rummaged through boxes as she spoke. "Speaking of, who are you going to be this time? I always liked the name Alexandra."

I hesitated. I didn't want to be someone else again; I wanted to be *me*. I was tired of running, tired of not feeling like a real person. I missed Alastrina.

"Well, here's a crazy idea," I said with hesitation. "I was thinking of being Alastrina Byrne."

Delilah's mouth dropped open. "As in, yourself?"

"Yeah, why not? I have a spare car here." I looked over to the black Mercedes covered up in the corner. "I could just drive for now, no flying, and then get new papers when I arrive."

Delilah smiled. "I actually think that's a great idea."

"Really?" I asked. "It's not too risky?"

"No," she said. "I have a really good feeling about this." Suddenly, she took a deep breath and added, "In fact, I know exactly where you're going now."

"Well, don't spill it too fast. It's not like I'm on the run here," I said, waiting for her to reveal my next destination.

"Belfast, Maine." She grinned so widely I thought she would pull a facial muscle.

"Why are you so happy about Belfast, Maine?" I said half-laughing. But really, I was intrigued. The name Belfast meant more to me than Delilah could know. I had been to a Belfast before and memories of those dark days filled my mind.

"This is it, Ally, I can feel it. What you're looking for is in Belfast."

"I thought it was in LA."

"LA was a stepping stone. All of this—giving up Mackenzie Jones, Nellie Freeman, or whoever else you were and taking back your own identity—it's leading you to Belfast."

"Why?" I asked.

"Oh, come on," she teased, "you know I have no clue. I just see it, I don't explain it."

"Wow, that's really not helpful," I remarked back.

"Time to go." She beamed.

I ripped the covering off the somewhat-new car. I'd bought it when I moved to LA because I was enrolled in Beverly Hills High School at the time, and Mercedes seemed to be the car of choice. Of course, I dropped out about two months later (high school for the tenth time . . . not so fun), switched to a moped so as not to be a slave to LA traffic, and stashed the Benz in the storage unit. Good thing, because here it was, ready to be my getaway car.

More importantly, it had a built-in GPS—because where the heck Belfast, Maine was, I had no freaking clue.

Belfast, Maine – April – Present Day

The Arrival

ON THE CUMBERSOME, three-thousand-mile drive to Maine, I started wishing my license wasn't so out of date and I could have flown instead: the most recent ID I had, which was not burned to a crisp, said I was born in 1980, which no airline in their right mind would let me use. "Oh, hi, sir, I know it says I'm almost thirty-five, but I recently had some work done . . . honest." Not all that convincing of a lie.

My mind was racing. I had been driving almost nonstop for three days (luckily, I didn't need much sleep to survive), and I began to wonder if the road to Maine would ever actually come to an end. Fear and panic had built a nest in the pit of my stomach. Delilah was sending me to a small town, but was that really the best idea? Small towns lacked the anonymity of big cities, and anonymity was often my best friend in the world.

Then, I finally saw it. The green highway sign read BELFAST: 15 MILES. *This is it,* I thought to myself. *A new beginning, a new life, and the reintroduction of Alastrina Byrne.* Hopefully this time there would be no deaths, no close calls, and no need to fear for my life . . . at least for a year or so.

I arrived at the entrance of Belfast with Cat perched in the passenger seat, a leather suitcase stashed on top of books, random weapons, a few household items in the trunk of my car, and a kernel of hope that this town would become a home, and not just a place that I lived. After all, isn't *that* what I was looking for?

Belfast was surprisingly cute. Small, but cute. Mom-and-pop shops, little cafes, art galleries, and a dock with real fishermen were harmoniously displayed in front of me. All of it screamed *New England Charm* in flashing red lights.

I pulled over to get a more personal view of my new city. I hoped Delilah was right about this.

As soon as I stepped out of the car at the end of Main Street, I could smell the sea, the fresh pine, and taste the saltiness in the air. The scent was pure serenity for my soul, and there was a calm eeriness to everything that happened around me. It was quiet here and everything moved in slow motion, not at all like Los Angeles. A child ran down the sidewalk. A storekeeper meticulously swept in front of his shop. A boatman tied his rope to the dock. I could hear nothing but the faint rustle of wind and the whisper of voices.

I stood there soaking up my new environment for an entire minute before I felt eyes on me. Unfortunately, arriving in a small town with an expensive car gets you noticed—which according to the English language is the *opposite* of blending in. I was so used to expensive cars in Los Angeles that the thought hadn't crossed my mind that in a sea of beat-up Fords and utility trucks, my new Mercedes yelled, "Look at me!"

The eyes of the observer continued to pierce my skin until my intense observation of Belfast was broken by a raspy, male voice from behind me. "Hello there. Do you need any help? You look a bit, er, confused."

I turned around to see a bearded, middle-aged man standing behind me wearing old overalls with a red flannel shirt underneath. He looked more like a lumberjack than a fisherman, but the smell gave him away.

"Me?" I replied stupidly. Of *course* he was talking to me—who else was standing around staring at the town like a tourist looking in from behind a pane of glass?

"No, I'm fine," I replied.

"Live around here?" he asked.

"Sort of moving in," I said with more confidence than before. He was just a *Lagga*, I thought—a human—but he was still creepy in an overall-wearing, serial-killer kind of way. Here I was, reveling in the quaintness of the town, all the while forgetting that small-town people are just plain odd sometimes. I wanted him to leave me alone, but I soon realized that would not be the case. I cursed Delilah and her visions under my breath.

"Nice car you have there," he offered. "I'm surprised your parents let you drive that thing around. I make my boy drive my old truck, just in case he wrecks it. He can have a nice car when he pays for it, I always say. Teaches him responsibility."

Oh, crap, I thought to myself. *Stupid Mercedes . . . where's the moped when you need it?*

"It's my dad's," I replied nonchalantly. *Now go away!*

"Just moved in, you say? Whereabouts?"

"Nearby," I said, trying not to give away exactly where I was headed. The last thing I wanted to advertise was my address. I mean, I may as well have started passing out fliers: *Hi, I'm an Imati—please come kill me!*

"I assume you will be attending Belfast High School, then? My son Carson goes there," he said with an eager grin, like his son and I would be instant friends.

"Um, no," I said as quickly as possible. He continued to stand there, waiting for me to elaborate. "I actually have to go. My dad is waiting for me. Nice meeting you, though." My urgent getaway conveniently failed to explain *why* I would not attend school there. I hoped I wouldn't see the bearded fisherman again anytime soon, considering I wasn't planning to throw any get-to-know-your-neighbor parties.

I left Main Street and cautiously pulled up to the gravel driveway on Bayview Drive to meet a real estate agent who was going to show me a house for rent. I was half an hour early, so I took the opportunity to scope the place out and check the windows, the exits, and most importantly, the visibility of neighbors. The more secure the house, the better.

As I surveyed the parameter, a wave of relief washed over me, soaking me from head to toe in its calm waters. I could tell this house was safe. It carried a familial sense, like happiness had once soaked through its walls. The white, wood-paneled home faced the coastline of Penobscot Bay. It was more perfect than I ever could have imagined. Up to this point I had only seen it on a virtual tour during a pit stop in New Mexico (the Internet—what an amazing invention), but the photos did not nearly do it justice.

I slowly made my way to the back yard, reveling in the architecture before me, when suddenly I saw a tall male figure darting into a small, wooden shed nearby. I quickly pressed my body up against the side of the house to remain hidden. Slowly, I peered back around. The man exited the shed just as quickly, only this time, he was armed. Dangling from his right side was a small axe. I watched him anxiously, wondering what his play was. He began to move closer and closer until he stopped a few yards away from me, faced a tree, and muttered something to it. *Odd*, I thought.

Then his arms swung up, and with a violent, swift motion they began to swing down. It all happened so fast: a rush came over me, an urge to save the tree. Without realizing what I was doing, I ran and lunged forward, knocking the axe out of the man's hands and tackling him forcefully to the ground, all the while screaming, "Noooooo!"

My face was in the dirt, and my right knee dug into his stomach as I got up. "Uh, sorry," I said and reached down to help him.

Without taking my hand, he rose from the ground and began brushing the leaves and dirt from his shirt, which was speckled with dried white paint. "Why'd you do that?" he asked, irritated; his accent was British.

"You were going to cut down the tree," I said, stating the obvious.

"Yeah. One of its roots is rotten. Ms. Rogers says it has to come down today."

"But it's an apple tree," I stated for the record.

The boy looked up at the leafy yet fruitless tree, confused. "How do you know that?" he asked.

"I can smell it," I said. "I really like apple trees."

"Rotten trees can't grow fruit. I'm cutting it down." He picked up the axe again.

"Stop! It's not completely rotten. It will grow back . . . trust me," I pleaded with him.

"Rotten is rotten. Sorry," he said. This boy was clearly delusional, and he knew nothing of apple trees . . . or redemption.

Our short battle over the tree was broken when an overeager blonde woman with thick black glasses appeared from the back door like a rabbit shooting out of its hole. She waved frantically, smiling from ear to ear and holding a thick folder. "Connor, there you are! I'm showing the house in about twenty minutes—is the paint dry? Are the fumes okay? You fixed the banister, right?" Her slew of questions ended abruptly when she noticed me. "Oh, hello," she said with a smile. "Are you one of Connor's friends?"

"No." I looked at Connor. "We just met," I said. Then I turned back toward the spastic woman and said, "I'm your five o'clock." I put my hand out to shake, but my five-foot, four-inch frame and lack of a parent quickly turned her bright, cheerful demeanor into a look of confusion.

"Well, hi there, then . . . again. I'm Kitty Rogers of Rogers Real Estate, and you are early!" She paused quizzically for a moment while sizing me up and then turned toward the boy with the axe. "Connor, thanks for everything, I'll be sure to tell your dad what a help you were." She glanced at the tree behind him, which was clearly not chopped down. "Why is the tree still here?" she asked.

Connor raised his eyebrows and looked at me. "She won't let me cut it down."

Kitty looked perplexed. "Oh. Okay then," she said awkwardly.

"I'd like the tree to stay," I said.

"Great, not a problem." She smiled through her gritted teeth. "Connor, you can go. Thanks again."

Connor walked away, frustrated. I had clearly stopped him from doing the one thing all teenage boys like best: smashing objects with weapons. I watched him saunter back into the house, and just as I was about to turn away, he glanced back. He held my gaze, trying to figure me out. I didn't notice before, but he was rather attractive—handsome, even. Then the moment passed, the way all intriguing moments do, and he left for good.

"Is your father on his way?" Kitty interjected, suddenly breaking my stare from Connor.

Once again, it was time for me to lie. Time to make up some story about who I was, why I was here, and why I was alone. I could tell her the truth: that my dad, my family, and most my friends are all dead. However, the practical, not-wanting-to-be-committed-to-an-asylum part of me knew better, and I went with the rehearsed lie.

"No, he's not. I'm Ally; we spoke on the phone. I'm Dr. Byrne's daughter. He's sorry he couldn't make it, but he just got sent to a very important medical conference in London. But I assure you, he gave me everything we need in order to rent the house—if we like it, of course." I smiled as widely and innocently as I could in order to seem trustworthy.

"He's not coming at all?" She looked even more confused than before.

"No. Not for a few weeks. He didn't know about London until the last minute, so unfortunately, if this doesn't work out I'll be stuck in Belfast with nowhere to live."

I gave her my best sad/helpless/destitute face. She looked at me with pity, uncertainty, and nervous speculation. She wasn't really buying it.

"By the way," I added, "we only use cash. I hope that's not a problem?"

I could see Kitty's face contort as she pondered her next move. She was skeptical, but also a shrewd businesswoman.

"Not a problem. We'll work something out," she said. "Follow me and I'll show you the property."

"Great," I said, and followed her into the house.

As I toured the upstairs and master bedroom, I felt more and more at ease. I slowly made my way to the attached balcony and looked to the vast ocean in front of me. I could hear the waves lapping below me and saw the orange halo of the sun slowly reaching the horizon. I peered below me to the wraparound porch, which was brilliantly illuminated by the setting sun, creating a glow on the freshly glossed paint. I looked back toward the room. There were wooden floors and huge bay windows for me to sit and read while I watched the world fly by. I was in love with it. This was a house I could have forever. Perhaps—the thought flashed through my mind like a lightning bolt—it could even be my permanent home. Even if I left for a few years and came back, it would still be mine. I had felt lost for such a long time, and so unable to put my life back together since Chile . . .

Stop! I told myself. Remembering was painful, and forgetting was impossible. I had spent the last century in pain. Chile had created a downward spiral for my life that I was just now getting out of, thanks in part to Delilah. It was a catalyst that had ruined everything I had stood for. I wanted to erase it forever, but still, even now, the image flashed into my brain: her doll-like face, her perfect cream-colored skin, a single curl falling to her rosy cheek, reaching past her amber-colored eyes. An image emerged of me holding her beautiful face in the palm of my hand. Her lifeless face lay there, frozen in my grasp forever. Memories can be dangerous, and I, more than anyone knew that. *Get a hold of yourself, Ally!*

I brought my thoughts back to reality, back to my new home and my new life. I would never forget what I did so many years ago, but I knew that somehow I must keep myself from drowning in its guilt.

I looked back toward the vast, seemingly endless ocean that was stretched out before me like a living portrait. Somewhere, thousands of miles away, was Ireland—my original home. The home I had not dared to go back to for over two hundred years.

Cork County, Ireland – 1740 – First Death

I SAT, HUNCHED over a small wooden table in my small stone house, gazing at my papa's Bible, while the waxy stub of a candle illuminated the words. I was staring at the front page where my name, scrawled in thick, black ink, stared back at me: *Alastrina Byrne—15th of March, 1723*. My father recorded all of his children's births inside its pages, even mine. Sometimes I stared at it, wondering what life was like before that date. Wondering if life was better.

The hour was late and we were all waiting for my father to return home. We couldn't eat until he came home: his rules. He was a ship hand and small farmer who worked primarily out of the docks in Cork. We lived in a small farming village just outside the city walls. It's important to note that my father did not like me. We did not look alike in any way, and he did not hug me like he hugged the rest of my family. Often, his true feelings emerged at night when he returned home, fueled by ale from Thistle's Inn. He was a very religious man, so I waited for him by candlelight, holding his Bible, hoping it could protect me. But it never did.

"Where is she?" he shouted as he burst through the thin, wooden door of our two-room house. "Where is my little yellow-haired girl?" His tone was filled with anger and resentment. Both of my siblings, Cordelia and Callum, had dark hair and fair eyes, while I stood out as the odd one in my family, because my hair was golden like honey and my eyes were as green as Ireland herself.

"I am here, Papa." I stood before him, grasping the large book with my head held high, despite the fear that rose in my belly.

"Ah, look at you." I could smell the ale on his breath and see the swagger in his stance. He was drunk. "Who are you?" he demanded.

"You know who I am," I said, "I'm Ally," but there was a quiver in my voice. I got my nickname Ally from my younger sister Cordelia, who had trouble pronouncing Alastrina as a child. Everyone called me Ally, except for my father.

"Are you? *My* Alastrina would not have this hair or this skin. There is something wrong with you—you are an imposter. Aren't you?" He slurred his words as he spoke. "Aren't you?" he screamed and banged his fist on the table.

"No, Papa, not an imposter." I tried to stay calm and to stand my ground, but my hands began to shake in fear as he inched closer to my face. His warm breath touched my skin. I stared into his icy, dark eyes and saw only hatred.

"What are you, Alastrina? Hmm? You can tell me." He moved his head to the right to whisper in my ear as my family watched in frozen horror. "Oh, I know—you're the devil!"

Then he stumbled away from me, into the room he shared with my mother, where he passed out fully clothed and slept like a bear in winter. This was a typical routine we practiced, as if preparing for a play, only the act was real and the feeling of being despised by my father was sickening. But for now I lucked out: he had disappeared without striking me, and we were finally able to eat. My stomach thanked him.

I woke up early the next day with Cordelia lying next to me. We shared a bed, which was fine, because when I cried at night it was Cordelia who rubbed my back and told me everything would be okay in the morning.

Trying not to wake my little sister, I snuck out of bed, put my leather boots on, and went outside to collect milk from our only cow. I wanted to get an early start to the day. The cool early-winter air pierced my skin and my lungs, but the day felt promising because it was market day. I always liked market day because I got to go to town and visit the other villagers. It allowed me to imagine what living in Cork would be like: living in a better house, wearing fancy clothes, and eating hot food every night. Some of our neighbors, who knew my father's ways (in the most horrible sense), would bring me an apple on market day when they bought my milk and cheese. I think it was out of pity, and they knew apples were my favorite.

As I methodically pulled on the belly of the cow, warm milk splashed into the metal bucket below me and my head started to sway. I was nodding off, still tired from my early rise, when suddenly I heard the neighing of horses and the pounding of footsteps coming toward me.

I was a few hundred yards away from the house at the time, thanks to the cow. She had wandered a ways off into the field, and I was forced to milk her where she stood. Just moments ago I was upset because I knew the buckets would be a pain to carry back, but now I was thankful, because something seemed desperately wrong.

From my position behind the cow, I could see three men on horseback descend from their beasts and storm into my home. I watched in horror, unable to move my feet. A back door was suddenly splintered from the inside, like something had been thrown against it, and screams from my mother and sister echoed through the air.

Not thinking clearly, I immediately sprinted toward the back of the house. What I was going to do when I got there, I had no idea. These men, even from a hundred yards away, reeked of danger. Why they would attack a peasant house with one cow eluded me at the moment.

My lungs burned by the time I reached the door. I ran inside, but it was too late. Everything was destroyed. Tables were turned over, pieces of the stone wall lay shattered, and broken dishes littered the floor. But the worst was the blood . . . it was everywhere.

I saw my father's body first, lying near the front door, his shirt soaked in blood. He was clearly dead. My brother Callum, only fourteen, was near him, slashed at the neck, lying limp on the floor. Cordelia was still in our bed, but now red-stained sheets surrounded her. At least she was killed while resting; it seemed better than being awake. The men who murdered my family in a manner of minutes had momentarily disappeared, but rather than escape, all I could think was: *Where is my mother?*

I ran into her room and found her lying on the other side of her straw-filled bed. She wasn't dead yet, but a large gash on her stomach was bleeding profusely.

"Mama!" I ran over to her. She was panting, desperately trying to breathe. "Please Mama, please don't die." Tears poured down my cheeks.

My mother looked up at me, her eyes wide with fear. She pulled me in close and whispered, "Alastrina, when you wake up from this, you must go to the well out back." She struggled to get the words out. "Look under the loose stone on the inside wall—there's a parcel for you. It's yours, Alastrina. It is the key."

I had no idea what she was talking about. Wake up from what? Perhaps the brink of death had made her mad.

Suddenly, I heard large boots approach me from behind, but before I could turn around I felt the cold sting of metal pierce through my back and come out the other side. My ears started ringing, and sharp pains ripped through my body. I looked down and saw the blade sticking through my guts.

"*Nooooo!*" my mother screamed. All I could do was fall forward, on top of my mother's bloody torso, as she cried out in pain. *This is happening. I'm going to die*, I thought to myself. Then I felt her hand come up as she gently stroked my face. "Alastrina, remember what your name means. Your father gave it to you. He wanted you to have it."

Before I could register what she was saying, I felt an even larger hand shove me to the side like I was of no more importance than a dead dog. I rolled off of my mother and onto the dirt floor. The man, dressed in black, straddled her and pushed his hands deeper into her wounds. She cried out in pain.

"Tell me where it is!" he demanded.

"I don't know what you want," she managed to choke out.

He grew angrier than he already was. "We know Asher was here. Give us what he gave you." The man's voice boomed when he spoke, and for the first time I saw true evil in the flesh.

Then a second man came in, looking even scarier than the first, with an unshaven face and a large scar that stretched across his cheek. "What are you doing?" he shouted to his partner in crime. "I cannot read her if she is dead, you fool."

The first man, who must have been a simple mercenary, huffed as he got up, angry at being stopped mid-torture. The second man, the one in charge, leaned over my mother with an evil look on his face. "Now we will learn everything you know."

Surprisingly, at that moment I saw my mother smile. She looked up at the man who had massacred her family, and she beamed with rare confidence. Finally, she spit in his face and hissed back, "Never." With that last word she fell back and died.

The man got up, frustrated, and came for me next. I saw his newly healed scar and his dark eyes looming over me. He stared at me for a moment, but I was already losing my grip with reality. My eyelids felt heavy, the gash on my stomach stung like a thousand little needles piercing my skin, and my hands were soaked with my own blood as I tried to cover my wound. I knew I wasn't going to last much longer. As my eyes closed and the room grew dark, the thought went through my head that I would miss market day, which was my favorite day of all.

Belfast, Maine – May – Present Day

Nothing But Time

Time, for most people, is a gatekeeper: it tells them when to wake, when to sleep, when to grow up, when to move on, and when to die. It lets experiences and memories into their lives and constantly pushes them forward. For me, time is like a mythical creature, constantly lurking in the shadows but never visible. To me, it has become merely folklore, a figment of the human imagination, and I no longer believe it is really there or ever existed at all. Therefore, when I wake up, I do not plan my day or check off a list of things to do. I merely wander, trying to fill up an endless void of time. Of course, Delilah was sure that I would "wander" into something in Belfast, but unfortunately, I had no idea what that was.

It was a Tuesday morning—not a particularly important Tuesday, just a regular Tuesday like all the ones that had come before it—when I decided to take a walk to the center of town. I still didn't know why I was here, but I kept my eyes peeled for a sign, a reason Delilah had sent me to Belfast, and on this regular Tuesday, I walked right into one.

Ironically, the sign was a literal one—a wooden sign, hanging above me on the sidewalk. The familiar face staring back at me caught my attention: the Green Man. The ever-familiar figure appeared, carved into the wood, staring down with his kind eyes and a face made entirely of leaves. He was the pagan symbol of rebirth, and he told me to walk in.

The store I meandered into was a coffee shop; the smell of roasting beans, sweet treats, and a roaring fire filled the air. There were bookshelves, brown couches, and a dark wooden bar. More importantly, as I glanced toward the chalkboard menu, I saw they had apple cider. I was sold.

I took a deep breath and approached the coffee bar. I should note, at this stage in my life I am not a super-friendly people person. I am suspicious, anxious, and untrusting, mainly because I've had too many close calls with unsavory characters, and I try to limit my conversations with people to only necessary situations—like, say, ordering a drink, which is what I was about to do. It's not that I'm socially awkward, but I do have to worry about slipping up when talking to Laggas and avoid saying things like "This one time in Paris, during the Revolution . . ." or "Hey, remember when the West was won . . . fun times." Thus, it can be exhausting to put myself out there. But Delilah said Belfast was going to be a more permanent stay, so it had to happen sometime, right? I needed to build a life here, and that started with standing in a coffee shop and ordering a drink, just like any other person.

"What can I get you?" the dark-haired girl behind the bar asked me with a giant grin on her face. She seemed overly excited.

"Large apple cider, please," I said. *So far, so good.*

"No problem. It'll be just a minute—grab a seat." She scurried off to grab the cider and I took a seat at the end of the bar.

As I waited for my drink, I turned my attention to an older gentleman sitting on the other side reading a newspaper. He was attractive for his age, I noticed. He looked up and met my gaze. "The apple cider is delicious here," he said, and then gave me a "cheers" with his own cup. A very small-town kind of gesture.

"Oh, good," I said. "It's my favorite." He smiled back at me, but didn't say anything more, so I continued to wait for my cider. Not more than five seconds passed when my phone rang. It was Delilah.

"Hey, Dee," I said, trying to keep my voice down.

"Ally, how's it going there?" she asked. She was checking in on me. She had decided to stay in LA, rather than follow me to Maine. Something about it not being her time yet.

"Good, it's good." I turned away so that I was out of earshot from the man at the end of the bar. "Hey, Dee, does the Green Man mean anything to you?" I asked.

"Um . . ." She thought about it for a moment. "Eat your veggies?"

"Not the Green *Giant*, the Green *Man*—the Pagan symbol of rebirth?"

"Ohhhh!" she exclaimed. "No."

"Great. Not very helpful," I said.

"Why?" she asked. It was an obvious follow-up question.

"There's a coffee shop here in Belfast called the Green Man, and it just . . . it felt important." I didn't know how to explain myself, how to explain why I'd walked into the shop. Delilah clearly wasn't getting any signals from the name.

"Well, follow your instincts, Al. Who knows?"

The counter girl suddenly popped back up and put a steaming hot cup of cider in front of me. "Hey, I gotta go, Dee. I'll call you later." I put the phone down, eager to dive into warm apple goodness.

"Enjoy!" The counter girl beamed as the copious amount of bangles dangling from her wrist clinked together. "Oh, hey," she added. "Would you like a blueberry muffin? On the house."

"No thanks," I declined. I didn't really need to eat that much—just a few times a month or so to keep from feeling hungry, since starvation couldn't kill me. Plus, a blueberry muffin didn't excite me in the least.

I took a sip of my hot cider. The man at the end of the bar was right: it was delicious. Just when I thought the moment couldn't get any better, a little bell rang and the door opened behind me. I felt a gust of wind hit my face and my ears suddenly perked back. I heard footsteps walking toward me.

I turned around to see who was causing this electric reaction, and standing in the doorway, about six feet tall, was someone I actually recognized. Connor—known to me as the tree-killing boy with an axe—was less than twenty feet away. I looked down into my cup, hiding my face. Fortunately, he either didn't remember me or was purposely choosing to forget. Who could blame him? I *had* attacked him mid-swing. The coffee girl intercepted him first.

"Hi there, Millie. I like your hair today," he said, which I assumed referred to the red streak blazing through her otherwise jet-black mane.

Millie, as Connor had called her, was instantly flustered. "Oh—ha—thanks, Connor! Just trying something new."

"It's nice," he smiled. "Can I get a bagel with cream cheese, triple espresso, and a double cappuccino for my dad?" His familiar British accent echoed around my head and I suddenly found him even more attractive than before. You would think holding an axe would have been more my style, but something about him this time was different. He seemed more . . . vulnerable.

"Sure thing, Connor, coming right up." Millie's face told me that I wasn't the only one who was mesmerized by this very tall and good-looking guy. I was sitting on a wooden counter stool almost right next to him, but I couldn't get my mouth to move so I could utter even the simplest hello. I mean, what would I have said—"Sorry about the tackle"? That's no way to start a conversation. I was clearly staring at him, turning away, and then staring again. Not very subtly, mind you.

He had dark brown hair and crystal-blue eyes. He wasn't fair-skinned, though; more olive-toned, even bronzed. His face and his jawline were so chiseled it looked like Michelangelo himself had sculpted him. He was more than good-looking, he was intriguing, with just a slight hint of ruggedness that made him seem dangerous. All the hairs on my neck stood up, and I got goose bumps when he left. The room started to spin, my head was dizzy, and I had to lean my elbows on the counter to compose myself. These feelings were strange and out of place. I hadn't felt dizzy in a very long time. In fact, I didn't realize I could still *feel* dizzy.

"Are you okay?" Millie, the counter girl, asked. She was staring at me with a look of concern splashed across her face.

"Yeah, I'm fine, thanks." I took the opportunity to pry about tree-boy. "Hey, who was that guy that just walked in? Connor?"

"Oh, that's Connor Winfield. He is so amazing. A little weird sometimes, but still amazing—and British!" Her entire face lit up when she talked about him.

"Yeah, I assumed as much from the accent. Why is he here in Maine?" I probably should have introduced myself before bombarding the poor girl with questions, but I felt desperate.

"Oh, he lives here, duh! He goes to Belfast High. He just moved last year from London with his dad. I think his name is Quinn or something. He is super strict; he never lets Connor do anything. I mean, with a face like that the boy could have been prom king, except his dad would never go for that, so he wasn't even nominated. He was on a short list, but nothing official—"

"So he doesn't get out much?" I interrupted. Millie, I was beginning to realize, was a bit of a rambler.

"Nope, and that's an understatement. Sometimes he comes here for breakfast, and once in awhile I see him walking around the town, but he doesn't have any friends, and he doesn't date. Trust me, every girl has tried. Well, 'tried' in the sense of pined away from a distance . . . but he doesn't really talk to anyone. Well, he talks to me, but that's only because he has to . . . you know, to order . . . nothing special."

"Right," I said as I contemplated the rapidfire burst of information.

"I'm Mildred Alden, by the way"—the red-streaked coffee girl put out her hand for me to shake—"but my friends call me Millie."

I met her hand with mine. "Alastrina," I said, "but my friends call me Ally." It felt good not to lie.

Even though we had made the proper introductions, I didn't ask her any more questions. I couldn't get Connor out of my head. I wanted to know more about him, talk to him, and be near him. He was a magnetic force that I was innately drawn to. After that Tuesday, I took more walks around town and made even more trips to the coffee shop. I convinced myself the walks were to better learn the layout of Belfast, but subconsciously I knew it was because I wanted to accidentally run into Connor.

But I didn't run into Connor. Millie was right; he really didn't get out much. However, each time I went into the Green Man, I saw the same gentleman who had told me the cider was delicious (duh!), sitting at the end of the bar, reading a newspaper. Something about him seemed off—so, clearly, I had to find out what it was.

"Hello again," I said as I sat down a few chairs away.

"Hello," he said. Millie approached me, but the man spoke up first. "Large apple cider," he said to her. Then he looked at me. "Am I right?"

"You're right," I smiled.

"You're new in town, yes?" he asked, his face half in a newspaper.

"Yeah. Really like it, though. Cute town," I said.

"That it is," he replied, almost cryptically. Like he knew something about the town I did not. I took a moment to get a good look at him. He was about fifty, rugged-looking, and when he smiled he had a twinkle in his eye. Of course, another word for *twinkle* could be *conniving*. He was curious-looking for sure, with his light blue eyes, square jaw, shaved head, and stern physique. He dressed modestly: white collared shirt, tan jacket, and slacks. His demeanor seemed antiquated, like he was from another era.

The man folded up his newspaper, put it on the bar, and placed a small book on top of it to weigh it down. I thought he was signaling that we were starting a conversation. So I conversed.

"What are you reading?" I queried.

He smiled. "Just the *Belfast Times*. There's some road construction out on Highway One and the local church is having an ice cream social next Wednesday. Exciting stuff." He was making a joke. I found his candor amusing.

At that moment, Millie came back with my cider. "Would you like to try our cranberry-orange scone?" she asked.

"No thank you," I said. For some reason, she was always offering me free food. I think she wanted us to be friends.

"Hey, Millie," the man at the end of the bar began, "can I get two apple turnovers?"

"Sure thing," she said. "Coming right up." Then the counter man turned back toward me.

"Apple turnover?" he asked. "I ordered one too many, and they're baked fresh," he offered with a charming smile.

"I can never say no to an apple turnover," I said, but with an air of caution attached. You know that moment in "Snow White" when the evil stepmother offers up the poisonous apple? Well, his gesture felt a little like that.

"Great," he said, obviously pleased I'd accepted his offer. "Bill Barnes. Nice to meet you."

"Alastrina Byrne, but I go by Ally." Behind the counter I saw Millie pout a bit. I always rejected her free food.

The apple turnovers came, and Bill and I ate breakfast together. Partaking in the ritual of breakfast with small talk and pastries was always a comforting feeling. Like all was right in the world. Like you could start off your day without feeling alone.

"These are delicious!" I exclaimed. "Thank you for offering." By this time I had moved two stools down.

"My pleasure," Bill said.

I wondered why he was being so nice to me. I mean, I knew why I wanted to talk to him: because I was suspicious, and a tie-him-up-to-a-chair interrogation was not a viable option. But why did he want to talk to me?

I continued the polite, neighborly conversation. "How's the book?" I asked, pointing to the book resting on top of his newspaper.

"Intriguing," he said and held it up for me to see. It was *The Stranger* by Camus, in the original French. "Have you read it?" he asked.

"Yes, actually," I replied. He seemed in awe of that, probably because I looked so young. I decided to take the opportunity to probe into Bill's life a little deeper. I mean, who reads an existentialist French book about a murder at ten o'clock in the morning over cider?

"*Parlez-vous français*, Bill?" The question—*Do you speak French?*—clearly threw him a curveball. He looked stunned, and his chin almost hit the floor; obviously, French was the last thing he expected from me.

"Yes, in fact I do," he replied. Not in French. A bit of sorrow shadowed his words and I took the cue to switch back to English.

"Me, too." *Obviously; why else would I have asked?* "It's an enchanting language," I added, but my words hung heavily in the air and created a sudden shift in Bill's demeanor.

"Where did you learn French, Alastrina?" Now he sounded inquisitive rather than curious.

"Um, I had a French nanny growing up," I quickly lied. "And you can call me Ally."

"Alastrina is an interesting name, though. Don't hear it much these days, if ever." Apparently my "trying to figure Bill out" had turned into *him* figuring *me* out.

"That's why I go by Ally," I replied curtly, now regretting the entire conversation.

He went on, not bothering to acknowledge my nickname of preference, or my curt reply to his remark. "You mentioned you just moved in, right?"

"Yeah," I said. *Again.*

"So you'll be here in Belfast permanently?" he asked, and suddenly that nagging suspicion that camped out in my gut telling me not to talk to people grew larger.

"I suppose so." *As long as no one tries to kill me*, I thought.

"So you'll be headed to Belfast High School, then?" His inquisitive face flashed a smile. "That will be fun, getting to be the new kid."

The new kid? Seriously? No one likes being the new kid. And is that really what he wanted to know—where I was going to school?

"Being the new kid is never fun," I shot back. I needed to control the questioning. "And I'm not in high school," I added. Not to mention my list of Top Ten Places to Spend Eternity did not include BHS.

Bill could obviously read the sudden annoyance on my face and he changed the subject. "I used to live in Paris, you know, I loved it," he began. "In a small apartment near the Sorbonne. That's why I like to read books in French . . . I never want to forget it, you know."

That's interesting, I thought. Bill seemed so worldly and now here he was in this tiny town, just like me.

"I know what you mean. I loved Paris too," I said as I tried to picture myself there more recently, but the image was escaping me, so I trailed off and ended with, "It really used to be something."

"Is it not still?" he asked, a little suspiciously.

"Oh, of course," I said in response to his question. "I just haven't been there for a while. I'm sure it's still fantastic."

"Sure is," he said longingly.

"Tell me about your time there," I asked. "Did you fall in love?"

"In Paris, everyone falls in love." He smiled as he spoke. "But mine was the tragic, Shakespearean kind."

Bill Barnes – Paris, France – Spring 1909

As THE RAPIDLY moving train gradually slowed to a complete stop, Bill's heart began to race. In fact, it was beating so fast he thought it might explode. Of course, that's only because the heartbeat itself was new to him. Overcome with excitement as the train pulled into the Gare d'Austerlitz on the left bank of Paris, Bill knew he was home at last.

The journey from South America had been treacherous. He had risked everything, including his life, in order to be with his fiancée—the beautiful Marisol, a woman from Barcelona he couldn't wait to get back to. His journey had taken three years, but in the end, he knew it would be worth it.

Bill grabbed his single leather suitcase, which was now worn and tattered from years of traipsing around the back slums of Chile, and burst through the train doors onto the platform below. The sounds, the smells, and the people of Paris—they all seemed different now. Maybe it was because he was seeing them with the eyes of a man in love . . . or maybe because, for the first time in centuries, he was seeing them through the eyes of a human.

Bill wanted to breathe it all in, take a moment to revel in his newfound life, but there was no time. As soon as his feet hit the road outside, he took off. He ran alongside the River Seine until he reached the *Quartier Latin*. He cut a hard left. Just a few more blocks and he'd be home. Marisol knew he was coming; he had written her daily.

Suddenly he saw it: the little white building with the little blue door. He took a moment before knocking. It had been years. Would she still love him after all this time?

Before his hand could reach the wooden face of the door, it swung open— and standing in front of him was the most gorgeous creature he could imagine:

the familiar dark hair, longer now, amber-tinted eyes, and a white dress flowing gracefully behind her from the soft, spring breeze.

"Is it really you?" Marisol asked in her thick, Spanish accent.

"It's me." Bill smiled and swept up his soul mate into his arms, spinning her around the foyer of their little home.

Marisol laughed and whispered in his ear, "I knew you would come back to me. I could hear you running. I could hear your heart beating before you came."

"Because you love me?" Bill asked it as a question, needing desperately to hear the answer.

"Because I will always love you." Marisol beamed.

The two ran upstairs to make love, to bask in each other's scent, and to make up for three years of lost time. Bill knew the time apart had been worth it. Without completing his task, he never could have had a life with Marisol. It would have been too dangerous. But now—now that he had successfully become human—he could have everything he ever wanted.

Hours later, Marisol lay in bed next to Bill, eating strawberries. She handed one to Bill. He took a bite and smiled. "This is the most delicious strawberry in the world."

Marisol giggled. "You are a liar."

Bill wrapped his arms around her and the bowl of strawberries spilled out, littering the bed with fruit. "No, it's the best. I swear on my life."

"You remember those strawberries in Marseille, the ones we ate when we first met? You said they were the best in the world."

Bill laughed. "Perhaps strawberries simply taste better when you are around."

Marisol put her lips, half covered in strawberries, to Bill's. "I agree."

After the love and lust and excitement wore down, the two fell asleep in each other's arms. Bill, for once, was able to close his eyes and soak in the feeling of happiness. The pain was finally over, so he lay there peacefully until the sun rose and the sounds of morning woke him up.

But sadly, when he opened his eyes, the bed felt cold—and Marisol was gone.

Bill shot up in a panic and quickly glanced around the room. Nothing was remiss. Everything seemed in its place. Except his true love.

"Marisol!" he shouted. But was only met with silence.

Then he looked at her pillow and saw a small white note, which had fallen onto the sheets. He opened it and was then faced with the worst news he'd ever received in his very long life.

Belfast, Maine – May – Present Day

Heirloom

"WHAT HAPPENED TO her?" I asked, now genuinely interested.

"Oh, I don't know. I suppose she died . . ." Bill's voice trailed off, lost in his memories.

That's weird, I thought, *to just assume she died*. There were holes in Bill's tale: he never explained when he lost Marisol or how old he was. It appeared he was excluding some noteworthy details, but "How very sad" is all I said.

"After Marisol, I left Paris forever; it was too painful to stay." Bill was clearly a bit on the melodramatic side.

"So you haven't been back since then?" I asked.

"No. I figure I'll go back someday, if the time is right." He had a calculating look on his face, like he was thinking of a checklist he had to accomplish before his return to the city that had taken away his true love.

"I'm sure that time will come. A city is just a city, just stones and walls and people. It's Marisol that you loved, and Paris was just the stage." I was being profoundly poetic, so much so that Bill returned from his trance of memories with a look of surprise.

"That's very wise, Alastrina." He stared off a little, past my eye-line, and said it to himself more than me. Then he added, "If I ever forgot her name, I think I would cease to exist."

Those tiny words hit me like a ton of bricks. I thought of my own mother, my beautiful, murdered mother. I had forgotten her name years ago. Had I ceased to exist?

I was silent for a moment. I composed my thoughts while trying hard not to completely give away the sorrow Bill had just reminded me of.

I didn't know what to say, so I said the first thing that popped into my mind. "I wish I could love someone the way you loved Marisol." He didn't realize just how much I sympathized with his pain. "You won't forget her, I can tell."

He placed a hand on my right shoulder in a gesture of familiarity. "Thank you, Ally. I truly believe you when you say that." I guess he had finally remembered my nickname.

"You are a very curious girl, Ally, and wise beyond your years."

I smiled, not sure how to take his remark. Was he suspicious of me, or simply complimentary? Then he took a long look at the chain around my neck, and for a second it seemed like he recognized it.

"You know, that is a striking necklace you are wearing. It looks very old," he commented.

I looked down at the chain resting on my chest while the suspicion alarms went off in my head. "Oh, thank you," I replied, trying to hide my discomfort in his observation. "It has been in my family for years. Just an old antique, I guess." I downplayed its value. I wanted to avert the conversation far away from my ruby necklace—the necklace I had owned since becoming immortal, so many years ago.

Cork County, Ireland – 1740 – New Immortal

I AWOKE SUDDENLY, thanks to a blinding streak of winter sun shooting straight through a window above my head. I quickly sat up to move away from the bright light. When I looked around the room, everything was the same. My mother lay next to me, blood-soaked and dead.

I leaned over her to try and wake her, but the body had gone cold. She had been dead awhile. *How long have I been asleep?* I thought. Then I remembered something and looked down at my own clothes. They, too, were covered in blood. I lifted up my linen shirt to search for a wound, but there was none. Was it all my imagination?

I ran out to the other room. There in front of me was my slaughtered family, unmoved. I didn't know why, but I didn't cry. I wanted to, but I couldn't. Suddenly, I was more angry than sad. The rage of losing everyone I loved boiled up inside of me, and I let out a violent, anger-filled cry. *"Ahhh!"*

When I stopped screaming, nothing had changed. Nothing was better. The house was quiet, soaked in the silence of death. I sat down, unsure what to do next. I stayed like that through the night; I just sat there, staring at the wall. The sun rose again, and then set again, and yet I remained frozen. Part of me thought I was dead, too. A few days passed, maybe more. Then it occurred that I couldn't let my family just rot away without a proper burial. I needed to get rid of the bodies.

I carried their remains to the back field. The cow was still grazing around, probably half frozen and wondering where I had been. I took the shovel from the shed and began to dig. I dug and dug and did not stop. I must have looked like a madwoman, but I didn't care; I needed to cover them. The sight of their dead faces staring back at me was too much. Finally, when four holes were finished,

I put them in, one by one. I barely noticed the snow that was falling around me. I didn't even feel the cold.

I placed Cordelia, Callum, and my mother into the ground, said an old Celtic prayer mama taught me, and then covered them with dirt, rocks, and snow. It was definitely not a proper burial, nor the type of funeral they all deserved. As for my father, I buried him, too, but I said no prayer for his soul—it was my only form of revenge.

I stood there for a moment in the snow-covered field, staring at the lumps of earth in front of me. Beneath them were my family's bodies, but from the surface it was just earth . . . just stones and dirt. They were officially gone, and I was completely alone.

I walked back into my house even more confused. It felt emptier now. I waited sadly for a death that would never come. I did not sleep. Or eat. Or drink. Or do anything at all. I sat in my house, looking at the fireplace that no longer burned, and stared at the cold, leftover ashes. *Maybe I am in hell*, I thought. I did not feel cold, I did not feel hungry, and I did not die.

I began to go a little insane. My mind raced with a frenzy of unwelcome thoughts: *Maybe I died of shock. Maybe I was never really alive. Maybe I never existed at all*. All of these questions, and no answers. I couldn't focus and I couldn't bear to move. I was stuck in the center of the room, shaking, eyes still glaring at the fireplace. *Where am I? What am I? Where is my family? Are they really dead? Am I a ghost?*

Suddenly, I jumped up and sprinted toward the wall. *Bang!* My corporeal body crashed into the stone and I bounced backward. *Not a ghost, then*. I sat back down in the center of the room and retook my position at the empty fireplace. Days passed, maybe weeks, maybe just hours—I was not sure. When you no longer need anything to survive, you are no longer aware that you are alive.

After what felt like an eternity, the onslaught of pure insanity was interrupted by a faint knock at the door. "Alastrina? Is anyone here?" The front door opened with a slight creak, and I could hear footsteps coming toward me. Heavy winter boots slowly thumped on the frozen dirt floor. The sound rattled against the stone walls in the room, and then it stopped. I felt someone touch my shoulder. "Dear child, you are alive! I knew I saw you a night ago. Is everything alright? Are you hurt?"

I couldn't move, and it took me a few seconds to realize that someone was addressing me. I could oddly hear the heartbeat; the rhythmic sound filled the room. I hadn't heard a heartbeat since I had woken up. The sound seemed deafening and frightening at the same time. *Are heartbeats usually that loud?* It meant one thing: I was not dead.

"Yes, it's me," I said softly. I hadn't spoken for days and it was strange to hear my voice again. Still staring towards the ash-filled fireplace, I added, "I am fine, but my family is dead." I am not sure why I said it like that, but the man must have known already because the walls were still covered in their blood.

"Mary and I assumed you were all dead," he said as he tried to explain why no one had helped us, why no one had come to save us. "We heard men come on horseback, violent, strong, capable men, and then they vanished just as quickly. I wanted to check on you, on all of you, but I was frightened, Alastrina, I didn't know if they would come back. If they were the King's men."

I still didn't turn around, but he continued to talk. "Then, I thought I saw you in the field . . . digging?" His voice shuddered a bit when he said "digging," as if he knew instantly that it was for their graves. Like saying it out loud made their deaths a reality. He placed a hand on my shoulder. "God has a plan for us all, child, and I can assure you that they are at peace."

He clearly did not see the way they died.

I inhaled and momentarily let go of my anger. I needed help. So I looked up for the first time since the man had entered and Seamus, a neighboring villager from a few houses away, stared back at me, half-kneeling behind me. My eyes locked on his, and the combination of fear, pain, and sincerity in his face jolted me back to life.

I jumped to my feet. The frozen confusion and rage morphed into sudden hysteria as I rejoined my body from another world. This whole time I had been drowning in fear, not really aware of where I was or what I was doing. Seamus's familiar presence made me realize that reality was still surrounding me: this is not limbo, this is not hell—this is life, and life is hard.

"Seamus, it's good to see you," I exclaimed. "It was horrible. They came in, they killed everyone . . . Callum, Cordelia . . . my mother. I wanted to stop them, but I couldn't. I . . ." I trailed off, remembering that I, too, had been stabbed, remembering I, too, was wounded, and remembering blood was still covering my shirt.

Seamus saw it too and asked me the obvious question. "Oh, dear child, are you still hurt?"

I looked up. "No, no, I'm fine," I said and then came up with my first of many lies. "It's not my blood."

Seamus put his arms around me, trying to comfort me and soothe me like a father, or I assume like what a father *should* do. Except for a twinge of nerves in his touch, I felt at ease at once. For the first time since the massacre, I felt like I was part of the world again. Somehow, I had survived. When death was upon me and had felt so imminent, it had spared me. But I was different. I had woken up a different person altogether.

The sound of his voice broke my train of thought. "Ally, how did you manage to . . ." he stammered a bit, unsure of his own query.

"To what, Seamus?" I looked up at him fearfully, worried that I would have to answer a question I had no answer to.

"To dig the grave? The ground here in the winter is so hard. I had to cover my son with rocks because I could not move the earth. How did you, a mere child, manage to do it?"

I froze. I was afraid to tell Seamus the truth: that for some reason, despite all logic, I had a newfound strength, did not need food like I once did, and had more power than ever before. I felt inhuman, like a terrible freak. It all felt so supernatural. If Seamus had noticed in such a short amount of time, then how long would it take others to notice? The villagers were all so superstitious—what would they think? What did I think? Fear consumed my thoughts as I imagined the townsfolk tossing stones, shouting obscenities, and calling me the devil as they chased me out of Ireland.

"I'm not sure, Seamus, I don't even remember doing it." I could sense my words did not put him at ease, but seeing my anguish he let it go for the time being.

"You can come stay with Mary and me." He said it earnestly enough, but I am not sure if he meant it.

"I don't want to be a burden." The truth is I had nowhere else to go and no one left who loved me, so without Seamus I was no one.

"It's not a burden, child, we would love to have you."

Before leaving my one and only home, I gathered a few of my things, and then I remembered something. Before my mother died, she had told me to go to the well out back and look for a parcel.

"Can you wait a minute, Seamus?" I asked. "I need to say good-bye to the cow."

"You can bring the cow, Ally," he said. "We can put her in our field tomorrow."

"I know, um, but she's cold, she needs extra comfort." Seamus looked at me like I was insane.

I didn't much care, and I sprinted out the broken back door and ran to the well. I looked down into the deep, dark hole that reached far beneath the ground. For a moment I thought about jumping, but shook the thought from my mind. I had more important things to do.

I used my hands to feel the inner side walls. All the stones seemed solid. I walked in a circular pattern as I moved around it, rubbing my hands up and down the inner stones. Suddenly, one of the stones rattled. I grabbed it, moved it back and forth to wriggle it out, and felt behind it, and there *it* was: a small package wrapped in leather. I opened it faster than I had opened anything in my entire life.

Inside was a silver necklace with a bright red stone in the center; it was far too expensive and ornate to be my mother's. The amulet, which hung from the bottom of the delicate, silver chain, was a triple spiral. I had seen the shape before. The ruby-colored stone was set in the center of a triangle, and on each side a spiral shot out and coiled around itself. The flat sides of the three spirals were carved with intricate Celtic knots. It was the most amazing silverwork I had ever seen. Under the necklace was a small, leather-bound book about the size of my hand and a note in unfamiliar handwriting:

I knew this day might come. The necklace will protect her. I love you.

I tried desperately to remember my mother's final words, searching for some clue to explain the cryptic note. She had told me to find the package and to remember my name, and that my father wanted me to have it, but this note was not in his hand. This package was from someone I didn't know. *But why was it here and who wrote it?*

The image of my mother lying on the floor bleeding to death flashed into my mind. The wound was still painful and I had to force myself to focus.

I opened the small book that was lying next to the necklace. The first page was blank save for one small word written on the bottom right corner, "Lazarus." I wasn't sure if it was a word or name. I flipped to the next page, but it was written in symbols and a language I could not read. I kept flipping and all the pages were like that, completely incomprehensible. Sadly, it gave me no answers. Something about the message itself still bothered me immensely: *It will protect her.* The message said *her*, and it made me wonder *whom* it was talking about. I came to two very vague conclusions. First, my mother knew something that I didn't, something important. Second, the book and the necklace were vital to this knowledge, but I didn't know why. My mother's last words once again echoed around me: the package was mine, it was meant for me, and that meant the warning in the note was meant for me as well. *But why would I need protecting . . . and from what?*

Belfast, Maine – May – Present Day

Star-Crossed

I COULD FEEL the weight of the ruby necklace sitting heavily on my chest, pressing against my skin. Bill kept looking at it, apparently trying to figure out where he had seen it before. For a Lagga, this amulet would mean nothing, so the only thought that came to mind was one of malicious intent: *could he be an assassin?* I thought. *Was my cover blown already?*

But I quickly snapped out of it, *No, of course not. Stop being paranoid, Ally. It's a ruby, for God's sake; anyone would stare, even a Lagga.* I changed the subject back to him.

"Can I ask you a question, Bill?" My voice was hesitant. "I apologize if it's too forward."

"Anything," he said with a hint of curiosity and excitement in his voice.

"Why did you come to Belfast? Of all the places you have lived and traveled, why come to a small town in Maine?"

He took a moment to reply, carefully choosing his words. "Hmm . . ." He paused. "I suppose I came here for the same reasons you did. I felt lost, and something about Belfast told me I was home."

I looked at him stunned. My jaw almost fell to the floor. *Lost? How did he know I felt lost? What was he, psychic?* My expression gave me away, the feeling of paranoia returned, and he began to backtrack.

"Oh, er—I mean, why does anyone move? It's to start a new life. To find a new home. That's what I meant. I came here to start my life again." *But you didn't say that,* I thought, *you said that I moved here* and *I felt lost.*

I decided to let it go, for now. I was still nervous from my Los Angeles exit and needed to realize that not everyone around me had something to hide. Besides, I liked talking to Bill, even if at times it felt awkward. It was important to keep an ear to the ground in a small town, and you can't do that without friends. Plus, his talk of heartache and loss made me feel closer to him, connected through our suffering. He felt like an old soul.

That day I went home and reflected on Bill's tale of love and loss with Marisol. I wondered what he wasn't telling me about her. Where did she go, and how does someone just disappear? All of my questions about Bill got me to thinking, and I began to contemplate my own experiences in life.

I had struggled with my beliefs for years; my mother was a Celtic pagan, a fact she hid from my very Catholic father, and after two centuries I had dabbled in almost every religion, even Scientology (thanks, LA—you really suck). Anything to shed light on my existence further than I already knew.

As confused as I was about my place in the world, it pained me even more that I didn't know love—or, at least, that I had forgotten it. It was as if I was missing out on something everyone else seemed to cherish. I had lost everyone I ever cared about, but at the same time I never felt like my heart was ripping in two or that I would die without someone, like Bill did with Marisol. Maybe I didn't have the ability to love anyone like that, or worse, maybe no one could really love me. *Well, that's depressing.*

The next morning I walked to the Green Man again, expecting to see Bill there, but when I arrived he was nowhere to be found. I was disappointed because I was actually craving human interaction. *Now what?* I thought to myself.

Of course, without Bill, Millie saw her opening. "Hi there, Ally!"

"Hey, Millie."

"Three times in one week, must be our lucky day." Millie was behind the bar smiling anxiously as she said this. She was a nice enough girl, a little too perky for my taste, but since there was no one else I thought I should take the time to be social and converse back.

"Oh, yeah, I'm on a real cider kick this week." I paused for a second. "Hey, last time I was in here, did you say your last name was Alden? As in the Alden House from down the street?"

Millie looked surprised that I remembered. "Yeah, that's my aunt's place. She runs the inn there. Good memory."

"It's a beautiful house, hard to forget," I said. Then I asked her what I actually wanted to know. "Um, you don't by chance know where Bill is, do you?"

"Bill? No, he usually keeps to himself. I don't really know all that much about him; I only work here in the summer, since school is out. He usually comes in every morning, but sometimes he disappears for a few days." She laughed. "It was really sweet that he was talking to you though, with you being new in town and all."

"Yeah, he was nice," I said and looked down to stare at the thick paper menu.

"So, Ally, I've been dying to ask you, are you going to Belfast High in the fall?" Millie inquired as I continued to stare blankly at the list in front of me. "I'm going to be a junior—maybe we'll have some classes together!"

I looked up at her eager, innocent, brown eyes. She so badly wanted me to be a normal girl that would go to high school with her, study for finals, and talk about prom dresses. I wanted to be that girl, too. Sometimes I thought I could be, but other times I remembered all the things I'd seen, all the things I'd done, and I found myself split between my seventeen-year-old face and my three-century-old mind.

"High school? No, I don't think so. I actually attended a private school, so I'm all set with my requirements." Another lie. My life was built on lies.

"Private school? Where?" she continued. "Los Angeles? That's where you're from, right? I have a cousin in LA. Maybe you know him."

"It's a pretty big city. I'm sure I don't." Millie was making me nervous, with all her questions and overt perkiness so early in the morning. I guess after spending nine months in LA, I wasn't used to people being so friendly. Then I heard the door open behind me; the same familiar bell rang out as before. I suddenly got excited, but when I turned around it was just a woman.

I continued my routine of visiting the Green Man in the mornings. Sometimes I saw Bill, and we chatted over apple turnovers, but sometimes he wasn't there. Who I really wanted to see was Connor, but I was starting to think he had walked into the coffee shop just as a figment of my imagination sent to torture me with what I couldn't have. Then, one day, logic and reason began to find me (like always). Connor couldn't possibly be a day over eighteen. What would we have in common? He was learning about WWII, whereas I was alive during WWII. It could never work, obviously, and I knew that. I almost never let myself get caught up in lust and attraction because I knew the outcome would be tragic.

I decided to leave it alone, not that I didn't totally keep thinking about him, but I took fewer walks and stopped giving myself chances to run into him. I reasoned it was for the better. After all, I was Imati; there were rules that I couldn't ignore, and I was pretty sure falling in love with a human boy would not go over well with the Eternal Council.

Paris, France – 1757 – Becoming Imati

WHEN YOU ARE constantly running, the only thing you know how to do is run.

The hour was well past midnight, and the air carried with it a crisp bite that only fall can bring. With King Louis XV constantly taking court at Versailles, many nobles had permanently moved their residences to just outside Paris's city walls. As someone who made a living through thievery and walking in the shadows, that was exactly where I needed to be. Tonight, however, I would find a different kind of treasure, one that was irreplaceable.

With a bag of jewels stuffed in my bodice, I easily leapt from the roof of the *comte d'Orsay*'s manor home, onto the soft ground of his gardens. I'd been in Paris for over seven years and found the best way to survive was to have a lot of coin. I still didn't know what I was . . . but I managed to get my hands on some rare Venetian glass, and I learned quickly that my face remained the same and my body stayed unbroken even on the brink of death.

I came to this discovery many years ago, when I stabbed my hand with a dagger just to watch it bleed. Simply to see what the wound would do. To my shock, it bled, but it was not red and warm like human blood. It was silver. Only not *just* silver; it looked like cold, liquid metal simply rolling off my skin. The wound closed, and all was fine again.

I could not die. I knew this for a fact as well. I was stabbed twice in the highlands of Scotland with an English bayonet, mortal wounds that shot straight through me. Just as when I was murdered in Ireland, I merely woke up again, perfectly strong. I used the strengths to my advantage, and in France, where peasants were starving and armies were uprising, money and power was key.

I sprinted out the back gardens toward the front gate of the d'Orsay estate, but as soon as I hit the main road I felt a shadow lurking behind me. As I got closer to the town of Versailles, I started making more turns than necessary and deviating from my route. I abruptly turned a corner onto a side street when a tall, stoic figure magically appeared right in front of me. I turned quickly on my heels, knowing I had to run. I would run and run until he was gone—or until I was forced to kill him.

But this time was different. As I sprinted through the tiny streets and turned another corner, there he was again. He was everywhere, like air. I stopped dead in my tracks and took him in face to face. Clearly, after all these years, I had met my match, an otherworldly opponent.

"*Qu'est que vous-voulez?*" *What do you want?* I asked as I drew a dagger from my side. I was never unarmed. He remained silent, and it was in that void of sound that I felt fear. Scared of the unknown. I could sense that he was faster and stronger than anyone I had ever met. Maybe even me. He carried an air of regality, and he stood so straight he must have been well above average men's height.

"*Parlez-vous français, Monsieur?*"

"*Oui*," he replied, finally breaking his silence. "I am looking for a mademoiselle named Alastrina Byrne. Do you know where I can find her?" he asked in a very calm manner, not at all fazed by the dagger in front of him.

"*Porquoi? Qui peut demander?*" *Who is asking?* I suspected that he already knew who I was, but why would he be looking for me? Why would *anyone* be looking for me? I had been chased out of every place I had ever lived with sticks and fires and stones. I belonged to no one and nowhere. I did not trust him for a minute.

"My name is Tegan and it's imperative that I find her." He cautiously glanced around to make sure no one was in earshot. "I am told that she is in need of guidance."

Tegan was a strange man with a peculiar manner, and he spoke with an intoxicating cadence. In fact, he wasn't really a man; more like a god. He was too beautiful to be real. His long golden hair was tied back into a ponytail, as was the fashion, and he spoke with such confidence that I couldn't help but be awestruck by his presence.

"Guidance . . . for what?" I inquired, still confused by his abrasive confrontation.

"Well, that is something I can only discuss with her. Do you know where she is?"

He had chased me down several streets, so I assumed he knew who I was and was reluctant to show his cards. I, too, could be guarded. "Perhaps," I replied nonchalantly. "She doesn't live around here, but I could probably track her down for you. I know everyone in these parts. Would you like me to give her a message?" I stared him down as I said this, attempting to call his bluff.

"Yes," he said, refusing to give up the charade that we both knew we were playing at. "Tell her that I mean her no harm. I am simply here as a messenger. I have the answers she is looking for." He bowed slightly, as any gentleman would. "Thank you for your help, Mademoiselle." He turned to walk away.

He only took a few steps before I called after him, "Wait!" I wasn't quite sure what I wanted to say. Should I trust this man I didn't know? Eventually, curiosity outweighed everything.

"You're not here to hurt me?" I said.

"Never," he stated. "Besides, you are the one with the dagger."

"I am Alastrina," I replied confidently, "but you already knew that."

Tegan laughed, "Of course I did." His mood lightened, but only slightly. "I needed you to trust me so that I could explain myself without scaring you off. Chasing women through the streets of Versailles is not my forte."

"So what exactly did you mean by guidance? What are you a messenger of?" I asked.

"Alastrina, the fact that your face shows no scar of time and you have no inclination why means you could use my help. Don't you think?" I didn't respond. "Come, let's go back to your quarters so we may speak in private. I have a lot of ground to cover."

I was living in the *Quartier Latin* on the Left Bank of the Seine, which was twenty miles from Versailles and sandwiched between the dirty streets of Paris. Tegan—who, inconveniently, had no horse of his own—rode back with me, on "my" brown and white steed. I sensed he was uncomfortable sharing the beast beneath us, because he rode with a fierce determination, like he was eager to get there. As we galloped and the wind crashed through my hair, I became excited for the first time since running from Cork. I was finally going to come to terms with my situation and be rid of this curse.

We sat down at a tiny wooden table in the corner of my room, and I waited for the mysterious man called Tegan to speak first. A single candle burned between us, creating an illuminating glow around his fierce jawline. His face portrayed godly strength.

"I come on behalf of the Eternal Council," he began, as if I knew what that was. "We have been waiting for you for a very long time. Now that you are an Imati, I am here to guide you through the Mortal Realm."

"Imati?" I said. The word tripped over my tongue like a foreign language. "What is that?"

Tegan seemed concerned that I had never even heard of it before.

"It is your birthright, Alastrina. You are a descendant of an ancient race called the Imati."

His words were confusing and unfamiliar. *Mortal Realm. Imati. Eternal Council.* All these years I had survived, I suspected that I was something not human, but putting a name to it suddenly frightened me even more. Perhaps I wasn't ready to be *this* different.

I lost control of any composure I had mustered up since meeting Tegan. I angrily banged my fists on the table in front of me. "Tegan—I don't know what I did wrong or who I hurt, but I am sorry for it, and I don't want to be part of an ancient race. I just want to be cured."

He interrupted, "Please calm down, Alastrina." His eyes searched mine, like he was trying to force my body to relax. Tegan continued, "First of all, as part of the Imati, you are an immortal. You were born with it; there is nothing you did to make it so. Only in death can an immortal be born. When that happened for the first time, the elemental composition of your blood changed. It is a gift, Alastrina, but a very fragile one."

I interrupted his speech. "This can't be true, Tegan—it's absurd. You're saying I'm going to live forever?"

"I assure you, it's true." He paused. "And I think, deep down, you know it's true as well."

Do I? Random thoughts about my past swirled through my mind like pinwheels, haphazardly knocking into each other, and I blurted out: "That's why it is silver then—the blood?"

Tegan was confused by my non sequitur. "Excuse me?" he asked.

"When my wounds bleed, the blood is not red. When I was human, it was. It's bothersome, to say the least."

"How many wounds have you had?" he asked, concerned.

"Enough to know my blood is silver," I replied, not giving anything away.

"I see," he said and then paused for a second. "It's Imati blood. The closest element to it on earth is Mercury. But it's not from this world and cannot be recreated. I am surprised that was your first question."

"Well, it's not my only question. I simply wanted to know, and it was the first thing that came out." I suddenly wished I hadn't asked and had just let him finish his tale. My interruption was obviously unwelcome.

"It was a good observation, Alastrina." Tegan shifted in his chair, and there was another awkward pause. "In fact, in ancient China and Egypt, many kings and emperors believed Mercury to give eternal life, thanks to legends of the Imati having silver blood. The royals would bury themselves with it, hoping for immortality. Unfortunately, the kings were wrong and unwittingly buried themselves with an element that is poisonous to humans. For you though, your blood is what gives you strength and power."

"So you, too, are an Imati?" I asked, still curious why Tegan had been looking for me, how he knew so much, and why now.

"No," he said. "When Imatis are first reborn, we—my kind—come to find you, in order to guide you through your new life. Your people call me Tegan, and I come from the Sidhe."

I leaned back in my chair. "The Sidhe?" I said. "Like the fairies of the Tuatha Dé Danann from the Celtic legends? You live underground in mounds and have magical powers?" Once I said it out loud, it seemed a bit ridiculous. Tegan, I could tell, was more than a little insulted by my insinuation that he was some sort of mythical fairy.

"Sort of," he said while furrowing his brow. He shuffled in his chair, clearly uncomfortable at having to explain his power. "Not exactly like that. Those are what you say they are—just legends—but we *are* a race apart from yours. We can choose whether or not to be seen by mortals, and we act as Guides for the Imati in order to ease their transition to the world of immortality. In fact, you are more closely related to humans than to us, and therefore we will watch and assist, but we can never interfere with what fate casts in the Mortal Realm." He stared at my blank expression, probably wondering if he should continue explaining or if I was finally all caught up.

"I don't understand," I said, not all caught up. "I became immortal when I died, but I was always going to be an immortal because I was born with it?" I folded my hands in front of me to keep from fidgeting. This was a lot of information to digest in one evening.

"Yes, Alastrina. It is passed on through the bloodline. It does not reach every generation, and some families of the Imati are older and the bloodline is stronger." He looked around the room as he spoke, surveying my apartment. He seemed uneasy in my presence, but I couldn't imagine why. He was the one with all the knowledge, while I was the freak with silver blood.

I ignored his awkwardness and continued to ask questions. "So either my mother or my father was an Imati and passed it on to me?"

"Yes," he said.

"But I watched my mother and my father die—so it couldn't have been either of them."

He cleared his throat. "Yes, but that's exactly why I couldn't find you. Usually we are able to reach newborns within a year. Otherwise they can go mad not knowing whether they are alive or dead. But your line . . . it was lost."

I cocked my head to the side. "What do you mean, 'lost'? How do you lose a bloodline? Especially you—don't you have powers or something?"

He grimaced at my use of the word *powers*. "Well, I am not a god. I could only sense you, which means I couldn't determine your exact location. I would track you, feel you out, but then your energy would just disappear. It went on like this for years. One day I could feel you, and then the next day you were gone. I went back to the Eternal Council and they had no answers; they were sure you were alive somewhere. I started tracking you here in the realm, on the ground, by tracing the Imati family I assumed you came from, but the last living heir had no children. It was not until I heard of a massacre outside of Cork, and the young witch who escaped some time later, that I thought I might be close."

The memory of running away from Cork petrified me. I had been expelled from my homeland and told that I was the child of the devil; they had chased me with stones and fire. I could never go back, and to think of it was dreadful. "You went to Ireland? You were near Cork?" I was unable to hide the fear and unpleasantness in my voice, but Tegan failed to notice.

"Yes. I discovered, Alastrina, that the man you thought was your father was not. That's why I could not trace your bloodline." He leaned in closer and whispered, "I had no idea about your mother."

"I have a different father?" I said as both a question and a statement. I was only a little surprised. This news explained so much about my previous suspicions. My father had always hated me because he must have known I wasn't his. My hair was too golden and my eyes were too green. All the years of crying myself to sleep had been pointless, because he was never going to love me. Then the obvious reality hit me. "My real father is dead as well, isn't he?" Another loss, this time of something I didn't even know I had.

"Yes," Tegan said as sympathetically as he could. "He died shortly before your first death, I believe."

The memories of the day my family was murdered came flooding back. The distorted imagery twisted and turned with my mother's face and the fear in her eyes when she died. What had that man screamed at her? "*Where is it? We know Asher was here.*" They killed my family for a reason. They killed my family because of *me*.

My eyes instantly darted to the floorboard underneath my bed, where I'd hid the ruby necklace and the book my mother had left me. I hadn't worn it for quite some time in Paris for fear it would be stolen. This city was full of thieves and rats, waiting to ravage the weak and vulnerable. The necklace must have belonged to *him*, to Asher. He knew I existed, but he never found me. Maybe he was too scared to find me? Or, more than likely, he was trying to protect me, like he wrote in the note. Tragedy sunk in and my hands began to fidget in my lap, despite my efforts to calm them. I stared past Tegan, not wanting to meet his eyes in such a personal moment of sorrow. Now I had two fathers, but both were dead. My mother, my sister, and my brother—all were still dead. Only I was born with this curse, and only I would have to be alone forever. I grabbed an apple that was sitting on my table and bit into it. The crunching sound calmed me. Tegan looked at me oddly.

"Wait," I said as a peculiar thought occurred to me in between bites. "Why couldn't you sense me? Why did I disappear—is there something wrong with me?" Like always, I was somehow different. Even as an immortal, I was defected. My father knew it, and now so did Tegan.

Tegan sighed because he had clearly pondered the same question. "Honestly, I don't know. It has perplexed me for all the years I have been searching for you. And now I find you here in Paris, robbing noblemen. I should have been with you. It must have been painful . . . to die, and then to wake up again, not knowing."

I looked away. "It was," I said, and I continued to chew on my fruit. I chose not to elaborate further, for those years between Cork and Paris were too painful to think about: full of fighting, madness, and uncertainty.

That is how Tegan saved me. He gave me answers that I had been searching for all these years. My soul started to feel more at ease and less tragically contorted from complete ignorance and isolation. You'd be surprised how comforting it is to realize there are other people like you, even if you don't know them personally.

"How do I die?" I finally asked. Obviously, that was the most important question.

"If someone cuts off your head, then you will reach second death, and never come back."

"That sounds painful," I said, grossed out a bit by the imagery.

"Not as much as if you were human. Your tolerance for pain is much higher."

"I figured," I replied, remembering stabbing myself in Scotland and being lit on fire in Cork.

"You are also stronger, faster, and more agile. But you are not invincible."

"What about food? I don't really eat that much. Can I starve to death?" I only asked that particular question because I had seen the hungry people of Paris and their dead bodies rotting on the streets. Starvation was a cruel mistress indeed.

"You need very little," he said. "You can go weeks, and you will start to feel hungry, but the hunger can't kill you."

"Good," I said with a sigh of relief, finishing my apple at the same time.

"Obviously, you are eating," Tegan remarked.

"Mainly apples," I replied. "I like them, although they are not that good here in Paris anymore. Sometimes rotten."

"Interesting," Tegan said. "Another thing is"—he hesitated—"and this doesn't apply to all Imati, but some can control metal from a distance." He stared at me waiting for a response, like he was gauging my reaction to see if I already knew that.

"Really? How?" I asked, thinking that I definitely did not have that particular ability.

"They just do. You'll know it if you have it." He was being very cryptic.

"Do you think I have it?" I wanted him to say yes. I wanted to be special . . . the good kind of special, the one with more powers.

"I don't know. There is something different about you. I am not sure what it is." He was determined not to elaborate on what exactly made me different and whether it was good or bad. "Which leads me to the last bit of information," he added.

"What?" I suddenly became nervous. Tegan was even more serious than he'd been before. Which is equivalent to a lot of seriousness.

"The Eternal Council has rules for Imati that you must follow, and if you do not, there can and will be consequences."

"What is the Eternal Council, exactly?" I asked, not particularly wanting to hear the rules.

"They are the ancient and powerful Sidhe, Alastrina, and they live in the Immortal Realm. But they see everything. It is their job to keep the balance of power within the realms and to make sure that Imati do not abuse their immortality."

Tegan went on to explain that some Imati lose touch with humanity so much so that they regard humans as dispensable, mere pawns to be used for their own aspirations. Certain members of the Imati, in the past, had become corrupt and took human life without a second thought or a morsel of regret.

"The Sidhe," he continued, "are against this." His voice was stern and authoritative. Apparently, the Sidhe felt that members of the Imati were not gods and had no right to torture and abuse mankind, thus Tegan had been thoroughly disappointed that I was stealing from humans. Little did he know that stealing was not the worst thing I had done in the last decade or so, but now was not the time to explain what my previous life had been like. According to Tegan, life was a slippery slope, and I was on my way to losing all sense of morality.

"First you steal jewels, and then you will steal more, and want more. One time you might even take a life to get what you want, and then another—where does it end? You cannot use your power irresponsibly, Alastrina; you must be respectful of this world and everything that is in it."

Tegan did not explain to me exactly what would happen if I became corrupt or went against any of the rules the Eternal Council had laid out, but I knew in my gut that whatever it was, it would not be good.

Belfast, Maine – June – Present Day

Chance Encounter

I HADN'T LEFT my house for a week. I had watched every movie I owned and reread a few books I had brought with me; sadly, I was becoming bored in this one-stoplight town. Even Delilah had failed to call, probably knowing I wasn't up to anything, and I think Cat had burrowed himself upstairs in my closet somewhere trying to get away from me. I needed to get out of the house, so I googled bookstores in Belfast (thank you, Internet) to find some new material and discovered one that carried specialty and rare books exclusively. I decided my no-more-walks-in-hopes-of-finding-Connor rule need not apply, considering I was venturing out for a valid and legitimate reason.

The specialty bookstore, called the Old Professor's Bookshop, was cute but dusty. Surprisingly I didn't recognize a lot of the books, which meant they must have been very rare since I had read a lot. The shopkeeper was an old man with glasses, *fitting for an old book store*, I thought, as he welcomed me in. He wore red, faded, suspenders and looked like he hadn't changed his outfit since nineteen thirty-eight. In fact, I think I actually remember that outfit from nineteen thirty-eight.

"Do you have any books written in Gaelic?" I asked him, trying desperately not to seem suspicious. But come on, Gaelic? What can I say; I was feeling nostalgic.

"Gaelic?" he slowly responded. "Don't hear much of a request for that these days. Try the back corner there. Lots of rare foreign language books over there, mostly just collecting dust."

I scanned the back corner of the store. There was a large cedar bookcase that took up an entire wall and was covered in books from all over the world, written in tons of different languages. I was mesmerized by all of them, and it made me a bit sad that by the looks of this place, no one in Belfast was eager to read them.

Then I saw it. Halfway down the aisle, a small leather binding stuck out with the ever-familiar Gaelic lettering written in gold filigree. I reached for the book, when all of a sudden another hand got in my way. Neither of us got a firm hold on it and the book dropped to the floor. I saw now that it was *Tristan and Isolde*, one of my favorite medieval legends. The poem was an oral story, not often written down, so it was a rare book indeed. I eagerly went down to pick it up and found myself face to face with Connor Winfield.

"Oh, sorry—did you want this book as well?" he asked in his charming British accent.

Say something clever, I thought. "Um, yes," is all I replied. *Wow*. Not exactly what I had been going for. I was at a loss for words. My mouth was dry, my throat felt like it was swelling, and I was (dare I say it) nervous. This *boy* made me nervous. I finally found words to speak when it dawned on me that Connor could read Gaelic. Now I was both nervous and suspicious.

"Hey . . . it's you!" he said. "The girl that attacked me."

I smiled nervously. "Yup . . . that's me . . . girl by day, tree-saver by . . . well, day also."

"It was a good tackle," he added. I took it as a compliment.

"Are you sure you were reaching for *this*—the tale of Tristan and Isolde?" I asked him curiously. I wanted to steer back to the fact that he might be able to read a dead language.

He stammered a bit. "Yes, well, it's for the summer reading list. I thought I would get a head start."

I looked at him in disbelief. "Belfast High School makes their students read medieval legends written in Gaelic?" I wasn't sure if he could sense my sarcasm.

"No, not exactly," he replied. "We are studying medieval history next year and this story is on the reading list. I chose to read it in Gaelic because they were out of all their other copies."

Obviously. I could tell he was lying, because his eyes were shifting and he kept clearing his throat at awkward moments.

"You know, I could ask you the same question," he added. "Why are *you* reading a book written in Gaelic?"

"Aversion Tactics 101," I replied. "Turn the accuser into the accused."

"Avoidance Tactics 101," he rebutted. "Answer a question with more questions. Or, in this case, more accusations."

"Valid point," I added. "But I am also Irish," I said confidently, "and Gaelic is technically still our language." *That ought to shut him up.*

"Really? You don't look or sound Irish. What is your name?"

"Ally."

"That's not Irish," he said mockingly.

"Fine. Alastrina Byrne, if you must know. It's actually Celtic for—"

"Defender of Humanity," he said, cutting me off before I could finish. "Quite a name you have to live up to, Ms. Byrne."

Now I was *really* suspicious. "How do you know what my name means?"

"I know a lot of things," he said with a cocky smirk. If he weren't so good-looking, it would have been irritating. *He thinks he knows a lot of things, but I doubt he knows anything about me.*

"Well, you can have it if you want," he added as he handed me the book. "I already read *Romeo and Juliet,* so I thoroughly understand the whole concept behind star-crossed lovers."

I pushed it back at him: "No it's fine. You need it for school or whatever."

When he took the book from me, he touched my hand lightly and his face changed expression, but only for a brief second. "Right, for school," he nodded in agreement. Then he continued, "Speaking of, will I be seeing you there?" He was clearly amused by this thought, and the corners of his mouth turned upwards into the most pleasant smile.

"Sorry, where?" His smile was so distracting that I hadn't actually been listening to anything he had just said.

"Belfast High . . . you are in high school, right?"

I stumbled over my response. "Um . . . er . . . yes." *What? What was I saying?* Now I would have to enroll in school just because a cute boy—who, by the way, looked older than seventeen—asked me if he would "see me there." *I am so stupid. What am I doing?*

I tried to speak again. "I mean . . . yes, I am in high school. I think . . . what I meant to say was . . . I might go to Belfast High, if I am still here." This conversation was going horribly, to say the least.

"Well then, I hope you are still here. You're much more interesting than any of the other girls I've met," he said with his boyish grin.

"Oh, in Belfast?" I assumed. "Yeah, it's a pretty small town."

He flashed his smile again. "Ha, no!" He chuckled. "I meant . . . *ever*."

Ever! Wow, that was a good line.

"Oh, and by the way, my name is Connor, since I never officially told you."

I swooned. I actually swooned. I hadn't felt like this in a hundred years. Connor had the ability to make me lose all control of what I was thinking and doing: rare, for a Lagga. He was intoxicating. He should have been born a prince. Maybe he *was* a prince. I was speechless. I mean, was he really talking to me? I turned around, just to make sure there wasn't a prettier girl standing behind me who he was actually having this conversation with. No, it was just us; in fact, we were the only ones in the entire store.

It's funny how I'd been looking for him for two weeks, and then all of a sudden he just turned up in the bookstore. Perhaps the stars had aligned and it was fate. I began to reason with myself that if it had been a serendipitous event, then the Eternal Council would have no objections, because it was not their job to interfere. I knew that humans and immortals have relationships all the time and nothing happens to them. Maybe it wasn't so much of a *rule* to not fraternize with them as it was just . . . frowned upon.

I decided to take my chances, and if I were to see Connor again, I would put forth my best effort to be less socially awkward—and not use words like *aversion tactic*.

Belfast, Maine – July – Present Day

Butterflies

IT WAS THE middle of July in Maine, and it was hot. Since I am an Imati, I don't sweat, but I can still feel the heat, and Maine might as well have been boiling lobsters in the balmy air. I had not stopped thinking about Connor since our last conversation—which was not enjoyable, since I had not seen him since then, either. I slumped into the Green Man that morning and ordered an iced apple tea (they made it special for me) in order to mentally stave off the heat a bit and pretend the cold liquid against my throat might actually make a difference. Millie and Bill were surprisingly eager for my arrival. Well, it was surprising that Bill was eager; Millie was excited in general.

"Ally! I am so glad you are here—I have excellent news!" Millie practically tackled me as I entered.

"What is it?" I replied, unenthused. The only news I was really interested in was Connor, or of course news from Delilah, but I knew she was dry on both fronts.

"The annual Belfast Celtic Festival is this weekend and Bill here said he was going to go with us—yay!" She clapped her hands and jumped up and down.

"The what with the who now?" I asked, confused.

She put her arm around me. "The annual Celtic Festival. Hello, we are in *Belfast*, named after the city in Ireland; there is Celtic history all around us!" She was pointing with her other arm to an invisible "history" she apparently saw.

"There is?" I said sarcastically.

"Yes! OMG, it will be so much fun. There's jousting, music, dance, games—everything you could imagine. It is like living history." Her eyes became wider and wider as she spoke.

Living history! I thought. *I am living history.* Little did Millie know that as part of the Imati and having been born in Ireland, I was the closest thing she knew

The Imati

to Celtic history. I wanted no part of this festival. In fact, there was no way I wanted to relive my days in Ireland or see it gimmicked up with fake costumes and anachronistic errors. If anything, the festival would be too much for me to handle. Ireland was the place where I was murdered. It is where I buried my mother, my brother, and my sister. It is the place that betrayed me. I began to fidget; it was my own natural reaction to uncomfortable feelings of sorrow. Ireland was a constant open wound of a place I both loved and hated.

"Um, no thanks. I don't think I can go." Millie's face dropped as if I had sucked the life right out of it.

"But you have to come!" she pleaded. "We're all going!"

"Yeah . . . um . . . er . . . I don't think so. My dad is coming in and he wants to take me to Portland." I really did not want to go to the festival. Feelings for me are often confusing, mainly because as an Imati, I have trouble exhibiting them. They get all muddled up inside my head and I can't properly identify with them. But my feelings about this festival and the mention of Ireland were crystal clear. I did *not* want to go.

Millie stared at me, ready to call my lie about Portland at any second. "Oh, really?" she asked suspiciously. "Well, if you can't go, then you can't go." She took her moment, and added, "I wonder if Connor will be named the winner of the highland games again. What do you think, Bill?"

Bill jumped into the conversation in order to back her up. "Oh, yes, he made quite a showing last year, especially for the new kid in town. Stronger than most all the men here, and to think, he was only sixteen or seventeen at the time. What a lad!" Bill pumped his fist in order to emphasize Connor's grandeur at the games.

My ears perked up. "Connor was there last year?" I tried to play it cool, but I was obviously interested.

"Sure was," Bill continued. "He won almost all the highland games. Great hand-eye coordination; never seen anything like it. I'm sure he will want to defend his title again."

I weighed my options: feel depressed over my past, or try to have fun and possibly get to run into Connor? After about thirty seconds of pondering the repercussions of this decision, the thought of Connor trumped the memories. *Wow, I'm definitely in trouble.*

63

I pretended to come up with a solution to get out of meeting with my fictional father. "Well, I can always tell my dad to reschedule father–daughter Portland day. I mean, it seems like this festival is real important to the town and all, so I should probably go and show my support."

Millie smiled. "Yeah . . . town pride . . . that's it," she said with just a faint hint of sarcasm, as if she hadn't known all along that as soon as she mentioned Connor I would be there with bells on.

The festival was like nothing I had imagined. The town really went all out for their Celtic heritage. I always assumed Maine would be more into a lobster fest of some kind, but apparently that was in August. I was right in my "town support" argument; it seemed like everyone was there. Of course, I didn't really know any of them besides the few I had seen in the coffee shop.

I walked past rows of tables lined with arts and crafts. Local restaurants came out to show off their take on Irish cuisine. Some people were dressed in costumes and others were just there to observe. The sound of Irish folk music played throughout the air I walked, and there was a general gaiety to the affair. I was actually glad I came. Millie was glad, too. I could tell by the way she wouldn't let go of my arm and every sentence that came out of her mouth started with "OMG, Ally, look at this . . ."

Just when I thought it couldn't actually get any better, Connor showed up. I saw him from across the lawn. He was standing with a tall, muscular man who resembled him but didn't look old enough to be his father. We locked eyes. He smiled and waved, but just as I was about to walk toward him, I accidentally smashed into a highland-themed horse that decided to cross my path and fell backward.

"Oh, great," I said as I rubbed my head and pulled myself up.

"Eek, Ally, are you okay? There's a horse there—didn't you see it?" Millie said as she brushed grass off my back.

"Obviously not," I said, irritated at my own clumsiness. *What is happening to me?*

"Well, the good news is that Connor is here. The bad news is that he totally saw you slam right into that horse's side and he is walking over here right now." She was clearly more concerned for my cool factor and less about whether I was injured or not. *Wow*, I thought. Some member of an ancient race I am. *Why am I so nervous around him?*

"Hey Ally, looks like you tried to tackle a horse this time," Connor said with a mischievous grin.

"Yes, well, I'm glad to see you didn't bring your axe or I'd have to take you down, too." I shot back. The man behind him glared at me when I said this and I realized he thought I was serious.

"It's great you're here though, it's so nice to run into you again." He glanced back at the muscular, glaring man who was now at his side. "Um, this is my dad . . . Quinn."

I looked at the man Connor called his father. I was definitely skeptical. There was no way Quinn could be more than thirty years old. He was handsome, just like Connor, and while they both had dark hair, they didn't act related. I smiled at him and reached for his hand. He did not take it or smile back. "Nice to meet you." I said the words, but obviously did not mean them. It was not nice to meet him; he sent a chill down my spine. Quinn, I could tell, did not like me. Connor looked uncomfortable.

"Dad, Ally is actually Irish." He turned toward me for confirmation. "Isn't that right, Ally? She can read Gaelic." As the words left his mouth, I wondered why that was the first thing he'd said.

Quinn's eyebrows rose slightly, and he was obviously intrigued by the statement. Then he returned to his icy composure. "Fitting for the festival, I suppose."

Those were Quinn's first words to me, and they weren't actually directed at me, more so at Connor. I replied anyway.

"Yeah, I am really excited to see some appreciation of Celtic and Irish history." Somehow I managed to say it with a straight face. Then I turned toward Connor. "I hear you are somewhat of a legend now in the highland games?"

Connor's face beamed with pride. "Well, you know, last year was difficult because I was new, and I didn't know the tricks—"

Quinn interrupted him before he could finish. "Connor, I am going to take off. Make sure that you are home within an hour."

Connor began to protest, "But Dad, I signed up to compete again, and there is a bonfire later tonight with—"

Again, before Connor could finish, Quinn interjected, "No buts, Connor. You have one hour."

Connor acquiesced, but he didn't seem defeated. "Fine, I'll see you at home." He and I stood there awkwardly as Quinn departed.

I decided to break the silence. "Gee, that was intense," I said as soon as Quinn was out of earshot.

"Yeah, my dad is a bit strict, as I am sure you've heard. He doesn't really want me to socialize with kids my age."

Lucky for him, I'm not his age, I thought. Maybe Quinn would let Connor hang out with me if he knew I was actually quite the mature adult . . . but on second thought, probably not. I was a little too mature, if you know what I mean.

"So I guess you have to leave in an hour, then? That doesn't give us much time to do anything," I said, disappointed.

"Yeah, well, just because I have to be home in an hour doesn't mean I can't come back." He glowed with a rare confidence that I had never seen in someone so young.

"Won't your dad get mad?" Millie interjected. I had completely forgotten she was even standing there. The sound of her voice startled me.

"Um, yeah, if he were to find out." He grinned.

"Oooh, snee-*kay*," Millie said enthusiastically, as if Connor had somehow just gained ten cool points. Like he needed them.

"So we have one hour to chill," he added. "I say we get some of that awesome funnel cake with blueberry jam and watch the jousting contest." The spark was back in Connor's blue eyes, as if the thought of freedom from Quinn was his greatest gift.

"Funnel cake? Is that even Celtic?" I asked.

"No, but it's delicious!" he said. Then he leaned in so close to my face that I could feel his warm breath on my ear, and he whispered, "When I sneak back for the bonfire, you and I can finally have some alone time."

At that moment I really wanted to come up with some cool-sexy retort, but all I managed was, "Okay."

There was no doubt in my mind that the night would be amazing, despite my rusty flirting abilities. If only we were required to dance a waltz, flirt with fan gestures, or drink champagne, then I'd be more prepared. Despite the nervous twitch in my fingers, though, Connor made me excited about the thought of starting a new journey in my new life—one possibly full of romance, which was a feeling I had long forgotten.

Belfast was turning out to be a much more enjoyable place than I had thought possible. *Thanks, Delilah.*

Journey to the New World – 1792 – Liberté

WITH THE INVENTION of the guillotine, Paris had become a dangerous place during the Revolution, even for a member of the Imati like myself. Getting my head cut off meant instant death for me, just as it did for a human. While in Paris, I had discovered two life-changing things. First, Tegan, my Guide, had become a welcome presence. He bought me a new, larger, place on the other side of the river Seine and stayed with me for several years until I had settled comfortably into the life of a proper, non-thieving lady. Then he would pop in and out of town whenever I managed to find my way back to Paris to check in on me. He also clued me in to the fact that time was on my side, and valuables tended to increase in worth. Then the Revolution, while at first seemed like the coming of enlightenment and free thought, turned into a bloody massacre, and Paris, for me, was over.

Which leads me to my second discovery in Paris: other Imati. Since I had the fortune of having a Sidhe Guide with me when the Revolution spiraled more toward bloody and less toward liberty in the 1790s, our home became a safe haven for Imati who were evading the guillotine as well. It was my first real encounter with other immortals, and that excited me greatly. However, the few that stayed with us were much older than I and didn't deem it quite as exciting to socialize with me—but the few conversations I managed to have with them were *somewhat* successful. If by successful I mean total and utter disaster.

"The Revolution is a bit out of hand," I said to Cornelius one afternoon as he sat in the downstairs sitting room. He was a very powerful and ancient Imati. Not even Tegan knew his exact age, but he said that his family carried one of the strongest bloodlines.

"Yes, I believe it is," he replied, and then he left the room.

Two days later: "It's so hot today. The stench of Paris is becoming unbearable," I said from my window seat as I fanned myself and stared out into the dusty, boisterous *rue Saint-Martin*.

"Yes, I believe it is," he said again, and left the room. I became convinced that he did not actually speak my language and could only muster those five words. My other conversations with the other immortals followed the same pattern: I would make small talk, and they would leave the room.

I complained to Tegan that Cornelius and the other Imati did not like me. His reply was that I was reading too much into it and too concerned with being liked.

"Imati, and immortals in general, tend to stick to themselves. They are lone wanderers. They have survived for centuries and have learned not to become attached to people—even other Imati." Tegan grabbed my shoulders and looked straight into my green eyes, signaling that what he was about to say was important, so I listened as carefully as I could.

"Alastrina, you must understand that for them, this is temporary. This house, this city, and everything in it mean nothing. When you live for such a long time, and you see so many things, you learn to disconnect yourself from them as a way of protecting yourself. After a certain amount of time passes, you start to lose the ability to feel. Cornelius and the others here are very old; that is how they were able to find me. Do not take it personally that they are not eager to become your friend. If anything, the thought has not even occurred to them."

"I understand," I said somberly, and I did, except for the "losing the ability to feel" part. I didn't want to lose any of my emotions or my ability to feel. Of course, with no family and no friends, I was quickly becoming aware of how possible that was. In fact, the more I thought about it, the harder it became to remember the last time I had really *felt* anything. It was obvious that my human relationships and connections to the world had all but disappeared.

That was the last I asked Tegan about the others and the last time I tried to make conversation with them. Then, one day, Cornelius was gone, and I have not seen him since. All he left was a note that said he was headed to Argentina in the New World and that it would be safe there for Imati.

Tegan took me to Bordeaux at once so I could catch a trade ship heading to the Americas. He did not board it with me, and I was not sure when or if I would see him again. Tegan did not have the same attachment to me as I had to him, and if he did, he made no mention of it. We said our good-byes in the dead of night with a simple hug. If I were human, I would have cried. I was sad to be parted from him, but the *feeling* of sadness actually made me happy, and I tried to hold onto it for as long as I could. I knew that I would be different from them. I vowed to myself to defend my own humanity.

The ship I traveled upon was called *Liberté*—ironic, since it was carrying slaves to French colonies in the West Indies. I had never made a long journey by sea, and under the circumstances, my maiden voyage was less than ideal. I am not sure how Tegan convinced them to allow me aboard the massive wooden ship at the port in Bordeaux, but whatever he did, it must have been expensive, since it was not customary to have a young girl on deck for the eight-week voyage. Sailors considered women bad luck aboard a ship. The crew seemed suspicious of me at first, but under the current situation of the Revolution it was not entirely rare to have refugees fleeing France under the dark cover of night. There was another family on board as well, which put my mind at ease. I didn't speak to them, but at least I was not a young girl completely alone with forty crewmen. I was also thankful not to be below deck with the rest of the "cargo," but I was less than pleased with my current state of affairs. Once again I was by myself, beginning a new journey in life and unsure of where exactly I was headed.

At night I slept in a tiny space on a roped hammock. The ship rocked back and forth methodically, almost peacefully, except for the motion-induced sickness that affected many of the crewmembers and passengers. After a few days the smell of seawater began to fade, and the foul stench of humanity clouded the air. The rhythmic rocking of the ship was interrupted only by the desperate cries from the condemned that traveled beneath me. I counted my blessings every day of that journey that I was not in desperate need of food, water, or sleep. I saw what happened to the unfortunate souls who did need those things, and needless to say, half of the human cargo traveling with us never set foot in the New World. Their souls would be forever lost at sea. Somewhere, their families would mourn them, if they, too, were not already dead.

From the port in Saint-Domingue, I had to catch another ship to the Southern Americas, in particular to the port at Buenos Aires in Argentina. Cornelius had given us a specific destination in his note, and Tegan was insistent that my crossing take me to Buenos Aires and nowhere else.

"Alastrina, listen to me," he had warned. "I don't care how long it takes or how tiring the journey is. You are to go to Argentina where you will be safe. Nowhere else, understand?"

"Safe from what?" I asked. It's not like I was the easiest person to kill. I was frustrated that he was treating me like a child.

"From anything. What does it matter? Just promise me you will head to Argentina, okay?"

"I promise," I said, and I meant it, but I was skeptical. What was Tegan—or Cornelius, for that matter—protecting me from? Was France or anywhere else that much of a threat to me?

I felt weathered after two months at sea, and the thought of getting on another ship was unbearable. Saint-Domingue was a heavenly paradise, with blue waters and crystal-white, sandy beaches lined with tall, almost branchless tress that I had never seen before. At that moment, it was the apple in my Eden. Part of me wanted to stay, but the other part was actually scared of Tegan's warning and the promise I had made to him. Tegan was the one person in the world I trusted, and betraying him was simply not an option.

The second journey was much shorter, and thankfully I was not aboard a slave ship. However, I made sure to wear my mother's necklace for good luck. Tegan's other words, from our conversation in Paris, began to haunt me on the journey south. He was right: the longer I lived, the more tragedy I would see in the world. The images of my transatlantic crossing should have disgusted me more than they did, but I was able to block them out and disassociate my life with what was happening aboard that ship. *Was this a skill acquired by all Imati? Should I really consider it a skill?* In Ireland I had witnessed death and betrayal, in France I had seen a bloody war firsthand, and aboard the *Liberté* I had seen a complete disregard for human life. My own family had been slaughtered. In seventy years, I had witnessed countless humans die from both natural and unnatural causes. What would I see in another seventy? How could it get worse? It seemed that the curse of the Imati—of immortality in general—was that they could live long enough to see the entire world, but by the time they discovered it, they would no longer care.

Thoughts of despair clouded my mind as I reflected upon my own life up to this point. However, when not reminiscing or overthinking my present circumstances, I was genuinely hopeful. It was like I was torn between two completely different thought processes. One was burdened by suffering. The other, the one I was only just discovering, was focused more on the present and was much less sympathetic to the trials of others. I was beginning to understand more clearly Cornelius's state of mind.

I felt less and less every day for the human lives around me. It was not a choice I made; it happened slowly, over time. I did not even notice it until I had landed in Buenos Aires and suddenly became excited for my new adventure in the New World. Thoughts of revolution, the guillotine, and lost souls at sea were far behind me. Every thought of despair I had with me I left aboard the ship from Saint-Domingue.

Belfast, Maine – July – Present Day

Falling

THE BONFIRE WAS about to begin. Everyone carried wood to the beach and made a big pile in the center of the sand. To the right of me, the ocean looked ominous and dark. To the left, I could see and hear the lights and laughter of a town in the midst of a summer celebration. Some locals poured in from Three Tides Bar, drunk on draft beers and Jack Daniels, and eagerly added more logs to the fire while simultaneously preparing their metal prongs for s'mores. The intoxication of the night was palpable. The flame of the bonfire was lit and a stream of black smoke climbed into the night sky as the people applauded. The fire was quickly hot and roaring.

I might have appreciated it more if I hadn't been so nervous. The thought of alone time with Connor was downright frightening. I was excited and scared all at the same time. I sat on the log waiting for him, hands folded in my lap, with my right leg pulsing up and down. *Where is he, anyway? Maybe he couldn't get away. Maybe he needs help.* Ugh. The thought of Quinn punishing him angered me. Poor Connor.

A voice called out from behind me, "Ally, there you are! I was looking for you." The accent was unmistakable.

"Connor! You're okay. I was worried." My voice was a little too high-pitched for my liking.

"Yeah, of course I am. Why wouldn't I be?" *Oh, right.* I had forgotten that all my concerns were simply in my crazy, neurotic head. Now I just seemed overly eager to see him. *Great.*

"I mean, how did you manage to escape Quinn's grasp?" *That's a cover,* I reasoned.

"Ah, well, I would tell you, but I'd have to kill you. Sorry, love," he said with his infectious smile beaming. That wasn't the first time someone had said that to me, actually, only that time, they weren't smiling.

"Oh, I see." Connor was staring at me, waiting for me to say more. "Well, I guess I have a lot to learn from you then—especially in the art of escape. Maybe you should consider a career in espionage."

"Hmm, I hear that MI6 loves hiring eighteen-year-olds. Maybe I'll give it a go and head back to London immediately." He looked at me curiously, trying to gauge my response.

"MI6 is the British CIA, right?" I was double-checking my facts. These agencies were always changing.

"Yes, but much more effective." He laughed. Obviously, he wanted me to tell him not to go be James Bond and to stay in Belfast with me.

"In that case, maybe not. I think you are better suited for high school at the moment." Not wanting to give him the satisfaction of forcing me to admit that I wanted him to stay stateside, I quickly added, "Besides, London is a bit dull compared to Belfast. I mean, do you remember that funnel cake today? A-*maz*-ing!" I flashed a smile at him and tried, probably unsuccessfully, to look cute.

"You're absolutely right, that funnel cake was by far the best part of my day," he said.

"Hey! What about getting to hang out with me? Can I at least come in second?" I feigned offense.

"Second? Not a chance. Jousting comes in second."

"Not fair, I can't compete with weapons," I said, half serious.

He continued, "You are, of course, the front-runner for best part of my night . . . and this night is beginning to rank as the best night of my life." He chuckled slightly, as if he had set the whole thing up just so he could say that line. It worked, because I was completely charmed.

"Best night of your life?" I said with as much sass as I could muster. "I guess you haven't lived very long."

At that, we both began to laugh. My line had more truth to it than he realized, but I think Connor was more impressed that I was able to rebut his attempt at sweeping me off my feet. I could sense that he was the kind of guy that liked a challenge, and he was definitely the kind of guy that enjoyed a chase. I was happy to oblige.

The bonfire was the perfect setting for a quasi-date. Connor and I sat side by side on a chopped up piece of tree trunk. Our shoulders were touching, and I so badly wanted to link my arm in his. I wished it had been colder so a blanket would have been necessary. The best part was that we finally had a chance to speak to each other without Quinn or Millie butting in. That is, until someone else did.

I didn't know who she was or what she wanted, but just when I was getting comfortable with Connor, a little, blonde-haired, blue-eyed girl walked up, smiling from ear to ear.

"Connor! I thought I saw you over here!" she squealed.

Connor reluctantly stood up—or, at least, I hoped it was reluctance. As he did so, his arm left my shoulder and planted a small hug around the new girl.

"Hi, Rebecca," Connor muttered, and then turned to me. "This is Ally. Ally, this is Rebecca Munn. She goes to school with us. Or will, when you start."

I stood up. "Hi. Nice to meet you."

Rebecca looked me up and down, like a hawk analyzing its prey. She was a tiny girl, shorter than me, and about the size of a toothpick. In fact, I could snap her in half if I needed to. Wow; I was seriously jealous. *Snap out of it, Ally.*

"Hi," is all she said to me, and then she turned straight back to Connor. "So are we finally gonna have that boating adventure you promised me?" She said it like Connor was a prize she was still waiting to collect.

Connor smiled. "Soon, maybe. I've just been out of town a lot. Sorry."

"It's cool. You know how good I am on boats!" She laughed. I'm not really sure why considering it wasn't funny. Connor didn't say anything and there was an awkward pause.

"Anyway, I'll tell my dad you say hi!" she added, purposely rubbing it in that she and Connor had a past.

"Uh, thanks . . . I guess." Connor said. And then she walked away.

We took our spots back on the log. Our warm moment had dissipated with the entrance of Rebecca Munn. "I do work on her dad's house, that's it," Connor said.

"Cool. She seems nice," I replied.

Connor laughed, "She's not that nice."

I smiled. "Yeah, I didn't really believe it when I said it."

We were back, and for the rest of the time, Connor and I chatted uninterrupted. He managed to avoid answering most of my questions, and I had definitely mastered the art of circumventing the truth, so our conversation treaded more toward the trivial than the real. He told me about his favorite football team—Fulham—and that if he could have been anything in the world, he would have been a professional footballer.

"I swear, I could take on Christiano Ronaldo any day—I mean, if I had the proper training."

"And Christiano Ronaldo is who?" I'll admit it—I was a soccer fan, but definitely not a *fanatic* like Connor.

"Only Portugal's best player. Plus, he's a huge celebrity in Europe, like David Beckham."

"Oh! The Armani guy!" *His* commercials I remembered.

"Yeah, the Armani guy," Connor said, apparently a little disappointed in my lack of sporting knowledge.

I decided to diffuse my ignorance with humor. "Well, you could try, but you couldn't live up to his dashing good looks, so I am afraid he's got you beat."

"You think he is good-looking?" he inquired with some insecurity layered beneath his confident exterior.

"Well, I am a sucker for dark hair." He smiled at that; I was clearly a sucker for him.

"So Ally, in all seriousness, what do you want to be when you grow up? A rock star? A famous writer? A butcher, baker, or candlestick maker?" I laughed. Guys are always sexy when they are funny.

"I don't know," I replied, still chuckling, and I didn't. Connor's face suddenly seemed less than amused, and I began to reevaluate my response. I probably should have lied and said I wanted to be a teacher or something, but lying *even more* to Connor felt a little wrong.

The problem was, I had never really thought about it because it didn't really apply to me. There wasn't an opportunity for me to "do" anything, since I would never age. It's not like I could be a doctor or lawyer or police officer; I was technically too young for all those things, and too paranoid to want to stand out in some profession.

Connor still looked confused. "Well, if you could pick something, what would you pick? Anything in the world." His tone was both serious and optimistic. He *wanted* me to have dreams.

This question made me both melancholic and uncomfortable. I couldn't think of anything. I didn't have the desire to *do* anything. I was just surviving. It was all I knew how to do. Did killing *Seeker* assassins count as a career choice?

I basically repeated my first answer, but this time without laughing. "Um, I don't know. I don't really think about the future much."

"You don't have dreams or aspirations? You just want to be a kid forever?" He seemed to grow angrier. "The whole world is open to you, you can do anything, and yet you choose nothing?" He paused for a moment, trying to control his fury at my response, and then his voice turned to disappointment. "Not all of us have such pleasures, Ally. Not all of us have the luxury of choice."

Where was this coming from? What luxury? Connor seemed genuinely put off by my inherent lack of ambition, and the only way I could defend myself would be to reveal that I wasn't a normal girl and I was born an Imati. What kind of choice was that?

I shouted back, "That's not fair! I do want things. But after a lifetime of knowing your place in the world, knowing what you can't have, you give up. You settle for what you've got." I was riled up. I began to realize I had unsettled feelings about my own station in life, and I took it out on Connor. "Sometimes dreaming about something that can never happen is more painful than just accepting it—maybe you will understand that someday when you're older." *Ouch.* That was a low blow, not that Connor would understand the reference. I felt on the verge of tears. I was unintentionally revealing feelings I had wanted to unleash for centuries. I had clearly said too much and started to worry that my outburst would lead to questions I couldn't answer.

Connor just looked at me for a minute, perplexed. If I had the ability to cry, tears would have been running down my cheeks. I regretted my words instantly; I was afraid Connor would think I was a freak, or worse, some overly hysteric and dramatic teenage girl.

Fortunately for me, he didn't. He did the last thing I expected him to: he hugged me. He wrapped his large arms around my much smaller frame, and in that moment I placed my head so close to his heart that I could hear it beat. The sound, unfamiliar to me, was comforting. In his grasp, I felt safer than before and safe from the world and worries around me.

"Ally, I am sorry I got angry before. I didn't mean to . . . hurt you." His empathy was surprising, to say the least. He paused for a second while stroking my back. "And I do understand. In fact, I know exactly what you mean."

We sat there, together, in a perfect moment. From the outside, we looked like teenagers sharing a quiet embrace. In reality, we were both scared. There had been a truth in my words that I had buried within myself for a long time. There was also something about my statement that resonated with Connor. I knew I couldn't ask him about it, and so we continued to sit there and stare at the fire until the flame died and everyone started to leave. It was completely dark, now that the glow from the fire was gone, and the stars above us were clearly visible. The moon shone on the ocean water, and if the colors were changed from black and silver to red and orange, it could have been a sunset.

"Time to go home," Connor said. We hadn't spoken for at least thirty minutes; we were both oddly comfortable in silence. The weight of my words still hung in the night air. "Ally, I can walk you back home, if you want."

I looked up at him to respond, "No, it's fine. I can find it on my own. I like walking alone."

With that, I got up from the log, hugged him good-bye, and began to walk back to my empty house alone. It was a walk I was accustomed to, but this time, it felt worse. The sparkle of hope that Connor made me feel when next to him made the walk feel even lonelier. I wanted more. I wanted more Connor, more life, and the feeling of truly being safe.

Buenos Aires, Argentina – 1831 – New Family

BUENOS AIRES TURNED out to be an incredible city: a bustling port, with new travelers from around the world arriving every day, created energy in the air that was palpable. Fish merchants shouting the daily catch, children running across the decks to watch the ships sail out, the bell sound for a new arrival—all were the echoes of a living, breathing city.

Unfortunately, I had left behind one war in France for another one emerging in Argentina. Fortunately, as an Imati, this worked to my advantage. The city was at many times in chaos; invasions came from both the British and Spanish. I would leave Argentina whenever the fighting was too much, but I always came back. Since the last three decades had been plagued by political upheaval, it was fairly easy to stay unnoticed there, since both power and people came in and out like a cheap date. Alas, I was so in love with empanadas and Argentinean wine that the constant power change was nothing I couldn't manage.

By 1830, I had established a life for myself, complete with an apartment, a job as a seamstress, and friends. No longer was I alone. Scarlett, Rafael, Paulo, and I formed quite a little foursome in our two-bedroom apartment. To outsiders, we pretended as if we were married, as was appropriate for the time, but in reality, we were all family. The three of them were, of course, all Imati like myself. I had known them for several years now, and I truly started to believe that Tegan was wrong, that not all Imati want or need to walk this earth alone.

It was Scarlett who discovered me. She had been watching me for a while when she finally mustered the nerve to approach me. Not that a girl like Scarlett ever needs mustering.

The air in Buenos Aires that night was heavy and blanketed my skin. I didn't perspire in the humidity, but everyone around me glistened under the moonlit heat. I was sitting in an outdoor café, fanning myself while listening to classical guitar and sipping a fruity red table wine, when she sat next to me. She was beautiful. Her auburn-colored hair was pinned up in curls and her blue eyes pierced against her milky-white skin. The glow of the hanging paper lights behind her made her look angelic and exotic at the same time. She wore a red dress with a small white hat, in a fashion that was clearly her own invention. I was so mesmerized by her beauty I forgot to inquire as to why she sat down in the first place.

"*La música esta increíble, si? Me encanta mucha.*" She said how much she loved the music with a beaming smile that seemed to reach across her entire face.

"*Si, por supuesto.*" *Yes, of course.* I picked up the language a few years back, but my accent was terrible. Rolling my 'r's was actually quite difficult, especially for an Irish girl from Cork.

"*Parlez-vous français?*" Her French accent was impeccable as well.

"*Oui, bien sûr. Porquoi? Vous n'aimez pas espagnol?*" *Yes, of course. Why? You don't like Spanish?* I was much more comfortable speaking French and enjoyed it greatly, but I was also curious as to the purpose of the language test.

"What about English?" she continued.

"It's not my natural tongue, but I picked it up somewhere along the way. Unfortunately, that's almost all of them, so if you say something in Italian next, I'll be stumped."

She laughed, and it was infectious. I began to laugh as well—I had forgotten how good it felt. Scarlett was intoxicating. She had barely said a word and I knew absolutely nothing about her, and yet I couldn't wait to learn it all. She grabbed the carafe of table wine and poured herself a glass. I did not object.

She spoke as she poured. "I was only curious because I could not quite place your country. I wasn't sure which language you would respond in. The port has been bustling with foreigners for years now; you never know whom you might stumble upon. My name is Scarlett. What's yours?"

"Alastrina."

"Well, Alastrina, I think I would like to call you Ally instead. Is that alright?"

"My sister called me Ally."

"Well, that's fantastic, because I see us being the best of friends—as close as sisters."

Her sudden confidence in our future made me nervous. How could I tell her that I have no friends, no more sister, and there was no way she could be a permanent part of my life? The concern I was thinking was obviously plastered in my expression because her demeanor changed instantly.

"Listen, Ally, I know you're worried. But don't fret, child. I may look twenty, but I'm no Lagga, if you know what I mean."

I did not know what she meant. "Sorry, I'm not sure what you're referring to . . . Lagga?" I asked, confused.

"Oh," she chuckled a bit. "It's *our* word for 'human'; it means I'm not mortal. I was born in Spain—fifth of August, 1763, to be exact."

My mouth dropped open. She'd said *our*, as in *us*. She was Imati, just like me. *How could she be so open about it? How could she be so confident?* I stared at her, half wanting to run away scared and the other half curious to learn more. "Don't worry, darling, we have been watching you. We know you're one of us. We were simply waiting for the right time to approach you, and here we are. Voilà! Come, meet my friends." Scarlett reached for my hand to take me away, completely confident in the fact that I would follow her. She was, of course, correct. I was smitten.

That is how my new life as an immortal really began. Scarlett introduced me to Rafael and Paulo. Both were Argentinean, *porteños*, as they called themselves. Scarlett was half French and half Spanish. She had grown up in Barcelona. She never talked about her *first death*, but then again, none of us really did. The three of them lived in the present, and that was exactly where I wanted to be. They didn't care much for the rules of the Imati and had more fun staying in one place together than wandering alone.

Scarlett said I had a "certain glow," so they decided to watch me more closely. After much consideration they decided collectively to offer me a place in their family. I accepted immediately. I was tired of being alone all the time. The best part of my immortal life had been the few years I'd spent with Tegan in Paris. I thought of him like a father, but in the end he still left me. I might have been safer in the Americas, but I was still isolated from the world like a walking ghost, treading over the streets of Buenos Aires, never really leaving a mark. It was part of my identity to be invisible.

Scarlett and her friends were offering me a real family and some semblance of a real life. There was a childlike optimism that they all possessed, like the world was theirs for the taking, and all I had to do was jump on board. I jumped, but little did I know just how far I would fall.

Belfast, Maine – August – Present Day

Half Truths

I WAS HAVING lunch with Millie at Darby's, a local restaurant and pub, about two blocks from the coffee shop, and in between bites of her clam chowder and bread bowl combo, she was able to muster out a few interrogative questions about Connor.

"Come on, Ally, spill it—did he or did he not kiss you?" She asked with her mouth half full.

"For the last time, Millie, he did *not*. Seriously, if he does, you will be the first to know. That is, if I ever see him again." I was still concerned that I had scared Connor off for good.

"Oh, come on, I'm sure it didn't end that badly. Besides, he is probably dying to see you. You're gorgeous!"

I internally blushed when she said that. I didn't consider myself pretty, and I never paid much attention to my appearance. The truth was that since the bonfire, it had been two weeks, three days, and about fifteen hours since I had last seen Connor, not that I was keeping track or anything. I never gave him my cell number, call me cautious, and he never offered his, either. From what little Millie knew, his house wasn't exactly on the town's radar, and even though he knew where I lived, he never came knocking. All in all, it seemed like we were the only two people in the technological age not communicating, either because we couldn't, or worse—because we were scared.

"I wonder where he is all the time. What is he doing?" I pondered out loud, irritated by the fact that running into Connor haphazardly was next to impossible.

"People say he and Quinn go out of town a lot—business trips, family visits back home. Who knows. I mean, his dad is a freak!"

"Yeah, he is. Quinn is really creepy. I don't think I would risk going to Connor's house even if I knew where it was." I took a bite of my apple pie and imagined what his house looked like. It was probably a castle—or a fortress. In my fantasy, Connor was a knight, and I was a princess that needed rescuing. He would rush in and save me from some giant, evil dragon. In reality he was just a boy, and I would more likely be the one saving him from some terrible fate caused by any relationship he were to have with me. My daydream was brutally crushed by logic . . . stupid logic.

Millie put her spoon down mid-bite. "Oh, really?"

"Yeah, really," I said, but Millie suddenly had a mischievous look on her face.

"So if someone, say, had that information, you wouldn't want to know about it?"

Still imagining Connor as a knight and becoming desperate, I said, "Well, yes, but I thought you didn't have that kind of information."

"I don't, but I think I could find it out," she said.

I was instantly game. "What do you mean? Why didn't you tell me this earlier, like before I ate an entire pie!" Excitement washed over me, and suddenly my delicious, apple dessert was no longer appetizing.

"I didn't think of it, I just had a flash of brilliance like this very second." She started congratulating herself on her own cleverness.

"Well come on then, track it down, let's go!" I threw twenty bucks on the table and scooted out of the plastic green and brown booth faster than was appropriate for a restaurant exit.

I was surprised by my own enthusiasm, but I was dying to see Connor again, even if it was in a creepy stalker way. I couldn't stop thinking about him. He was like a drug to me, and I needed to get my fix. Just one look wouldn't hurt anyone . . . right? Plus, I should know where he goes. What if he's dangerous? I needed to protect myself before getting too close. It was reconnaissance.

I stood anxiously in the parking lot in front of Darby's as Millie called her friend Jane, who had asked Connor for help last year on the Advanced Placement European History exam. Apparently he was some kind of academic genius as well. However, Connor is notorious for not allowing anyone in his house, but since Jane's dad is a bit of a drunk and she dreams of going to Yale, Connor made an exception. Chivalry is always sexy.

"Did you get it?" I asked eagerly, as I paced in front of the restaurant.

"Yeah, yeah. Jane was hesitant, said that Connor had asked her not to give it out or whatnot, but I managed to squeeze it out of her anyway."

"How?"

"I saw her kissing Jason Parks earlier this year at the spring carnival."

"So?" Like I knew who Jason Parks was.

"So . . . her boyfriend wouldn't be too happy if he found out!" Millie was smiling at her resourcefulness.

"Wow, Millie, I didn't think you were the blackmailing type of girl."

"I'm not, but I feel so alive today. Come on, let's add breaking and entering to the list of crimes. Casa de Connor, here we come!" She high-fived me and then proceeded to sprint to my car. Whether I saw Connor or not, it was fun to have a friend in Belfast.

We slowly pulled up to a large and expensive-looking house on the outskirts of town, buried a little ways in the woods. It was definitely aged, but well maintained. The house itself was made of dark wooden shingles, contrasted against white-lined windows. The structure looked ominous, mainly due to its large size and the protruding dark forest silhouetted behind it. I felt the nerves inside me. My hands were gripping the steering wheel and my body felt frozen. *What am I doing here?*

"Come on, let's look inside." Millie had me park the car a few blocks away, and we strategically approached the house on foot. There were several windows on the bottom floor with small shrubs underneath them, which we used as cover. As we peered in, it looked like the lights were on.

"Looks like Connor answered your question about what he does." She pointed in through the open window to where we could see Connor and Quinn. "Looks like he stays at home with his dad. How boring," Millie said, unimpressed.

She was half right. He was at home, but it wasn't boring. All of a sudden, a knife appeared in Quinn's hand and he started to attack Connor. He lunged and missed. Connor turned quickly to block the blow coming from behind him. Quinn lunged again, this time slicing Connor's shirt, spinning around, and placing him in a headlock. Connor surrendered and then started to laugh. "You win again, but I'm getting stronger. Next time you won't defeat me so easily."

"That's why we train every day. No mistakes. No distractions, got it?" Half out of breath, Quinn patted Connor on the back.

"Yes. I know. No distractions." They began to fight again, this time with no weapons. After about thirty seconds of watching Connor take punches to the gut, I felt sick. No matter what he was, I knew one thing for sure: he was a liar.

"Come on, Millie, let's go. We shouldn't be here." I quickly got up from my crouched position in the bushes, brushed the dirt from my jeans, and pulled Millie up with me. We walked back to the car in silence and began to pull away.

The drive back was disheartening. I didn't know Connor at all. All I knew was that he was some gorgeous British kid who loved football, funnel cake, and, apparently, knife fighting with his crazy dad. What was I thinking, getting involved with someone so dangerous? I never should have let my guard down. I never should have trusted him. *I know better.* I was angry with myself for being naïve, and with Connor for being dishonest.

The road hummed underneath my Mercedes. I should have turned on the radio in order to break the awkward silence, but Millie beat me to it and in a frantic voice said what both of us were thinking. "Oh my gosh! I'm gonna say it, Ally—what the heck was that? Your boyfriend is a nut!"

"He's not my boyfriend," I said sternly.

"Well, aren't you scared? He was fighting his dad with a *dagger.* That is some serious stuff. It's not like they were fencing or something. There was choking and punching involved."

"I know. I was there, remember?" Millie's panic attack was starting to irritate me.

"What are you going to do? You can't date him—he'll kill you!"

I didn't have an answer. I wasn't scared; I had definitely seen worse. I was more concerned that I had allowed myself to like someone when I had known too well that I shouldn't. Seeing this whole other side to Connor reminded me why I don't get close to people: because you never know whom you can trust. Connor had secrets. I had secrets. There is no way that either of us could risk being exposed. I decided that my infatuation with Connor Winfield needed to end—before one of us wound up dead.

Argentina – 1836 – Lessons Learned

FIVE YEARS WITH my new family flew by. The more I surrounded myself with Imati, the more I loved being one. Ever since I had left Ireland I had been trying to blend in, when really I was meant to stand out. Scarlett knew this about herself and embraced it. She made her own clothes (hence my job as a seamstress) and the hats she sold were becoming quite fashionable in Buenos Aires society. The four of us did what we wanted when we wanted to. We drank wine constantly; if it took one bottle to make a Lagga drunk, it took about five to affect us. Scarlett and I would walk on the beach, vino in one hand and a cigarette in the other. Men would pass us and stare with their mouths open. We were never scared to be alone as two young girls, because we knew we could defend ourselves. Life was incredible, the days seemed brighter, the sun was warmer, and the hot nights were as intoxicating as the wine.

Sometimes Raul and Paulo would come home with expensive things, but I decided never to ask questions. It was their prerogative to live as they wanted to. They would disappear for weeks at a time and Scarlett said they were off gallivanting through every whorehouse in Argentina. I learned not to judge them, but rather to embrace their hedonistic lifestyle: dancing until sunrise, drinking until I passed out, traveling anywhere I wanted to go. The world and everything in it were mine for the taking.

Scarlett had begun seeing a wealthy businessman named William who split his time between Buenos Aires and Barcelona. He was only in town for a few months at a time, but that is what she loved about him.

"Does it bother you that you are just his mistress?" I asked her one day.

"Oh, Ally. You are so naïve sometimes. I get the best of everything—the jewels, the shoes, the breakfast in bed—and I never have to worry about commitment or any of that nonsense. I obviously cannot marry him; he'll be old within a few years." She was so sincere in her answer that I completely ignored the shallowness of her response.

"You're right; I guess I never think about it like that. And the Eternal Council—it never bothers them that you and Raul and Paulo have affairs with Laggas?"

"The Eternal Council? Ha! That is a myth to scare us. I remember when my Guide first told me about them. He was all foreboding and pessimistic, but honestly, they can't possibly *see everything*. Look at it this way: no one will hurt us for existing the way God and nature intended us to."

"You think the Eternal Council is a myth?" I asked, not really expecting a response.

There is no way Tegan would have lied to me. He was so insistent about the rules and obligations of Imati. Cornelius had said Argentina was the only safe place for Imati. There had to be an unforeseen danger out there. For Scarlett to laugh it off as just a story was ridiculous.

"Of course! How else would our Guides keep us in line? They just don't want us becoming more powerful than they are. They are jealous because we get to live in the Mortal Realm and they are stuck in the stuffy, boring Immortal Realm. They are scared of us, Ally, because we are stronger than they are and we know how to have fun!" She did a twirl around the room, her red scarf trailing behind her, like a small child dancing to no music.

"I don't know, Scarlett. I lived with my Guide for years and he was the most powerful person I had ever met; even the most ancient Imati looked up to him. He was like a god."

I winced because Tegan would cringe if he heard me describe him as a god.

"Well, then he is the only one. My Guide stayed with me a week and then let me go. He didn't care what I did or how I survived. Then I found Raul and Paulo and they became my family. Trust me, Ally, we aren't in any danger. I promise."

I decided to take a walk to clear my head. Maybe I didn't understand who I was as well as I had thought. Tegan had scared me into thinking that if I didn't follow the rules then bad things could happen, but he had never said exactly what those punishments would be. Maybe Scarlett was right; maybe there was no danger. Was it all just empty threats? Besides, my new family broke the rules all the time, and nothing had happened so far.

Two weeks later, Scarlett and I were meeting Paulo for a lunch near the docks. He had recently come into a large sum of money—probably made from dice and cards—and he wanted to take us out for food and high-society shopping. I wore my prettiest dress and showed off my priceless ruby necklace. It was to be a day of fashions, food, and fun. Just when we were about to leave, there was a knock at the door. Scarlett was in her room powdering her face, so I answered it, assuming that it was a delivery boy or something. I was almost right. But rather than a boy, it was a man.

"*Hola, Señorita. Hablas inglés?*" he asked in a terrible Spanish accent.

"Yes, I do," I replied in English. "Can I help you?"

"Yes, of course, my apologies, my lady. My name is Tucker James." His accent was British. He reached out to kiss my hand. His expression suddenly turned to one of confusion. Apparently, I was not what he was expecting. I pulled my hand away awkwardly.

"I am a friend of William's. Is there another lady of the house here?" He stuck his head halfway through the door and tried to look around.

"Um, yes. You must be looking for Scarlett. Come in." I should not have been so trusting. As he walked past me, he put his hand on my shoulder to thank me, but it rested there just a moment too long, as if he was waiting for something.

"She'll be right out," I said peacefully, but I felt strange being in the same room as him. He scanned the apartment with his eyes, surveying it like he was looking to buy. He made me nervous, so I kept my eyes on him at all times.

"Have you known Scarlett long?" he asked.

"Only a few years." I didn't appreciate his prying. He still had not announced the purpose of his visit. "What is it again that you wanted to speak to Scarlett about?"

"Oh, nothing, really. Just some news from William. It's not urgent." He took his hat off and made himself comfortable, which made me more uncomfortable.

"Did you say William? How wonderful—how is he?" As usual, Scarlett made a grand entrance. Her cream-colored dress covered in lace reached the floor, and she wore a magnificent hat to match, adorned with tiny pearls woven into the intricate lace detail. A few strands of her auburn hair lay at her shoulders, radiant against the lightness of the dress. Her lips were painted red to match. She was exquisite, and her beauty took Tucker back a notch.

"Scarlett, I presume? What a pleasure it is to finally meet you. William speaks about you often." He stood up to greet her.

"Oh good sir, you flatter me too much." She was reveling in it. I hadn't noticed before, but Tucker was extremely handsome and athletically built. Scarlett, no doubt, would claim him.

Tucker took her hand and ever so slowly brought it to his mouth to kiss. Just as before, he took his time when holding her hand, not wanting to let go of such an amazing creature as Scarlett. She was unnerving as always. However, this time, rather than looking confused, he suddenly looked pleased. Something about Scarlett assured him he was in the right place.

"You two are friends, then. You and Miss—I'm sorry, I did not catch your name." His attention was now directed at me.

"I didn't give it," I said from the opposite side of the room.

"Her name is Alastrina Byrne. And yes, she is my best friend, practically a sister to me."

"Ms. Byrne, it is a pleasure to meet you again. So you are not sisters, not related, then? You met here, in Argentina . . . yes, I *see* it now."

"See what?" I asked him suspiciously. My hands were behind my back, but they were prepared to grab a weapon if needed. Something was off about Tucker James.

"Sorry, look at me, rambling on about you two, when I came here to tell you about William."

Scarlett perked up. "Yes! I completely forgot—what did he say?" She clapped as she spoke.

"He said good-bye." Scarlett's face dropped. Her smile was instantly gone.

"What? I don't understand." Her face filled with fear and confusion.

"I'm sorry, Scarlett; as much as it pains me to deny the world your beauty, it is for the greater good to rid her of your evil."

Just then, Tucker drew a sword that had been carefully hidden under his long coat. Scarlett screamed. There was no time to think. As he was about strike,

I threw a chair at him. *Good job, hands.* He toppled over, but it would only buy us mere seconds.

"Scarlett! *Run!*" I screamed. "We have to go, now!" Together we picked our feet up and sprinted toward the other end of the room. We had almost made it to the door when Tucker was back up and on his feet again; Just as we turned the knob to exit, he slammed the door shut from behind us. Then, he threw me against the wall. I hit it so hard that pieces of paint chipped off and shards of plaster landed on my head.

"Ha! I knew it! I couldn't read you, but I knew you were Imati. No human could throw a chair like that."

Just as he finished his sentence, Scarlett kicked his feet out from underneath him. She had rediscovered her Imati strength. Tucker's sword slid across the room. Still recovering from the blow of the wall, I ran over to pick it up. I concentrated on the metal blade in order to pull the sword to my hand but was still unpracticed in the skill. I cursed myself for not training harder. Before I could reach the blade, Tucker swiftly threw Scarlett back, away from him, and lunged in front of me. I turned to see Scarlett face down on the floor. Clearly, he was prevailing. Tucker looked at me for a moment like he was reading my thoughts, and we both grabbed for the sword. I felt a large fist strike across my face; Tucker had punched me square in the jaw. It hurt, but I would recover. In a blur I looked up to see a flash of silver descending over me. Now I saw why he fought with a sword: he was aiming for my neck.

Just then, a large force burst through the door and Tucker was thrown backward. The next thing I saw was a silver streak, and Tucker James's head was severed from his body. It hit the floor with a loud thump, and a river of red slithered across the ground, like the snake he was.

"Alastrina! Are you okay?" The strong, yet musical voice was familiar.

"Tegan!" I jumped up from the ground. "You're here, and you saved me! Thank you, thank you, thank you." I held onto Tegan for dear life. I felt that if I let go, all would be lost and Tucker would magically appear from the dead.

"Where is Scarlett?" I frantically searched the room for her. She was still lying on the floor, barely conscious. "Scarlett—are you okay?"

"Ally?" She could barely speak. She had a streak of silver blood slowly creeping down her face from where her head had hit the corner of the armoire.

The wound had already healed, and the final drops of her shiny, metallic blood fell to the floor and beaded up into tiny balls.

"I think I'm fine . . . what was that?"

"That—was a Seeker," Tegan interjected. "He has been here for a few months now, obviously tracking you."

"A Seeker? What is that, and why would he be tracking us?" I asked. Anger started to boil inside me. *If Tegan knew about him, which he obviously did, why wait until now to tell me?*

"I am sorry, Alastrina. I should have told you about them. I assumed you would never be involved in all this."

"Sorry to interrupt, but if we are going to understand what happened, we need to stop with the obscure statements." Scarlett was always a right-to-the-point kind of gal.

"You're right," he said to Scarlett. "Seekers are assassins. They're similar to the Imati in that they are a separate race from humans, but they are still mortal. Their entire existence was created to hunt corrupted Imati and keep the balance of power. If an Imati is a plague on mankind, a Seeker is sent to end their life. They are stronger and faster than humans, but they die just the same."

"Wait a minute: they are just like us, but they don't possess immortality?" I asked, still confused by the recent events.

"Sort of. Centuries ago, the Eternal Council granted certain powers to a secret society they called the Seekers in order to keep the Imati living in the Mortal Realm in line. The Sidhe, myself included, are not to interfere in the affairs of mortals, so they needed humans to help them control the Imati. Over the centuries, those humans developed a power of their own."

Tegan continued as if he had rehearsed this speech a thousand times in his head. "Seekers are bred from a young age to find and hunt immortals. They do this by reading memories. Not thoughts, just memories. When Tucker touched you, he could see everywhere you had been and everyone you had met. He could tell your age and therefore knew you were not human. This is their greatest ability."

"He was trying to read our memories? That's why he was being so odd?" I suddenly felt violated.

"He couldn't read you though, remember?" Scarlett added. She seemed oddly suspicious of me. "When he threw you against the wall, he laughed and said that he couldn't read you but he knew you were still Imati." She stared at me like I was hiding something.

"Yes, that is strange, Alastrina. I also couldn't sense you. I have been in Buenos Aires for a few weeks keeping an eye out because I knew a Seeker was here, but today, I could not find you. I had to track you through Scarlett."

"So, what . . . I'm different, right? It seems like it's a good thing if Seekers can't find me," I added in support of my oddness. They were treating me like a criminal when I, too, was a victim in this situation just as much as Scarlett was.

"It is, of course. The question is, why?"

Tegan ended the conversation with that last statement and then took me for a walk, after Scarlett assured him she would be okay. He was obviously worried about me, so worried in fact that he had trekked halfway around the world to find me.

"Alastrina, listen to me. I sent you to Argentina to be safe from this. There is a lot more going on here than you can possibly understand. It was my hope that you would never be exposed to this part of our world."

"What are you saying, Tegan . . . I need to leave?" He was asking me to do the one thing I didn't want to.

"Maybe." Tegan sighed in frustration. "Scarlett and her friends are not good for you. They are young and careless. More Seekers will come. Also . . ."

"What is it?"

"Not everything is as black and white as I have made it seem, Alastrina. There are Seekers much worse than Tucker; they will kill for no reason at all. Each time a Seeker takes the life of an immortal, he garners that immortal's strength, which adds years to his own life. Some Seekers are on a quest for immortality, Alastrina, and they don't care how many they have to kill in order to get it." He kept repeating my name; I think to make sure I was paying attention.

"Tucker could have been one of those Seekers, then? He wasn't necessarily sent by the Council to kill us? Scarlett didn't do anything wrong." I wanted Tegan to see how good she was, for I could tell he did not trust her.

"Not yet, she hasn't. She is different from you, Alastrina. She takes what she wants with no remorse. I don't want to see you get hurt."

"I thought the Sidhe weren't supposed to interfere, Tegan. What you did was a crime to your people; you killed someone without even hesitating, which makes me believe that wasn't the first Lagga you killed. You come here to lecture me about my family, when they are the only ones who really care about me. No one loves me and everyone I loved is dead. I trusted you, and you kept all these secrets from me. How am I supposed to believe you now?"

What I said was mean. I could feel myself being mean. But I was still angry that Tegan had left me in Bordeaux and put me on a ship bound for an unknown country. *How could I forgive him for abandoning me?*

"You're right. It's not the first *human* I killed, and you shouldn't call them otherwise. In hindsight, maybe I shouldn't have done it, but your life was in danger. I have done a lot of things, Alastrina"—he took a moment, his voice steady—"but never have I risked my own fate for an Imati. You are different, and for some reason I feel an inherent need to protect you. I should have realized that from the beginning and told you everything rather than keeping you in the dark. I should have been training you and furthering your powers rather than keeping them from you."

"Thank you, Teg—"

He cut me off before I could finish saying his name. "However, *do not* think for one minute that I will always be there to save you. Alastrina, I need you to understand that if you make the wrong choices, or choose the wrong side, I will be powerless to help you. Please, listen to your instincts and save yourself. Separate from your new friends and stop using demeaning words for humans. I'm disappointed in you."

His plea sounded more like a demand than a suggestion. "And," he continued, "remember what I told you about certain Imati. You must start to train. You could have defeated Tucker if you could have controlled his sword." Tegan's use of the word *sword* suddenly triggered a long-forgotten memory. I knew how to handle a sword all too well, but only with my hands – not with my mind. Tegan kept talking, but I was only half listening. "Practice the ability to attract metal, because someday it may save your life. That is all the advice I can give to you.

Good-bye, Alastrina." He turned to walk away. Seconds passed in what felt like an eternity.

"Tegan, wait!" I ran up to him. "Was it Seekers who killed my family?" I asked. "They came with swords, and they were looking for something."

"What were they looking for? You never told me that," he said accusingly.

"I don't know." I lied to Tegan for the first time, feeling an inherent need to protect my mother's necklace and book. "It's all a little hazy," I added. "But one of them mentioned *reading* my mother before she died."

"Yes, then it must have been Seekers." Tegan paused. "Did he have the opportunity to do it?"

"No," I muttered somberly. "She passed before he got the chance."

Tegan sighed. "Alastrina, because of your father and because of who you were meant to be, you are never going to be truly safe. That is why you must take it upon yourself to learn protection."

I paused for a moment to take it all in—that my life was in danger, even as a human—and then wrapped my arms around Tegan's neck, the only safe place I had ever known. The corset I was wearing made it difficult to reach up, and I had to stand on the very tips of my toes, but it was worth it.

"Thank you," I whispered. And then once again he was gone.

Belfast, Maine – September – Present Day

Longing

AGAINST MY BETTER judgment, I enrolled in Belfast High School. I had gone a month without talking to Connor, and it had been over two weeks since I had spied on him at his house. Of course, attending the same school would make *not* seeing him more difficult.

The first day of school was like a movie playing in constant slow motion. I was very aware of everyone around me and acutely aware of my own actions. I was trying desperately not to stand out. At least I had a friend. Millie was very supportive and offered to take me to school so I wouldn't be embarrassed searching for my first class.

I sat in the second row of my Advanced Placement English class. Connor sat in the back. Of *course* in such a small school there would be only one AP English class. They passed out the reading list for the year: *The Great Gatsby*, *Pride and Prejudice*, *Wuthering Heights*, *Canterbury Tales*, and *Anna Karenina*. No mention of any medieval poems or *Tristan and Isolde*. Once again Connor had lied to me—but I had to be sure of it.

I turned toward a cute ash-blond boy sitting just to the left of me and tapped on his desk. "Excuse me?"

He looked over, but didn't say anything.

"Um, is this the entire reading list? Or is there more?" I whispered.

"Why would you want more?" he asked, suddenly assuming I was a complete nerd.

"I don't—I was just curious . . . was *Tristan and Isolde* ever on the list? Last year, maybe?"

"I don't know what that is . . . Tristan and . . . whatever you said."

"So, no changes, then? This"—I held up the reading list—"is all the books?"

The boy glanced at the sheet of paper in front of him and then back toward me. "Yeah, that's it."

Suddenly, the teacher glared at him. "Carson, is there a problem? Do you have a question?"

"No ma'am," Carson said nonchalantly.

"Very well. Less talking then, okay?" She went back to addressing the entire class. "Now, back to your first class assignment."

I stared at Carson for a moment while the teacher trailed off, wondering why he seemed familiar, and then it hit me. "Hey, Carson," I said as I tapped on his desk again. "Is your dad a fisherman?"

He looked at me dubiously. "Yes," he replied slowly. "Do I know you?"

"Um, no, just a lucky guess." I smiled, remembering the fisherman from my first day in town—the one I told I wouldn't be going to high school and whose son I pretty much vowed I would never meet. Yet here I was chatting with Carson, the fisherman's son, all because of Connor—who, apparently, was a big fat liar.

"Hey." Carson was suddenly addressing me again. "You're new here, aren't you?"

"Yeah," I said, while watching the teacher from the corner of my eye.

"You wanna go out with me?" Carson asked bluntly.

"What?" I asked, surprised. He continued to stare at me, so I quickly responded with a giant "No."

"Fine, you just seemed real chatty is all," he said, his ego clearly a little bruised. Then he turned away from me, and I realized high school was going to create a whole new world of problems.

After English, the rest of the day went fine, and by fine, I mean it was uneventful. Classes were boring; I had already learned this stuff a thousand times, and the teachers were as disinterested as the students. Millie invited me to sit with her at lunch in the gray and white cafeteria and introduced me to some of her friends. There was Talon O'Connell, a scrawny kid more into something called World of Warcraft than the actual world. Monica Samuels, who was so obsessed with yearbook committee she was already taking pictures, even though it was the first day. Another girl, with reddish-brown hair who carried a guitar, named Molly. And lastly, Chris, who was rather cute. I think Millie had a crush on him, because she kept throwing wrappers at him.

As soon as I sat down and the introductions were made, they all stopped talking and I could feel their eyes on me, wondering who I was. Chris broke the silence first. "So Ally, where ya from?"

"Los Angeles," I said, not bothering to elaborate or alleviate the awkward silence that followed.

Molly spoke next. "Why'd you move here then?" she said, more or less interested.

"My dad moved me," I replied. It went on like this for a few minutes. They all had a lot of questions, but my mind was searching for Connor, so I mostly gave one-word answers.

Then, Talon chimed in from across the table, "You're really pretty." His comment sort of hung in the air, doing me no favors whatsoever with this crowd.

Millie threw an orange peel at him. "Ew, Talon, don't hit on her."

"I'm not," he choked out. "She just is."

I felt awkward and uncomfortable. I had connected with Millie from the moment I met her and I liked being friends with her. But her friends did not give me the same warm fuzzies, so I sat there staring off into space, regretting coming to school at all.

Suddenly, Connor appeared, but he sat by himself on a long picnic-style lunch table reading a book. I found myself gazing at him uncontrollably.

"Just go over there and talk to him. Forget all the ninja stuff," Millie spat out as she nudged me with her elbow and chewed on a repulsive-looking hamburger. I also noticed, for the first time all day, that the streak in her hair was now blue instead of red.

"I'm not going to just go over there. Besides, he should come over here; he has no reason to avoid me," I said, resolute in my decision to remain seated at the other end of the cafeteria.

"Except that you are a distraction, and you heard what his dad said. Will you just go? All my friends think you're creepy just staring into space like that."

She was right. Her friends sitting across the table from me were now looking at me with perplexed, unwelcoming expressions rather than ones of joyful curiosity.

"Fine," I said, annoyed, and then added, "Thanks, Millie." But as soon as I got up, I saw that someone else had beaten me there, and I quickly sat back down.

"What are you doing?" Millie asked.

"That girl, the one that just walked up to his table—I know her," I said, slightly vexed by her sudden presence. I was whispering so Millie's friends couldn't hear me, but I could tell they were all trying to listen. Millie had warned me Connor was popular, so any move he made or people made around him was instantly noticed.

"You know Rebecca Munn?" Millie said, surprised.

"Yeah, why?"

"I barely know Rebecca Munn. We've been in the same class since kindergarten and all she's ever said to me was 'Move.'"

"Really? She's that bad?" I asked, even though I could already tell. "What's her deal with Connor?" I pried.

"I don't know. She tells everyone they went on a few dates, but I never see them together outside of school. I mean, she wishes," Millie snarked.

"She's really pretty," I muttered, slightly defeated.

"Oh, who cares about Munn. She sucks." Millie pointed. "Look, she's getting up. Go now! Go, go!" Millie shooed me away from the table.

"Okay, okay," I said and thought how truly great Millie was.

I walked over to Connor's table and sat down hesitantly across from him. He didn't look up from the book he was reading. Maybe he thought I was Rebecca coming to bother him again.

"Hi there," I interrupted, attempting to be as friendly as possible. "What ya reading?"

"*The Kite Runner*," he said, clearly disinterested in conversation. I had an urge to get up and leave before I totally embarrassed myself, but I decided not to be scared of Connor; he was just a Lagga, after all. Then he looked up, saw it was me, and just slightly changed his tune.

"Oh, I mean, hi," he added.

"So is that on the reading list next to *Tristan and Isolde*, then?" I asked. *Hmm, that was probably a bit confrontational.* His eyes darted from side to side. Then he smiled.

"Uh, no. I already read all the books on the reading list. This is for fun. As for *Tristan and Isolde*, I lied. You were pretty and I wanted to talk to you, so I reached for the same book." I was suddenly smiling. Darn his charming British ways.

"Well, what about now? You don't want to talk to me anymore?" I was nervous for his response. What if he really didn't want to talk to me anymore?

"Of course I do. It's just that we come from two very different worlds, Ally. My dad is really strict and wants me to . . . succeed. I'm not sure how to balance it all out, you know?"

"Yeah, I understand totally." I gathered my things as if to leave, but I took my time, hoping he would stop me; he didn't.

"I'll see you around, I guess," I said as I stood up. "I mean, in English and calculus and possibly if you have sixth-period gym."

I was completely serious, but Connor laughed. "Ally, we're going to see each other every day, several times a day. We'll figure it out, okay? You're basically the only friend I have here." Then the bell rang. "That's my cue. See you in gym," he said.

I left school that afternoon feeling a bit deflated. That was it. Connor was not as hung up on me as I had thought. Either that, or he was terrified of his father. Regardless, it was like he didn't even care. He barely spoke two words to me in gym—granted we were playing basketball and the girls were separated from the guys, but still. He could have made an effort. *Why did I care so much?* I hadn't been this obsessed with someone in a hundred years, and I knew how dangerous it could be. *Why was I letting myself fall into this trap again? Why now? Is this what Delilah wanted?*

Millie dropped me off at the coffee shop that had gone from her summer day job to her after-school job. Since it was afternoon, I was surprised to see Bill there. It was like he knew I was coming in.

"Hey, Ally, how was the first day of school?" he asked as I slumped down next to him.

"Uneventful," I said dryly.

"Aren't they all?" He laughed. I was instantly in a better mood thanks to his awkwardly dry wit. "Any new kids besides yourself?"

"Nope, just me. Why?"

"No reason, just wondering if any new families moved in. Anyway, I'm gonna head out of town for a week or so. I'll see you when I get back," he said as he settled his tab.

"Where are you off to, Bill? Somewhere exciting, I hope?"

"Oh, you know, anywhere is somewhere." Then he exited. I was confused. Apparently, so was Millie. "What does that even mean?"

"I don't know. Everyone in this town is nuts, Millie. Except you and me." But not even I believed that. I knew I was more nuts than all of them.

"Speaking of nuts, your favorite one is right behind you," she said as she pointed toward the door. Connor walked in and headed straight toward me.

"I thought I might find you here. Can we go for a walk?" he asked as if he assumed I would say yes.

"Sure."

We walked down Main Street and took a left toward the ocean. Even from a few blocks away, we could hear the waves lapping on the coastline. It turned from dusk to dark quicker than I thought it would. The night was slightly chilly from the onset of fall.

Connor didn't say much. He just talked about his day and asked how I liked school. It was all very pointless; he clearly had something else on his mind. I could feel the cold metal of my necklace against my chest where my heart should have been beating. I was nervous. *What does he want to say?* We stopped to sit at a gazebo a little further away from the coffee shop, no longer close to the center of town. It was only half lit due to a light bulb malfunction in one of the street lamps. He sat so close that I could feel the warmth of his body. I wondered if he could tell mine was cold.

His rambling finally ended and he got to the point. "Ally, I've been thinking about you a lot lately. Every day I'm not with you, I think about being with you. When you tackled me at the house that day, it was like waking up for the first time in my entire life. I wanted to know you, to talk to you, to figure you out. No one has ever had that effect on me before. It kills me not be able to be honest with you." His eyes were pleading with me to understand. Part of me wanted to jump up and say *who are you?* But the other part of me knew that I had to keep secrets from him as well and I shouldn't judge him for doing exactly the same thing.

"Connor, I get it . . . my life is complicated, too. Let's just be friends and see where that goes—no questions and no judgments." I was resolved not to push him into anything more; it was for the better.

He laughed. "Friends?" He found that amusing. Then he leaned in and kissed me for the very first time. It was short and soft, and he pulled away, but only so he could finish talking. "I want to be more than friends, Ally. Screw complicated."

This time, he kissed me hard and with passion. I should have pushed back but I didn't; I let his lips envelop me completely. I could feel that he wanted me, wanted everything about me. I loved that feeling. I remembered that feeling so well, and as much as the sensation scared me, I didn't want to let go.

Santiago, Chile – 1859 – Infatuation

AFTER OUR ENCOUNTER with the Seeker, Scarlett, Raul, Paulo, and I decided it was best to leave Buenos Aires. We traveled all around Brazil, Colombia, and Venezuela and then headed south to Santiago, Chile. Everywhere we went there was war, so we had to settle upon a life of uncertainty if we were to remain in South America. I was the only one who even considered going back to Europe. Scarlett believed that "Europe is over for the Imati, especially if that is where all the Seekers are." She still had not quite forgotten her brief stint with a second death. Raul suggested the United States, but Paulo said there wasn't enough culture or even a population to be a part of. Santiago happened to be the last city we were in while having this argument, so we settled upon it as an acceptably desirable location.

Chile was in no short supply of society or culture, and Scarlett loved it. She would constantly weasel her way into the grand parties of the aristocracy and charm some wealthy lord into bed with her. I tended to shy away from these events unless she absolutely insisted that I go—which is exactly what she was doing.

"Oh please, please, please come with me. It will be so fabulous!" She was on her knees giving me her most pitiful frown, hands folded in front of her in full-on begging position.

"Oh, fine, I'll go," I acquiesced.

"Great, because I already told them how beautiful you are and they are more or less expecting you there." Then she pranced off to continue getting ready.

"Scarlett!" *Why was I always falling for her schemes?*

We arrived at the most impressive gated mansion in Santiago, whose proprietor was named Antonio de Fuentes. He was a wealthy Chilean aristocrat, businessman, and hopeful politician. His son Joaquín was considered one of the best-looking bachelors in Santiago and possibly in all of Chile. I wore my most noble green dress to match my eyes, and although it was ostentatious, I wore my necklace as well in order to display some sign of wealth. As soon as I put on the gown I thought of my home in Ireland, thousands of miles and several lifetimes away. I remembered dreaming of wearing beautiful dresses and attending fantastical balls. At the time it seemed like all of my problems could be solved with some pretty lace and a string of suitors. How wrong I was, and how different my life had become.

Scarlett dressed in a dashing and regal purple gown, adorned with black lace on the bottom of her hem. The neckline was quite revealing. She was constantly pushing boundaries, but the attention excited her more than anything.

We were greeted with French champagne and spicy, red Chilean wine. We drank more than anyone, yet ended up the least drunk. Scarlett was there to meet with her latest beau, an Englishman named Andrew Rissman. He was twenty-four, rich, and excited to be away from the confines of his family back in England. He had only been in Santiago a year and had already made friends with Joaquín Fuentes and the rest of his aristocratic circle. Joaquín was statuesque with his large build, olive skin, dark hair, and green eyes. His father was Chilean completely, but his mother was Dutch. He was amiable and sweet while he gave us a grand tour of his family's home. He had studied at Cambridge and then returned home to follow in his father's footsteps. I was completely captivated by him. Scarlett, of course, noticed instantly.

"If you want him, just take him; it's easy," she whispered to me at the end of the tour, just as we were reentering the grand ballroom.

"*Hmmph*—maybe for you. I'm not that charming, remember?" I whispered back, fearful that Joaquín, who was only a few paces in front of us, would hear.

"Oh, stop wallowing. You are part of a gorgeous superior race, darling; you can do anything you set your mind to."

I have to say, she made a good case for it. I grabbed a flute of champagne from the closest servant, drank it in a single sip, and went straight up to Joaquín, determined to flatter him.

"Care to dance, sir?" I held out my hand, waiting anxiously for him to take it. My actions were quite bold, considering the time and place.

"Señorita, I've been waiting all night for you to ask me that." He smiled and led me to the dance floor, instantly taking back the lead.

The music was exhilarating, and I was enthralled with every note. The sounds and scents of the whole evening blurred my vision. Joaquín was inspiring, and every second I was near him I felt like I was reborn and experiencing life for the first time. He was incredible to look at and more incredible to touch. When we danced, I felt like we were flying. Finally, at the end of the night, he took me back to my quaint house in the bourgeois section of Santiago, away from the mansions, from the petticoats, and, most importantly, from the watchful eyes of others.

We entered my apartment and he gently undressed my many layers of clothes, taking his time with every string and button. His confidence gave away his experience. Finally, when the last lace had fallen and the anticipation was excruciating, he looked at me and held my face in his palm. "You are lovely."

My night with Joaquín was my first time to ever be with a man completely. I had sat by for decades, watching Scarlett and the others partake, and never had the desire to get involved. Now I understood why they were obsessed. It was invigorating to be so close to another human being, to feel so loved and connected all at once. His body and mine melted together as one, and we continued this dance until sunrise, when I finally fell asleep in his arms.

By mid-afternoon, I woke up. Joaquín was gone. The warm sunrise had transformed into a cold morning. There was a note on the pillow.

You are beautiful, mi amore. I will count the days until I can see you again.

I was in love. Infatuated might have been a better word. Scarlett was thrilled that I had finally done something interesting. She was starting to think I was abnormal even for an Imati.

For the next week I walked around beaming, happy to be alive. All of that quickly changed, as happy moments tend to do—for they are fleeting, and if you do not hold on to them they will quickly turn to misery. My misery became the printed words that were plastered in front of me. I was reading the weekly Sunday paper where, splashed across the society page, was a wedding announcement:

Sir Joaquín Fuentes will be married to the daughter of Lord Ellison . . . Miss Amelia Ellison . . . the ceremony will take place . . . the entire city will show up for such a magnificent . . .

I could barely read the words as their meaning turned my eyes to icy stone and clouded my vision. The room went dark. "He is engaged! To the daughter of a Lord!" I shouted from my chair for all to hear. There was a sketch of her in the paper beside the announcement; she was attractive and young. She was seventeen, just like me—except not like me. I was the mistress, and she was the soon-to-be "Mrs." *How could he do this to me?* I was furious and devastated at the same time. I had never been so mad in my entire existence. Even with two bayonet wounds in my back I had not felt the fury I felt at that moment. I wanted answers immediately.

I sprang out of my chair, ready to march across town. Scarlett put her arms out to stop me, "Ally, calm down! You knew going into this that it would never work. Do you think Lord Rissman and I are a match made in heaven? No! I am using him, and in return, he is using me. That is our way of life. In forty years, when you are still seventeen and Sir Fuentes is old and fat, you will care much less about this whole situation."

Of course Scarlett was right, but I didn't care. I was still mad. The feeling of abandonment and loneliness closed in on me like a suffocating cage. It had only been one night, but I had put so much faith and trust in him that to be deceived was inconceivable. *Did he not love me the way I loved him? Did what we have not mean as much to him? How could I be so stupid?*

I argued with Scarlett. "What are you saying—that I should just go along with it until he is through with me and tosses me out with last week's bread?"

She shook her head and glared at me like I was the most naïve girl in the world. "No, what I am saying is that you should go along with it until *you* toss *him* out with last week's bread. Do you see the difference? It's all about control, Ally. Take what you want when you want it, and then let it go." What she said made sense; I could string him along and keep the power. I didn't *need* him . . . but I *wanted* him.

We continued our affair for five months. His wedding came and went. I did not attend, nor was I invited. The only problem with my plan to take control was that I had no urge to toss him out. I wanted to keep every bit of him for myself. Our visits began to shorten. They went from four times a week, to twice a week, to twice a month. He was slowly slipping away from me.

I became obsessed with him, constantly trying to impress him and make him want me more. The harder I tried, the more he pulled away. I was lost for ideas. Scarlett and I decided to follow him and see where he was going when he wasn't with me. It seemed he was spending more time with his new little wife. She was quite pretty and grew cuter by the day. Her skin was cream-colored and smooth, and it further exemplified her youth. Her cheeks would blush pink every time Joaquín touched her or was near her. At night, when he would leave her, she would shed tears and cry herself to sleep. It was a zero-sum game, and my happiness was dependent on her sorrow.

Scarlett had gone along with my spying but was finally at her wits end. One night she threw a royal blue dress at me that she had just finished sewing.

"Put it on. We are going to a soiree," she demanded.

"I'm not going, Scarlett. He'll be there—you know that."

"What better way to keep the power than to flaunt your beauty and flirt with his friends?"

"Scarlett, I appreciate—"

"No, Ally, no excuses! You are becoming a pathetic excuse of a woman and of an Imati. You mope around all day, and your whole existence is defined by this mere child. This is ending tonight. Get up and put on the dress, or I will kill you. Seriously."

I didn't know what to think of her statement, but part of me believed her when she said that she would kill me. *Could she kill me?* I put on the dress so I didn't have to find out.

The party was just like all the others. Everyone who was anyone was there, plus any talented women who had managed to sleep their way in. Scarlett was happy to be out again. I danced with a few bachelors and made small talk with a few grand men. I could feel Joaquín's eyes on me the entire time. Finally he approached me.

"Stunning as always, *mi amore*. What brings you out here tonight?" He handed me a glass of wine and seemed pleased to see me, but I knew he asked the question because I was *not* invited.

"The wine, of course"—I took the glass to toast him—"and the company, maybe." I batted my eyes as I spoke.

"I always forget how gorgeous you are until I see you through the eyes of others." His voice was low so no one would hear. "And this dress—it should be a crime to look so delicious."

"Aw, feeling neglected and jealous, are we?" Mocking, I discovered, was always a good tactic to reel in an egotistical aristocrat.

"Charming." He clinked my glass to say good-bye. "I have to tend to my wife tonight, but perhaps tomorrow will be different." Then he walked away.

A newfound hope washed over me. He still loved me. Only his wife was in the way. I searched for Scarlett to tell her my good news, but had no luck. Instead, I found Amelia. In fact, she brazenly cornered me at the bottom of the staircase. She looked down on me, both figuratively and literally at the moment.

"Hello, Alastrina. That is your name, correct?"

"Yes. Hello." I didn't know what to say. *How did she know me?*

"How is my husband tonight?" She was quite brash for someone so young.

I swallowed hard. *Why was she so intimidating? Maybe because I was in the wrong? Maybe because she had the right to hate me?* All I knew is that I hated her just as much, and I wasn't going to let some child make me feel inferior. Scarlett had taught me to stand up for myself, so that's what I was going to do.

"He is fine. A bit lonely, I suppose." My words were weapons. *Take that,* I thought.

"Listen, Miss Byrne. I appreciate you coming this evening. However, my marriage would be much better if you weren't in it. Therefore, I am going to walk upstairs and dab some water on my face, and when I come back down, you will be gone." She was threatening me. She was not a day over eighteen and *she* was threatening *me*!

"You are very confident for someone so little," I replied calmly, but inside was pure rage.

"I don't have time for a war of words, Miss Byrne. I'm leaving now, and soon so will you."

With that she walked upstairs. I turned to leave, when Scarlett's words echoed in my head: *Take what you want when you want it.* I might have been ruining Amelia's marriage, but she was ruining my affair. *How dare she threaten me like that!*

I followed her upstairs. I didn't quite know what I would do when I got there, but I did know that I was powerful, and soon Amelia would know it, too.

She had stepped into a bedroom suite. I pushed the door open. She was staring at herself in the mirror, trying not to cry. For one split second I almost turned to walk away, feeling regretful and embarrassed, but then she spotted me.

"You! What are you doing up here?" She walked straight up to me and spit in my face. "I hate you," she said as tears welled up in her rage-filled eyes.

"You should not have done that," I responded. "I love Joaquín, and I loved him before he was engaged to you!"

She stepped closer. "He would never marry you. Look at you . . . you are nothing, just a whore who likes to play dress-up at pretty balls." She continued to stare me down, waiting for my next move.

A wave of fear washed over me. Then, I was blinded by my own rage. My hate for both Amelia and Joaquín spilled out at once. In one instant I was staring at her, seething with pain, and then the next moment her neck was in my right hand, her feet slowly rising off the ground. She was slapping my face with her free arms and trying to kick me. I continued to tighten my grip around her. Her eyes gave away her internal panic. She was struggling for life, fighting to survive. Then, her struggle slowed, until all of a sudden . . . she stopped.

I dropped her body to the tile floor. She lay there, motionless. A strand of hair fell across her porcelain face. Her amber-colored eyes stared back at me. A tear remained on her cheek. I killed her. No, not *killed*. I took my strength and my power and I *murdered* her. I wanted her dead, and I made it happen. I could do anything.

I felt sick. I threw up all the wine I drank that night. Once the wine was gone my body started heaving uncontrollably. The room was spinning. My hands were shaking. I had to get out of there. I ran out through the back window, but the room was two stories high so I had to jump and escape through the back gardens. When I landed, I fell and rolled a bit on the ground. The dirt and mud sullied my hands. I looked back at the house, where sounds of laughter echoed from the party. The bathroom lamp was still on. Amelia's dead body would stay there until a servant or maid found her. No one would place me in that room, no one would remember I was there. Her death would forever be a mystery to her family, and forever be a ghost in my past.

The next day, it was not Amelia's murder that made the front page. Instead, it was the tragic suicide of Joaquín Fuentes that splashed across the morning paper. Upon discovering Amelia's body, Joaquín had shot himself right next to her corpse so he could be next to her for all eternity. He had loved her so much he couldn't live without her. Amelia had been correct in her assumptions—I was *just* his mistress. In the end, I got nothing I wanted. In the end, I had become an evil person.

Tegan was right; too much power was a curse. As much as I would miss Scarlett and the rest of my family, I had to leave them. I no longer knew who I was or what I wanted. I felt more lost than ever. I waited two weeks to disappear, not wanting to draw attention to myself in connection with Amelia's death. One night, when they were all out dancing, I packed my things and wrote a good-bye letter. I told them I loved them, but that I needed to rediscover myself. I did not say why. I think some part of them already knew.

Just as I was about to leave, there was a knock at my door. Flashbacks of Tucker raced into my mind. *Had the Eternal Council sent a Seeker to punish me? Was this to be my tragic end?* I checked who it was through the peephole in the wooden door. To my surprise, it was a small, old, Indian woman who must have been alive for at least a hundred years. I fearlessly opened the door.

"Hello. Can I help you?" I asked her.

"*Buenas noches, señorita.* I am looking for Miss Byrne." Her voice was raspy and almost inaudible, but she seemed innocent enough.

"*Soy ella*"—I am she—"why?" I should have been more suspicious, since she knew my name, but I was in a rush to leave before everyone else returned. And really, what harm could a little old lady cause me?

Then, in a swift move, the woman reached under her shawl and threw a lump of dirt at me, followed by a brown, watery substance. It looked like mud but it smelled like sulfur. It splashed all over my dress and my ruby necklace.

"Excuse me! That was completely uncalled for," I shrieked back at her.

"You took a life, and now I will take yours." Then she started to speak in a language I had never heard before: "*Arisitia Callum Abbrevi Vivandun.*" Her chant was haunting and dark. I wanted to move, to slam the door, but I was uncontrollably frozen. I couldn't release a single muscle in my body. The smell of sulfur was making me dizzy.

"Who are you?" I whispered just as I was about to collapse.

"I am the *bisabuela* of Joaquín Fuentes, and because of you he is dead. Therefore, I curse you to die, and with these ashes, your life will be stripped from you, as it is a gift you took for granted." She threw a handful of ashes at me, and with that I passed out and she was gone.

Belfast, Maine – September – Present Day

Meant To Be

I WALKED INTO school the next day beaming from my night with Connor. I searched for him in English class, but he wasn't there. By lunchtime, I was worried.

"Do you think he is avoiding me?" I asked Millie.

"No, of course not. What did he say again—'You're everything to me, I think about you all the time'? Jeez, Ally, he is totally in love with you!" Millie was genuinely impressed that Connor liked me.

"Then where is he?" I said, concerned. I could feel the obsession beginning, and I needed to keep reminding myself to play it cool.

"I'm sure he'll be here tomorrow. Plus, he probably wants to ask you to the Welcome Back dance."

"Welcome Back dance? What is that?" I hadn't been to a high school dance in decades. I usually avoided them whenever I was in school; I usually didn't have any real friends or a boyfriend, so it was never an issue to miss it. This time was different.

"The dance next week, the one that has been advertised on all the posters and bulletin boards. The one the class president mentions every day in announcements." I stared at

Millie blankly. Clearly, I was not paying attention to the goings on of my classmates and school. All I saw was Connor.

"Oh, right. Remind me again?" I asked.

"Every year, there is a formal Welcome Back dance in the fall. The theme this year is Under the Moonlight."

"What a lame name," I laughed.

"We voted on it last year. It was my idea," Millie said.

"Oh, sorry . . . by 'lame' I meant . . . 'original.'" I tried to cover up my faux pas.

"I'm kidding, Ally! I hate the name, too." Millie smiled. Relief washed over me. I genuinely liked Millie and the last thing I wanted to do was offend her.

"So are you going?" I asked her.

"Yeah, and so are you. Even if Connor doesn't ask you . . . we'll go together."

"Sure. It should be fun, right?"

"Wow, I thought I was going to have to convince you more. I had a speech ready and everything. I'm glad you're more open to school stuff now," she added, happy to finally have me on board with the whole teenage girl thing. I decided not to mention that I was going in order to see Connor. I let her have her moment.

The whole week went by, and there was still no Connor. By Friday, the dance was the following night, and he had not asked me. Frustrated, I slammed my locker door shut and the whole wall rattled. Everyone turned to look at me.

"Oops," I said with a demure smile.

"Jeez, Ally, angry much?" Millie asked.

"Why hasn't he been here? Did I scare him off?"

"Are we talking about Connor again?" She asked, clearly sick of my moping. She gave me the same look Scarlett had given me about Joaquín.

"Sorry, you're right. I need to shut up. He's not here—"

"Ally, um," she interjected. I obviously wasn't listening.

I continued rambling. "I need to move on. If he wants to see me, he'll see me."

"Ally, shut up. He's right there." Millie pointed down the hall to where Connor was opening his locker. *Note to self: get a locker near Connor's.* My eyes grew wide, my body tensed, and I couldn't move.

"Aren't you going to go say hi?" Millie asked as she nudged me forward.

"No, he'll come over here." Just then he closed his locker, looked over at me, and began to walk my way. "See, here he comes," I added confidently. Then, from behind him emerged Quinn with a nasty look on his face. He ran up and tapped Connor on the shoulder to get his attention. Connor turned around . . . away from me.

"Why is Quinn here?" I said out loud.

"He takes parenting to a whole new level," Millie joked. Although she was kind of right; Quinn did take parenting to a whole new level. Quinn put his arm around Connor and I watched them turn the corner and leave the hall.

"And good-bye, Connor," Millie mumbled sarcastically under her breath.

"That's it!" I said, shocked. "I see him for five seconds and his dad takes him away. This is crazy!" I was furious and annoyed—with Connor, with myself, and with the whole situation. Dating was becoming annoying and we weren't even really dating. We had just one kiss. One awesome, amazing, life-changing kiss, but still. How was I supposed to see Connor if he was never around?

Just then Rebecca walked by, which normally I wouldn't notice, except that for the first time since the bonfire she stopped to talk to me.

"Hey, Ally," she said, her hair perfectly straightened and her lips perfectly glossed.

"Hi, Rebecca," I said. Millie's mouth dropped to the floor in shock.

"Have you seen Connor today?" she asked.

"No, I think he went home," I said coyly.

"Oh, bummer. I saw him this morning and he was asking me all these questions about the dance. I wonder why? I mean, has he asked you yet?" She was feigning concern.

"No, he hasn't asked me yet," I said through gritted teeth. Why was this happening to me? It was a school dance, I know, but all I wanted to do in that moment was shove Rebecca Munn's head into a locker and tell her that Connor was mine. Of course, I'd been down that road before, and it's never pretty.

"Oh, well maybe soon. Ta-ta." She waved her fingers delicately and pranced away.

"Ugh, I hate her." Millie chimed in.

I laughed, "She's not even worth it, Millie." I added, "Trust me."

"You're right," Millie began. "You know what you should do . . ."

"What?" I asked as I leaned up against my locker, irritated and forlorn.

"Get an awesome dress, show up to the dance, and have the time of your life. Believe me, you'll feel better."

"That's a great idea!" I said. Connor or no Connor, Rebecca or no Rebecca, I was going to rock that dance and stop feeling so pitiful. I am an Imati, after all . . . if anyone can dress to kill, it's me.

The next night, I put on my best (and only) cocktail dress, which still looked fairly new. It was a bloodred cotton and matched my ruby necklace. It had a heart-shaped top and small sleeves and hung just above my knee: short enough without being scandalous. I think it was from the early 90s, but I couldn't really remember. My memory of the last few decades was actually worse than from centuries ago. There was a big, fat black hole in it. Turn of the century, I could recount where I was, what I was wearing, and whom I met . . . or killed . . . but ask me where I was in 1949 and I'd have no idea. I threw on some high heels and red lipstick, took a look in the mirror, and, for the first time in a long time, was rather pleased with myself. Cat, who was curled up on the edge of my bed, gave a purring stretch of approval.

Before I left, I needed to do one thing first. Something about Connor just felt *off*. I knew I shouldn't, but I called Delilah.

"Hey, Ally," she said as she answered the phone. "How is Belfast?"

"Hey, it's great," I stammered, as I tried to quickly get to the point. "That's actually why I'm calling."

"Sorry Al, I still don't have a read on why it's important. I wish I did. I hope you're not going crazy there." *Too late.*

"No, it's actually okay. I wanted to ask you if the name Connor Winfield meant anything to you?" *Oh, no . . . what am I doing?*

"Hmm," she said. "Depends—is that even his real name?" she asked, half laughing.

"Yeah, it's his real name." *I think.*

"Can you describe him?" Delilah always needed visuals to get a better read.

"Um . . . eighteen, British, handsome." I blushed as I described him. It felt invasive.

"Hold on." I could hear Delilah breathing over the phone. She was channeling. Then, the breathing stopped. "Ally, I'm getting something."

I suddenly got excited. "Really? What is it?"

"He's *in* Belfast, yes?" she asked.

"Yeah," I replied. I wanted her to get to the point and just tell me we were destined to be together and he was the real reason I was sent here. I mean, *if* that's what she was getting.

"I'm getting . . . darkness," she said. "I think, maybe, he has a tortured soul."

Ugh. "What does that *mean*, Delilah?" Sometimes she used very new age phrases. It always reminded of me of when I met her in Las Vegas and she was using her third eye as a sideshow act for tourists. Little did they know they were getting the real thing.

"I don't know, I'm sorry. It's all blurry," she said, confused. "My advice is to be cautious. A storm is brewing around him."

"Great, thanks. I'll remember that." Delilah and I chatted for a few more minutes until she had to go. I hung up the phone a little more defeated. That was not what I wanted to hear, but it wasn't going to sway my feelings. I grabbed my bag off the bed to finally head to the dance, but Cat gave me an incredulous stare.

"Don't look at me like that," I said. "I'll be careful." He purred, but I could tell he was judging me.

When I arrived at the school, I was anxious from my call . . . and late. I'd told Millie I would meet her there at 8:30 p.m., and it was already 9:15. I was never good at being on time, since it usually didn't matter. The phrase "hurry up" wasn't exactly in my vocabulary. Everyone was already there, and I could hear the sounds of dance music blaring from the gymnasium. As I walked, my heels clicked on the pavement. I found the double door entrance, took a moment to compose myself, and walked in, ready to have fun, blend in with all the other normal teenagers doing their normal dance stuff, and forget about Delilah's foreboding read. How accurate could it be over the phone, anyway?

As soon as I opened the door my eyes were inundated with sparkly twinkle lights, papier-mâché stars and moons, and silver glitter sprayed on everything. The moment I began walking, my heels started clicking on the floor and people turned to stare at me—only they didn't just glance once and then look away. Something was wrong. They were all looking at me. *Do I have something on my face? Did I forget something? What is wrong with these people?* Something was definitely off . . . something about this dance was different. People continued to whisper and laugh as I walked by. I could see Millie dart at me out of the corner of my eye.

"Ally! You're here!" she said, as she looked me up and down. "Uh . . . what are you wearing?" she asked, concerned.

"A dress. I thought it looked nice," I said, although now I was not so sure.

"It does, you look great . . . but it's red," she said as she pulled me aside.

"Yeah . . . so?" Then I looked around. "Why is everyone wearing black and white, Millie?" It dawned on me that not a single person was wearing color in the whole place. It was black, white, and silver—but the silver was only from the glitter.

"Because this is the Welcome Back Black and White Dance . . . I thought you knew that."

I seethed with embarrassment and anger at the same time. "No, Millie, no I didn't know that. You said it was the Welcome Back Dance and failed to mention the whole *Black and White* part of the name!" I was doing an angry whisper.

"Did I? Sorry, I thought you knew . . . everyone knows."

"Well, I'm not everyone, am I? I should leave—I look like a giant bullseye."

"No!" she pleaded. "You look like a rose, that's much better than a bullseye. Come on, it's fine. You're hot and no one will care that you're in red. Look, everyone is dancing again."

I thought about leaving, but the amount of effort it had taken to get ready seemed like a waste of time if I went home now. Only one thing could salvage this disaster. "Is Connor here?" I asked Millie.

"Uh, yes he is. I've never seen him at a dance before. He must be looking for someone," she said with a wink and a nudge.

"Do you think he saw me?"

"Everyone saw you, Ally. You're wearing red at a black and white dance. It's not exactly subtle."

"Hey!" I took offense.

"Sorry, too soon?" She laughed. With that, she led me to the dance floor. Within moments, Connor began his approach, but not soon enough.

Chris, Millie's kind-of-cute friend, got to me first. "Hey, Ally, great dress." And then he asked the one thing I did not want him to ask at this very crucial moment. "Wanna dance?"

I contemplated rejecting him, but I felt bad, so I begrudgingly said, "Sure."

Chris grabbed me and we awkwardly started dancing. I had no clue what song was playing, but it was fast and upbeat and his hips tried unsuccessfully to sway to the rhythm. I noticed, as I became preoccupied with Chris, that Connor was surrounded by other girls, one of whom was Rebecca.

I noticed as she put her arms around his neck and leaned her face into his, taking over as his dance partner. But instead of meeting her gaze, Connor turned to look at me, and we made eye contact. He then smiled a smile meant only for me, so I smiled back. And as Chris kept bumping into me, twirling me around the dance floor every which way, I made sure to keep looking at Connor. We were separated, but not for long. When the song finally ended I made a beeline for him, eager to talk to him. But again, just as in life, I was met with a barricade.

"Hey, Ally."

"Hey, Carson," I said, frustrated. The music was starting up again, but this time it was slow and sensual. Unfortunately, my view of Connor was now blocked by the fisherman's son.

"Dance with me?" He sort of demanded it more than asked, leading me to believe that he was about as adept at current social norms as I was.

"I really can't," I said. But as I shoved past him, I saw Rebecca still dancing with Connor, only now she was leaning her head on his chest. Connor looked straight at me, apologetic, like it was somehow out of his control. I turned back to Carson.

"Alright, fishman, let's go." Never hurts to have a plan B.

Carson looked shocked. "Sweet," he said, as he gave his friends a thumbs-up. When he got close to me, I realized that he, too, kind of smelled like fish. This was the worst way this dance could possibly be going. After about thirty seconds of awkward swaying, I was about to call it quits when there was a tap on my shoulder. "Can I cut in?"

Connor had come to rescue me, and behind him I saw Rebecca Munn shooting me the stankiest stink-eye you could imagine.

"Of course," I said. Then I looked at Carson and, realizing I might be hurting his feelings, gave him a handshake consolation prize, "Um, bye, Carson. Thanks for the dance." He seemed okay.

Connor and I moved a few paces away only to stop in the middle of the dance floor. Then, he looked at me for a long second and simply said, "Hi, Ally."

"Hi," I replied. He was standing within a foot of me now. Everyone else was staring at us, waiting to see what would happen. I had waited all night for this moment, all week for this moment, and now that it was here I didn't know what to do.

"Do you want to dance?" he asked.

"Sure," I said, and he put his arms around my waist. Dancing, as I had discovered in the last few minutes, had definitely changed over the years. If this was a century ago we would dance ballroom style, but this was more like swaying in a breeze. My arms were around his neck, resting on his shoulders, and he moved me back and forth, slowly rocking like a long, musical embrace. I stared up at him, mesmerized by his beautiful face.

"Nice to finally get to see you . . . how are you?" he asked.

"I'm fine," I said awkwardly.

"Nice dress." He chuckled. "I guess no one told you about the theme?"

"Millie failed to mention it." I grinned.

"See, that's exactly why I like you. You're the only girl that shows up in a red dress to a black and white dance and embraces it. Brilliant." He smiled down at me.

"You like me?" I said nervously.

"Of course I do. Why else would I be here?" He asked.

"The delicious fruit punch and paper decorations?" I joked, but I was yearning for him to tell me just how much he really liked me.

"Well, that—and because I thought you would be here." Connor continued to dance slowly with me despite the fact that the music had changed to an upbeat dance-rap remix. He didn't let go, so there we were, swaying back and forth in a sea of people jumping, bumping, and grinding. I didn't mind.

"Sorry I was absent from school," he began. "Quinn wanted to take a trip." I felt like he was lying, but it would be stupid to ruin the moment, so I didn't ask where they went.

"It doesn't matter . . . you're here now." *And storm-free*, I thought.

Then I looked up and smiled. In Connor's arms I felt safe. I rested my head against his chest and listened to his heartbeat quicken. I could feel myself falling for him. He took his right hand and brought it up to the back of my head in order to pull me in closer. We were like two polarized magnets, drawn to each other. Each of us had a side that wanted to stay as close to the other as possible, but turn us around and we would repel . . . that's what it felt like. Despite logic, despite reasoning, and despite suspicion, I wanted to stay with him, dance with him, and feel safe in his arms. If there was some magical reason I was drawn to Belfast, I knew in my gut that it was to meet Connor Winfield.

Belfast, Maine – October – Present Day

Dangerous Liasons

CONNOR AND I saw each other as much as we could. School was an easy meeting place, but getting around Quinn was much more difficult. I was never allowed over to Connor's house, and I felt uncomfortable having him at mine, considering I hadn't exactly spilled the beans on the having-no-dad-and-being-immortal fact yet. Our first actual date after the dance was playing paintball, but mainly we hung out in class, took hikes up to Mount Battie over in Camden, and kissed as much as possible, in my car or the park or on the coffee shop couches. Connor was amazed at my hiking stamina and my ability to keep up with him on long runs. Sometimes I feigned exhaustion to keep up appearances. I was just as impressed with him—he was much stronger than I imagined.

Anywhere we were slightly alone we saw as an opportunity to get to know each other better, and every chance I got to be with him was amazing. Part of me was worried about what the future would bring, but my newly rediscovered teenage hormones pushed those thoughts as far back as possible. Sometimes, though, in the pit of my stomach, I could feel it aching me. This relationship obviously couldn't last forever. At some point, Connor would discover me, and who knows how he would react.

October was a beautiful time in Maine. The trees painted the sky red and orange, while the crisp autumn air provided more opportunities for warm hugs from Connor. On rainy autumn days, he and I sat in the coffee shop sharing hot apple cider and talking about nothing. It was corny, but it was cute. The only problem with our conversations was that neither of us revealed much about ourselves, so even though we spent a lot of time together, I didn't really know Connor. I knew he preferred toffee ice cream over chocolate, that he could remember the lyrics to every song ever written, and that his idea of the perfect day would be up in the mountains snowboarding in the morning and watching soccer while eating pizza with pineapple on it at night.

He knew that I was obsessed with cheesy movies, especially musicals, that I couldn't remember the name of any song but knew all the lyrics, and that my idea of a perfect day was taking a long jog in between napping, baking, and doing absolutely nothing. However, he didn't know about my mom or my dad, or if I had cousins, or what I did as a child. He never asked those questions, and neither did I. I didn't know what he did in England, where his mom was, or why he was really in Belfast in the first place. Part of me wanted to tell him my secret so we could truly have a relationship, but I knew better. I would have to settle for a half-life with Connor rather than nothing at all.

Everything was going as perfectly as it possibly could, except that deep down, both of us knew our relationship was heading somewhere much more serious, and neither of us knew how to handle that. Connor had decided unexpectedly one day that since we could never go to his house, the next step was to begin hanging out at mine.

While sitting in the Green Man, he suddenly looked at me with an inquisitive look in his eye.

"Okay, what do you want?" I asked so he would finally spit out whatever he had been thinking about all afternoon. "I know that look."

"Well, Ms. Ally, I was thinking that tonight, since your dad is out of town *again*, I could come over and watch a movie or something." He was both asking and telling me at the same time, since he was assuming my answer would be yes.

"To my house?" *Eek*, I thought. It barely looked like *I* lived there, let alone a fictional father. There was no time to think of a way to get out of it.

"Yeah, where else? I've been dying to see your place, considering I repaired half of it. Plus, we'll be alone, and movies are much more enjoyable that way." He smiled a half smile, knowing that would convince me.

"Ok, but we are still remodeling, so a lot of our stuff is in storage." *What a stupid excuse*, I thought. I hated lying to Connor, but I really had no other choice.

That night, I was anxious. Connor was coming over. Connor, with the supposed tortured soul, was coming into my house. It would just be the two of us. We had hardly done anything but kiss, since we were caged by the figurative jail cell that was our situation, but tonight there would be no obstacles, no bars to keep us apart. Just him and me. Alone. *Crap!*

The first problem was figuring out what to wear. Jeans, T-shirt, skirt, dress . . . pajamas? I didn't want to lead him on, but I wanted to look cute. I opted for a tank top and jeans: simple and casual meets slightly sexy. I took off my necklace, which I had been wearing almost every day; usually it was hidden under a T-shirt, but it seemed a bit too much for my ruby-colored spaghetti-strap tank top.

The doorbell rang. I eagerly ran to answer it, but then paused. I took a deep breath, calmed myself, and slowly reached for the doorknob to let Connor Winfield into my home. This was a momentous occasion in my life. I had never truly been courted by a gentleman, I had never been to prom, and I had never fallen in love in the romantic sense of the word. For the first time in my new life, I was opening the door to a completely new experience . . . and I was terrified.

Connor looked cute: long-sleeved navy blue and white Rugby shirt and dark jeans. Good choice. As soon as I saw him, I was at ease. He was supposed to walk into my life, I was sure of it.

He walked around my kitchen, my living room, and my family room and glanced upstairs.

"Is your room up there?" he said with his eyebrows raised and a slight gleam in his eye.

"Yes, but the TV is down here." I shot back an innocent smile.

"Great, I always say that the living room is the best place for a flat screen. Nice entertainment system, by the way. It's about the only piece of real furniture you have."

"I watch a lot of movies in my down time. Kind of a hobby."

He seemed fairly satisfied by my house and less suspicious than I had thought he would be. He was obviously too distracted by my awesome flat screen and PlayStation system.

"So, I brought *Pulp Fiction, Moulin Rouge,* and *The Notebook*—you pick." I was nicely surprised that he brought some of my favorite movies, especially since two of the three were clearly chick flicks.

"*Pulp Fiction,* definitely!" I replied. "I love movies with lots of guns."

He started laughing. "Good, because that's actually the only one I brought. The other choices were a test of what *not* to watch, and you passed."

"Very funny," I replied, not letting on that I secretly loved the other two as well.

The movie was perfect; we sat on the couch, my head resting in Connor's shoulder, our fingers intertwined.

"Aren't movies great?" I said as the final scene played.

"They're pretty awesome," Connor replied nonchalantly.

"I mean, considering people used to not be able to do this—sit and watch moving pictures. Technology is incredible."

"Moving pictures?" Connor laughed. "What is this, 1922?"

"Ha!" I said, surprised and embarrassed by my phrasing. It obviously wasn't 1922, but my remembrance of how life used to be compared to life now made me nostalgic. It also made me realize that I was loving my date with Connor, and I loved the everyday things in life, like movies, dances, school, and friends. For once, nothing felt complicated.

"Okay, time for ice cream!" I changed the subject and jumped up as the credits began to roll. Connor followed me into the kitchen. I grabbed the ice cream from the freezer, and Connor opened my fridge to look for drinks.

"Ally?" he asked.

"Yeah?" I replied.

He looked confused. "What's with your fridge?"

"What do you mean?" I asked curiously, having no clue what he was referring to.

"It's all apples," he said, sounding put-off.

"No, it's not." I walked over to show him how wrong he was. "Look—juice, pie, jam, bread . . . lots of regular food."

"Uh, Ally . . . apple juice, apple pie, apple jam, and apple bread . . . where do you get apple bread?" He looked at me like I was a freak.

"So I like apples. So what. I also like ice cream. So let's go back out there, away from the apple stuff, so you can stop looking at me like that."

"Like what?" He shut the door to my fridge of shame.

"Like I'm a freak."

"Aww, but you're a cute freak. That counts for something," he said with a smile as we walked to the living room.

"Gee, thanks," I said, smiling.

"Actually," he continued, "I have something to tell you."

He was suddenly serious. He motioned for me to come toward him. I put down the ice cream and he took both my hands.

"Ally," he nervously began. "I really like you. In fact, I've been thinking a lot about you and . . . me . . . together, lately." He smiled. "Like all the time. It's hard to explain, but sometimes when I am around you, I feel so out of control that if I let go for even a second I will lose all composure." He took a breath but continued his speech. "At first, it was hard for me to accept that. But now, despite the weird apple thing, I realize it's because we are so perfect for each other. I have never felt so close to anyone in my entire life. I think . . ." He paused.

"Yes . . ." I was waiting for him to say it . . . dying for him to say it.

"I think I'm falling in love with you."

Hallelujah! I thought. I couldn't believe my ears. No one had ever said that to me. It's an incredible feeling to be loved by someone else. Not because they are family and they have to, but because they choose to, independent of obligation.

"Me too," I replied instantly. "I mean, I feel the same way about you. I love you."

Then he kissed me like he had never kissed me before. Suddenly, he was moving me away from the kitchen doorway. He pushed my waist back up against the wall. His hands were around me, all over me; there was so much passion and love in that one moment that I completely lost all sense of where I was or what I was doing. It was just the two of us, melting together in our bubble of happiness. The world was spinning, yet time was magically standing still. Then the wave of passion broke and he pushed me harder against the wall, so hard that it hurt . . .

"No!" he yelled. Suddenly, it felt like all the air in the room had been sucked out. The two of us were suspended in the hallway, unsure of what would happen next.

I was in shock, and my body was frozen. *Did I do something wrong?* Connor looked at me furiously, like he suddenly hated me. He was breathing hard while in the midst of contemplating his next move; his eyes darted back and forth. At least a minute must have passed.

"Ally, give me your hand," he demanded. I gave it to him on command. I was reacting without thinking. He held it for a while, and then suddenly he opened his eyes. A tear fell down his cheek, but only one.

"Connor, what is it? What's wrong?" I was so scared. *Why was he acting so strange, so mean?*

"You . . . not you, not you, Ally . . ." He trailed off.

I grabbed his arm. "Talk to me—what happened?"

"You're an Imati!" He shouted it like it was a disease. "You are just like them, all of them. You killed her; I saw you. I saw everything."

I couldn't believe my ears, and I panicked. "Connor, please, I love you . . . I can explain . . ." Although I couldn't really *explain*; I was an Imati, it was in my blood, and his reaction to that seemed to be less than understanding. Delilah's words echoed in my head: *A storm is brewing around him.*

Am I the storm?

Connor then shoved me away from him so hard that I hit the floor. He just left me there screaming his name while he slammed the door shut on his way out.

Connor Winfield, I realized, was a Seeker.

The Book of Connor Winfield

To be or not to be: that is the question.

—*William Shakespeare*

The Beginning

MY EARLIEST MEMORY as a child was of being with my mum and my sister, playing in a large green field in a small town just outside of Bath, England. It was Sunday, and my mum had brought a football with her to the local park and we were kicking it around. I kept falling over, trying real hard to keep up with my older sis, who while only seven was quite a runner. My father wasn't there; he had died before I was born, so I never knew him in person. My mother was a force of nature. She knew I missed not having a dad, so I think she tried that much harder to remind me how much she loved me. At least, that's what I remember. She homeschooled me, always said she could teach me more than any teacher in a classroom could—and I believed her.

"Now Connor, love, what do I always say?" she asked, as she made me breakfast early one Monday morning.

"I can be anything I want to! Even a cowboy!" I was only five and completely fascinated with Western movies and the Hollywood version of outlaws and bank robbers.

"That's right. Don't let anyone tell you differently, son. You are a Winfield, and that makes you special." She handed me a bowl of cut fruit and oatmeal.

"Eat your breakfast, Connor . . . and remember who loves you?"

"You do," I said, smiling.

Every day she reminded me that I was special, and that I should never let anyone force me to do anything I didn't want to. She wanted my life to be of my own choosing. At such a young age, I never knew what she was talking about. She was always a little on edge, and she had this look in her eye that at any moment someone would emerge from the shadows and shatter everything she had built.

I didn't realize at the time that she was scared of me—of what I would become. What *they* would turn me into. I learned later that she had lost her brother and my father to the Seekers, and she was trying to protect her only son. Her way of helping me was to hide me. The day I turned five she began looking over her shoulder, fearful that they would find her. It was a crime to keep a Seeker child hidden from the Masters after the age of five. The small town proved a vital cover for nine years, but one day our luck simply ran out.

I was out with some mates playing dodgeball at the park when the sun began to set. I was late getting home. I knew my mum would be pissed I was coming home after dark, so I thought I would try to sneak in through a back window. When I got inside the house, she wasn't alone. I slowly crept in, trying hard not to make a noise. No way did I want to get in trouble again; I was always coming in late and muddy right before dinner, and my mum couldn't stand it. I thought I would try to get upstairs before she noticed me. Out of the corner of my eye, I saw her in the front room speaking to two large men. She was completely distracted by them, her gaze as cold as ice, yet covered with fear. They looked like coppers, with freshly pressed suits and black ties, but I couldn't be sure. I was only nine. Their conversation felt intense. I wondered if I was in trouble.

"Please—leave my house now. I have nothing to say to you." She was pleading with them; her desperation filled the air. "I am not who you think I am. If I had a son, wouldn't he be here right now?"

"Is that an invitation for us to look around, then?" The one on the right was staring her down.

"No, it's not. I don't have a son. I never had a son and I certainly wouldn't want one, considering the circumstances." She stared at them like she was trying to make them believe her, but at the same time she looked shaken. I didn't know why she was lying to the two men. Maybe she was so mad at me for being late she disowned me? I was always giving her problems, goofing off and never doing my schoolwork.

"Mrs. Winfield, we're not stupid. We know you have a son; your late husband spoke of him in his final hours, God rest his soul. It's alright that you chose to run away after everything you have been through. The Masters understand the circumstances and are willing to forgive you for this little protection spell you have been using, but only if you turn him in now. We'll catch him up on every-thing he needs to know and he'll be safe. We promise."

"I won't give him up. You cannot have him." A look of defeat permeated across her face. She stood up to face them. "Besides, I know what you did, and I know you'll kill me the second you get the chance."

Suddenly, I was scared at the thought of watching my mum die in our living room.

"Listen, you little witch, we've been rather cordial through this little dance, but all we have to do is read you and we'll know everything—even *you* can't fight that. Out of respect for the late Mr. Winfield, we haven't done so . . . yet. So please, cooperate."

"You haven't read me yet because you can't." My mother spit at their feet. "So don't feign respect for my husband, you monsters!"

Still trapped in the kitchen, I walked closer so I could hear better, and then, *bang!* I accidently knocked a metal pot off the counter. Suddenly my mother turned to me, her eyes wide with fear. I was frozen; the room was silent except for the slight clanging of the pot on the kitchen floor. My mother looked back at the two men, and then back to me. *"Connor, Run!"*

The two men bolted after me. Instinct took over my body. I hopped back out through the window I had just snuck in through. I ran as fast as I could, through the yard, down the street. Past Old Man Yeardley's house, which was as far as I usually went in that direction. I ran and ran until my lungs burned and my legs felt as heavy as lead. I was only nine and I couldn't run fast enough. A large hand grabbed the hood of my pully and yanked me to the ground.

"It's okay, son. Are you alright?" He was out of breath and seemed genuinely concerned for my well-being. "We're not going to hurt you. We're going to take you home, to your new home. Understand?"

I didn't understand. *Where am I going? Who are these men? What about my mum, and my sister?* The newly formed pit in my stomach and goose bumps running up and down my body told me that I would never see them again. I was only nine, and I never got to say good-bye.

Orientation

MOST SEEKER BOYS arrive when they are five to begin orientation into the Brotherhood. The Masters enroll them when they are young, so they don't remember what it's like to live in the real world and, most importantly, so they do not have any remaining familial ties that could jeopardize a mission. Most parents are happy to send their sons off because it means they are gifted, that they have a higher calling in life, that they have been endowed with the strength of Seeker blood. I, however, was almost ten when I arrived. I missed my mum and my sister Ophelia greatly. I wanted nothing to do with the Academy of the Brotherhood.

We arrived at a castle somewhere in England. I had been in a car for two days, blindfolded. My captors said it was for my own protection. When I got out, all I saw were grazing sheep, fields, and gates: large, oppressive, iron gates. Gates that said once you went in, you did not easily come out.

A surprising thing happened when I arrived at the Academy: I was welcomed with open arms. It's like they had been waiting for me all the years I had been absent and were rejoicing at my homecoming. There was even a banner with my name on it: "Welcome Home Connor!" I was taken aback by the lengths these people had gone in order to make me feel at ease. Once everyone applauded me and we had cake, the students (all boys, I noticed) began to hustle about their normal day. Some ran off to class, others wrestled outside on the lawn, older boys were sword-fighting in a weapons class, and several students were reading what looked like giant leather-bound handbooks. I was intrigued by the magic and festivity of it all. My life was about to change. I was scared. Everything seemed exciting except for one small detail: I had technically been kidnapped.

Since I was already nine, they put me in an accelerated one-on-one tutoring course and kept me separate from other boys. The first step was to test my abilities. I'd first realized I could read memories when I was about six. My mother and I had been out walking, and she'd taken my hand to lead me across the street. Suddenly, images of her and my father had flashed through my brain.

"Mommy, where did daddy's scar come from?" She dropped my hand immediately and knelt down to look me in the eyes, making sure to hold my gaze.

"What did you say, Connor? Who told you that?" She started frantically looking around.

"No one . . . I saw it. It was right here." I pointed to my left cheek where my father's scar was.

She started crying and pulled me in so tight I couldn't breathe. "I knew this would happen. I knew you would be special. I'm so glad you're with *me*, Connor."

That's when my mother started giving me Seeker lessons of her own, although at the time I didn't know what a *Seeker* was. She wanted me to know my skill to the best of my advantage. She warned me to never let others in and taught me how to protect my own thoughts. She taught me that reading people's memories was invasive, and that I should only do it when absolutely necessary.

I missed her immensely during testing because everything reminded me of her. I missed our lessons. She was a much more patient tutor than the professors here. As the days went on and I made less and less of an effort, my tutor, Mr. Dawson, became acutely more aware of my depression and lack of interest in his teachings.

"Connor, concentrate, please. I don't want to be here all bloody afternoon!" He slammed a stick on the corner of my desk, frustrated by my lack of effort. "Now, take my arm and tell me what you see."

I closed my eyes and concentrated. "I see you, in a classroom, teaching young boys."

"Okay, good. Be more specific; what am I saying, listen to me, hear my memories."

"I can't hear you, I just see you."

Lie. I was lying. I could see everything. I could see him when he was four and his dad took him out on a sailboat. I saw him when he was eighteen and he snuck away from his mentor to meet a girl. I saw him when he was in Paris hunting Imati. I saw and felt everything about him—instantly.

"What do you mean you can't hear me? Try harder, boy!" Mr. Dawson was getting angry.

The less I could read, the more frustrated he became. He was suspicious of me. He grabbed my head to read my memory of his memory, a skill which I later learned takes years to acquire. I faked it and showed him the classroom scene. He was temporarily satisfied.

This went on for a week, until finally he had enough. The next day Mr. Dawson took me in to meet a Master of the Academy they called Master Grey, though I don't think that was his real name. I had only been at the Academy for two weeks and it seemed as if I was already being kicked out. Good riddance, considering expulsion was my only plausible escape plan.

Mr. Dawson practically dragged me by my neck through the large wooden door that led to Master Grey's office. He bolted through it like a bat out of hell, his anger and frustration echoing against the walls.

"This boy is either extremely powerful and purposefully pulling a ruse on me, or he is the worst Seeker we have ever known! I can't work with him anymore. It's too bloody late." Mr. Dawson had reached a new level of anger. "Damn that witch!" His eyes looked about to pop out of his head at any moment.

"Oh, come now, Gregory. You knew the boy's father and uncle; he comes from one of the most powerful lines. Plus, there is the small matter of his mother . . . he can't possibly be the worst. There must be a deeper-set problem here, don't you think?"

I looked up to get a better look at the Master. He was seated behind a large chestnut-colored desk, and large pieces of stained glass made up the wall directly behind him. His office was adorned with old books, and knightly crests were mounted around each wall. It all felt very ornate and ancient.

Then, Master Grey addressed me directly. "Connor, are you happy here? You do *want* to be a Seeker, don't you?" His demeanor was calm, and his smile captured his entire face and reached to the furthest corner of every wrinkle he had. His jovial energy was the exact opposite of Dawson's.

I looked away and kept my eyes to the floor. "I guess so" was all that came out. What was I supposed to say? The truth was that I missed my mother, and the mention of her name reminded me of all her warnings. I had a feeling that these were the people she'd been protecting me from.

"You guess so? Ha!" Master Grey laughed. "The boy has a sense of humor." He directed the last statement to Mr. Dawson. My mentor, however, looked confused by the Master's comment. "Connor, you have been given a gift. You are part of an ancient, secret society. It is your destiny; do you understand how important and special that makes you? Some boys would die for this opportunity, and you couldn't care less."

Pangs of guilt slashed across my chest. He was blatantly highlighting my complete lack of respect for their rules and the disinterest I held for their sect. Still, I didn't feel connected to their institution, and I couldn't shake the feeling that I was here against my own free will. My parents hadn't sent me to this school; I was forced to be here. This wasn't my home. Out there I had my mother and my sister. In here I was completely alone.

"Connor," Master Grey continued, "I have a solution. There is someone I would like you to meet." Just then a dark-haired young man entered his office, right on cue. "This is one of our most prized graduates and one of the most talented trackers we have seen in over a century. Meet Quinn. He will be your new mentor."

"Hello, Connor." He reached out to shake my hand. "Great to finally meet you." He was young and handsome. He looked a little like a younger version of my dad, or at least what my dad had looked like though my mother's eyes. When I shook his hand, I was tempted to read his memories, but that would have been rude. I made sure to block most of mine.

Quinn and I left the Master's office so he could show me around and teach me about what being a Seeker really meant. The first thing he did was take me to the grand library. I hadn't really said much, but he seemed perfectly comfortable walking in silence. Inside, we climbed up a large spiral staircase. Books filled the room from floor to ceiling. We walked past row after row until we hit the back wall. Quinn grabbed a book from the shelf and a secret door opened.

For a kid, this was pretty cool. I felt like we were on a secret mission to save the world. Quinn had caught my attention. As we walked through the passageway, we came face to face with a giant lock. Quinn used a key he wore around his neck to open it and we walked through the gold-inlaid wooden door.

The room smelled of ancient parchment mixed with too much dust. I felt like I had to sneeze but held it back.

"Where are we?" I asked as my eyes widened with curiosity.

"The Vault of Last Wills and Testaments. Whenever a Seeker enters a major battle, he writes a letter to his family just in case he is not triumphant in his quest. This is known as his Last Will. This is one reason we knew to look for you."

"Why did you bring me here?" I asked, but deep down, I already knew. He was going to show me the will of my father.

"Here it is. *Dannon C. Winfield.*" Quinn reached up and grabbed a leather tube. "*C* stands for *Connor*, just in case you didn't know that." He smiled and handed me a rolled-up document with a broken wax seal.

"I'll leave you alone. Just come out when you're done."

I sat down to prepare myself for what I was about to read. When I opened the letter, an eerie feeling washed over me. To me, my father was a ghost; I could see him through memories but he had never addressed me directly. I always saw him through the eyes of others, never through my own.

I scanned the will. Then, at the bottom of the page I could make out my name in large script letters.

To my son Connor,

I have yet to meet you, and in the case that you are reading this, I suppose I never did. I would like to take this opportunity to tell you that you are loved. There are a few things you can be sure of, young man: you are strong, truthful, proud, and most of all loyal. You come from a long lineage of Great Seekers, many of whom became Grand Masters in their generations. My unwavering loyalty to the Brotherhood will be my greatest legacy, and I hope it is a tradition which I can pass on to you, my only son. Through your veins runs the blood of valiant warriors who sacrificed their lives to the greater good of justice and the preservation of all that is good. Connor, never forget your name and never forget your heritage, for your destiny is the greatest thing you can ever hope to achieve. Lux et Veritas. Godspeed, Sir Winfield.

Your devout and loving father,
Dannon

I held onto the letter in front of me, utterly speechless. For the first time in my life I heard the voice of my father. This entire time I had felt like an outsider, like I didn't belong in this place with these people. The truth was, I was meant to be here. Only my mother wanted to keep me away from it, but my father wanted me to embrace it. I felt torn between two worlds: the one I was taken from, and this new world, which offered me a life of bravery and sacrifice. Maybe if I gave it a chance, I would learn to love it just as much as my father had. Maybe I could be a great warrior one day as well.

I left the vault to go find my new mentor. "Thanks, Quinn. I never knew my father." He smiled back at me, knowing he had just changed my life forever.

"I never knew mine, either; thus is our curse." We walked a few more steps, and then Quinn paused. "Just so you know, Connor, the Winfields are one of the most respected Seeker families. Around here, you are as close to royalty as we get. Why do you think we made such a big to-do about you finally coming home?"

"Really?" I beamed.

"We have been waiting for you for five years, kid. Come, let's go make a copy of that letter so you can always have it."

I suddenly felt powerful. The letter was stamped with the Winfield crest in the upper left corner. The face of a lion stared back at me.

I was a Winfield. I came from a long line of powerful Seekers, and this was my destiny. I vowed from that day forward that I would dedicate my life and blood to the Brotherhood. I was finally ready to begin my training.

Blood and Sweat

MY FIRST YEAR in the Academy was primarily focused on academia. I had to learn the rules of being a Seeker, the purpose of our existence, and why hunting Imati was an ancient tradition in the pursuit of justice. While the handbook was at least four hundred pages long, two main rules were plastered to the front page:

i. Hunt and kill all Imati who have been condemned to death by the Eternal Council

ii. Never read another Seeker unless deemed necessary for your safety or the safety of others.

Halfway through my first year, a letter came that said my mother and sister had tragically died in a car accident. I cried for several days. I never got to say good-bye and tell them I loved them, that I missed them every day, and that being a Seeker wasn't as bad as they had thought. Quinn went with me to the funeral. I didn't recognize anyone at the cemetery. Every night, I reread the copy of my father's letter to me to remind myself why I was there.

By my thirteenth birthday, I was completely integrated into the Academy and the ways of the Brotherhood. Longing thoughts of my mother and my sister running around and baking meat pies had disappeared. I still never felt as warm and loved as I did when I was little, but the Academy was starting to feel like home. My days and thoughts were consumed with weapons, tracking, hunting, and killing. I was turning into a soldier, and I loved it. I became skilled in the sword, the Seekers weapon of choice for the decapitation of our enemies. I also learned how to use a dagger, a bow, and a staff. We had improvisational weapons classes, as well, in simulated real life situations. Anything could be a weapon: a carpet, a lamp, even a bed sheet. One simply had to know how to utilize it.

Quinn became like a father to me, and he was constantly at my side. He made me train harder than all the other boys . . . including my roommate Lawrence, who managed to go through more than one new mentor each year.

Any opportunity for free time was bogged down with a new task or a new lesson. Quinn was my most trusted companion, but also constantly around like a shadow that would never leave. The only secret I had not let him in on was my ability to falsify memories. I thought the secret skill might come in handy in the future, and while I trusted him, I didn't trust him, or anyone, that much. Words of my mother still echoed in my head.

Quinn was never suspicious and always praised me for my abilities. He was especially impressed with the speed of my reads. I could instantly see the past of anyone I chose to read, and as I got older, the reads became stronger. Eventually my read morphed into a living history. When I read someone, time stood still, and I was transported into their past. Their thoughts, feelings, emotions—everything they did or felt was in me. My body became a vessel that worked at lightning speed. Quinn had never seen anything like it and took me to the Grand Masters to share my gift. It was ironic, considering that three years earlier I had been brought in because I wasn't performing up to par; now I was excelling beyond my classmates. The Grand Masters logged Quinn's description of my power in a big black book and sent me on my way.

"That's it?" I asked on the way out. "I don't get a medal or anything?"

"No," Quinn replied. He did not seem concerned with the Master's lack of praise for his discovery.

"A pie?"

"No."

"Maybe an extra banger at dinner . . . nothing?"

"Nothing. You get nothing, Conner. Your ability is your reward. Learn that."

The meeting accomplished what Quinn had set out to do. I was placed in advanced classes for the rest of my time. Quinn wanted me to accomplish as much as possible in school so that by the time I graduated I would be given clearance for special assignments.

Lawrence thought he was nuts. "Wait a minute, mate," he started in on me as soon as I got back from the meeting. "You did something great—like completely extraordinary—and they're giving you *more* work?"

"Yeah, pretty much," I said and plopped down on the bed across from him. Lawrence had been my roommate since I arrived at the Academy. We could choose someone else after the first two years, but we always stayed together.

"Doesn't seem worth it, if you ask me."

"Good thing nobody asked you." I threw a tennis ball at him.

"Hey, watch it." He threw it back, and I caught it. Then he added, "Why does Quinn ride you so much? What does he want?"

"Something about my clearance needing to match his when I graduate, so we can stay together. Same assignments, that sort of thing."

"It's peculiar. I get that you're good, man, but it's like they brought him in just for you."

"I guess." I threw the tennis ball up in the air, playing catch with myself and thinking about Lawrence's comment.

I appreciated all the time Quinn put into my training and hoped one day to live up to his expectations. I was, however, curious about his great interest in me. I loved him like family, but most of the other students moved on to other mentors after a year or two, and no one stayed with their mentor after graduation. It seemed as if Quinn was keeping me all to himself, like a prized hound in a dog show.

When I was fifteen, I reached a milestone. I only had one year left of the Academy before I was released into an apprenticeship in the real world. During my apprenticeship, I would experience a real life hunt and kill. Quinn, I was aware, had already requested to be my permanent mentor, so I knew when I graduated I would move with him to London. In my last year, I also faced a rite of passage: unbeknownst to me, fifteen was the age at which Seeker students were tested in the room of Blood and Sweat.

The room had always been a myth to underclassmen, a mere urban legend. Perhaps it was because older boys never confirmed it, or perhaps because the whole school would revolt if they knew the myth was true, but no matter what the reason for its "legend" status was, no one talked about it. Therefore, the night they came for me was a night I was completely unprepared for.

It was three in the morning. I was sound asleep in my bed, drooling on my pillow and dreaming about completely destroying Lawrence in combat training that day—he was a good wrestler, but I was better. Then, out of nowhere, my door violently burst open and three men attacked me. They were completely cloaked in black and wore white masks so that their faces were indiscernible. I felt a sharp prick on the side of my neck as they shoved a needle in it, I felt a drug surge through my body, and then I was unconscious. Most of it was a hazy, black blur. I woke up in an unfamiliar room, bound and gagged.

The area was cement and bare except for the small metal chair I was tied to in the center. The three men entered, still masked.

"Connor Winfield, you have been captured and charged of crimes against the Imati race. How do you plead?" The center figure spoke, but I did not recognize his voice. He removed my gag so I could respond.

"What? Who are you? This is bollocks. Let me go right now!" I shook my chair to try and release the ropes that tied me to it, but it was a fruitless effort. I was trying to show them I wasn't scared. *What's the worst they could do? I mean, this is a school, right?*

Just then, a large fist came across my face. The one on the right had just clocked me straight in the jaw. It felt like my whole face was instantly swelling.

"Shit, guys, you're all in a piss-poor mood. I was just trying to sleep, and now here we are in a grungy basement. Do the Masters know you are doing this?"

Another punch, this time from the other side. Then a side-palm came down on the left part of my clavicle, causing my shoulder to go numb for a brief second. I hunched over in my chair from the pain.

"Connor Winfield, you are a Seeker, and this is a crime against Imati. How do you plead?" they asked me again. This time I knew not to be a smart-ass.

"Not guilty." *Slap.* A hand smacked my right cheek. He was not wearing a glove. I realized that if I could anticipate a slap, I could read the attacker and learn his identity.

"How do you plead?" My head was still throbbing from the previous blow.

"Not guilty." Another slap. Instant read. It was Greg Dawson, my first mentor. He must have been promoted from professor to torturer. I'm sure he was getting a kick out of this.

"Lying will get you nowhere; tell us everything we need to know about your kind and the pain will stop." This was obviously some kind of test. If real Imati had snuck into my room, they would have killed me already, not chatted me up like a schoolgirl.

"Okay, you win. I'm guilty. When I was twelve, I stole the fire extinguisher from the Grand Hall and sprayed it all over the back lawn." I chuckled. It hurt to laugh, but it was worth it to piss them off. "Wow, I feel much better. You're right, honesty is the best policy."

This time, they untied me, lifted me up, and removed my chair. Standing was proving more difficult than I had thought it would be. It did not get easier. A punch to the gut. I was on the ground. Then the kicking began. They were looking for a good ruck, but I didn't want to give them the satisfaction, so I curled up into a ball on the ground until I passed out.

I awoke in the same room, once again tied to the chair. My face was caked with dried blood and my right eye had swelled to the point where I could not see out of it. Somehow, I needed to gain the upper hand—which seemed a little daunting, considering I was half beaten and tied to a chair.

This time, only one man entered. I recognized his voice from before; it was definitely Dawson. I had an idea. Dawson was an uptight, egomaniacal asshole, and I knew I could break him.

"Well, it seems like the little boy woke up from his nap," he said sadistically.

"Can I have some water?" I coughed. "Or tea with lemon, if you have it?" My attempt to be nonchalant and mock the hell out of him was inhibited by the fact that my throat was so raw I could barely speak.

"What was that? I could barely hear you, chap." Dawson sounded pleased with himself and clearly enjoyed torturing me. "Only a coward would curl up in a ball rather than fight."

"Oh, yeah, it was real courageous of you to fight a beaten kid three to one." I took a second to catch my breath. "You're just a wanker like all the others."

This time there was no brute force to punish me. I was slightly relieved, but also terrified of the unknown. Then, Mr. Dawson walked behind me to retrieve a machine that was plugged into the wall. He attached two electrical wires to my ears. He pressed a red button. My head shook violently. The room went black.

I was awake again. "What do you know about the Academy, Mr. Winfield?"

"What Academy?" I said. He pressed the red button. The electrical charge was lower this time, probably so I wouldn't pass out.

"The Academy, Mr. Winfield. Where is it located?"

"We're in it, you idiot. It's right here!" More electricity flowed through my head. The pain was excruciating.

"Stop playing games, Mr. Winfield. Answer the question!" His voice sounded irritated.

"I'm surprised they let you teach kids here, Dawson, considering you were such an untalented reader. On the other hand, I guess that saying is true: those who can't do . . . teach."

"You little—" Dawson pushed the red button.

My head was spinning from the last shock, but I couldn't help but give him one final blow. "It's okay, I'm sure Victoria still loves you. She always said she would wait for you." I tried to laugh as I spoke. "Oh . . . sorry, no she didn't; she left you. Sorry to hear that, mate. Women are tough."

He pushed the red button, my face felt like it was on fire . . . and then . . . I passed out.

Don't take it personally. He obviously read you from a distance . . . or when you hit him. Either way, that makes him powerful. He was able to instantaneously read your whole life in a split second . . . Calm down, Gregory. He was being tortured, for God's sake. If you were him, you would have said anything to get at the guy pushing the button, too . . . I know, I know, but we can't punish him for using his power in an extreme situation. He passed the test with flying colors; his tolerance for pain was astounding. Let him go, but tell Quinn to watch him; we don't want Connor switching sides on us. He could be very dangerous.

Though groggy, I caught most of what Master Grey said at the end. What did they mean, switching sides? Was that even an option?

London

A FEW MONTHS after my sixteenth birthday, I graduated from the Academy, and a ceremony was held on the back lawn. Only family members who were directly involved in the Seeker world were allowed to attend, for security purposes. No one came for me, since I had no family. However, Quinn was there, which was cool. I could tell he was excited that I was finally done. He had already resigned from his mentorship at the Academy so that we could leave upon my graduation.

I said good-bye to my friends. Lawrence was the most difficult to leave behind. He had been a mate of mine from the beginning, and he felt like a brother to me. Unfortunately, we'd been given very different assignments. He was headed to an outpost in Brazil and I was staying in London. Most likely I would never see him again.

"Well, it's been good, Connor." Lawrence hugged me with a firm pat on the back.

"Yeah, glad we stuck it out," I said, returning the same gesture.

"Look, if you're ever in San Paulo, be sure to find me, yeah?" he said with a grin laced in sorrow.

"Of course . . . wouldn't miss it." The words were hard to mutter. "Bye, mate," I said, and with that, I turned to leave.

"Oh, and one more thing," he shouted. "Good luck with Quinn . . . watch yourself." He held my gaze as he spoke.

"I will," I said, and then walked away.

Quinn and I shared a flat overlooking Hyde Park. It had obviously been paid for with money from the Academy, because neither one of us could have afforded it. It was modern in design, with three bedrooms and an office. It felt a little oppressive, with its stainless steel appliances and black marble countertops. We probably didn't need anything so large or expensive, but I decided to leave my complaints at the door. As soon as I saw the hot tub bath in the master bedroom, I was sold on it.

"Hey, Quinn, have you seen this thing? It's got jets in the bath. Isn't that fantastic?"

No response.

"Quinn . . . where are you, man?"

I found him in the office, looking intently at his computer. "Quinn, are you alive in there?"

"Connor, yes, I'm here. Listen, we don't have much time. The first assignment just came in. I'm printing it out."

"Assignment . . . for what?" *It's time to work already?* We had literally just arrived. I hadn't even tried the new bath jets yet.

"For us, Connor. We have an Imati to track. I need you to focus and take this seriously. This isn't school anymore." Quinn grabbed the papers and shot up from his desk.

His words came at me fast, and I barely had time to process them. By *track* he obviously meant *kill*. All the years at the Academy, I had dreamt of this moment; the time had finally come to hunt an Imati and to fulfill my sacred duty as a Seeker. Rather than excitement, however, I felt . . . nauseous. I ran to the bathroom and threw up all over the new, marble sink.

"Connor! You alright?" Quinn had run after me and was standing in the doorway of the bathroom.

"Yeah, I'm fine. Just a nervous stomach." In reality, I was scared shitless. Was Quinn going to make me do the killing?

"Look, I know the feeling. The first time is rough. Don't worry—I'll be there with you."

Quinn packed our bags: tracking equipment, weapons, rope, food, and lastly, two swords. He put his sword under his coat and tossed mine to me. "Time to go."

We got in the car and headed north toward Cambridge. Apparently, the Imati we were tracking wasn't in London. Quinn handed me the piece of paper he had printed from his computer. "Here, read this." I took the paper and stared at the writing in front of me.

Attention:
Your next assignment is located in Cambridge, England. Male. Appearance: 25.
Age: 95.
The Eternal Council hereby condemns the offender for crimes against humanity rang-
ing over the past twelve years, first occurring in Paris and several throughout England.

"That's it? This is all the information we get? How are we supposed to find this guy?" I asked. This was ridiculous. What did the Council expect us to do, just show up and find some guy who looks twenty-five in a town with a university? Everyone looked twenty-five.

"Well, young Connor, that is why we call it 'tracking,' not 'showing-up-and-killing.'"

Wow, Quinn made a joke!

I still wasn't convinced. "What did he do, exactly? This assignment sheet is rather vague. 'Crimes against humanity'—what does that even mean? Did he kill someone?"

"Probably," Quinn said calmly, obviously not concerned at all. "Look, Connor. We don't make the assignments. We carry them out, like soldiers. That's our role in this."

I knew he was right. We were sent on missions, like MI6 agents with swords. We didn't need explanations. We were trained to kill, and kill we would.

"So what do we do? How do we find him?" I asked as I started picturing myself as the new-and-improved James Bond.

"You'll see. Trust me. Once we get there, your training and instinct will start to kick in."

Quinn had so much confidence in me I couldn't help but feel empowered. *Go with your gut, Connor.* My Bond persona came back: Winfield, Conner Winfield. I laughed inside. I was suddenly excited.

We arrived in the town of Cambridge. We parked the car and I got out. It was pleasant outside, but with a cool chill in the air. The wind hit my face and I breathed it in like a life force. I was in hunting mode.

"Let's walk," Quinn said from behind me. "Just feel it out, Connor."

"*Use the force*," I replied sarcastically. Quinn didn't catch the *Star Wars* reference.

I walked past townspeople, students, and tourists. I paid attention more to the young males, but I knew I wouldn't rely on my sight to guide me. I kept walking in any direction my gut told me to. I walked for hours, but I did not tire.

It was dusk when I came to the White Horse pub on a side street, a little ways away from the town. Something told me to walk in. I entered and the room was bustling with patrons drinking pints of beers, clinging their glasses and chowing on typical pub fare. The smell of fried food was somewhat repulsive. I walked up to the bar to order a pint.

"Newcastle, please." I had to shout it in order to be heard over the ruckus of drunken men.

"Oy, make that two," a voice came from my right. "Sorry, mate, been waitin' ages for the bartender, thought I'd just tack on to your order."

"No worries. I'm Connor." I held out my hand.

"Westin. Nice to meet you." I shook his hand. "You a Cambridge boy?" he asked as I let go of his hand.

"No. Just visiting some friends. How about yourself?" I asked, pretending to be interested. He was just a mortal, I took a mental note.

"Me too. In fact, here he is, man of the hour. This is my good mate Charles. Smartest man at Cambridge. Just aced all his final exams. I swear, they practically throw pounds at him to study here."

"Nice to meet you, Charles. I'm Connor."

"Please, it's Charlie. Only my dad and Westin here call me Charles."

I reached out to shake his hand and read him like a book—a big, fat, voluminous book. His father did call him Charles; painful memories there. His dad would come home at night completely sauced and decide that young Charles was to be his punching bag. One day he beat him unconscious almost to the brink of death. Charlie moved out as soon as he could and enlisted in the military.

Right about the time he did, Germany invaded Poland, and Charlie fought the Nazis with the best of 'em. Definitely not mortal. I kept my cool. Little did Charlie know that he was about to die.

Something gave me away; maybe it was my inexperience or the way my heart changed beats when I read him. I had never come face to face with an immortal before, and I couldn't help but feel starstruck, like I was meeting a celebrity. Charlie must have picked up on my interest in him, because his guard was suddenly up. He carefully set his beer down on the bar.

"Listen, Westin, I'll be right back, got to make a phone call outside. Nice meeting you." He walked away. I followed him.

Quinn was waiting for me out front. Charles turned right, back through the alley. "You'd better catch up."

I started to jog in order to move faster. I turned toward the ally. There was no one there. I ran back to Quinn.

"I lost him," I said, frustrated and out of breath.

"So what should you do now?"

"I don't know . . ."

"Connor, dammit, think! You read him, didn't you? You know everything about him. He can't hide from you."

He was right. I did read him. I saw him move to Cambridge, I saw him in class, I saw him studying at the library. I saw his apartment, the address, where he keeps the spare key . . . I saw everything.

"Let's go. He lives on the south side: Fitzwilliam Street, number two-oh-eight. There is a key in the plant on the front stoop."

I waited for Charles in his apartment. Quinn stayed outside. I heard the door unlock. It had been at least an hour since I last saw Charles. He probably wanted to make sure no one followed him home. I heard footsteps: they traveled down the hall, to the kitchen. The fridge door creaked, and I heard the crack of a fresh bottle of beer being opened. He was vulnerable and completely unsuspecting. The TV came on. I came out slowly from the shadows.

"Charles Wooten, you have been charged with crimes against humanity and are hereby condemned to die." The words flowed out of my mouth like butter, smooth and perfect. I surprised myself with my own composure.

He jumped up from his recliner. "I knew you were a bloody Seeker; you got that look in your eye when you touched my hand. You people are a disgrace." He said as his beer flailed about in his hand, half spilling on the floor.

"Us? I am a Seeker of justice. That makes me honorable, unlike you. I saw you kill your father. You used your power for evil, and that makes you one of the corrupt."

I drew my sword.

"What the hell are you doing? Put that thing away. You think *you* can kill *me*? What are you, eighteen, nineteen years old? I have a century of combat under my belt, friend. You can't kill me."

I swung. I missed. He kicked me from behind. I felt a lamp crash over my head. *Dammit—my first assignment and he hits me with a lamp.* I got up to face him, but now he had a weapon. Swords clashed back and forth. Only an Imati would hide a century-old sword under his couch. I sliced his shirt; he sliced my coat. The room proved a difficult battleground, full of furniture and breakable items. His swordsmanship was impeccable and he was starting to gain on me. I felt my back growing closer and closer to the wall. Then I remembered something. Three days ago, he had crashed his car and smashed his left knee. He was healing quickly, since he was an Imati, but it was a weakness.

I roundhouse kicked him hard, so hard I heard his knee crack. He fell to the floor. This was it; this was the moment. I drew my sword above my head and came down with perfect precision. His head made a thumping sound when it hit the floor. Silver blood flowed from his neck. A sudden rush of power and energy flowed through my body. It was a high like I had never felt before. All my wounds and all the pain were suddenly gone. I was refreshed, rejuvenated, and more powerful than before. The feeling lasted for a minute and then was gone. I had completed my first kill and was definitely ready for more.

False Memories

A WEEK LATER, I was still beaming from the hunt in Cambridge. Quinn said most graduates take at least six months to actually kill an Imati without the help of their mentor. I knew he was proud of me. All I could focus on, though, was the power. The instant surge of energy I felt after the kill was intoxicating, and I couldn't wait to get my next fix.

"It was so incredible! I feel so alive. It—"

"I know, Connor. His energy source transferred into yours, and you grew more powerful." He was obviously annoyed that I was still talking about it a week later.

"Yeah, but it was more than that. It was like I took on more than just his energy. I handle my sword better, I feel smarter, and somehow I started understanding quantum physics."

"What do you mean?" Quinn got that quizzical look on his face, like he was trying to understand something without letting me know he was actually confused. "You think you took on his mental capacities as well as his life force?" he asked, both intrigued and slightly jealous at the same time.

"I don't know . . . does that happen?" I felt like I had said too much. Maybe I should keep my new skill a secret. God forbid I should break some kind of Seeker code I wasn't aware of, considering I'd never fully read the four-hundred-page handbook.

Quinn squinted his eyes a little, a look he often got when he was pondering new information. "There have been instances where Seekers, for a short period of time, will carry on memories of the Imati they killed. The Grand Masters believe that life experiences become imprinted into our life sources, so it would make sense for you to temporarily share some of his past."

"Well, that explains it, then." I felt relieved. I wonder why he hadn't mentioned that before.

"Keep an eye on it. It's supposed to be temporary." I nodded to signify that I understood. Quinn continued to stare at me for a few more seconds and then looked away. He was suspicious of this new talent, and I knew he would watch me like a hawk.

Six months went by, and the condition didn't go away. For every Imati I killed, I picked up new skills. Some stuck with me more than others, but I decided not to tell Quinn. This meant I was keeping two secrets from him: my ability to falsify my own memories so other Seekers couldn't read me accurately and my ability to absorb more than just the energy force of my immortal slayings. I wondered how many secrets he had from me.

There was really no reason to distrust Quinn, just an uneasy pang in my gut that constantly told me not to get too close. He was, however, the only family I had, and the only reason I excelled in the Brotherhood as much as I did. Over the months, we grew into a familial routine: cooking dinner, reading together, going to football matches, and of course, hunting. The more time we spent together as *normal people*, the more I let my guard down.

Life was primarily filled with hunting: Scotland one weekend, Dublin the next. We even went to Paris a few times. I was always surprised how many immortals lived among humans. They held jobs, they drank coffee, and they rode the tube. They were everywhere, and each time I killed one I saw their crimes, their corruption, and the despicable acts with which they plagued mankind. I became more and more zealous and more convinced that if the corrupt were not stopped, all would be lost. By my tenth kill, I truly felt like a seeker of justice. Quinn and I were an unstoppable team. The closer we became, the more I forgot about all the secrets I had from him. Maybe one day I could tell him, and then we truly would be brothers.

"Prague was brilliant, man. Two Imatis in one trip. The look on his face was priceless. What an arse he was, too. I saw all those women he raped; it was disgusting. He deserved everything he got."

I was still riled up from the recent hunt in the Czech Republic. I had never seen Prague, but instantly I fell in love with the medieval, brightly colored buildings and winding cobblestone streets, not to mention the booze was cheap and absinthe was everywhere. Quinn had been to Prague tons of times—Imati love the vibrant, multicultural city, filled with whores and liquor—so he was less excited about the recent adventure.

"They always do. They should all be killed . . . and they will be. One at a time." Quinn's eyes were black and appeared cold as marble. He truly meant what he said.

"Well, all of the corrupt ones, at least—right, mate?" I chuckled to hide my nervousness at his response.

"No . . . all of them." He paused to explain himself. "Connor, even if they are innocent, at some point they will become corrupt. It's in their blood. It's better to kill them now than to wait for them to commit their crimes."

"Like a preemptive strike? Guilty before proven innocent?"

"Exactly. It's better them than us. You'll see . . . we're at war."

I had never heard Quinn speak so candidly about killing all the Imati before. Obviously he was beginning to trust me more, which made me feel proud, but at the same time, his hatred for the entire Imati race scared me a little. I wanted to seek justice, not create a justice for crimes that didn't exist. What Quinn was talking about went against all the ideals created in modern society. People should not be punished for crimes they have not yet committed, and to judge them for what others of their kind do . . . well, that was plain racist. Quinn was talking genocide. I didn't know what to say, so I excused myself.

"I'm going out for some orange juice, we're all out . . . I'll be right back." I had to leave the flat in order to clear my head. I was sure that the Imati I had killed deserved to die. *But what about Quinn? How many has he killed? Were all of them guilty?* These thoughts made me sick to my stomach. All of a sudden, I was questioning my entire existence as a Seeker. *This is ridiculous*, I thought. We don't kill without reason. We are the Brotherhood. There are rules.

I took the tube on the way back from the market and couldn't help but look at all the humans sandwiched in the car, going about their mundane lives with no worries of guilt, or murder, or righteousness. A girl stood next to me holding a book in one hand and flowers in the other. Quietly reading, she was paying no attention to her surroundings. A mother in front of me played with her child and read him all the ads on the side of the wall. A kid came by and asked if I wanted to buy a chocolate bar. None of these people had killed anyone. I felt alone.

I looked at the girl again; she looked vaguely familiar. Dark hair, soft features, almost doll-like. She intrigued me. I was jealous of her. She had a normal life. The train stopped suddenly and she was thrown into me, knocking the flowers and her book from her hands. For a second she was on top of me. As soon as she touched me, I felt a magnetic force between us. She squinted her eyes and looked at me for a second as if trying to recognize something.

"Are you okay?" I asked her while trying to get up.

"Um, yes . . . do I know you?" She still had that puzzled look on her face.

"No, I don't think so . . ."

"Are you sure? Where did you go to school? Saint Paul's?" She wouldn't leave my line of sight.

"No, I'm not from here . . . maybe I just have one of those faces." She did not look satisfied with this answer.

We both went to pick up her flowers, and she grabbed my wrist with a purpose and stared at me intensely. I didn't know how to react. And then her eyes opened wide, and I could see that they were grey-blue with specks of green. Her mouth dropped. She took a deep breath and whispered, "Connor?"

How did she know my name? I had no time to think.

"My name's not Connor." I shoved her back a little and started to walk away.

"Yes it is. I know you." She continued to follow me, but I did not look back. She really did not know how to take a hint. I exited the subway car and kept walking. People bustled by us as I frantically searched for an exit sign.

"Don't leave, Connor," she shouted from a few yards back. "It's me, Ophelia . . . your sister!"

All the noise and chaos suddenly stopped. I turned to look at her. She stared back at me with a pitiful look of hope in her eyes. She was smaller than me now, but I could tell she was the same girl I used to race in the fields with, the same sister who used to throw strawberries at me and spit in my cereal. I wanted to hug her, to run to her and embrace her, but something stopped me. It felt like the whole world was holding me back from running toward her. Images of her funeral flashed into my head, her burial site, her gravestone, the yellow daisies

I had brought the day I watched them put her in the ground. All of these memories were real; this girl standing in front of me was a lie.

"You're not her." I was trying to convince myself more than convince her.

"Yes I am. How could I not be? I know you; I know you are Connor Winfield."

"You're dead!" I screamed.

A few strangers turned to look at me telling this innocent young woman she was dead. "You can't be Ophelia . . . I went to your funeral, I put flowers on your grave." My words shocked her. She clearly had no idea what I was talking about.

"What? That's a lie, Connor. Whatever they told you is a lie. They tried to kill us after they took you and we ran away. They wanted to punish Mother for keeping you for so long. We escaped on a ferry to Amsterdam and went into hiding."

Her expression then changed from consternation to pure joy. "I can't believe it's you . . . it's really you!" She ran up to touch my face, but I grabbed her wrist to stop her.

"Stop it! You're dead, I know you are. I saw the coffin. I saw them bury you!" She backed up.

"Did you? Did you see my body . . . or just the casket? What can you really believe, Connor? You are a smart boy—did you really think they were just going to let what mum did slide? She hid you for over four years. She was never going to stop looking for you and they knew that. They knew if they killed us, we would no longer be a threat."

"It's not true, it can't be true!" I was angry at her for telling me these lies. Who was she to insult the Academy, to insult my existence, to shame our father?

"Dammit, Connor, read me! You can do it. I can't lie to you, remember? You're a Seeker." She held out her hand for me to take. Her confidence was frightening. She'd clearly inherited that from my mother. I read her, and she was right. They did try to kill her, and my mother. I hadn't seen my mother in seven years, and there she was in all of Ophelia's memories. The hiding, the fear, and the constant paranoia . . . all because of me. I had ruined their lives.

"Connor, we must go now. You can come with us; we'll run away together. We have a plan to make everything right again. It will be like it was *supposed* to be." There was a sense of urgency in her voice, and she took my hand to lead me away.

"Wait." I backed away a little without realizing it. "Run away? I can't . . . my life is here, in London. I'm a Seeker, Ophelia, that's my duty. I took an oath and I can't just abandon the Brotherhood. I have a calling."

"They tried to kill us, Connor! What is it that you are fighting for?" She looked disappointed and betrayed all at once.

"It's more than just you and me. There are greater battles being fought. I need to be here to fight them." I couldn't believe what I was saying. I felt so bound by duty and honor that the idea of leaving with Ophelia seemed impossible. I missed my mother and my sister, but that was the old me. My life was now something greater than that; I meant something. I knew that if I left, I would miss hunting; I would miss the rush and the power that came with it. A big part of me loved the Brotherhood, and for the first time I saw what a hold they had over me.

"I can't believe you. They lied to you, Connor; they made you believe we were dead. Who knows what else they are capable of? You would really choose them over your family?" She was clearly dissatisfied over the choice she knew I would make.

"*They* are my family." As soon as the words came out of my mouth, I could see the disgust rise in Ophelia's face. Tears welled up in her eyes, yet she did not let them break. Her fists clenched and she composed herself.

"Well then, I hope you love them as much as we loved you, Connor. I am sorry we were not enough." She walked away.

As soon as she was gone from my sight, I felt a lump of remorse in the back of my throat and at the pit of my stomach. *What have I done?* I'd just lost my sister again, all in order to remain a Seeker. What was I going to tell Quinn? Quinn who came with me to the funeral, Quinn who had been lying to me all these years? *Who can I trust?* I was suddenly more confused than I had ever been. The journey home took longer than usual. I was moving at a snail's pace; every fiber of my being was weighing me down and telling me not to go home. What was I going to do?

I walked through the front door with a heavy heart. My feet felt like they were made of lead. My head was pounding from overthinking my life's choices, or lack thereof. Was I just a pawn in a game I didn't know I was playing? Quinn was there, waiting for me at the table.

"Connor, you're back. I have news." He cut himself off. "What's wrong?" he asked.

"Nothing, just tired from the Prague trip. Wiped me out more than I realized." I tried to add a reassuring smile.

"Where's the juice?" Quinn always paid attention to details.

"I dropped it on the train. A guy ran into me, knocked it out of my hands. No problems. Just decided to come home because I was tired." I started to walk away, but Quinn continued the conversation.

"Well then, rest up, because you need your energy for the big move." He seemed more excited than usual.

"Big move? Where to?" I asked, hoping for it to be far away from London, in light of recent events.

"Belfast, Maine."

"Maine? Why . . . what could possibly be in Maine?" I couldn't imagine that moving to a small town in Nowhere, USA would be of any interest to the Brotherhood.

"Everything," he said with a devious smile.

Ophelia Winfield, Present Day

Dear Mother,

You were right. Connor remains in London with Quinn. He seemed genuinely concerned for my well-being, but not enough to leave the Brotherhood behind. Everything you said is true, and I feel with all my heart and soul that now is the time to act. Everything is in place and we are more than ready. Please, leave word with the white doves. I will meet you in Heaven.

With love,
Ophelia

New Beginnings

I COULDN'T SLEEP. The new house in Belfast did not feel like home. It was located off of a small dirt road in the middle of the woods. The trees knocked against the windows at night, making a creepy scratching noise. Ophelia's plea would not leave my mind. The image of her walking away troubled me. Three months into my new life in Maine and I still didn't know what we were looking for. *Did I make the right decision by coming here? Should I go? No . . . I can't leave, there is too much at stake. What is at stake? Why are we here?* Every night was the same battle . . . I was fighting myself more in Maine than actual Imati.

On the plane to the States, Quinn explained we were looking for the Holy Grail of Imati, a person who knew everything and who could help the Brotherhood finally become what it was meant to be. What exactly it was meant to be was unclear. After several months of false leads, we had only been in battle three times. All three Imati we killed were far outside of Maine, even as far west as Colorado. This did not seem to bother Quinn at all, but it sure bothered me.

"Aren't there other Seekers in the States that can kill this one?" I asked as we were loading the car to Denver. "It's not even our region. I have missed the last two weeks of school as it is; people think I'm weird disappearing all the time."

"No, not for this kill. Only us. I have a lead," Quinn said curtly. "Besides, who cares what teenage mortals think?"

"I am a teenage mortal!" I snapped back. Quinn laughed. I continued my whining. "You always have a lead, and then it's nothing. What is the point?" I sounded like a stupid kid.

"Connor!" Quinn shouted back. "That's enough." He glared at me intensely; his head looked as if it was about to boil over with anger. We didn't get along as well as we used to. Maine had changed him. We trained harder than ever before;

he was constantly on me to improve and not ask questions. He was obviously preparing me for a war I didn't care was coming. I was no longer as obedient as I used to be. The move was wearing on us.

"When did you become a whiny little twat, Connor? Who cares what your schoolmates think? They are worthless. Who cares if we have to go to Colorado? It's your job and your duty to the Brotherhood. If you don't want this life, then leave."

There was a silence, and the distance between us became an ocean.

"I am serious, Connor. Decide now: get in the car and live the life you were meant to—the life destined to you—or pack your bags and be . . . a teenager."

I reached for the door, sat down, and strapped in. I was silent for an hour. I was furious. He was treating me like a child, and thus I was acting like one.

Finally, I spoke. "Dammit, Quinn, I want this. I love the Brotherhood . . . but you can't drag me around America looking for a ghost. You have to give me something to grasp on to, man . . . I'm losing my faith."

What I said was true; I was losing it.

Quinn stopped the car. "Fine," he said as if he was relinquishing his greatest secret. "There is a way, Connor, for us to become more powerful, to live longer and have more strength than you could ever imagine. The Brotherhood has been searching for a way to improve ourselves for centuries to fight the Imati at their own level. We have always failed. Then, a few decades ago, something happened. A link to the other world was found, a bridge to the Immortal Realm. If we can find this bridge, then we can have everything."

I was confused. "We are looking for a bridge?" I asked.

"No, not literally . . . the bridge is a person—well, sort of." He stuttered a bit. "We don't know what he or she looks like."

"So we really are looking for a ghost, then, searching blind," I said, knowing that Quinn would get frustrated with my mockery.

"Blind, no; foggy, yes. Listen, I get leads, we have sources. All my sources say that Belfast is Mecca . . . these other hunts are to learn more about Belfast, get it?"

"Sure, I get it." *What's not to get? We're looking for something that we've never seen before based on a story decades old.* My faith was not exactly restored in that moment.

"One question," I said.

"Anything," Quinn said sounding relieved now that the burden of his secret plans had finally lifted off of his shoulders.

"What do you mean, live longer?" I paused, choosing my words carefully. "How long is *long*?"

Quinn stared at me, gauging how much trust and faith he had in me as his pupil. "Forever," he said. Then he started the car again, and we drove off to find another lead to a bridge that we could not see.

Carinthia Winfield – Nineteen Months Ago

Dearest Ophelia,

Heaven can wait. We must bide our time a little longer. While we are prepared to the best of our knowledge, it is what we don't know that plagues us. Connor is no longer in London; he and Quinn have moved to America. We must not go there . . . yet. There is something I need to show you in Paris first. Please come; you know where.

All my love,
CW

New Friends

Belfast, maine proved to be a very sleepy town. Despite Belfast being a larger Maine city (and I use the term *city* loosely), I was accustomed to London, Paris, Prague, and thousands of other places that were more intriguing than a fishing port, one-stoplight town. After almost a year, I was feeling a bit . . . bored. The leads had stopped for the last few months. Quinn and I almost never hunted anymore. We spent most of the time training, training, and training some more. He had turned our house into a military-style facility complete with sparring rooms, weapons facilities, and backyard obstacle courses. Luckily for us, the surrounding forest cover hid our endeavors from prying eyes.

The more time I was in Belfast, the more time I had to spend at school. While I did not want the other students to think me weird for my absence, I realized I wanted even less to have to be around them. I could not relate to any of them. I was a trained killer, fluent in three languages, and part of an ancient secret society devoted to hunting the corrupt and unjust. They were simply . . . mortals. They fussed over exam scores and lunch menus, football games and dances. The girls were the most annoying; they fussed and fawned over me despite my utter lack of interest in or complete silence toward them. For some reason, a sixteen-year-old girl can talk, uninterrupted, for twenty minutes straight without realizing the other party has yet to say a word. I was not a total ass; I would smile and nod, then send them about their day. No one ever ate lunch with me, and Quinn did not allow me to go anywhere after school, unless it was some random chore he decided I should partake in. He had a lot of rules for town life: be liked, but stay under the radar. He also did not want me getting attached to anyone. So far, that was not a problem.

However, sometimes at lunch, when I was feeling particularly vulnerable, I would watch the other students and feel a slight pang of jealousy. Couples kissing in the hallway, a girl crying that her boyfriend cheated on her, two girls hugging from their recent *A*s in geometry, a jock wearing his letterman's jacket—scenes of lives I would never have flashed in front of me every day. I was an imposter in this school, and during the hours from eight a.m. to three p.m., I felt completely alone.

Then, school let out for the summer and I was free . . . except now I was stuck with Quinn 24/7. Any chance to get away suddenly became a godsend. One morning, Quinn was hungry and there was no food in the house, so I quickly offered to run to town for some breakfast. I took the longest route possible and decided that the coffee shop in the center, where there was less parking, was the best bet. The longer I was out of the house, the better.

As I slowly walked down Main Street, I began to contemplate my own existence, something I was very keen on these days. I hated being with Quinn all the time, but I hated school as well. I wasn't a normal teenager . . . I was caught in this purgatory between the Brotherhood and a human existence. Belfast made me feel further from the Brotherhood. At least in London we were hunting, and I didn't have to pretend to be a student. The big city made us anonymous. Here I was constantly struggling with two identities, and it was driving me crazy.

I was so caught up in thought that I didn't realize I had passed the coffee shop. I backtracked three blocks and went in. Millie was standing at the counter, smiling per usual, and completely overexcited to see me. Despite her perkiness, I was fond of Millie; she had a sunny disposition that made talking to her enjoyable. Plus, she wore so many bracelets that they rattled when she spoke. I only noticed because the noise was so apparent.

"Hi, Millie," I said and ordered my usual. Then, out of the corner of my eye, I saw a familiar face sitting at the long counter. The tree-saver from Bayview Drive glanced up at me long enough for me to see the emerald color of her eyes juxtaposed with the golden color of her hair. She looked otherworldly. There was a hollowness in her face, like she had seen one too many bad things in her young life. Something about her drew me in. When I looked at her, the room was quiet, my fears were gone, and the worries that had been plaguing me not five minutes before dissipated before my eyes. I wanted to talk to her, learn her secrets, to say anything, even just hello . . . but she turned away and stared into her cup. The last time I had run into her she had knocked me down in a single blow, so I knew she had a power about her. I wanted to introduce myself but couldn't. *Amateur*, I thought, *scared of a girl*. I took my order and left. I glanced back through the window once I got outside and saw her frantically talking to Millie. Maybe she was asking about me, maybe not.

When I got home, I felt the need to tell Quinn about her, but I decided that would be a bad idea considering he would probably have her killed or something. It made me sad to distrust Quinn so much, and the more I thought about it, the more I was pulled away from the bubble of serenity and intrigue the new girl had created for me and right back into my dark world.

"Connor, you're back . . . that took a while." Quinn's voice had an accusatory tone.

"Yeah, not much parking in the summer on Main Street, sorry, but I got your joe right here." I sat down across from Quinn, who was reading a scroll. *Finally!* I thought. *Time to hunt.*

"I have good news. We are going to Canada . . . Montreal, to be exact. There is a gang of Imati up there wreaking havoc and we have been called by the Brotherhood to hunt them."

"What did they do?" I asked.

"Oh, the usual—steal, kill, rape." Quinn was lying, I could tell.

"The usual?" I asked skeptically. *Why doesn't he trust me?* "Quinn, just tell me what they did. What does the letter say?"

I grabbed it from the table before he could stop me. I could tell he wanted to get angry, but if he did he would be admitting he was hiding something. The letter was different from the others. It had the seal of the Brotherhood, but it also had a crest in the lower right corner I was unfamiliar with, and it was signed *G. Dawson*.

"This isn't an order to hunt; this is a lead, isn't it?" I tried to remain calm. I felt like I should be angry but I wasn't. Part of me was excited, a new lead. Maybe Quinn was right all along and we were finally going to find this elusive bridge to the Immortal Realm . . . whatever that was.

"Professor Dawson is your source?" Quinn looked at me like that information didn't matter. "He hates me. He tortured me in school, for Christ's sake!" I hated Dawson but knew I needed to remain levelheaded when speaking about him. I was a little shocked at my own self-control when mentioning Dawson's name.

"I know you're mad, Connor, but—"

I stopped him before he could finish. "I'm not mad, Quinn, I am . . . interested." He looked at me, puzzled, assuming I was going to throw another *you don't trust me* tantrum. "I want to be involved. This sounds legitimate. If this trio knows anything about the 'bridge,' I want to make sure we find it before they do. That's our job, right?"

Quinn looked at me with so much pride and adoration in that moment that part of me felt badly for conning him. As soon as I saw the name 'Dawson,' I knew I was being watched more carefully than I had originally thought. Flashbacks of the room of Blood and Sweat hit me, and I remembered Master Grey's words while I was in and out of consciousness: *Let him go, but tell Quinn to watch him; we don't want Connor switching sides on us. He could be very dangerous.* Quinn had to believe that I was on his side . . . whichever side that was.

"You never told me that Imati would be looking for the bridge as well, Quinn. This all makes sense now; we have to stop them from finding it."

He bought it completely. "Yes! Exactly, Connor. I had no idea you would be able to handle all of this. I misjudged you. I'm glad we are on the same page. Pack your bags; we have to get on the road tonight."

"How long are we going for?" I asked, already knowing the answer.

"As long as it takes," he replied. I wished I could have said good-bye to my mystery girl, but I had no way to find her; I didn't even know her name, not to mention she barely knew I existed. Thoughts of her were pushed from my mind. I needed to focus on everything Quinn said and did in Montreal, because I was finally being let into the inner circle of the Brotherhood, and to me that meant everything.

Light and Truth

MONTREAL WAS LIKE being in France; the Québécoise were everywhere, and everything was in French. I felt like I was back in Europe. Being out of Belfast was a breath of fresh air.

The first three days we were in the city, we did surveillance. We already knew where the Imati were living, but during a hunt, it's important to get down their routines, know their every move. When we arrived at our hotel, Dawson was waiting there. I had not seen him in over two years, since I had left the Academy. He looked exactly the same. He still was not as powerful as Quinn or I, but something told me knowledge was his best weapon.

"Hello, Connor." He shook my hand: a sign of trust, as he was assuming I would not read him. I respected that. I shook back.

"Greg, nice to see you again." He smirked at my use of his first name. He was no longer my professor.

"Quinn tells me you are all caught up now. Welcome to Montreal, and congratulations."

"Congratulations?" I asked. "On what?"

"I haven't exactly told him yet, Dawson," Quinn added.

"Told me what?"

"Oh, come on now, Quinn, it's important . . . it's tradition."

Dawson reached into his pocket and pulled out a little platinum ring with the same crest I had seen on the letter. In the center was a sideways 8, the symbol of infinity. "Welcome to Lux et Veritas," Dawson said with a smile, and then out of the blue he hugged me.

"What is it?" I said, still confused and fidgeting to put the ring on.

"Light and Truth, Connor. We are a secret society within the Brotherhood—the oldest and most powerful of them all. Your father was a member, and he wore this ring, as do we all. You should feel very honored."

He placed his hand on my shoulder. I did not read him. I suddenly felt more bound to him, once again connected to the Brotherhood.

"My father was a member." I said it more like a statement than a question. I remembered his Last Will; right before his signature, it had said *Lux et Veritas*. I did feel proud. Quinn and Dawson were letting me into their society. The new-found love and respect we shared clouded my judgment, and I forgot to ask *why* there was a secret society within a society.

After four days of surveillance, it was time to strike. I was sent in first. My target was the girl. She was beautiful, with auburn-colored hair, blue eyes, and fair skin. She carried a charisma with her that was overtly intoxicating, and I knew I needed to focus extremely hard when I was around her. Despite the warmish weather, she was almost completely covered. She wore black leggings with a long-sleeved white sweater tied in the center with a large brown belt. Her boots were brown as well. She even wore gloves. I approached her on the street, in public, where she could feel safe, and addressed her in French.

"*Excuse me, miss? I am lost; do you know where Rue Pierre-de-Coubertin is?*"

"*Rue Pierre-de-Coubertin is not near here, sorry. You should just get directions to the Olympic stadium. Is that where you are going?*" She spoke perfect French.

I replied in English. "Um, yes, do you know how to get there?"

I went to hand her the map and place it in her hands. She took it and quickly took her hand away. I couldn't read her through her gloves. Now I knew why she was covered; she was prepared.

"*Je suis désolée*—I am sorry. I am new here; I do not know my way around yet," she said sweetly.

I was at a loss. I needed skin contact, and clearly I had to go to plan B.

"I'm Connor. I am new as well; just moved from London, actually. How about I take you out for a drink and we can talk about all the places we don't know how to get to in Montreal?"

She laughed. I felt drunk she was so enchanting, but in a different way than my mystery girl. I could tell this fiery woman was bad news, that she could devour men with a smile. I was mesmerized.

"You are very brave, Connor, asking a strange woman you just met for a drink. How do you know I won't hurt you?"

"I am willing to take my chances," I replied.

"I'm Scarlett."

I chuckled, trying to be as charming and whimsical as possible. "Of course you are! What a most perfect name." Then I held out my arm for her to take. "Shall we?"

"We shall . . . not."

Even as she was rejecting me, she was still delightful. "I fear this is not the last time I will see you, Connor. You are looking for something that I don't have and I don't want. I know why you are here. I have seen you before. I have seen many of you before. Montreal for me was a safe haven, and now it too has been compromised. Whatever you heard, whatever they told you . . . what you want is not here."

She turned to walk away. Then she did the strangest thing: she walked back up to me, looked straight into my eyes, and whispered not more than one inch from my ear, "I am not a nice girl. Do not follow me. I have killed many Seekers, Connor, and I don't want to have to kill one as handsome as you." Then she kissed me straight on the mouth. She knew I would read her. I was so taken aback by her behavior that I was not prepared for it. She was like the siren that drew Odysseus into her cave. I barely caught her life. I saw her in Paris, and New York. I only caught the last few weeks in detail; everything else was a blur. I saw her in South America, I thought, and maybe in a large house, but only in smudges. It was my worst read.

What did she want me to see? Something recent, obviously; she caught me off guard for a reason.

I looked up and she was gone. After that encounter, all the other Imati we had been watching were gone. They knew we were coming, and they knew what we wanted more than we did. Scarlett had given me a clue, and I couldn't figure it out. Most of the images of her were in France: meetings, shopping, killing (she was right, she wasn't a nice girl) . . . was she helping me or hurting me?

I went back to Belfast more confused than when I had left. Every day of my life seemed to add more questions with no answers. Dawson blamed me for losing Scarlett. He let us go back to Maine and would not disclose (at least not to me) his next destination. Quinn reassured me that he understood the Imati were prepared for us. "We need to be more careful and plan better next time. The problem is these damn leads from Dawson come so late. By the time we get there, they are already gone." He was frustrated.

"Don't give up, man. Scarlett knew we were looking for something, and she obviously wanted to separate herself from it. From the looks of what she has done . . . if something is scaring her off, it has to be big."

"You're right, Connor, good thinking." My last statement seemed to put Quinn at ease.

"Looks like I'm finally doing some good around here, eh?"

"Connor, you are irreplaceable. Trust me."

Alastrina Byrne

SUMMER WAS IN full swing once we got back to Belfast. June was humid, and it made sitting around unbearable. Quinn and I were taking the day off from training. He was using his time to study manuscripts and letters; I was using my time by sitting around and playing video games while simultaneously watching sports matches and ordering pizza. We had two TVs in our living room. One was connected to satellite so we could get all the good football matches, and the other was strictly set up for PlayStation and Xbox. I may be a powerful Seeker, but on my off days I liked to be a lazy eighteen-year-old bloke . . . especially since off days came about once every blue moon.

"Don't lift your knee—dammit, man! Quinn, you should see this; Ronaldo shanked another ball over the crossbar. I swear, if he doesn't start scoring, Real Madrid is going to be in huge trouble. They'll have to bring Beckham back from retirement."

"Connor, be serious." Quinn looked up from his studies. "Beckham became worthless as soon as he moved to Los Angeles. Too much sunshine in Hollywood."

"Right, mate." I laughed. For a brief second we were brothers, chatting over a match and making fun of elite athletes that could run circles around us. I felt at home, and then I was snapped out of it by Quinn's next question. "Connor, how good is your Gaelic?"

"It's okay, I guess—why?" I continued to watch the match, only half listening.

"I am trying to read this letter, but it's centuries old and completely in Gaelic. Do we have a translator?"

"Yeah, but it doesn't have Gaelic. It's a dead language, mate."

"So is Latin," Quinn said, "but it's still important. Maybe you could run to the rare bookstore, pick up some stuff in Gaelic we could use to translate . . . or they might have a dictionary."

"Really? You think so . . . in this town?" I was not convinced, and I really wanted to finish my game.

"You would be surprised, Connor. This town is full of eccentric things." Quinn was being cryptic again, which I hated, and which also meant he was close to discovering something. I begrudgingly grabbed the keys and went.

The old man in the store pointed me to the back, and to my surprise, I saw the blonde mystery apple-tree girl once again. I became unexpectedly excited. I went to the other side of the shelf; she was in the foreign book section. Interesting. She was clearly looking for something specific. I watched her for a few moments, and then started to approach from the other end. As soon as she reached for a book, I reached too. The book fell. *Perfect*, I thought.

"Oh, sorry—did you want this book as well?" I asked, knowing fully that she did, and that in reality I did not. I looked down and saw that she was reaching for a book written in Gaelic; interesting and ironic, really. *If only I could ask her to translate for us. Not really the best line for a first date: "Hey want to come translate this old document we need in order to kill people and save the world?"*

"Um, yes," she said, sounding nervous. I don't think she recognized me as the guy she had violently shoved to the ground to save a tree. I decided to remind her.

"Hey . . . it's you! The girl that attacked me." A little forward, maybe, but my ego was still bruised.

"Yup . . . that's me . . . girl by day, tree-saver by . . . well, day also." She looked embarrassed, which I found rather amusing.

"It was a good tackle," I added, which, in all fairness, it had been. Maybe a little too good.

After some more awkward conversation, interrogation tactics references, and slightly witty exchanges, I found out her name was Alastrina Byrne. The strikingly beautiful, green-eyed, golden-hued girl was Irish American, or so she said. Really though, what modern, Americanized Irish person still spoke Gaelic? There was something off about her. She fidgeted when she talked to me, and she seemed a little unsure of everything she said, like she was gauging my response . . . or lying. Her awkwardness, however, was comforting. The more awkward she was, the more charming I became. She intrigued me because there was a darkness in her eyes that gave her an old soul. She did not come off as seventeen, but I guess neither did I; I've seen and done too many things. I offered her the book and she refused. When she shoved it back at me, I touched her finger ever so slightly so that my hand barely grazed hers. I read her . . . I knew I shouldn't, but I wanted to learn her secrets and figure out why she was so strange.

I got nothing. I was shocked and confused. I wanted to grab her and shake her and see her memories, but I held myself back. I continued the conversation as if nothing had happened; in reality, nothing did happen, and that's what was so discomfiting. I quickly ended the banter with a compliment to her; the truth was that I needed to leave as quickly as possible because I was a bit shaken by my inability to read her memories. Her mind was a locked box for which I had no key.

I turned to walk out of the store and shouted back my name, which she had never asked for. I left with the Gaelic copy of *Tristan and Isolde*. Really this would be quite useless, but at least I was not coming back empty-handed. *Who is this girl, and why couldn't I read her? She was blank: no memories, no images, not even a smudge. Is she even human?* I left thinking about how much I wanted to see her again. Both of us were clearly drawn to each other, and it seemed like that was exactly where we shouldn't be.

Distractions

.

THE NEXT TIME I saw Alastrina—Ally—was weeks later at the Celtic festival. I assumed she would be there, which is why I dragged Quinn along (since he wouldn't let me go alone). He was still upset that I'd won last year's games. He thought it would be more beneficial for me to blend in and not show off my unnatural strength.

My meeting with Ally did not go as planned; I did not mean to fall in love with her so quickly, and I was utterly unprepared for it.

She sat next to me on the log, gazing at the fire, her golden hair illuminated by the flame. She looked absolutely regal. She had no idea how striking and attractive she was. That's what I liked about her. The fact that I couldn't quite figure her out made her seem like a puzzle I was trying to solve, a game I couldn't beat. A game that was interrupted by Rebecca Munn.

I saw her prancing over from a few yards away and knew exactly where she was headed. Rebecca was what you would call hot. Really, really hot. But she was also the most annoying, vapid girl on the planet and had made it her life's mission to date me—which I despised. The last thing I wanted was Munn ruining my Ally time.

"Connor! I thought I saw you over here!" she said with a wide-eyed grin.

Crap. It's happening.

"Hi, Rebecca," I muttered as I stood up to say hello, not having the balls to blow her off in front of Ally—whom she was clearly aware of. So, like a normal person, I introduced the two, not that I wanted to. I needed Rebecca to go away. Luckily, after about two minutes of icy conversation, she did.

But when Ally and I took our seats back on the log, I felt that the encounter with Rebecca Munn had put a damper on the mood. I wanted to reassure Ally that the tiny girl with the killer ass was not a threat in the least, so I blurted out,

"I do work on her dad's house, that's it." Not very smooth, but it got the point the across.

Ally smiled. "Cool. She seems nice."

I shook my head. "She's not that nice."

To which Ally responded, "Yeah, I didn't really believe it when I said it."

Excellent. Smart and funny. This girl challenged me in a way that no other girl could. For the rest of the night we chatted like old friends, except that she constantly managed to circumvent my questions and never gave me a straight answer. She was obviously hiding something. Still sitting by the fire a little while later, I took the opportunity to figure her out, find out what she wanted. But to my surprise, it was nothing at all.

"So Ally, in all seriousness, what do you want to be when you grow up? A rock star? A famous writer? A butcher, baker, or candlestick maker?" She laughed at my joke, despite the fact that it was rather lame.

"I don't know," she said, still laughing, but I wanted her to answer the question. What did she want? Who was she deep down?

"Well, if you could pick something, what would you pick?" I asked again. "Anything in the world."

"Um, I don't know. I don't really think about the future much." She said it blankly, like it didn't matter. Like *life* didn't matter. This upset me.

"You don't have dreams or aspirations? You just want to be a kid forever?" I was irritated. What was she hiding from? "The whole world is open to you, you can do anything, and yet you choose nothing?"

I became angry. This whole time, I had been trying to figure out a girl that couldn't figure herself out. She had every opportunity available to her—unlike I, bound by destiny and bloodline. No one had given me a choice whether or not to be a Seeker; it was simply decided for me. It wasn't that I didn't love the rush and excitement of it all, but part of me knew deep down that I had been chosen, and therefore could not do the choosing.

I continued my tirade. "Not all of us have such pleasures, Ally. Not all of us have the luxury of choice."

I yelled at her for taking her options for granted—like another version of Rebecca Munn—and she almost started to cry; but the look on her face was not simply of sadness, but of anger and frustration. Suddenly, she had a spark, and

her voice overflowed with unfulfilled passion. The fire inside her as she continued to speak brought back that initial feeling of lust I had for her.

Then she added, "Sometimes dreaming about something that can never
happen is more painful than just accepting it—maybe you'll understand that
better when you're older,"

What did she mean by that? I was shocked by her response but pleased to
have lit a fire. Obviously, she had a tortured soul hiding beneath her golden exterior. In that moment that I fell in love with her. I wanted to hug her, kiss her, save
her, and keep her safe forever. I slowly put my arms around her and apologized
for getting so upset. She must have forgiven me, because she put one arm behind
my back and rested her head near my heart. There we were, sitting near the fire,
embraced in a moment neither of us could figure out.

The pain that she felt, I felt. Every ounce of her being seemed to be holding
back secrets and her anger was deep-seated and uncontrollable, like a wild animal
caged in for far too long. There was something she wasn't telling me, but I didn't
push it. I let her sit in my arms, hoping that for just a moment she would feel safe.
I offered to walk her home and she refused. I was afraid I had ruined everything
with my reaction to her apathy toward life, but I couldn't help it. I was caught off
guard . . . and feeling slightly bitter. I was worried I would never see her again and
never get a chance to tell her how I feel. To tell her that she is not alone.

For the next two weeks I moped around, barely even speaking to Quinn.
I sat in my room, I worked out, I trained—all the normal stuff—but I was distracted. I couldn't get Ally out of my head. I wanted to rescue her from whatever
was plaguing her. That was my job, to fight evil, and there was something bad
in her life that she needed help with. If only she would let me in. Again, I was
confused. Quinn apparently had had enough of it and finally confronted me.

"Connor . . . what's wrong? You've been a ghost. Where's your head?"

"Nowhere," I said, only half listening to his questions.

"Well, *nowhere* is not good enough. We are in the midst of a discovery here,
mate, closer than we have ever been before." He gave me a reassuring pat. My
guard was down. "Is this about that girl, Ally?" he added.

"What?" *How would he know that? I always cover my memories of her . . .* "Did you
just read me?" I asked him. I was angry. Quinn was invading my privacy, and I
was so distracted I let him into my head.

"Connor, I only read the last two weeks, I swear. You need help. You are losing touch with reality."

"I am fine."

"No—you—are—not. This girl is one of two things, Connor: she is either worthless or dangerous. Either way, you can't have her in your life."

I looked at him quizzically. *What a presumptuous conclusion he has come to,* I thought.

"Think about it," he continued. "If she is just a girl, then it can never work, and she'll end up dead hanging around you. Is that what you want? You want her to get hurt?"

"Ally is not like that . . . she is different." I knew she was, and Quinn knew she was too.

"Exactly. Say she is different—then what is she, Connor? She is not a Seeker, and if she is not a Seeker, then she is dangerous to you and me."

Quinn was right. Best-case scenario, Ally was a normal girl. Even I had my suspicions of her. She had too much to hide for someone so young. She was burdened by something, and I didn't know what. What if she was dangerous?

"I suggest you stay away from her . . . for her sake. We don't want her to get hurt, Connor. We live in a dark world; don't put that on someone else."

I couldn't tell if Quinn was threatening Ally's safety or genuinely concerned with bringing her into this life. Either way, I knew I couldn't see her. I knew I loved her, I knew I wanted to protect her, but I also knew I had to let her go.

The next day, Quinn and I packed our bags for New Orleans. There were a few weeks before school started, and Quinn said he had a new lead. I thought he just wanted to get me out of Belfast, but regardless, I was happy to have my mind on anything but Alastrina Byrne, and hunting was always the best cure for depression.

Familiar Faces

ONCE AGAIN, WHEN we arrived in New Orleans, Dawson was waiting for us. "Welcome to Sin City," he said enthusiastically.

"That's Las Vegas, Dawson, not New Orleans," I replied.

"Well, it's here, too; this is a melting pot of corrupt Imati and humans alike." His face irked with disgust at the thought of the Imati infiltrating the old city.

Dawson was probably right. New Orleans was a vibrant city, caught in the middle between its sordid past and its destroyed present. The blend of Creole and Old South, mixed with deep-rooted jazz and blues, combined with the devastating effects of Hurricane Katrina, made New Orleans a complete hodgepodge of culture, eccentricity, and poverty. The people were intriguing and carried with them an energy I had never seen. Dawson believed Imati loved cities like New Orleans because most of them had passed through here decades if not centuries ago, and to them, it still felt like home.

We walked down Rampart Street and arrived at a snow-white manor house in the French Quarter. The big house with its large front columns loomed over me, as if to say that something lived in this city that was far from my reach. *Enter with caution*, it warned. This was my first time in the South, and I felt a little uneasy about it. New Orleans reminded me of the type of city Scarlett would reside in. She could stay out all night basking in the unbearable summer heat, which would not have the slightest effect on her immortal skin. I could see it now . . . she would dance her way into men's lives, con them, love them, and leave them . . . sometimes for dead. She was a poison.

When we entered the house, I realized I had been there before. The pictures that lined the walls were of Paris and arranged in a manner which seemed all too familiar to me. *That's impossible*, I thought. I had never been in the South—but someone I knew had. I'd been thinking about Scarlett in New Orleans because Scarlett *had been* in New Orleans. She had stayed in this house. That's why it made me uneasy. Images I saw in her memories that I assumed were of France were actually of New Orleans. What was she trying to show me?

As I walked, the floorboards creaked beneath me. This house was old, and thanks to Scarlett, eerily familiar. My room was done in green wallpaper, with a giant antique-style mahogany bed in the center with white sheets and white pillows. The furniture was all dark wood except for the random leopard-print bench at the foot of the bed. I had never paid so much attention to detail before, but I felt like I was in a living video game, looking for clues. Scarlett had shown me New Orleans, and I needed to start picking up on her missed messages. Regardless of whether it was a trap, I was hooked.

I went into the bathroom; the tub was pink, and the wallpaper was the same green as the bedroom, but this time adorned with flowers to match the bath. None of this looked familiar.

I tried harder to remember the fleeting images Scarlett had shown me. I sat down on the leopard bench. *What an ugly piece of furniture. How out of place it is.* I concentrated on everything I could remember. How had Scarlett been able to block me out so well? I took a deep breath. I should have had my guard up. I closed my eyes and concentrated to try to remember. *I see her in the house, walking up the stairs, turning right . . . one, two, three doors down . . . she enters . . . she tapes a letter to the bottom of the bed frame . . . What's in the letter?* My first clue.

I ran out of my room and down the stairs. I retraced her steps exactly. Door one, door two, door three . . . I knocked. Dawson answered. "Connor, what a surprise." He was perplexed by my sudden arrival at his door.

"Dawson. You're in *this* room?" So much for my plan to secretly find and read the letter myself.

"Yes. Obviously." He looked at me oddly. "Why are *you* here, if you didn't know this was my room?"

There was no time to waste. I was too eager to find the letter to explain myself properly. "I have a lead; I need to look under your bed."

I walked over to the large antique bed (the same as in my room) without waiting for his permission to enter. He couldn't stop me anyway. "Found it!"

I said, more excited than I had ever been. I half expected it not to be there. Scarlett must have just been in New Orleans when I saw her. Why did she want me to have this? She's not on *my side*, is she? What *is* my side?

"How did you know that was there?" Dawson asked me as he grabbed Quinn from his room across the hall. "Quinn, look what our boy found."

Quinn entered, hardly fazed. "A letter? How? Where?" He was always straight to the point. No time for frivolities.

"Under the bed. It was from Scarlett's memories, from when I read her in Montreal," I explained.

"Good work, Connor. You're learning to focus more than ever." Quinn began to translate the letter, which was written in French, out loud.

Scarlett,

I hope this necklace finds you well. It is the greatest gift I can give to you. I trust you know how to use it. It will protect you always. It is one of the last remnants of the old society that I have, and I am bestowing it to you, my most trusted companion, for I no longer need it. They are coming for me, but I fear not, because the gate has been revealed. Remember what your purpose is, and good luck with the search. If I were you, I would burn this letter.

Bisou Bisou,
C

"Who is *C*?" I asked.

"My question is: what does the necklace do? I couldn't care less who gave it to her," Dawson retorted.

Quinn, ever the logical thinker, spelled it out for us more clearly. "Here is what we know: Scarlett was given a necklace with some kind of power. Scarlett was a given a secret letter she was told to burn. Scarlett is in search of something that has brought fear to her friend. Scarlett did not burn the letter, and not only that, but she purposely hid it and told us about it through Connor."

"So the real question is," I interjected, "why does she want us to know she has it?"

Quinn made a slight noise. "Hmm . . ." is all that came out, but then he was silent for a minute, thinking. Quinn was onto something. "What if she doesn't?"

Dawson and I looked at him quizzically.

"Why else would she show me the letter?" I said.

"Maybe it was a mistake. You are a very powerful reader, Connor. Probably the most powerful of all the Seekers." Dawson gruffed at this, but Quinn paid no mind. "Greg, be serious. You know he is."

Quinn continued his explanation. "Maybe she thought she had you beat, she got cocky, she assumed you couldn't read her at all. Maybe you seeing the blurry images you did was a mistake, and she left the letter for someone else, not expecting you to see it. You only received recent images. Whatever was protecting her, well, you beat it unknowingly."

Quinn's theory sounded right. Scarlett hadn't been sending me messages; she thought she would be a completely blank read. She was using power we don't have. Power she wants to keep hidden. Power she is still searching for. New Orleans was turning out to be our biggest lead, and we had only been there one day.

Over a dinner of traditional Cajun cuisine, Quinn and Dawson were busy contemplating who the letter could have been from, while I was taking a break from searching Scarlett's memories to gaze upon the patrons of New Orleans. The streets were still full well after dark, and the sounds of jazz echoed throughout the air. The hustle and bustle of the pedestrians combined with the luminescent red lights gave New Orleans a hallucinogenic characteristic. Everything was accentuated: laughter, street cars, blaring lights. Nothing seemed real.

Just when I thought the city couldn't be more strange, I looked out the restaurant window and saw a familiar face walking along the street. I jumped out of my seat and ran outside. I don't know why—usually I would shy away from seeing townsfolk outside of town—but something made me get up and rush out the door. I flung my hand above my head and yelled out, waving frantically like a lunatic.

"Bill! Bill! Over here—it's Connor!"

Bill Barnes stared at me in disbelief. I stopped running and stared back, realizing he wasn't moving closer to come meet me. I ran over to him, but once

I got there, I didn't know what to say. I don't even know why I was so eager to see him, but my gut told me to find out.

"What a coincidence, huh? What are you doing in New Orleans?" I asked Bill, who I had never actually had a full conversation with before.

He laughed a nervous Santa-type laugh. "Oh, you know . . . I was about to ask you the same thing!" Which did not answer my question.

"I'm here with my dad, Quinn, end-of-summer-vacation type thing. My uncle Greg is here, too." I pointed into the restaurant where Quinn and Dawson were still deep in conversation, barely noticing I had left the table.

"Oh, that's very nice. I am here to visit my niece, Cynthia. She is in the fourth grade. Her step-mom lives out here, so I don't get a chance to see her much." I felt like he was lying. His statement was over-detailed, as if to make up for the fact that is was false. Why would he lie, though?

"Well, then do you want to join us for dinner? We have room for one more," I offered, knowing he would refuse.

"No, but thanks, Connor." He went on to say something and then stopped.

"What is it?" I pushed. I was curious to know why he was here. I mean, what are the odds?

"I was going to ask you how Ally was doing. I know you two are friends, and, well, sometimes I worry about her . . . all by herself in that house. She can be a bit of a loner, you know."

The mention of Ally's name put a pit in my stomach. I hadn't talked to her for a few weeks, and I missed her. The idea of her being alone made me miss her even more.

"Uh," I stuttered, "I don't know, I have been out of town a lot. I didn't realize you knew her so well."

"Oh, I don't—just some conversations here and there. She's easy to talk to . . . and there is something special about her that makes me feel at ease."

I knew what he meant. There was an awkward silence between us in the midst of a bustling street. People rushed past us, and red lights turned to green. Neither of us moved or said a word. We were both in New Orleans for reasons, it felt like neither of us could disclose. I broke the wall of silence and distrust with a goodnight and held out my hand for a shake. Bill refused. "I am a bit sick, the flu, pretty contagious, better not to shake hands, son." He gave me a little good-bye salute and stepped into a cab. I think Bill knew more about *me* than he was letting on. I went back into the restaurant to finish my dinner.

"Who was that?" Dawson asked me as soon as I sat down. "No one," I replied. "Just an old townie from Belfast, here to visit his niece."

Choices

SCHOOL STARTED IN the fall. The air outside was crisp and constantly smelled of apples and cooked pie. Training had increased tremendously since the summer trip to New Orleans, but it was okay, because for the first time in my life, I cared about someone in an unfamiliar, exciting, can't-stay-away-from-her kind of way . . . and nothing could ruin that.

It was a rough start, I'll admit it, but after I returned from the trip and high school became an everyday occurrence again, it was harder keeping myself from Ally than just giving in to her—so that's what I did. After the Black and White dance, I dove in head first and asked her out on an actual date, but now that the moment had finally arrived, I was pretty bloody scared. I wasn't sure exactly how to act on this *normal* teenage endeavor, and honesty certainly wasn't on the menu. The Academy had trained us for a lot of things, but let's face it: I grew up in a school full of mates and was completely unprepared to entertain a girl. That's why I picked an activity more in my comfort zone: paintball.

"Glad you could make it," I said as Ally popped out of her Mercedes. *Nice car,* I thought.

"Of course . . . wouldn't miss it!" she said with a huge smile.

"Are you sure this is okay?" I asked. "I mean, have you ever shot a paintball gun before?"

"Paintball gun? No . . . but I'm sure I can figure it out." She seemed confident.

"That's the spirit." I put my arm around her shoulder and we walked to check in.

The field was pretty great: full of obstacles, hay bales, and old trashcans, dilapidated in a way that made it cool. I was pumped. Ally seemed happy, yet quietly reserved. We checked in, got our black jumpsuit-style uniforms, and picked a team color: green, per Ally's request. *Still trying to convince me she's Irish, I guess.* We gathered round to hear the instructor's rules.

"Alright, my name is Anderson. I am your referee today. Welcome to Rapid Fire." Everyone cheered.

Ally looked up at me. "This is gonna be fun," she whispered and then continued to listen to the rules.

Anderson, who looked like an ex-marine turned paintball enthusiast, explained how it worked. "You are in teams of two, and there are a total of six teams. You will battle each other until the last team standing wins. Pretty simple. You can get hit up to four times, then you're out. However, there are special metal boxes hidden around the field with small badges inside. Red badge gives you one extra hit and yellow gives you two. Comprendo?"

Everyone clapped, excited to start. I didn't pay attention to the whole "badge" deal because I knew I wouldn't get hit. I am a professional hunter, after all. Anderson then gave us ten minutes to strategize and learn how to load and fire our guns.

"Alright, Ally, I can show you how this works." I'll admit, it felt good to finally be the one who knew everything.

"Great." She smiled. She didn't seem nervous at all.

I put the hopper on the gun, loaded the paint, attached the tank, and showed her the quick-fire trigger. I pointed to a target in the practice area and hit the bullseye. I didn't want to seem egotistical, so I kept my pride in the shot to a minimum, but I'm sure she was impressed. "The goal is to create a straight line from the barrel of the gun to your marker." I handed her the other unused gun. "Wanna try?"

Ally grabbed the weapon, repeated exactly what I did, and was locked and loaded within ten seconds. "Got it." She beamed. Then she lined up her shot, pulled the trigger, and hit the mark so perfectly it actually landed on top of my splattered green paint. Not exactly what I expected.

"Wow, that was good. You sure you haven't done this before?" I asked, surprised.

"I might have been around a few guns in my life," she added coyly.

"Right, then . . . I guess we're ready." I gave her a fist-bump to say good job. She looked a little confused by it.

Then, suddenly, the air horn blasted out and Anderson began to speak again. "Alright, troops . . . enter the arena, find a spot, and at the sound of this horn, let the games begin."

Ally and I went inside, crouched behind a hay bale, and waited for the start signal. My adrenaline was pumping, not just for the game, but for everything. This girl was getting more amazing by the second; she could shoot a gun, she was down to play sports on a first date, and her aim was pretty badass. I was definitely sold on Alastrina Byrne . . . if only I didn't have a sneaking suspicion she was hiding something major—like *where* all of these skills came from.

I looked over at her and saw that she was surveying the grounds, counting the obstacles, and making note of other players. She turned back to face me. "This isn't a good spot; our line of sight is blocked by too many things. We should move more to the right . . . behind that wall over there."

"We can't move until the horn." I said.

"I know—when the horn sounds . . . sprint." Then she checked her weapon, put reserve paint in several different pockets, and took a breath. I smiled.

Then—*erhhhhhhhhh*—the horn went off. Ally darted away and I followed her; she was quick. We slid behind the new wall and reassessed. People were sprinting everywhere. A yellow member ran across the field; I fired and nailed him in the back. Ally followed my fire and hit him ten yards further away. We both turned back to face each other.

"Nicely done," she said.

"You too," I added. I had a feeling we were going to win.

It went on like this for a while: run, shoot, duck, shoot, run some more. We were everywhere, and each step of the way Ally was by my side, pulling her weight times ten. It was amazing to be in battle with someone and know that person liked you, wanted to protect you, and totally had your back. For a second I imagined what it would be like if I told her who I was. Maybe she could handle it; maybe she could protect herself. If I ever bothered to imagine having a wife and family someday, it would have to be with a girl like Ally, since Seekers don't come in the female variety.

It was down to two teams: green and orange. We were on opposite sides of the field, and Ally and I had each taken one hit. Mine was on my left arm and Ally's was on her left thigh. We took a moment to strategize.

"I say we flank them from both sides and just keep shooting until we criss-cross and end up back here," she said.

"That's kind of suicide; they'll be shooting us dead-on," I said.

"Shooting a moving target . . . zigzag your run."

"That also means we're shooting while zigzagging." She was nuts.

"Yeah," she replied like it was no big deal.

"We're gonna get pelted," I pointed out.

"Eh, it's just balls of paint, right?"

Yeah, paint that freaking hurts when it hits you, I thought. I wasn't thrilled to go kamikaze on the orange team. Of course, I clearly couldn't back down, so my response was, "I'm in if you are."

She smiled. "Okay. Make it to the first barrier, pause, and then when my hand goes from this"—she made a square fist—"to this"—she pointed two fingers forward—"it means go."

"Yeah, got it, Rambo," I said as she turned to look at her first cover spot.

"Oh, one thing," I added, and then grabbed her and turned her to face me. "If we're about to die a vicious paintball death, we should say good-bye." She looked confused. I reached for her face, kissed her lips, and then kissed her some more. For a second I thought about throwing out a white flag and just spending the rest of the time making out—it seemed less stressful—but then it ended, as all good moments do.

"We should say good-bye more often," she smiled.

"I'll say good-bye to you as much as you want," I said and I kissed her again. "You ready to destroy some orange team?" I asked.

"Oh, yeah."

With that, we sprinted to our respective spots. Suddenly, being across a field from her felt like we were separated by an ocean, and my body was pulling me to go back, to never leave her side, and to never leave the fire and warmth she provided. I was definitely going to have to blast these guys quickly so I could get back to the Ally part of my day.

She put her fist up and then gave the signal to charge. I ran as fast as I could; paint balls came flying at me. I rolled at one point to avoid being shot; Ally did the same thing. I changed my steps, dodged to my right, then to the left, and began shooting. Ally and I got there at the same time, both firing away. The orange team didn't know what hit them. We bombarded them with completely accurate shots: *bang, bang, bang.* Ally and I crisscrossed in front of them and kept shooting until we were in the clear. We made it back to the center of the field and ran into each other's arms.

"We won, we won, we won!" she said as she jumped up and down.

"I got hit—count 'em," I said a little too frantically.

She looked at my black jumpsuit. "Three hits. You're still alive."

I checked her out. "Three hits . . . you're still alive, too."

She laughed. "Trust me, I know."

The orange team, made up of Belfast High's lacrosse captains Reese and Dave, came sauntering out from behind their barricade. They were covered in green splat. It was everywhere, as if slime had exploded on them. They limped over to congratulate us, but they looked mad.

"You know it takes four hits to kill out, not twenty, Connor," Reese said as he walked up.

"Sorry, Reese. I guess I got excited." I shook his hand. "This is Ally."

"Nice to meet you," she said to Reese. He didn't respond; he was too pissed that she was a girl and better at paintball.

"Hi, I'm Dave" Reese's losing partner chimed in.

"Ally."

"Well, Ally, I'm gonna be bruised for a week, so thanks," Dave added.

The two began to walk away, until Reese yelled back, "Hey, aren't you that freaky new girl in school?" They both laughed.

"Watch, it man," I said, but Ally quickly grabbed my arm.

"It's fine, Connor." Then she looked to Reese and Dave, who still thought it was hilarious, and said, "Yeah, but aren't you that guy who just got his ass kicked by a girl?" The two instantly shut up and walked away. Ally and I stood there for a moment and then looked at each other.

"Oops," she said. "I guess he's mad."

I laughed. "That was classic. Now, how about some celebratory pancakes for all your ass-kicking?"

"By all means," she said, "lead the way."

Ally and I headed to Darby's for some post-game grub. We slid into the plastic booths, dirty, tired, and sweaty. It was brilliant.

"They have really fantastic blueberry pancakes here," I said, knowing that Maine was Mecca for blueberries and the whole town practically swore by them.

"Uh-huh," Ally muttered as she mulled over the menu. She kept turning the pages, looking unenthused, until she hit the back and then let out, "Oh, wow— they have apple pancakes with cinnamon-apple-maple syrup! I can't believe that. I've never had apple pancakes before."

"Me neither. Must be seasonal," I assumed, not quite as impressed.

"Wow, this is amazing." She seemed super excited about it. We ordered and fifteen minutes later were scarfing down some serious pancake grub. Mid-bite, Ally looked up at me and put her fork down.

"Today was really fun," she said.

"Yeah, it was." I looked at her, beautiful even with messy hair and a pound of pancakes in front of her.

"No, I mean, really fun." She sounded serious. "Like, I haven't had that kind of fun in . . . forever."

"I know what you mean," I replied just as seriously, so she would know I meant it. Then we continued eating.

I thought about what Quinn would say: that I was falling too quickly, that Ally would be a distraction. I didn't care. All I knew is that I had more fun running around a hayfield shooting paint with a girl I barely knew than I'd ever had in my entire life. That meant something. This girl meant something, and I chose right there at Darby's that I would do anything to keep that safe.

Kill or Be Killed

THE NEXT SIX weeks of my life were amazing. Despite the stress of juggling my "Ally" life with my "Quinn" life, I really was happier than I had ever been. I was training better, kissing better, and just plain being better at everything. Ally was perfect. Well, not *perfect*, but that's just why she was so perfect. She was interesting and intriguing. I was constantly figuring her out and never got bored. Our relationship was reaching a new level, a level I had never known existed, and I was anxious to finally tell her how much I loved her.

Tonight would be the night. I was finally on my way over to her house for the first time and reveling in the thought of being completely alone with her. She had never invited me over before, and this case was no exception; I had more or less invited myself. I knew she was nervous about me seeing her place. I wanted it to fill in some blanks for me . . . like where her dad was all the time, what she did at home, or anything that would give me some clue as to who she was. Most likely, though, we'd just make out a lot.

I paused for a moment before I knocked and took a deep breath in order to calm myself. She answered the door after a few seconds, and I entered. It put me at ease when I sensed she was just as nervous as I was. I was curious about what lay inside these walls, what secrets she was hiding.

She barely had any furniture. The dining room was completely empty. There were no boxes, or moving supplies, or any evidence of remodeling like she had said. It looked like she barely lived there. I checked the kitchen; hardly any food. The house was big and clean. Other than that, it was unremarkable. She did have a large entertainment system and a PlayStation. *She just keeps on getting better.*

After we watched the movie, I had to tell her I loved her. It was boiling up inside me and was about to spill over. I followed her into the kitchen, trying to find the courage to talk to her. Suddenly, my throat was dry and my palms were sweaty. *Not a good sign. Maybe water first, then the embarrassing revelation of feelings.*

I opened her fridge looking for something to drink but was shocked at what I saw. "Ally?" I asked, suddenly distracted from the daunting task of expressing my love.

"Yeah?" she replied innocently.

"What's with your fridge?"

"What do you mean?" she asked, confused.

"It's all apples," I said. How could she not know? Her entire food supply was apple-flavored everything. It was weird. I knew she always drank apple cider at the coffee shop, and I saw her excitement over apple pancakes, but this was ridiculous . . . and kind of freaky. Suddenly, the day she tackled me was starting to make more sense: she was saving an apple tree.

"No it's not." She denied it as she walked over. "Look—juice, pie, jam, bread . . . lots of regular food."

She clearly had an addiction and couldn't see the truth to her oddness. I just kept staring at her as she tried to defend it. The she added, "Stop looking at me like that." She looked hurt.

"Like what?" I asked as I shut the door to her weird little secret.

"Like I'm a freak." She was obviously offended.

I smiled, "Aww, but you're a cute freak," I said, not wanting her to feel bad; in fact, if that were her only freakish secret, I'd be more than relieved. "That counts for something."

"Gee, thanks," she said, smiling again. This was it; this was the opening to tell her. *Now or never,* I thought.

"Actually, I have something to tell you." I grabbed both of her hands and took a deep breath, my palms still slightly sweaty. "Ally, I really like you. In fact, I've been thinking a lot about you . . . and me . . . together, lately. Like all the time. It's hard to explain, but sometimes when I am around you I feel so out of control that if I let go for even a second I will lose all composure." I wasn't sure if she understood what I was trying to say, but the words and feelings just kept pouring out of me. "At first, it was hard for me to accept that. But now, despite the weird apple thing, I realize it's because we are so perfect for each other. I have never felt so close to anyone in my entire life. I think . . ." I paused.

I was suddenly scared to go on. What if she didn't love me as much as I loved her? What if I was putting myself out there only to be rejected? What if she was not who she said she was . . . or, in her case, didn't say? She egged me on. She knew what I was thinking, and she refused to let my doubts stop me.

"I think I'm falling in love with you." There; now it was out there for the world to hear.

"Me too," she replied instantly. "I mean, I feel the same way about you. I love you."

Suddenly, a wave of relief and ecstasy washed over me. I wanted her more in that moment than I had ever wanted anything in my entire life. I lost complete control. Her neck, her mouth, her hands; I kissed everything I could touch. I threw her against the wall, trying with all my might to hold back my strength, but I could tell I was losing touch with reality. Ally was a drug I wanted to revel in, to lose myself in completely. My hands were everywhere, and the more she responded, the further I pushed. Images began to flood my mind.

I could see her lying in a grass field surrounded by wildflowers; I saw her dancing a waltz in a decadent ball gown, her golden hair half pinned, and half flowing behind her. I saw her gazing up at the Eiffel tower with complete joy and jubilation on her face. I kept kissing her, wanting more, seeing more. Suddenly, I realized the images I was seeing were not merely a hallucination. They were not a dream conjured up in the moments of passion. They were her life. Her *immortal* life.

Instinct took over and I pushed her off of me, violently. I couldn't think, I couldn't breathe, and all I could do was act. "Ally, give me your hand," I demanded. She acquiesced, completely unaware of what I was or what I was trying to do. She was a deer waiting to be hunted. Wide-eyed and confused, she sat perfectly still while I read her completely for the first time.

I saw her with Scarlett. Scarlett, the poison from Montreal, the temptress of New Orleans . . . Scarlett had trained her. My Ally, my innocent Ally, was corrupt. I saw her murder that child. I saw her sexual escapades. I saw her suffering. I saw her being chased by angry villagers, I saw her on battlefields stained with red, human blood—her victims' blood. I saw her on a horse, riding ferociously in the desert. I saw and felt her depression, her loathing, and her fear. Images were fluttering in and out; completely non-sequential, as if time itself had no definition in her life.

Then, I saw the old, heartbroken gypsy woman curse her with ashes of death. Suddenly, my mind went somewhere else, somewhere dark and violent. I could see nothing but death and the disappearance of life. I felt a surge of heat pass through me and it burned my thoughts. The heat penetrated from my skin to my veins and left a blanket of darkness in the air. I felt like I had died, like the air had been sucked from my lungs, and then just as quickly as it came it was gone.

I was once again back in Ally's memories, back in her devastating history. I saw her loneliness; I saw her suicide attempts in New York—her wrist-cutting, her drug-snorting, and her self-hanging. These images were distorted with more black spots popping up everywhere, like she was managing to block certain memories . . . or as if they'd been lost.

Everything I did not want to see, I saw. Once again, I saw her in the field in Ireland surrounded by wildflowers. That was the girl Ally wanted to be, and that image was most prominent. I also saw myself through her eyes, how she saw me . . . rugged, trustworthy, and safe. She saw me as a prince. She adored me.

Only a minute had passed, but I could feel and see everything in her entire life. I felt the jealousy and anger she felt for Amelia, I felt the revenge she wanted to take on Joaquín. I felt her sense of betrayal when he killed himself for his true love. Something passed through me in that moment. South America was a black stain on Ally's life and brought with it something I had never felt before. I unleashed something and I had no idea how to control or stop it. I had to get out of that house, away from the darkness, and away from her.

My read ended with the shrill sound of her screams. The fear in her voice was unfamiliar to me.

"Connor, what's wrong?" she asked, panicked and confused.

I didn't want to hurt her, but I shouted back at her. Everything was such a blur I don't even know what I said; probably something awful. All I could think was that it was my job to kill her. *As soon as Quinn finds out who she is, he will hunt her. Why is she in Belfast? Is she the one we are looking for?* I was torn between my own oath to kill her and my need to protect her. How could she have done all the things she had done? I was so confused, more confused than ever before. My confusion quickly turned to anger. If I didn't leave, I knew I might regret what I was prepared to do.

"Connor, I love you . . ." She looked like she was crying. I pushed her down and ran out the door.

I ran as fast as I could back home, leaving my car at her house. My feet moved faster than ever before, and by the time I ran the two miles home, I was out of breath. My head was clouded with anger. I stormed through the door so quickly I didn't realize Quinn would be right there. I practically knocked him over; he grabbed my arm to stabilize himself.

"Connor, whoa, slow . . ." he trailed off. His expression turned stone cold. He was reading me.

I pushed him away. "Quinn . . . I know what you are going to say, but—"

"No buts, Connor! Ally is an Imati—this is unforgiveable. We have to kill her." He was dead serious. More serious than he had ever been in his life, because he knew I would fight him on it.

I slammed my fist on the table next to me. "You had no right to read me, Quinn, this is not your fight—"

He cut me off before I could finish. "You knocked into me, Connor; you were careless and the read was unintentional. You're practically advertising your emotions. I know this is not my fight, but I took an oath to the Brotherhood, and so did you; do not forget that."

"We don't have to kill her. She didn't even know I was a Seeker. She knows nothing. I read her completely. She barely even understands what it means to be an Imati. She has been so alone for so long and kept so far under the radar that her people barely know she exists."

This was true; I wasn't just trying to save her life from Quinn. Ally, it seemed, had managed to stay completely away from her own people, except for her brief stint in South America. She was a loner even in the immortal world.

"It doesn't matter. Why is she in Belfast, Connor? Coincidence? I think not." Quinn was standing his ground. "Don't you get it? We were sent *here* for a reason, and then what do you know . . . the girl you couldn't read happens to be an Imati. Don't you think that is suspicious? Why the sudden change—what happened?"

"I don't know," I said, defeat in my voice. Quinn, once again, was right: why could I suddenly read her, when I couldn't before? Ally possessed the same power that Scarlett did. This meant she did have connections. Connections I couldn't see. She had power I was completely unaware of.

Quinn knew what I was thinking, because he was thinking the same thing.

"Connor, you have to kill her. If you don't, I will." He stared at me point-blank, making sure I knew that he was not bluffing. "Connor, she will kill you now that she knows you are a Seeker. I am sure of this. I will do what I have to in order to protect you and the Brotherhood."

Quinn grabbed his sword and headed for the door.

"Stop!" I yelled back.

I put on my jacket and hid my sword beneath it. "I'll do it," I said in a controlled and calm manner. I stepped outside.

The night air was cold against my skin. Fall was in full swing, and the full moon created an eerie white glow against the pavement. I closed the front door behind me and started my journey to Bayview Drive in the middle of the night with every intention of walking into that house and beheading the first girl I had ever loved.

The Book of Alastrina Byrne

Belfast, Maine – October – Present Day
Nine Of Swords

CONNOR'S DEPARTURE SENT a shock wave of terror through my body. I lay on the floor screaming for what seemed like hours. I loved him, and he left me. I did not feel sad, or angry, or mad, I just felt completely out of control—like the whole world was spinning and no one was there to stop it. I didn't realize I could cry, but I did. I cried so hard that I could barely drag myself up the stairs to my bed. I lay there, and for the millionth time in my life, I wished I was dead. I wished that I could die like everyone else. I felt nauseated. My body was shaking. I would never see Connor again, I was sure of it. I fell asleep under my covers, shivering from the cold night air. Hopefully, I would wake up in the morning and realize it was all a dream.

I was asleep less than an hour. The image of Joaquín floated in front of me. I had not thought of him in a while, but there he was, mocking me. I reached out to touch him, but nothing in my body moved. It all felt so real, but I soon realized I was still asleep. This was a dream. His face disappeared, and in an instant I was in a bright field filled with white and yellow daisies, sprinkled across green, green grass. Then the world shifted; the sky went from bright blue to gray, and the wildflowers all turned black and disintegrated into the ground. Black smoke filled the sky and ashes began to rain above me. They covered the floor. I put my hands up to touch them, and they settled all around me until my skin, my hair, and my clothes were all covered in ash. A voice echoed in the background, "With these ashes, your life will be stripped from you."

I woke up in a sweat, gasping for air. I could feel the crushing weight of my blankets on top of me, the purple and green comforter practically choking me. Maine in the middle of October was cold, but suddenly, I felt like I was boiling.

I ripped my body from my bed, trying desperately to break free of the hot pain. Cat sprinted away to hide in my closet, frightened by my spastic urgency.

I violently threw the sheets to the floor. The heat should have subsided, but it didn't. I realized it wasn't the covers that were hot—it was me. I was burning up. My insides felt like a sea of hot lava, and with every heartbeat, my blood pumped the burning fluid through my entire body. I could feel every ounce of it as it reached my toes, my legs, my arms, my heart, and . . . my heart? I froze.

With my feet planted firmly on the wooden floor of my second-story bedroom, I placed my hand up to my heart. It was beating rhythmically like a drum. The burning sensation coming from within my body continued to swirl around violently and drops of sweat ran down my neck, highlighting the dark conclusion I was slowly coming to. I wiped my sweat-drenched forehead, which caused my hand to become soaked in my own bodily fluid. I could not remember the last time I had sweat. It suddenly dawned on me—I was becoming human again.

I had not moved from my position in what felt like an eternity, and as I looked around I saw the covers still strewn about the room as if there had been a robbery. Other than my abrupt awakening and tossing of the comforter, the rest of the room was eerily still intact. Only *I* had drastically changed. I tried to relax and calmly and rationally take in my previous thought with more clarity and understanding. I was *alive* again. I had lost my immortality.

I couldn't believe my own thoughts. *How could I be mortal? That's impossible.* I had tried to kill myself a million times and nothing had worked. Maybe the solution was a broken heart. *That's stupid.* I ran downstairs, once I reached the kitchen I realized I was out of breath. I had forgotten what it felt like to truly breathe. I searched frantically for a knife. I ran to the drawer just to the right of the sink. On the way there I stubbed my toe on the center island.

"Ow! Shit!" I screamed in pain. "Crap, crap, crap . . . it hurts." The pain was excruciating. I guess I forgot what mortal pain felt like, too.

I grabbed the steak knife, and without thinking, I sliced it straight across my left hand. It was the only thing I could think to do. Worked in Scotland; might as well work now.

"Ahhhhhhhhhh!" I screamed so loud my ears rang. The pain was sharp and excruciating. Blood started pouring out from my palm . . . red blood. Not silver.

Not cold and metallic, but red and hot. *Oh my God*, I thought, *I really am human again*. I searched for a towel to stop the bleeding. The pain was worsening, and the cut ran deeper than I'd hoped. Deeper in the dangerous, possibly-need-a-doctor sense. Did I even own Band-Aids?

A wave of concerns flooded my mind. *Was everything a dream? Was I ever really immortal? Maybe I'm just crazy*. Nothing in this house looked ancient. My clothes were normal. This scenario reminded me of Ireland and my *first death* and how I thought I was insane. *Back to square one*, I thought.

I walked out of the kitchen into the hallway. I saw my necklace sitting on the end table near the couch next to my cell phone. I had taken it off right before Connor had come over. My necklace, my wonderful trustworthy necklace—it was still there. I wasn't crazy. My life wasn't a dream. I went to put it back on, when I noticed something different. The stone in the center had cracked. Now the neklace I had managed to keep safe for hundreds of years, the only remnant of my father, of my immortality, was damaged. Not to mention, I didn't even remember dropping it; in fact, it was exactly where I had left it just hours before. *Strange, that means something broke it*. With that thought, my devastation turned to concern and an eerie feeling came over me. I hung the necklace around my neck. It felt heavier. The image of ashes raining from the sky quickly filled my thoughts and I was officially freaked out.

I decided to take a minute to sit down, clear my head, and call Delilah. If something was wrong, she should feel it . . . or see it . . . or do whatever it is she does.

The phone rang, like it had so many times in the past year. *Pick up, Delilah, come on. Pick up. If I ever needed you it's now.*

Her voicemail clicked on and my heart dropped. "Hey, it's Dee. I'm off the grid right now—you know what that means."

Great. That meant, "Figure it out yourself, sucker," because Delilah was off at some Order of Ajna thing in God only knows where and completely unreachable. Perfect timing for me to, you know, *become human again*. Why hadn't she seen *this* coming? *She* was the one who sent me to Belfast. *She* was the one who said I was special. *She* was the one who said I was powerful. Becoming human definitely didn't feel very powerful to me.

Delilah – Las Vegas, Nevada – Two Years Ago

DELILAH ENTERED THE Hard Rock Hotel and took a deep breath of the freshly pumped oxygen. She always loved the smell of casinos, mainly because it was the smell of money. Gambling was her ATM. As a member of the Order of Ajna and as a great seer, she could bet on anything—and win.

This trip was different, though; she wasn't here for the cheap drinks and slot machines. She was here on official business. She perused the casino floor looking for someone in particular—someone who had come to her in a vision.

Suddenly, the energy fields cleared and a girl about twenty yards away from her playing blackjack caught her attention. She sauntered over to the table and sat down. It was a five-hundred-dollar buy-in. *Great*, she thought as she cashed in for chips. *I should really get an expense account for these gigs.*

Delilah turned to get a good look at her mark. She looked no older than eighteen, blonde hair, green eyes, beautiful. She must have used a fake ID to play. She also noticed the girl was on a huge winning streak, with several thousand dollars' worth of chips piled in front of her. Delilah was drawn to her instantly.

The dealer dealt the first round of cards and shouted out, "Seventeen," as Dee's hand was revealed. A normal person might hold, but not Delilah; she knew the next card was a three. "Hit me," she said without hesitation. Out came the three and she won with a twenty.

The girl sitting next to her shot her a suspicious look. Then there was a second hand and another win for Delilah. After about twenty minutes of this "good fortune," the green-eyed girl cashed out—her winning streak interrupted by Dee—and walked away.

Delilah grabbed her chips and walked after her. "Hey, wait up!" she said. The girl turned around cautiously. "Do I know you?" she asked.

"No, but I know what you were doing back there," Delilah said cryptically.

"Really?" the girl said, smiling. "What would that be?"

"Counting cards," she accused. "I watched you; that's how you were winning."

"You're mistaken." She sloughed off the accusation and added, "Besides, once you showed up, I stopped winning, remember?"

"That's because I cheated," Delilah brazenly confessed.

"Excuse me?" The girl looked shocked that Delilah would admit to such a crime in the middle of a casino floor.

"Yeah, I knew what cards were coming . . . I'm psychic like that." Delilah reached into her pocket and grabbed a purple and gold business card. "See: Delilah the Psychic."

The girl grabbed the card and eyed it skeptically. "Why are you telling me this?"

Delilah hesitated. It was now or never; she needed to reveal her trump card. "What are you doing here, Alastrina?"

The girl's eyes almost popped out her head and her entire body stiffened. "I think you've mistaken me for someone else."

"I haven't, I assure you . . . it's Alastrina Byrne, yes?"

The girl took a step forward. "How do you know my name?" she asked angrily.

Delilah pointed to the card. "Psychic . . . remember?"

"Look, this has been really fun, but I have to go find a new game—and a new casino, considering this conversation is probably being bugged."

Delilah smiled. "Wow, you really are paranoid."

"Yeah, good thing too, since I have a stalker." Alastrina motioned toward Delilah. "Not to mention we're in a Vegas casino run by the mob. They don't take so kindly to cheaters, so thanks for blowing it."

Alastrina walked away toward the outer casino floor. She was faster than Delilah realized and began to disappear into the crowd of gamblers. *She was getting away.* "Hey, stop, wait!" Delilah yelled as she ran after her. This was proving to be a pain in the ass.

The girl turned and hissed back at her, "Leave me alone!" The sound of slot machines echoed in the background.

"I know you're an Imati." Delilah's words cut through the nonsense and hung in the air for a moment longer than she expected. Alastrina instantly stopped, let out a sigh of frustration, and then slowly turned around.

"What do you want?" she asked, defeated. This wasn't the first time someone had called her out and she was tired of constantly running from people, constantly changing cities, and constantly hiding from who she was.

"I was sent here to find you, to help you." Delilah pleaded with her, "Please just listen to what I have to say."

Alastrina looked at the twenty-something, amber-eyed girl in front of her. She wasn't sure what to think. *Could she really be psychic?* Finally, she broke her silence and gave a definitive, "No." But then she added, "You're gonna need to prove yourself first."

"What?" Delilah looked at her dubiously. "Did you miss the whole blackjack thing?"

"I saw it. Not impressed—so come on." Alastrina walked into a boisterous sports bar, where they were taking bets on horse racing. "You make me twenty thousand dollars in the next twenty minutes or I walk."

Delilah was more than game. "Coming right up!" She beamed at the thought of proving herself. It didn't take twenty minutes; all it took was three races and Delilah had it in the bag.

"Impressive," Alastrina commented as she counted her money at a leather booth inside the bar.

"My turn for demands," Delilah said. "What are you doing here, Alastrina?" It was the same question she had asked before.

"Raising money." Alastrina smiled while holding up the cash. "In fact, you and I should go into business together." Delilah was not amused. Alastrina read Delilah's frustration and got momentarily serious. "Look, I needed to make some more cash so I could disappear for a while, okay?"

"What are you running from?" Delilah asked the question, but she already knew the answer. What she wanted to know was if Alastrina knew the answer too—that she was running from herself.

"What aren't I running from?" she replied somberly.

"That's not an answer, that's a question." Delilah made her try again. "Listen, you can be honest with me, because I already know when you're about to lie."

Alastrina paused. "You must know what it's like, for an Imati," she began, as she unexpectedly let her guard down. "We don't belong here and we never will."

"Have you tried? Have you tried to live a normal life?" Dee asked.

"Yes, of course," Alastrina exclaimed. "But the moment I get too comfortable, the moment I start caring about people, it all just goes away. It goes away when other people grow up and I don't. It goes away when other people die and I don't. I don't know what I'm supposed to do anymore. Where am I supposed to go?"

Delilah stared at her. "Alastrina, you must know you're special." She said it earnestly enough that Alastrina believed Delilah believed it, but she still did not believe it herself.

"What?" she asked, confused.

"My order—the Order of Ajna—sent me here to find you. You play a major role in this world." Then she added with a grin, "So congrats."

Alastrina looked at her skeptically. "I guarantee you, I play no such role."

Delilah almost burst out of her seat. "You do, though! Why else would I be here?"

"The ninety-nine-cent buffet?" Alastrina quipped.

Delilah laughed, "Well, at least we know you can crack a joke."

Alastrina became lost in her thoughts and stared down at the pile of money in front of her; it was tangible proof of Delilah's abilities. If Delilah could see into the future, then why shouldn't she be able see Alastrina's future too?

Alastrina looked up suddenly with a new, more important question on her mind. "Do you know when I'm going to die?" she asked.

Delilah felt a cold rush take over her body, a physical reaction to Alastrina's question. She had no clear answer.

"I cannot see your death," she began, "but you are an immortal, so that makes sense."

Alastrina sighed, disappointed by her response. "There has to be an end to forever, though, right?"

Delilah was pained by the question. The truth was, she saw many deaths for Alastrina, and all a result of different paths she might choose to take.

"Alastrina, let me be clear: there is a reason you are here. I don't mean here in Las Vegas, I mean a reason you are still alive. You *mean* something, I can feel it. I'm just not sure what it is yet."

Alastrina furrowed her brow and leaned across the table, fiddling with a ripped-up paper sugar packet as she spoke. "I don't remember who I am anymore."

Her words dropped on Delilah like a bomb. She had not expected that to come out of her mouth.

"What do you mean?" Dee asked. She had never heard an Imati say that before. In fact, Imati usually had the best memories.

"I have these holes in my memory. I can't remember where I was fifty years ago. There are these dark spots. I feel like I'm missing something. I just . . . I've been wandering around, going from city to city, school to school, and I just keep moving, and I just keep wishing that at some point, it would stop. That time would just . . . stop."

Delilah had known that Alastrina had a tough life—a tough couple of lives, actually—but she hadn't realized how bad it was, how lost she felt.

"That's why I'm here," Dee began, attempting to bring some sort of comfort to Alastrina's dark existence. "This world cannot afford to lose you," she continued. "My people tell me, and I was never supposed to tell you this, but they say that you're the most powerful Imati in the world, and it's vital to keep you alive."

Alastrina started laughing. "Me? Wow, that's . . . wow, I needed a good laugh. Thank you."

"I'm serious, it's true. So from now on, we stick together and you do what I say so we can figure this whole thing out."

"By 'thing' you mean my life?" Alastrina asked.

"Yes. So if I say jump, you say . . . ?"

"Why?" Alastrina muttered.

"No," Delilah replied. "You say *how high*."

Alastrina chuckled. "So you and I stick together and I find out why my existence matters?"

"Yes." Delilah let out a sigh of relief, realizing she had finally gotten through to her.

Alastrina smiled. "Jeez, where were you two hundred years ago?"

Belfast, Maine – October – Present Day

Red Blood

WITH DELILAH NOT available to help, I realized I needed to help myself. I looked down and saw that my hand was still bleeding. The towel I used to wrap it was completely soaked through with my new red blood. It was a constant reminder of my sudden predicament. What was I going to do? The other person I wanted to turn to for help had violently shoved me to the floor and slammed the door in my face. I didn't know where to find him regardless. Everything felt hopeless. I couldn't be mortal . . . I didn't know how to be mortal. I felt hopeless.

Just as my head was coming together, I could hear footsteps outside my front door. Then, it swung open in a violent rage. Connor Winfield had returned to my house, and he didn't bother to knock this time.

"Connor!" I jumped up excitedly, then immediately began to back away behind the couch when I realized why he was there.

"Alastrina Byrne—you have been charged with crimes against humanity and you are sentenced to die."

Did he really just say that? My eyes grew wide as I saw Connor in all his Seeker glory. He drew his sword from beneath his coat and walked toward me. All the times I had wished for my life to end and here it was playing out in front of me. Being killed by the love of my life was not the ideal way to go, but at least it was slightly poetic. Shakespeare would be proud. A piece of me gave in completely. I backed up against the wall near the couch, closed my eyes and prepared for death.

I felt my waist hit the flat surface behind me; I remembered the same feeling from when Connor was kissing me. He had pushed my waist back and used the wall for support. That wall once again became my support. I wanted Connor back, *my* Connor. Not the Seeker, but the charming boy I loved. I didn't want to die; I wanted to be there to kiss him, to be next to him. I wanted life. I no longer had my Imati strength to carry me, so in my desperation I pleaded for my survival.

I dropped to my knees and literally held my hands in front of me. I had done this before. Blood flowed down my wrist and onto my arm. It dripped onto the surface of my rug, leaving sticky red dots everywhere.

"Please, Connor . . ." I was half crying, half speaking. "I love you so much . . . I don't want to die . . . please . . . don't do this . . ."

He dropped his sword. I heard the comforting thud as it landed on the rug.

"Ally, you're bleeding." He grabbed my arm, his tone giving away how shocked he was to see me with human blood all over my body.

"Yes," I said, still sobbing.

"How are you bleeding, Ally? Your blood should be . . . well, silver," he said, sounding just as confused as I was.

"I know. I woke up and I was . . . human. When it happened, it felt like I was suffocating, but breathing at the same time—I can't explain it."

I looked into his blue eyes, hoping for sympathy. I got nothing but him staring back at me, so I continued. "I was confused, so I stabbed myself with a knife just to make sure."

He laughed, but I could also see that he had started to cry, because tears welled up in his eyes. "You stabbed yourself just to make sure? That is so stupid." His smile comforted me. If Connor was smiling, then I was smiling.

"I know," I continued. "I don't know what happened. I lost my—" I stumbled over my words. They were harder to comprehend than I realized. "My immortality."

Connor looked at me with a strange expression. He didn't know what I was thinking, and I could tell his mind was searching for answers.

"You're no longer an Imati." He stated it for the record.

"I guess not," I replied.

He picked me up off the floor and brought me to my feet. Then he grabbed my necklace—I had put it back on—and held it in his hand, suddenly examining it more closely than he ever had before.

"Where did you get this?" he demanded.

I told him I had always had it, ever since Ireland, and that it was an heirloom. He already knew that; he had seen it before.

"Ally, I have to go." He turned to walk away from me.

I screamed after him. "What? You can't leave me . . . not like this! What am I going to do?" I was begging him for help because I was helpless.

"I don't know . . . I can't."

"What?" I screamed. "You can't what?"

"I just can't look at you the same way." *Ouch*. It was harsh, and it hurt more than I thought it would.

"Connor, please! It's still me. Don't walk out that door." I couldn't bear the thought of losing him, but it was a reality all too true. "If you still love me, you'll stay."

"Ally." He grabbed me and placed his large palms square on my shoulders. "I can't." Then he turned to leave, and once again I was alone.

Belfast, Maine – October – Present Day

Hopeless

CONNOR HAD LEFT me. Connor, who told me he loved me, had left me. I looked down at my hand and saw it was still bleeding. My house was eerily silent, and the air hovered around me like a thick blanket. It took all my strength just to get over to the couch and sit down. I stared at my flat screen. The movie Connor and I had watched was still in the DVD player, so the cartridge sat on the ground, empty and unmoved. Everything around me was exactly as it had been a few hours ago . . . the only thing that had changed was me.

As I took a moment to breathe, there was a knock at my door. I didn't answer it. There was only one person in the world that could make me answer that door, and I knew it wasn't him.

Slowly, I heard the knob turn and the door creak open. Apparently, I had left the door unlocked. A chill went up my spine. I sat there frozen, waiting for the intruder to reveal themselves. Footsteps echoed from the foyer, and then a familiar voice rang out. "Alastrina? Are you here?" A moment's pause, and then, "Hello . . . Alastrina?"

"In here," I said from the couch. I still couldn't move. Two seconds later Tegan was standing in front of me, looking more statuesque than ever. My body registered what my eyes were seeing and finally released me. I jumped up and put my arms around Tegan. "Oh, Tegan, it's so good to see you! You will never guess what happened. I need your help, I—"

Tegan held me and comforted me like a child. "It's okay, Alastrina, I'm here." His actions were warm but his words were laced with ice.

I let go in order to get a good look at him. He was not thrilled to be standing in my house. I could tell something was not right. "Tegan?" I asked discerningly, "What's wrong?"

"Alastrina, as you may have noticed, something has changed." His face was like stone. He chose his words carefully, I could tell.

"I know," I said. "*I* changed." I looked at him before continuing in order to brace myself for his utter shock at my news, but he showed no emotion. "Didn't you hear me? I am different now, Tegan. I am . . . human."

He took a moment before responding. "Yes, I know. I could tell as soon as I walked in the door. That's why I am here."

"You can fix it!" I screamed happily. A wave of joy passed over me. It was the first good news I'd had since my death-defying experience. Just when I thought all was lost, Tegan was once again here to save me.

"No, not exactly." He cleared his throat as if to start a rehearsed speech. "Ally, I am here to say good-bye. You no longer require my services, and on behalf of the Eternal Council, we apologize greatly for whatever difficulty this may bring to you—"

I interrupted him, "What? Tegan, no . . . what are you saying?"

He continued his speech, disregarding my objections. "Unfortunately, since you are no longer a member of the Imati and are in fact human, we cannot engage in your . . . existence . . . as that would be interfering in the lives of mortals." And then he added, "I'm sorry."

I was stunned. The one time I needed help more than ever, and Tegan was leaving me forever. He could help me if he truly wanted to, but he didn't. He was too bound by his duty to the Eternal Council. I began to get angry. Connor was loyal to the Brotherhood, and Tegan was loyal to the Council. *Who was loyal to me? Who would keep their promises to me?* I was not going to take this lying down.

"Tegan," I said calmly, "I need you. Please; I am mortal for the first time in over two centuries. I already sliced my hand open and practically bled to death. I don't know how to live in this fragile body. I have lost all my strength, all my abilities—everything. I have *no one.*"

I waited for his response.

"We should take you to the hospital."

"That's it? That is all you have to say? Help me! Change me back!" I demanded.

"I can't!" he yelled back.

C T Hillin

206

C T Hillin

For one who doesn't show much emotion, he suddenly had a fire in his belly. "I don't know how, nor do I have the ability." All hope drained from my face. Tegan could finally see that I was hurting.

"Ally," he walked up and put his hands on my shoulders, just like Connor had done. This was the good-bye stance, apparently.

"Something happened. Your energy disappeared. I thought you were dead. I came here thinking that you would be gone, and when I walked in, I could sense that you were human. I was relieved to know you were alive . . . but this has never happened before. The Eternal Council can't fix it; I can't fix it . . . we don't fully understand what exactly went wrong. I'm sorry."

Tears streamed down my cheeks. Tegan wrapped his arms around me to hug me. "Come on, I'll drive you to the hospital."

"And then what?" I asked, still sobbing quietly.

"And then I will say good-bye, and you will never see me again."

He said it all so matter-of-factly, like he was reading the minutes from a business meeting. To me, Tegan was a constant; he had saved me in Paris and trained me. In my mind, I thought I was as important to him as he was to me. He had always been there right when I needed him, and over the years I truly felt our relationship was based on a familial love. If I had felt alone when Conner left, I felt even more alone now. I was completely stripped of anyone, human or non-human, who cared for me.

On the drive over to the hospital, my mind began to wander to distant, far-off places I had not thought of in centuries. I began to look over my experiences, my choices, and my regrets. I gazed out the car window and watched blurry trees blow past my face. My eyes twitched back and forth, trying to get a clear picture of them. It was mesmerizing. My trance was broken when a small pebble from the highway flew up and hit the windshield, creating a tiny crack.

"What was that?" I asked Tegan as he was driving, breaking the silence that had been between us since we got in the car.

"A rock," he said. "Just a rock."

Cork, Ireland – 1742 – Outcast

AFTER MY FAMILY was murdered, Seamus and his wife allowed me to stay in their home and join their family. I never asked them for help, but they gave it selflessly and willingly. At first, there was an apparent awkwardness to the situation. Seamus' son had died, so his wife, Mary (I remembered *her* name), was hesitant to take me in as her own. However, after a few weeks she warmed up to me, and soon thereafter she treated me like a daughter. Every night she would braid my hair, and tell me a prayer before I went to bed. I remembered it well:

May you see God's light on the path ahead
When the road you walk is dark,
May you always hear, even in your hour of sorrow,
The gentle singing of the lark.
When times are hard may hardness
Never turn your heart to stone,
May you always remember when the shadows fall—
You do not walk alone.

Then, she would kiss me on the center of my forehead and leave me to rest. It was a sweet gesture, and one I remember enjoying thoroughly. Unfortunately, she did not know that I was unable to sleep. This became the worst part of my day (or night, I might say): lying there in the darkness, trapped in a bed I did not need, under blankets that felt like woolen chains. The house was so small that it would be noticed if I woke and walked around. Questions would be asked. So I lay there, silent and still, alone with my thoughts, until the sun rose and I could once again come to life.

Seamus became the father I never had. He genuinely cared for me and took an interest in what I was doing. He clued into my strength pretty early on and started to use me for farming and manual labor. I rather liked it. Mary and Seamus seemed satisfied enough: I didn't eat much, I'd come with a cow, I paid for my keep in chores, and I was generally pleasant to be around. It was not until a year had passed that the unsettling feeling they kept harbored deep in their guts began to show its face.

The more time went on and the more my physical appearance didn't change, the more cautious they became. They were not sure how old I was, but they did know it was beginning to be the time for me to marry, to have children, and to essentially leave them. I always skirted around the subject; I never wanted to meet any men, and I definitely did not have any plans for what to do with my life. I also began to get tired of lying in the tiny bed all night, so I would sneak out and make it back before sunrise. I was a fool to think they didn't notice, because they did, and one day Seamus and Mary decided to confront me.

It was just moments before the sun came up when I pushed open the wooden door to the house. As soon as I walked in, I noticed the fireplace had been burning, and the chill that usually accompanied the morning air was weakened by its burning embers. Seamus and Mary were sitting on my unoccupied bed, waiting for me to return.

Seamus spoke first. "Alastrina, whereabouts have you been all night?"

I didn't know how to respond. I hadn't been up to anything, just roaming the woods, climbing trees, and gazing at the stars.

"Nowhere. I just needed some fresh air," I replied, trying to sound as innocent as possible.

Seamus looked me over and then looked to Mary; obviously, she was more concerned than he was. She urged him to continue, but he sat there silently. She decided to take the interrogation into her own hands. "Alastrina, 'tis not proper for a young woman to roam the streets at night and get up to God knows what." Her eyes began to light up, not in a jubilant, loving manner, but in a fire-and-brimstone sort of fashion. "People are startin' to talk. They say they see you at night, walking past their homes, sometimes barefoot, like a wee wild woman, like some sort'a banshee creature."

I thought about this for a second. It was true, sometimes I forgot to wear shoes, but I didn't need them, and the dirt felt good between my toes. How could they understand this? How could I explain to them that I was different?

"I'm sorry . . . sometimes . . . I sleepwalk," is all I said.

Mary exploded, "That's 'cause you have the devil in you. You barely eat, you don't sleep, and you work all day. You're possessed . . . either that, or you're a witch!" Seamus was clearly uncomfortable at his wife's use of the word *witch*.

"Mary, hush now." His voice lowered into a whisper. "The neighbors'll hear you. We can't have 'em thinking Alastrina here is a witch."

"Ooh, they already think it, Seamus, and if we don't do somethin', they'll start thinking we're her servants to the devil himself." Mary's voice raised an octave as she tried to make her point while whispering.

Frankly, I was a little shocked. "I'm not a witch!" I cried, although as soon as I said it I began to doubt myself. The truth was, I didn't know what I was. Maybe I was a witch, but if I was, it wasn't the devil kind . . . I was the good kind. If that existed.

Seamus became the voice of reason. "Of course you're not a witch, Ally. We're just concerned. You have been here for more than a year, and we love you dearly . . . both of us. Like a daughter"—his voice was comforting, and he flashed me a timid smile—"but you have to admit, you're a little peculiar for a girl."

Seamus always had a way of knowing I was different and trying to accept me regardless, which is exactly what he was doing now. This was the moment, I thought. I had to tell them.

"I know," I said, and I began my tale. I told them how everyone had died, except me. How I had woken up scared and confused. I told them everything; even that I had no heartbeat and wasn't sure if I was really breathing at all. At the end of it all, Mary looked horrified. Seamus was less so. He seemed frightened, yet intrigued. He stood up, looked down at his wife and across at me, and said one thing: "Well, we're family, and if one of us is special, that makes us all special." Then he exited and went back to bed. Mary followed him out of the room. She made sure not to walk too close when she passed by me. I had let go of my secret, and except for Mary's cold exit from the room, I finally felt at home. My body relaxed and my spirits lightened. In Seamus's home I felt safe.

The feeling did not last. Mary was suddenly very cold to me. A few weeks went by, and she no longer said her prayer to me at night or combed my hair. Before, her words had been so comforting: *May you always remember when the shadows fall—You do not walk alone.* To me, she was now the shadow and I was again alone. She also made a point to put a rift between Seamus and me. She wanted to distance him from me. Whenever he would ask me to come and work, she would send me to town. If he needed help in the field, she would find a chore inside that was more important. I was never alone with him. She would drag me to church and sit between us. At dinner, she would only direct the conversation to him. She was no longer my friend; in fact, she was becoming my enemy.

Mary was scared of me, I knew it, but she tried not to show it. I began to feel unwelcome in the house that had saved me, the house that had become my home for almost two years. I could not help but be different, and the more I had let Mary in, the more she had pushed me away. I knew the time was coming that I would have to leave, but I wasn't ready. I had nowhere else to go. Seamus knew that, and he assured me that I could take all the time I needed. Mary did not agree with her husband, and her disdain for her circumstances bubbled and bubbled, until one day when they boiled over.

That day at supper, before we had taken a single bite, Mary picked up her glass and made an unprecedented toast.

"To Alastrina," she said as she held up the cup and looked at me, "for being such a peculiar houseguest. We're sorry to see you go, but alas, this'll be your last meal in our home. Cheers, me love."

Only Mary drank, despite the fact that she was already drunk. I sat in my chair frozen. I looked at Seamus, who was just as shocked as I was. The room was silent except for the sound of Mary eating. I refused to be the first to speak. Seamus tapped his wife lovingly on the wrist. "Mary, let's not be hasty. Alastrina is welcome to stay here as long as she needs, or until she can find a new home."

Mary put down her food and looked up at her loving husband. "No, Seamus, she is not. I will not have this devil child in me home any longer. If you do not command her out, I will!"

Just then, Mary rose from the square wooden table and marched over to my bed with my few things. She ripped the sheets off and threw the pillow on the floor. "Look here, she doesn't even need this. Why do we have a bed here if she doesn't sleep? 'Tis a waste of space." She was beginning to look like a madwoman on a rampage. The more she tossed around, the more fervor she gained. She walked over to me and took the food away. "What a formality; she doesn't hardly eat. Why do we do this? She has us under her spell. Seamus, look at her—she is a witch!"

Seamus and I sat there like ghosts, observing Mary through a pane of glass, unable to speak to her or reach her logically. Unfortunately, she crossed the line.

"That's it, little girl; get up and get out of me house!"

Mary grabbed me by the arms and hair and started to drag me out. At first, her actions seemed so ludicrous I did not fight back, until I realized that she was dragging me out the door . . . literally. Without much realization of how strong I was, I grabbed her hands from where they had shackled me and tossed her across the room.

"Enough!" I screamed. "You have no right to abuse me like this—to kick me out of this home. I will not be treated like an animal."

My own rage was shocking even to myself. I was even more shocked to see that when I thought I had merely shoved her off of me, I had in reality thrown her so hard that she flew across the room and hit the wall behind her.

Seamus sprung from his chair to help his wife. I fully took in what I had just done. "I am so sorry, Mary!" I ran over to her immediately. "Please forgive me, I did not mean to . . . I mean, I did, but I didn't know . . ." I looked at Seamus, worry painted all over my face and eyes. "Seamus, I would never hurt her. Surely *you* know that." My eyes pleaded with him to understand. He said nothing. His eyes were cold; the love and the trust were gone.

"You need to leave."

I got up. I grabbed a sack and placed a few of my things inside. I slowly walked out, my head hung low, my shoulders slumped. I didn't know where to go, so I went to the woods where I usually spent my nights and lay on the hard soil. A few pebbles dug into my back, but they did not hurt. I had made a great mistake and did not know how to control my strength. I gazed up at the night sky. It seemed like a billion little stars looked back at me. I thought about how much I disliked Mary, but how much I loved Seamus. I would miss them greatly. I was sure he would forgive me. I decided that in the morning, I would go back, apologize, and ask for forgiveness. All would be better once the sun came up, and a new day could wipe the slate clean.

The cool air turned warm. The trees above me were alive with the sounds of morning birds. The sun began to sparkle through the branches and reflect off of the morning dew that had fallen on the leaves. The world seemed peaceful, and I felt relieved that some distance had been placed between me and the horrible incident from the night before. I got up, stretched, and began to walk back to the village. I would beg Mary to take me back, and Seamus would no doubt support me.

When I turned down the dirt path and saw the first house at the entrance to the village, I felt a cold shiver run up my spine, and my ears perked back like a deer sensing a hunter. I moved with caution. Something was not right. The town seemed empty. I kept walking, but there were no people. The morning fog had enveloped the houses and the fields were still covered by its haze. It was early, yes, but not so early that everyone should be asleep.

Suddenly, I heard a bell ring, and then a small voice shouted from a window, "There she is . . . there she is . . . she's back!"

Just then, a horde of townspeople emerged from the shadows. In front of me, at least ten men walked wielding sticks, rocks, and flames. I turned around and there were ten more behind me. From every side, from every house, everyone within a mile had made it. They had all been waiting for me to return, to walk right into their trap. They knew I would come back; they knew that this was the only place I knew.

I was trapped, with nowhere to run and no one to save me. I looked into their eyes and realized they were going to kill me. They had been indoctrinated with rumors about me for a year. They all believed I was a witch. It was just a matter of time before a mob formed. Mary must have galvanized the masses while I was away. She must have told them how powerful I was and how it would take an army to defeat me. I was more scared than I had ever been in my entire life.

I fell to my knees in the middle of the angry mob and put my hands out in front of me and pleaded for their kindness, their absolution.

"I beg you, I am just an innocent girl. I mean you no harm. I just want to live in peace. I have done nothing to you."

A murmur rose from the crowd. "You're a witch," I heard, along with "The devil owns ya . . ." "She doesn't age . . ." "She wanders in the forest casting spells . . ." "She's dangerous—look at her eyes."

They all said something. They were all angry with me, although many of them I had never even met. I saw the crowd part and Mary stepped forward. Her face and arm were bruised. She was limping.

"You . . . are a witch!" she screamed. "I have seen it with me own eyes, and felt it."

Before I knew it, she pulled out a rock and threw it at me. It hit me directly on the shoulder. I barely felt it, but the emotional weight of the action was unbearable. The woman who I had considered a mother had just cast a stone at me with the intention of killing me. I scanned the crowd for Seamus, but he was nowhere to be seen. No one else had yet dared to throw a stone. They looked at me in silence to see if I would retaliate to Mary's action. I just stared at her, hurt and confused. Then, from behind her, I saw the familiar face of Seamus. He stood over her like a shadow. There was no kindness in his eyes. If I was expecting him to save me, I was wrong. He placed a hand on Mary's shoulder, and with that action, he chose his side.

I had known for weeks that at some point, it would be Mary or me. I knew he had a life to think about, and that I was not his daughter and it was not his job to love me. However, I never thought, in all my years, that it would end like this: with me, kneeling in the dirt, begging for my life, and him idly standing by.

Then, unexpectedly, he moved. The crowd was watching him. He took his free hand and revealed what was hidden behind his back, and then without warning, and without even a flicker of remorse, he threw the second stone. The rock came hurtling at me with more force than Mary's, and it hit me straight in the left eye. I recoiled from the force of it and my face hit the dirt. His was the rock that started the frenzy. The mob went wild and began pummeling me with stones.

While it is hard for me to feel great pain, it is not impossible. My body began to soften and I could feel bruises forming underneath my skin. Rock after rock hit me, and there were so many that they piled up around me. I was caught in an onslaught and could not move. Each time I went to get up, another stone hit my face, or my chest, or my arm. I felt death wrap around me. I could see it moving toward me, calling my name. But alas, it would not come; it was trying to find me but couldn't. I begged for it, I called for it, and yet nothing. I remained intact and alive.

After a while, the rocks formed a pile on top of me, and the townspeople grew tired. "She cannot die," I heard one say from underneath the cold stone.

"She is still alive . . . she is a witch, a witch!" said another.

"Look, she doesn't bleed proper . . . it's silver, it's the devil!"

The rocks stopped and they took a moment to plan their next move. Suddenly, I heard, "She must be burned." It was Mary's voice; I could recognize it even in my half-conscious state.

The rocks above me began to move. A hand reached down to grab me and pull me out. I must have looked dead; I shudder to think how swollen my face was. Then I saw a flickering light moving in front of my half-closed eye. It got closer and closer, until suddenly, my clothes were on fire and my skin began to burn. Burning I could feel, and burning was painful. The circle was tightly formed around me and I could not get out. The flames enveloped my clothes . . . I began to roll around to put out the fire. More men came with more torches; they wanted to restart the flames I had just extinguished. They wanted to finish the job.

It was time to fight back. If I could not die, then I refused to lie down and be tortured for eternity. I was weakened from the previous beating, but I knew I had to start channeling my strength. As one man approached, I got up and lunged at him like a wolf. I did not know how to fight. My legs straddled him as I clawed and bit him until he was able to push me off and run away. Two more men came at me, and I used the same primal instinct to fight them off. I was stronger than they were, faster, and my teeth were sharper. I bit off an ear, and I could taste the blood. It was salty and smelled of copper. I spit it out, red blood dripping down my mouth. The ear lay in the dirt, near the pile of stones. I looked at them in all my madness and all my rage. The crowd was horrified, their mouths gaped open. If they weren't convinced before, then all of them now believed I *was* the devil.

I picked up a few rocks and threw them at the crowd. They all began to run. Seamus, for a brief second, looked at me, and the loyalty and kinship were completely gone. This is how he would always remember me . . . bloodthirsty, dirty, and savage. Then the moment passed, and his fear carried his legs all the way back to his home.

I stood in the middle of the village, alone. My clothes had been torn and ripped, and my body was covered in ash and blood, some of it not my own. I found my sack, half trampled, on the road. I picked it up and ran away. I ran and ran until I could run no more. I collapsed onto the ground many miles from Cork and from my village. For the first time, I was scared of myself and scared of what lay ahead.

Belfast, Maine – October – Present Day

New Truths

TEGAN AND I entered the hospital. Both of us were like fish out of water, lost in a maze of white halls. I had never been in a post-millennium hospital before, and from the look on his face, neither had Tegan. We approached the front reception desk with blank expressions, confused and overwhelmed at the same time. The woman behind the desk looked at me unpleasantly. When she saw my hand, her face turned from annoyed to horrified. I suppose the amount of blood that had run down my arm and onto my clothes made it look worse than it was.

"Did he do this to you?" the overweight, manly-looking nurse asked as she eyed Tegan up and down.

I could tell he was uncomfortable with being stared at. Usually, he didn't allow Laggas to see him, but since I was with him (and now human) he more or less had to. I now see why he had never felt inclined to show himself. Under the fluorescent lights of the hospital, he almost seemed to glow, and his blond hair was shinier than it had ever been. Perhaps I had forgotten what Tegan looked like since it had been so long, but he truly was beautiful.

"No. Of course not," I said, still half staring at Tegan in wonderment. "I did it. It was . . . an accident."

The judgmental nurse said, "Mm-hmm," and threw a stack of papers at me. "Fill these out; we need insurance, date of birth, driver's license, and social security number."

"Um," I began, looking as sweet and helpless as possible, "I don't have any of those things on me. Can't I just see a doctor?"

"You don't have insurance?" she asked, as if I was the most unintelligent person on the planet. "What about you?" She turned her attention to Tegan. "Is this your daughter?" He didn't respond. "Sir, excuse me?" she asked again.

Still nothing. Tegan was not used to mingling with Laggas. He obviously didn't care for it.

"No," I interjected. "He's just a friend."

I knew we were getting nowhere with this woman. "Look," I said in the harshest tone I could find, "I am badly injured and I need help. This is an emergency room, and I have an emergency—so please, do your job and find me a doctor!"

The woman looked a little shocked that I suddenly had the gumption to yell at her. She grabbed a different form, one that read Uninsured Party at the top, and sent me down the hall to the urgent care clinic.

Tegan and I walked into the room and saw ten other people waiting to be treated. *This could take a while*, I thought, and I sighed in frustration at this bureaucratic system that I was glad to have avoided for the last fifty years. I was relieved that Tegan was still with me, considering I was terrified to be alone. We grabbed two empty chairs in the center of the room, and then I heard someone call my name from the back corner. Lo and behold, there was Bill Barnes in the waiting area, reading a book.

"Bill," I said, my voice shaky. "What a surprise."

"I was just thinking the same thing, Ally. What a coincidence; a few months back I run into Conner in New Orleans, and now here I run into you in a hospital. Constantly seeing people out of place, I guess."

The mention of Connor's name was like a big fat punch to the stomach. The wound was still fresh, but I pushed it out of my mind, not wanting to dive back into that emotional trauma just yet.

Bill was staring at Tegan, as was everyone else, but his looked more like an expression of recognition than of awe. I decided to introduce them.

"Bill, this is my friend Tegan. Tegan, this is Bill. He frequents the same coffee shop I do . . . and, uh, he's my friend."

Neither of them held out a hand. Bill just nodded his head. "Pleased to meet ya, Tegan." Then a female nurse came out and called Bill's name. Bill left with her but promised he would stick around and wait for me to say good-bye. I told him he didn't have to, but he insisted.

Once Bill left, Tegan decided it was time. "Alastrina, I am afraid this is where I say good-bye. The doctors here will help you, and I see you have a friend to look after you." He placed one hand on my shoulder as he towered above me.

"Tegan, please, you don't have to go just yet. At least . . ."

He stopped me. "Ally, it's time. You are never going to be okay with me leaving you, so whether I go now or in an hour does not make a difference." Of course, he was right.

I started to cry again. What was I going to do without Tegan? He saw my difficulty with just going to the doctor. I didn't have any papers, no date of birth; all of my forgeries were way out of date. Why couldn't he see that just leaving me here in this place, mortal, was like sentencing me to death?

"Please don't abandon me here—not like this!" I grabbed him and held on tight. I thought if I squeezed hard enough, he wouldn't let me go. I was wrong. His large arms and supernatural strength easily lifted out of my grip.

"Alastrina, stop it. This is not like you. Do not lose sight of who you are and where you come from."

"But I don't know who I am." Fat tears fell from my chin onto the floor. I was not used to so much liquid pouring out of me. I felt totally out of control, and that frustration made me cry even more.

"You are an Imati. Regardless of what color your blood is, or how much you hurt, you will always be an Imati. If you forget that, then you truly will lose yourself." Tegan's words carried weight. That fact that he still acknowledged me as more than human was a compliment from him. I wish I could have felt the power of his words more than I did, but all I could think was that my blood was now red, and my wound would not heal.

With that last statement, he turned and walked away. His long strides took him across the room, out the door, and down the hall to the exit sign. This scene had been played out before: once in Bordeaux when he put me on a ship to the New World, and once again in South America when he first saved me from the Seekers. However, in all the times he'd said good-bye, I always knew deep down that it wasn't the end. I knew he would come back. This time was different. I was human, and I no longer had a place in his world.

I had an urge to run after him, to make him stay, but my feet wouldn't move. My heart told me that Tegan really did love me, but my mind felt otherwise. My mind saw the difficulties that lay ahead, the dangers that awaited me around every corner, and it insisted that if Tegan did love me, he would not have left me. I began to lose hope. Tegan, my lifeline to the immortal world, was gone.

I sat back down in my chair and waited for my name to be called. I looked down at the wound on my hand. Not my worst injury, but still, it didn't look good; the cut was not sealing itself up. The open gash made me think of every time in my life I had felt truly hurt.

My thoughts flashed back to the brutal slaughter of my family. Then I saw Seamus throwing the second stone. I watched Joaquín lying in bed with Amelia. I saw Conner with his sword drawn, standing above me. Finally, I saw Tegan walking out of the hospital doorway. Everyone in my life had left me. No one really loved me, and if they did, they died. My presence was like a plague, killing everyone around me while the survivors fled for their lives. Now here I was, stuck in a mortal, corporeal body, coming closer to death each second that I lived. Just then, Bill came back out and interrupted my silent, pathetic moping.

"Alastrina! Good you are still here—I wanted to talk to you." Bill sat down next to me.

"Bill, you really shouldn't be around me," I replied. "I'm cursed." I added a slump in my shoulders so he would think I was kidding, even though I was really starting to believe it.

"Oh, Alastrina, let's not be dramatic. You're not cursed," he said with a mischievous smile. "But after meeting your friend there, I realize I can let you in on a little secret . . ." I lifted my eyes toward him, feigning interest.

"What?" I said, none too eagerly, wondering how meeting Tegan had clued Bill into something about *me*.

"Well, you may think *you're* cursed, but me . . . I really am."

And then Bill Barnes told me who he *really* was, and just how important Marisol had been.

Cayden Remier – Santiago, Chile – Winter, 1909

CAYDEN REMIER FRANTICALLY walked through the streets of Santiago. The medieval construction of the small cobblestone pathways made navigating the old town almost impossible. *Did the man say to the left at the square, or to the right?* He suddenly couldn't remember the directions the *abuelito* had given him. Cayden was frantic; he knew he didn't have much time before they figured out where he had gone—and why.

He arrived at the Plaza, where five streets beamed out like giant sun rays. He went left, down a small street he knew was Avenue Cristobal Colon because of the market stalls on either side. The dirt path dusted up his shoes. A woman selling chickens practically shoved one in his face, and he could hear eager vendors on either side of him shouting their goods for sale. Cayden missed Paris; he had been gone now for three months, and the journey was taking longer than he expected. He desperately wanted to get back to Marisol, his true love, and knew that this was his last and only chance.

Finally, he saw it: the door he was looking for, red with a cross in the center. It was the only door painted red on the whole street. This had to be it. Cayden walked in; not nervous, as he had been in many a bad situation, and not fearing for his life, because he could not die, but instead, he walked in excited. He knew what he wanted, and he was willing to do anything in order to be with Marisol. He wanted to grow old with her, to have children with her, and most of all, to wake up next to her every morning and tell her how much he loved her.

The apartment was small. An old woman sat in the center of the room at a round wooden table with a stack of cards in front of her. She had silver hair and her eyes were glazed over with a white film. The room was lit with candles and incense burned from all four corners. It smelled of sandalwood and lavender.

Dead chickens and jars of random reptiles hung from the ceiling. This woman was a gypsy.

"*Yo se* . . . I know why you have come," she said without looking at Cayden. He walked forward and sat down at the table.

"Then you can help me? You are the one they told me about?" he asked hopefully.

"*Si, si,*" she replied. "But I must warn you, I have never done this to one of *your* kind. I do not know what will happen."

Cayden eyed her, debating in his mind whether the reward was worth the risk.

"*Yo comprendo,*" he said. "I am very willing, please, anything you need to do—you have my permission."

The old woman got up from her table and grabbed a brown velvet bag from a box. She walked over to him and told him to stand up. "*Arisitia Callum Abbrevi Vivandun.*" The old woman spoke in a language Cayden had never heard before, which was surprising, since he had lived almost everywhere. She reached into the brown bag and threw some dirt on him, and then took a vial from the table and poured a brown, watery substance on his head. It smelled like sulfur and he was momentarily repulsed. Lastly, she added, "With these ashes, I strip you of your life." Cayden gave her a look of confusion for a second, wondering if it had worked, until he suddenly passed out, hitting his head on the table as he collapsed.

He woke up some time later, in pain, with a large welt on the left side of his head. A big smile reached across his face. He ran up to the old Indian woman, who was sitting once again at her table. He picked her up and hugged her.

"Do you know what this means?" he said, grinning. "This means I am hurt. Look at my head—there is a bump!" The gypsy was confused, so Cayden continued. "This means I am mortal . . . I am *human*!"

Belfast, Maine – October – Present Day

Souls

AFTER BILL TOLD me his story, I was taken aback.

"What does that mean?" I asked him. "*You* are Cayden . . . you're an Imati?"

He looked at me and laughed. "Yes, I am Cayden, but I'm *not* an Imati. Weren't you listening?"

The truth is, I was listening, but I had no idea what he was talking about. He wasn't a Seeker, and he mentioned his immortality, so I assumed he was Imati.

"I'm a *Saturo*, Ally—a Souljumper. Haven't you ever met one?"

"No," I responded, waiting for further explanation.

"I have no body of my own; my soul is a separate entity. I jump from vessel to vessel, so this body you see me in is not the same as Cayden's or any of the other people I was before."

"Oh," I said, still not on the same page as Bill—or even in the same book, for that matter. "So what happens to the person, or soul, that was in there before you?" I asked, fearful of his reply. I had a hunch I already knew what happened to them.

Bill hesitated. He waited to catch my eye, and then he simply said, "They die." My frozen expression prompted him to continue his explanation. "As a *Saturo*, my soul enters and overtakes theirs, and they cease to exist. That's why I enter Laggas. Imati and Seekers and everyone else would be able to fight back, but not Laggas. They barely understand the concept of *soul*."

"You call them Laggas too?" I asked Bill. "I thought that was *our* thing."

He laughed. "The Imati stole that term from us, you know . . . but it's true, the humans do lag in the soul department." Then he smiled. "Don't worry, you're still just Ally to me."

I thought about what he just told me. *I barely understood the concept of soul.* This was the first time I had ever met a Souljumper like Bill, and frankly, it freaked me out. What else was out there? How had I been alive this entire time and never really seen this whole other world? I had so many questions but didn't quite know how to ask them. Was Bill mortal now? How long had he been alive? Why did he exist? Questions were swirling through my mind, and Bill's cryptic answers didn't really help. He must have noticed I had zoned out, because he snapped his fingers in my face in order to bring me back to reality.

"Snap out of it, Ally!" I looked at him to prove that I was listening.

"I'm okay," I said.

"Jeez, Ally, you really are the most humanlike Imati I have ever met. That must be why I didn't quite understand who you were."

I squinted at him. "What is that supposed to mean?" I felt a little offended.

"Well, you don't act like an Imati . . . you *act* and *live* like a human. Ironic, considering the meaning of your name: Defender of Humanity. Somehow, you've managed to retain all of your human qualities and completely keep yourself out of the immortal world."

He looked at me in wonderment, like I'd retained my mortality despite all odds. "I think it has something to do with that necklace of yours."

"My necklace?" I touched the now-broken ruby necklace draped around my neck. It was the only thing I had really managed to keep after all these years. I knew it was special, but I had no idea why.

"Yeah. If I am correct, that necklace has a protection charm on it—and it's one of the keys," Bill said, eyeing the amulet sitting on my chest.

"One of the keys to what?" I responded, curious to know his explanation and wondering why he'd never mentioned it before. He had seen my necklace plenty of times.

"Ally . . . seriously?" He looked at me as if waiting for me to say I was kidding. I stared at him blankly.

"A key to access Imati power. You see, there's a book called Lazarus that holds all the powers of the most ancient Imati, but it's written in code, so a scroll is needed to translate it. They're held together in a chest that can only be opened with one of four keys. I am pretty sure that necklace is one of the keys."

"You are not serious, Bill," I said, mainly because I didn't want it to be true. But I also realized that inside the leather book I held was written the name Lazarus, the only readable word in it, and that my mother had also called my necklace a key. If my necklace was powerful, if the book I held was powerful, then that meant I'd been carrying around the very things that led to the murder of my family by power-hungry Seekers. Of course neither of them came from a chest. That must have been lost centuries ago. Suddenly all my problems, the downward spiral of my existence, could be traced back to the mere possession of these objects.

"Yes, I'm very serious. I went to South America looking for that book. I wanted to make Marisol immortal so we could be together forever. I gave up my own immortality looking for that chest. I lost everything, Ally, and now I am cursed to live as a mortal with a soul that can't die because I couldn't find the Book of Lazarus. I have never been more serious about anything in my life."

Bill's face was filled with anger and grief. I hadn't realized how important this was to him, and he hadn't realized how devastating it was to me. Plus, I still couldn't comprehend why *I* of all people had ended up with the rare objects Bill was looking for.

"Sorry," I said meekly. "It's just that I don't fully understand everything you're telling me." I looked at him, hoping that my apology would bring down his frustration a bit, and then continued, "I mean, you're saying there is a book inside a box that contains all this power, and that the necklace I have had for two hundred years opens it? You have to admit, this is all really new to me." I was playing a bit dumb hoping to squeeze more information out of Bill.

"Well, it shouldn't be," he snapped back. "You should have been exposed to all of this a long time ago. There is a whole world out there that you are supposed to be a part of, but instead you are completely naïve to all of it."

"I'm sorry, Bill. No one ever told me this; no one told me any of it! I went years being an Imati without even knowing that I had died. I wandered the streets not knowing if I was in heaven or hell, or what was happening to me. People chased me with pitchforks and tried to stone me to death and burn me alive. I went a little insane, okay?" *Oh, and no one clued me in that the little leather book I carried was full of secret ancient spells.*

Tears of frustration started coming again. I really was going to have to get used to this whole crying business and try to control my emotions more. Bill did not know how to react, so he stared at me awkwardly for a second and then patted my leg in an attempt to be comforting. I shifted a bit in the plastic and rubber waiting room chair. I felt utterly out of place.

"It's okay," he said softly. "I just assumed since you were Imati you knew this, but I was clearly wrong. I'm sorry."

I wiped the tears and snot from my face. This conversation was becoming more serious by the second, and I realized that by the end of it, my life was most likely going to change. I decided I needed more answers if I was going to wrap my head around what I really was and what all of this new information really meant.

"What do you mean you went looking for the Book of Lazarus? That you wanted Marisol to be immortal?" I pried.

"The ancient Imati figured out a way to *create* immortality in a non-Imati. It was their defense against Seekers and Souljumpers who assassinated them at the request of the Eternal Council. When their numbers were dwindling centuries ago, they practiced an ancient form of magic that garnered its power from other realms. Once their power was too strong, too dangerous, they decided to guard the spells, and use them only when necessary. Only the royal Imati families held the keys to the chest, where the book and scroll were kept, and those keys offered protection to whoever bore them."

As I listened to Bill talk, I was wide-eyed. There was a history and a purpose to my people that I had never realized. The fact that I had ended up with the necklace meant something. It meant that *I* meant something.

"You wanted to be with her forever?" I queried.

"Yes," Bill replied, suddenly somber as he remembered his one true love. Then his eyes started to water and tears fell from his eyes to the clean, white hospital floor. "She was my soul mate."

Cayden Remier – Paris – Spring, 1909

CAYDEN STARED DOWN at the note where Marisol's head should have been. Anger boiled up inside him as he read the devastating words: "You have been summoned to the *Abbaye de Maubuisson*. Come before night falls, or Marisol dies."

Cayden crumbled the note in his hands and threw it across the room. One day he'd had with Marisol before the Souljumpers found him—just one day—and now, to save her, he would have to meet his death. He never wanted it to play out like this. He simply wanted to be human. He never meant to break their rules or go against the Eternal Council, but when he tried to reason with them, when he asked permission, they refused to let him go. He'd had no choice.

In a fury, Cayden tried to barter for a horse to make the ride, but he was short on time, so he simply stole it. It was a slow horse, mainly because it had been beaten its entire life and forced to walk on death-soaked cobblestones. But Cayden knew the deserted Abbey was a good forty kilometers northwest of Paris and a horse, any horse, was necessary.

A few hours later, Cayden arrived at the long dirt path lined with trees leading to the abbey. It hadn't been used in a while and was overrun with weeds. Cayden traveled along the road with a heavy heart. He had no idea why *Saturos* would choose to kill him in a thirteenth-century-monastery, but it seemed ironic considering the peaceful surroundings.

Cayden descended from his horse as he arrived at the dilapidated building. The abbey had been wrecked in the French Revolution, like so many things, and after one hundred years it was turning to rubble. He left the horse untied, knowing he would never need it again, and walked through one of many openings.

As Cayden stepped over stones and broken glass, he wondered where Marisol was . . . or if she was even still alive. After several minutes of wandering and going nowhere—for there was nowhere to go—he heard footsteps. Then, out of the shadows appeared an old friend.

"Cayden, you made it," a deep voice spoke out.

"You know me, Rupert, always the punctual type," Cayden replied, unfazed. Rupert was a former brother in arms. Perhaps he wouldn't die today after all.

"You know why you're here, don't you?" Rupert asked, now fully revealing himself in the midafternoon light.

"To bring Marisol home," Cayden said.

"No. You broke the rules, Cayden. I wish there was another way, but there isn't." Rupert slowly moved forward, like a pawn changing squares in a chess game.

"I asked the Council to give me mortality and they said no. What choice did I have? I found another way, and now I am human. Let me live, Rupert," Cayden pleaded.

"The Council said no because it was an impossible request. We, Saturos, are too valuable to lose. You know that," Rupert paused. "And now you've gone rogue, which is even worse. Now you are the enemy."

"I'm just a human, Rupert. Like all the humans you saw die here, I will bleed red and I, too, will die." Cayden remembered that Rupert had been in the abbey during the Revolution and had seen countless lives destroyed. The memory had clearly left a mark.

"Well, only if that gypsy did her job right."

"Where's Marisol?" Cayden asked. "Let me see her first."

Rupert smiled. "As you wish." Rupert turned around and bellowed out, "Franz. Bring her here."

Franz, a Souljumper Cayden had never met before, brought out Marisol. She was wearing the same white dress from yesterday, only now it was torn and dirty. Her hands were tied and her cheeks stained with tears.

Cayden was fuming. "Do not hurt her, or I swear you will not live to see another moment."

"Calm down, brother. You are in no position to be making threats here."

"Fine, then—what now, Rupert?" Cayden asked, frustrated.

Rupert strutted forward. "You say the gypsy made you human? So you can no longer jump on your own?" he inquired. He was now standing within three feet of Cayden. Marisol and Franz were still several paces behind.

"I can't jump." As Cayden spoke, Marisol's face contorted with confusion.

"Let's see, shall we . . ." Suddenly, Rupert pulled out a dagger and stabbed Cayden in the thigh. Marisol screamed, despite the cloth gag stuck between her teeth.

Cayden composed himself. "You see?" he said through the pain. "It's bleeding and it does not heal. This body is mortal."

Rupert chuckled in amazement. "Look at that. The gypsy is more powerful than we thought." Rupert turned to face Marisol. He walked over to her and put the knife to her cheek. "Witness your true love," he said looking toward Cayden. "He did this for you."

Marisol said nothing. Tears ran down her face.

Growing frustrated by the second, Rupert screamed at her, "He was an immortal! But now, look at him. He's human. Like you." Rupert ripped off Marisol's gag. "Say something!" he demanded.

But Marisol spit on his face and said the only thing that came to mind: "You are nothing."

"I am nothing?" Rupert mocked. He took the dagger and slit open his left wrist. Marisol watched in fear as the wound closed as if nothing was ever there.

"That's what I am," Rupert said, pointing to his healed arm. "I am invincible. But your lover, Cayden, he gave it all up for you. Thinking he could have a life with you. But now, he's going to watch you die."

Cayden screamed, "No, Rupert! Do not do this. We are friends, remember?"

"I have my orders. Remember when that used to mean something?" Rupert put down the dagger as Marisol squirmed in her restraints. But then, he did something unexpected and untied her.

"You can have one last good-bye, as my *friendly* gift to you," he said, seemingly sincere.

Marisol, finally free, ran to Cayden, who was still bleeding on the ground. As she ran Cayden opened his arms to take her in, but the moment she got there, something happened.

From the corner of his eye, Cayden saw Franz collapse to the ground as his body suddenly grew limp. In the same moment, as Marisol ran, she jerked forward as if pushed from behind and flew violently into Cayden's arms. Her eyes lit up gold, and then filled in like pools of black. Her body convulsed. Cayden screamed, "*Noooooo!*"

"Rupert, get him out of her. He cannot do this. You cannot have her soul." Cayden realized Franz had jumped freely into Marisol's body, overtaking it, fighting her soul to the death, until her vessel would be his. Her soul would be crushed and cease to exist.

"Jump in. Fight him off, Cayden," Rupert said, amused.

"I can't. You know I can't jump anymore!" Cayden yelled furiously.

"And that's the proof I really needed," Rupert smirked.

"No, not her. Not Marisol. She deserves more. She deserves . . ."

But Cayden trailed off, as Marisol's eyes suddenly opened and she grinned. But it was not sweet. In fact, it was sinister, because it was no longer her. Marisol was gone. Forever.

Cayden cried out in pain. His leg was torn and his heart was broken. Rupert walked over to him and bent down to his line of sight. "Cayden Remier, under orders of the Eternal Council, you are hereby sentenced to death."

Cayden looked up at his old friend. "You will pay for this, Rupert. You and the Council."

"We'll see," Rupert said, and then he took the dagger and slit Cayden's throat. Cayden bled out and died for the first time.

But then, minutes later, Cayden woke up with a blinding headache in unfamiliar territory. It was nighttime and it was freezing. He was wearing long underwear and the fire in his tiny room had gone cold. He stood up, and knocked over a bottle of vodka when he did so.

He did not live here. This was not his house. He was lost. He looked at some books on the shelf; all were written in Russian. One of the many languages he knew. He stumbled around, found a match, and lit a lamp. Pictures, postcards, letters—all written in Russian. He ran outside his door. He was in a hallway, clearly in an apartment-type dwelling. An old woman walked up the spiral stairs. She shouted at him in Russian, "*Please, Alexie, put on some clothes, you buffoon!*"

Cayden looked around; he was the only one on the hall. *"Me?"* he asked in Russian. The woman walked up to him, sniffed around his neck, and said, *"You are drunk, you idiot. Go to bed."*

Cayden grabbed her. *"Where am I? Who am I?"*

The woman slapped him. *"Enough is enough. You are Alexie the drunk, and this is Moscow—unfortunately. Now get to bed."* She walked away mumbling.

Cayden ran back into his room. He looked in the mirror. Large brown eyes, bushy, lice-filled beard, bruises on his eye from a bar fight, most likely. This was not Cayden's young, well-structured face. It was Alexie the drunk. Somehow, Cayden had jumped. The gypsy had cursed him, made his body human. But his soul—his powerful, *Saturo* soul—remained intact. Only now he had no control of where he went or how he got there.

He would remain Alexie until someone killed him. And then, he would jump again.

Belfast, Maine – October – Present Day

Heritage

I DIDN'T QUITE know what to say. Bill was cursed in a most awful way. I thought life as an Imati was hard, but he'd been through so much. I realized I felt even more connected to him now. I was not used to sharing so much with someone so otherworldly, someone who might actually understand my own feelings. Except for Connor, I was not used to being so close with someone—and here Bill was crying his eyes out to me, letting me in on his deepest secrets, hoping I could console him. All I could do was listen. I had no practice in this. After all, I wasn't really human.

The room remained silent as Bill remembered and I thought about Cordelia, Callum, my mother, and even Amelia, who had died at my own hand. Death was everywhere for us. And I knew, deep down, immortality's only true companion was the death of others.

Then Bill took my hand and squeezed it. "Enough of this sadness, Ally. It's time to go." He got up and pulled me up with him. "We can bandage you at my house."

"Why at your house?" I said, reluctant to leave the place of bandage professionals.

He grabbed my arm and started to pull me out of the hospital. "You are the one I have been waiting for, Ally. I know it. We have been brought together for a reason, and that reason is to find the Book of Lazarus, to make everything right again." I didn't know what he meant by that. *Ugh—why was he always so cryptic?*

"Bill, wait!" I shouted while releasing myself from his grip. "I can't just go with you."

He stopped and looked at me. "Why not?"

It was a good question. *Why not?* Why couldn't I go? What did I have to do, except be human and live out my days until I died . . . again? "Because . . ."

I stammered. "I don't know; I am human now." That seemed like a good enough reason to me to avoid danger at all costs.

"Exactly!" He said excitedly, "Once we get that book, we can make you immortal again."

"We can?" I asked, not entirely sure how I felt about this prospect.

"Ally, only your body is mortal, but your soul . . . that's still Imati. You are destined to be a great Imati, and for some reason it was taken from you. Now we are going to get it back!"

Huh, I thought. *Destined to be a great Imati—me?* Now he sounded like Delilah. I hadn't really lived up to that yet in all my years of existence, and here Bill was selling me on it, convincing me of my own fantastic destiny. It was obvious that he wanted the book as much for his own reasons as he did for mine, which he was reluctant to admit to.

"But what about Connor?" I interjected once we had made it to the hallway, just a few yards shy of the exit sign.

"What about him?" Bill asked, perplexed.

"He's a Seeker," I said. "He practically tried to kill me."

Bill stopped in the middle of the corridor. "That explains so much," he said quietly, to himself. His expression turned from thoughtful to concerned in the matter of seconds.

"This could be a problem. He and Quinn are here for a reason, then. Now that they know you're an Imati, they will try to kill you. Or torture you. It depends."

Oh, great, I thought. *Now that I am mortal, I'm in even more danger than I was as a supernatural Imati. Now that I can't defend myself, everyone wants to kill me.*

"Look, Ally, all I know is that we need to leave—now! Seekers are trackers, and they will be looking for you. Even your necklace can't protect you."

That was that. Bill grabbed my hand and pulled me to the exit sign. We burst out of the double doors. The sunlight was blinding. By this time it was midday. I saw my car in the hospital parking lot. The last time I'd sat in it, Tegan had been with me. So much had happened in the last twenty-four hours: Connor was a Seeker, Bill was a Souljumper, and I was mortal. Now, suddenly, I was on the run from killer Seekers—*again*—and searching for a book I was pretty sure I already had possession of.

If I had trusted Bill more I would have told him, but as naïve as he thought I was, I had learned a lot in the last day, most of it revolving around the phrases "nothing is what it seems" and "trust no one." For all I knew, Bill could be the enemy. He was a powerful Souljumper who had been everywhere, seen everything, and been crossed one too many times. What did he really want with the book, how pissed off at the Council was he, and how dangerous did that make him? And, more importantly, what the heck did "Even your necklace can't protect you" mean?

Cayden Remier – Madrid, Spain – 1906

CAYDEN REMIER ARRIVED in Madrid with an anxious heart. The love of his life was growing older by the day; therefore, he felt the pressure of time on his back with every step he took through the old city. He had come to Madrid on a whim, a mere hope that what he needed he would find. With all of his years of service as a Souljumper to the Eternal Council, he was sure they would help him in his one time of need, but no; they had refused his request for Marisol's immortality and his subsequent request to regain his humanity. Through soft feints and whispers he had heard tales of Imati power, and now he had come to Madrid in search of them. He knew of several Imati living in the Spanish capitol from an unlikely source—a Seeker.

He had run into James Winfield in London and formed a fast friendship. James spoke of spells, ancient magic, and the ability to create immortality from nothing. He said the Seekers were hunting all ancient Imati who possessed the power in order to put an end to their ability to cause chaos and destruction. Cayden himself had nothing against Imati; he knew them to be heartless, hedonistic creatures, only concerned with their own well-being, but as an immortal himself he knew what a slippery slope that was, and how easy it is to fall under the spell of eternal life. He listened to James in order to learn, but he never planned on using an Imati for his own personal benefit.

He arrived in Plaza Mayor and gaped at the grand baroque-style buildings, which surrounded him like a prison. The square was hot and crowded. The sun beat down on the cobblestone street and reflected the heat back onto him. *What a dreadful city*, he thought to himself. He imagined the center of the square as it had been decades ago: a place of execution and the Spanish inquisitions. So much blood had been shed on these stones, and here he was, prepared to add more. Out of the corner of his eye he saw his contact.

"Hello, James," Cayden said discreetly, not making eye contact with his friend.

"Cayden—good to see you made it to Madrid. Are you ready?" James asked.

"Yes, where is he?" Cayden eagerly waited for his instructions. The fear he had felt five minutes before had made its way from the back of his throat to the pit of his stomach. He knew it was spreading like wildfire.

"Cayden, I must tell you . . . *he* is a *she*." James said as he looked at his immortal friend, trying to gauge his reaction.

Cayden's mind raced. Was he truly prepared to do this? James knew that as a Souljumper Cayden must have done horrible things, but to torture another soul for personal profit is always a tough order to swallow.

"It's fine," Cayden remarked quickly. "I am ready."

The sudden news that it was a woman waiting for him was disheartening. Hopefully she would not resemble Marisol in any way, and if she did it would take all his strength to get from her what he needed.

"Good," James said. "Top floor, to the left. It's the room with the red ribbon on the handle. Just to warn you, she is a wily one—just arrived from South America less than a year ago. Be careful."

"I will," Cayden said.

With that, he turned and approached the massive east-facing wall of the square. He entered the first door and climbed the wooden staircase to the top. He could hear his own footsteps as he walked through the hall, carefully checking each door for a red ribbon. Finally, he could see it: only three doors away. He approached, turned the handle, and walked in.

The fear was now in his throat, his stomach, and worst of all his heart. In the middle of the room, secured to a chair with metal chains, was a beautiful, slender woman with fiery, copper-colored hair. She was blindfolded. Immediately Cayden feared for the twisting, metal chains that acted as her restraints. He knew some Imati to be so powerful they could manipulate metal objects around them. Then, the thought occurred to him that *this* Imati must not be that powerful, or else the Seekers would never have risked such a fate.

Cayden approached her, sat at the foot of the bed in front of her, and undid the scarf that wrapped so perfectly around her heart-shaped face. He revealed her crystal-blue, almond-shaped eyes. Cayden was temporarily taken aback by her presence. She flashed him a smile, and then head-butted him straight in the nose, followed by an onslaught of spitting and profanities, which she flung at him like a hailstorm.

Cayden immediately stood up. "You Imati bitch!"

Scarlett laughed at him. "Oh, please, you Seeker whore! You all are worse than we are . . . how dare you chain me here for days. As soon as I am loose, I will kill you, and you know it."

James was right; she was wily, with a burning temper that matched the color of her hair. Cayden took a moment to straighten himself out and calm his nerves. "I am not a Seeker," he said proudly, "I am a Souljumper."

Scarlett looked at him, suddenly fearful. "*Saturo, Saturo, Saturo!*" she shouted.

"What do you know of that word? Only the old ones call me *Saturo*," Cayden replied, revisiting his original thought that she may know more than she was letting on.

Scarlett spit on the floor in disgust. She knew that even she was in over her head if they had brought in a Souljumper. She knew them to be deadly creatures who could take any form, and she also knew that if Cayden really wanted to, he could jump into her own body and fight her soul to the death. When a Souljumper takes a soul, there is no afterlife, no continuation of being; the soul simply ceases to exist. A chill ran up Scarlett's lower back and created small goose bumps on her arms. *That's odd*, she thought. His presence was shocking her body into fear, which was an emotion she had absolutely no control over.

Scarlett continued to glare at him and waited for him to speak first. She had no idea why he was there. She assumed that if he'd been sent to kill her, it would have happened already. Cayden paced around the room, making sure to keep a reasonable distance between himself and the woman. Finally, he spoke.

"There is a way," he started, not sure exactly how to phrase his request, "to grant immortality. The Imati have perfected it, and I want to know what it is."

Scarlett replied, "Why do you, an immortal, wish to have immortality?"

"That is not the point," Cayden said to her. "You know how to do it, and you are going to tell me."

"I am not telling you anything, dirty *Saturo*, unless you give me a reason to."

Scarlett had an air of confidence about her that was intimidating to Cayden, yet it was also irritating enough to make what he had to do next more bearable. Cayden reached under the small metal-framed bed, which was directly north of Scarlett, and pulled out a leather sack. He reached into the sack and came out with a small club. Cayden looked at Scarlett, but there was no visible fear in her eyes. "This is going to hurt," he said. With that, he struck her across the face with his small, handheld club. Knowing that she was an Imati, he struck her two more times. No silver blood ran across her face—*yet.*

Scarlett was not one to easily give in. "You can hit me all you want to, but until you cut off my head, I will feel nothing."

"Just tell me how to do it, how to make a mortal an immortal, and this won't go any further." Cayden felt that pleading might actually get through to her.

Scarlett's mouth turned upwards, and she smiled faintly. "I get it," she said. "You love someone; that is whom you wish to give immortality to."

"Don't speak of things you know nothing about," Cayden replied harshly. His words were like little daggers, piercing Scarlett's rough demeanor.

"I know all about love of *Laggas*," Scarlett said. "We use them, and play with them, and then we discard them. That is exactly what you will do with this one. Just give it time; she'll die soon, and then you will forget all about her."

Cayden took the club and started beating Scarlett, first on the face, then the shoulder. Then he used his bare hands until his knuckles were briefly stained with the metallic substance that protruded from her face. Even her blood was beautiful, as its remnants streaked her hair and dripped down her cheek onto the wooden floor beneath her, where it gathered into a perfect pool of silver. "Don't talk about Marisol that way!" Cayden screamed as he continued the lashing. "You don't know her, and you will never know her!" By the time he stopped, Scarlett was still, temporarily unconscious from Cayden's blows. He was stronger than both a human and a Seeker, and Scarlett was not prepared for the beating.

When she awoke Cayden was once again sitting on the bed in front of her. She lifted her eyes, which were crusted with dried silver beads of blood. Part of her felt bad for him, the other part wanted to kill him. "There is a way," she muttered, "but I don't know it."

"You are lying," Cayden accused, knowing she would purposefully try to fool him.

"Fine, don't believe me. All I know is that the power is very old, very hard to achieve, and no Imatis of today remember it. It is all kept in a book they call Lazarus, which has been lost, or hidden or something."

Cayden had never heard this before. He'd never heard the name Lazarus. He still wasn't sure he trusted her. He grabbed a small silver dagger from the leather sack on the bed and held it to Scarlett's throat.

"If you are lying to me, I will kill you . . . slowly . . . with this tiny dagger, one inch of your neck at a time."

"I am not lying." She coughed up silver blood and spat it on the floor. "I can prove it."

Cayden waited for her to continue, wondering if she was about to send him on a wild goose chase or if she genuinely feared for her life.

Scarlett began to speak again. "But you have to help me."

"Not possible," Cayden responded. "I can't let you out of here. I was lucky to be granted this time with you; the Seekers will have my head if they knew I helped you escape."

"You'll just get a new one. Besides, do you want to save your true love or not?" Scarlett asked, already knowing the answer. She held the trump card, and that was Cayden's biggest weakness. "Fine," he gave in, "but first tell me exactly how you can prove your theory about this book." Scarlett shuffled in her chair, trying not to show the excruciating pain she was still in.

"We must go to Iglesia de San Nicolás. Inside, there is a map and a letter that prove the existence of the book and the location of the scroll. Once you find it, you will have access to all the Imati power you can imagine."

"If you have access to this map, why did you hide it in a church? Why didn't you use it to find the book yourself?"

"First, because *I* didn't hide it there," Scarlett said. "And second—I can't read the map."

Belfast, Maine – October – Present Day

The Return

Bɪʟʟ ᴀɴᴅ ɪ ran to my car. There were hardly any vehicles in the parking lot and barely any people around. I jumped in the driver's seat, thinking how ridiculous this all was. I started the car and buckled my seatbelt. The county hospital sat directly off of Highway One, so the drive to Bill's should be short, I thought. Then, out of nowhere there was a frantic banging at my driver's side window. "Ally, Ally, stop!"

Connor's face was slightly sweaty from running and stricken with fear and urgency. He was trying to pull open my car door but it was locked. He shook the door handle but it didn't budge. Bill looked at me and screamed, "Drive!" I began to put the car in reverse and drive away, but Connor followed. He leaped onto the hood of my Mercedes SUV, straddling it like a lizard on a sun rock. He continued to bang on the metal hood, and the sound ricocheted through the windshield straight into my gut.

"Please, Ally, stop the car!"

I looked to Bill, then to Connor, then to Bill. His eyes said everything: *Ally, drive this car with him on the hood or he'll kill us both.* I gave Connor one more look. His eyes were pleading with me to listen to him, to forget our fight, to forget everything I had learned, and to trust him. I stopped the car, got out, slammed the door shut, and forcefully marched over to him.

"What is wrong with you? You try to kill me, you leave me, and then you jump in front of my car!" I was screaming like a lunatic; clearly my passions were getting the best of me. "I should have just run you over!"

Connor looked hurt, then angry. He was still panting from the commotion. "Run me over? You're an Imati! I should kill you right now—you have been lying to me this entire time. I trusted you." He looked hurt again.

I knew he didn't want to kill me and that he regretted reiterating that option, but I also knew he was struggling with his own decision to keep me alive. I asked the obvious question. "Why did you even come back?"

Connor's eyes darted to the right, and then he stared at the ground for a moment. The fall air made me shiver as I waited for his response. "Ally—Quinn is going to hunt you, and then torture you, and then kill you. He doesn't care what you are now; he thinks you are more powerful than you are letting on and this whole being a mortal thing is a ruse. We have to get out of here."

"I thought you couldn't look at me the same way, remember?"

"I can't—I can't shake what I saw Ally. The killing, the running—the murder." Connor struggled as he remembered my past. He looked as if it physically pained him to think of me like that. "But," he added, "I know who you are, and you're a good person, and the thought of you dead is worse. I came back to tell you that you're no longer safe here."

Suddenly, Bill shouted from the passenger seat, "I already told her that—we were escaping until you jumped on our car!" Apparently, he had been listening to the conversation.

Connor yelled back, "Well, I was *trying* to save her too!"

"Yeah, great timing," Bill loudly muttered. "And now that *saving her* is out of the way, let's go so we don't have to save her again." Bill slammed his door.

Connor then looked to me, suddenly part of the team again. "So where are we going?"

"Bill's house," I responded. "He has a map."

"For what?" Connor asked as we loaded back in the car, all sense of urgency dissipating regardless of the fact that we had wasted more time.

"For the Book of Lazarus" Bill responded, taking the words right out of my mouth.

"We need the book so Ally can get her immortality back." Bill gave me a wink that told me not to tell Connor he had his own reasons for wanting the book, which even I was still a little unclear on.

"Oh," was all Connor said.

From my rearview mirror, I could see him slump back in his seat and stare out the window. Something about that news seemed to bother him, because his face became pinched with worry and despair in a matter of seconds.

Carinthia Winfield – The Sorceress – One Month Ago

Dearest Ophelia,

You see now what the prophecy has given us. Heaven is closer than we think. The Doorway is in Belfast, all we need is the Key . . . and I know just where it is. Arrangements have been made. Tell the White Doves, and ask for their help—they know what to do. I'll see you soon. Love.

—CW

Belfast, Maine – October – Present Day

Hill Of Tara

I STARED AT the old map Bill had placed in front of me. It was more of a diagram than a map. The paper was faded and made of some kind of animal skin, beige and soft. There was a date in the upper left-hand corner which read *1700* in ink script. The map was old; in fact, it was older than me. The more I looked at the images, the less familiar they became. When Bill had first placed it on the table, I thought I had recognized the patterns, and then in an instant that feeling was gone.

"This isn't a map, Bill—it's just circles and squares," Connor said, frustrated. "It looks like blueprints or something, with no rhyme or reason!" Connor was still upset from learning that Bill was a Souljumper, which meant he was both stronger and more powerful than Connor . . . or used to be, anyway.

"I told you I couldn't read it. I've had the stupid thing for a century. I trekked through half of South America trying to decode it. After a while, I figured I needed help, but I never actually trusted anyone enough to show it to them."

Bill and Connor continued to stare at it and argue what it could be. Then it hit me: *blueprints.* It was so simple, and so obvious, I was surprised that Bill did not recognize it. I must have seen those shapes a million times. In fact, I'd stood on that ground; I had been there before, only many, many years ago.

"I've got it!" I said, interrupting their boyish quarrelling. "It's just like Connor said—blueprints—only not of a building." They both looked at me like I was speaking another language. "It's what the earth would look like from above. Only one place in the world has markings like that, and yes, they were there in 1700—"

"Ally!" Bill interrupted. "Spit it out . . . I've already waited a century."

"The Hill of Tara, in Ireland," I said, pleased with my own detective work. I remembered seeing the shapes many times when I had researched my homeland in one of my many stints in college. I went through a phase where I wanted to know everything about where I had come from and to understand everything that had happened there when I was alive.

"Ireland!" Connor said, apparently not pleased by the idea of traveling all the way to Europe for some kind of treasure hunt. "I don't get it." He continued, "I'm pretty sure Quinn also wants whatever is there, and he specifically sent us to Belfast, *Maine*. I mean, how do we even know that whatever is there is actually still there?"

"We don't," I said. "Most likely it's gone. That place has been excavated dozens of times. But," I emphasized, "whoever originally had this map might have figured out the location; ergo, they might know who has the scroll, right?"

"And Lazarus," Bill added. "That's more important."

"Right," I said. "The book and the scroll . . . we need both." I debated telling them right then and there that I had the book, but decided against it.

Bill picked up his car keys and walked toward the door, "Well then we need to find Scarlett, because she gave me the map and the letter in Madrid." Bill said.

"Scarlett?" I questioned. "*My* Scarlett?" I looked to Bill for his answer.

"I don't know . . . fiery redhead with a powerful punch?" He rubbed his forehead when he spoke of her like he was revisiting an old injury.

"That's her," I said. I hadn't imagined Scarlett alive and in the present in a long time. Now, after all these years, she was coming back into my life. The girl who taught me how to live, how to love, and how to kill was going to help me regain my immortality. Hopefully, this time, I would hold onto my soul.

"What letter?" Connor interjected, getting straight back to business. Bill put down his keys and walked over to the bookshelf where he had kept the letter. It was dated the 14th of April, 1701, and it was, surprisingly, written in English.

Cornelius,

Here is the map. Your Destiny lies in Death. I pass this on to you now. Please keep it safe. The amulet is for your protection. Carry it with you, and use it wisely.

All three of us read the letter silently. Each of us kept our reactions to ourselves, not wanting to give away too much information. Obviously, we all still had trust issues. I took a deep breath and decided to go first.

"Cornelius, if it's the same one, is a very old Imati. I met him once in Paris, during the Revolution." I let out a chuckle. "Hey, I can actually say that and it's not weird."

Connor and Bill just stared at me, not understanding my joy in the sentence.

"Anyway," I continued, "he was the one who told me to go Argentina for safety. The words *Destiny* and *Death*, capitalized, probably refer to the Stone of Destiny at the Hill of Tara, which must be where the scroll was buried at that time. Whoever made the map must have been the keeper of the book and scroll." Connor and Bill did not react. My cards were on the table. It was their turn.

"Fine." Connor began, "If I am not mistaken, Scarlett has the amulet, similar to Ally's mentioned in the letter. Someone left it for her in New Orleans very recently, and she is actively using it. Cornelius must have given it to her; therefore, she is still very much in touch with him."

"How do we know it's the same one as in the letter? Bill said there were four keys." I asked, looking toward Connor.

"I don't know." He said perplexed.

We both looked at Bill, waiting for him to spill the beans on whatever the letter had revealed to him and shed some light on the situation.

"That bitch! She must have lied to me—of *course* she could read the map, and she knew Cornelius already had the book and scroll. She used me to get away!" Bill was furious. His face had turned a new shade of red, and he was seething through his teeth as he ranted on about Scarlett and how her day would come.

"Bill!" I screamed. "Focus . . . what can you tell us from the letter? Do you have any new information?"

"What? Sorry." He was still frazzled and worked up from the realization that Scarlett had duped him a century ago. "No, nothing new, just that we need to find Cornelius in order to find that book—and, therefore, we need to find Scarlett first."

"What about the keys?" I asked?

"Yes, there are four. If Scarlett has one it's probably from Cornelius." He said, as if that was obvious.

"How do we find her?" I asked.

"She is in Montreal, or at least she was a few months ago." Connor quickly responded.

I stared at him, wondering how he knew her, why he had met her, and what he had done with her. I was insanely jealous that Connor had met Scarlett. She was so stunning he must have been awestruck by her. *Was this before or after he met me? What did they talk about? Why didn't he kill her?* So many questions swirled through my head, and yet none of them were pertinent to the situation at hand, so I kept quiet. I was successfully learning to control my emotions. I would ask him later. Right now, we needed to get to Canada.

Montreal, Canada – October – Present Day

Friend or Foe

BILL, CONNOR, AND I loaded into my Mercedes SUV and headed to Montreal. What a group we made: an ex-Imati, a cursed Souljumper, and a rogue Seeker, all of us sworn enemies and now all of us fighting together. None of us completely trusted the other, because at one point or another, all of us had lied; thus the car ride was less than eventful, and we let the radio do the talking. It was not until we got close to Montreal that Connor's tracking skills became apparent. He knew exactly where to go without even looking at a map, down to the tiniest detail, remembering even the exact number of trees we would pass on a given road. I was actually impressed, and it made him sexier than he already was, though I was still hurt and angry with him for leaving me in my time of need. No doubt Quinn and Dawson knew what I was and were now after my head because Connor had spilled the beans. I couldn't quite shake that betrayal but knew I needed to focus on the positive: Connor had come back, and he was trying to help me. *I think.*

We arrived at Scarlett's apartment midday. Connor wanted to take time and scope out the surrounding streets and buildings and also to wait for visual confirmation that she still lived there. I was pretty sure she did—Scarlett had no problem returning to dangerous places; she liked the thrill of it all—so I had a different plan. I jumped out of the car and began to walk across the street with the intention of knocking on Scarlett's door and simply asking her about Cornelius. Before I could go two steps, Connor was in front of me.

"Ally, stop. Think about what you are doing—you can't just walk up to a deadly Imati warrior and expect not to be killed." His hands were square on my shoulders preventing me from moving forward.

I knocked his arms to the side and pushed past him. "Connor, she is not a deadly Imati warrior, she is my ex-housemate, practically a sister. I really doubt she'll kill me." I continued walking, then turned around halfway across the street and said, "If you feel that strongly about it, come with me." Connor hesitated, so I egged him on: "Unless you are scared . . ."

That got his feet moving. "Bill, let's go, out of the car. We are going with Ally."

"How did I get dragged into this?" Bill asked. "I thought I was the wait-in-the-car guy."

"Not anymore, Souljumper, it's your time to shine," Connor said with a smirk.

"May I remind you that this *body* is mortal!" Bill retorted.

I walked ahead and ignored the so-called strong men behind me. I knocked on the door. Suddenly, my stomach dropped, and I became very nervous. My hands began to twitch. What if she did want to kill me? What if she hated me? How would I defend myself? I heard footsteps, and my heart froze.

Scarlett, like a beam of light, answered the door. I had forgotten how flawless she was. It had been well over one hundred years since I had seen her. She looked exactly the same.

"Alastrina . . . oh my, Ally! You have come back!" She smiled a smile that reached across her entire face and took me into her arms completely. She hugged me for a while, a genuine, I-love-you-and-am-glad-to-see-you hug. "I missed you, darling . . . things have not been as fun without you." All of my fears washed away, and I began to relax. Suddenly, Scarlett's expression changed and she looked at me like I had just put a knife in her back. "Ally," she said sternly but with a smile, "you brought friends."

Connor and Bill appeared behind me and timidly looked at Scarlett. They were obviously scared of her. They had never been that scared of me; why was she so intimidating to them? Why was I not?

"Yes," I began, "but they are not here to hurt you. We just need your advice." My voice felt shaky as I tried to explain myself.

Bill interrupted, "More like we need information than advice."

"Thanks, Bill," I said dryly.

Scarlett laughed her infectious laugh, "Of course, of course, come in, all of you. Even you, Connor . . . although I believe the last time I saw you I told you never to come back." Her words cut him like knives, and for the first time I saw a genuinely frightened Connor Winfield.

He cleared his throat, mustering up all the confidence he could. "Actually, if I recall, you said not to follow you. Which I didn't. You never mentioned not coming back."

Scarlett, always impressed with anyone who stands up to her, enjoyed this answer greatly and replied, "My mistake, then. Please sit."

We didn't have time for small talk and catching up about the last hundred years, so I cut right to the chase. "Scarlett, we need to know where Cornelius is. He has something, and we need to get it." I am not sure why I didn't mention the book or the scroll, despite the fact that I knew that Scarlett knew what I was referring to.

Scarlett sat in her wooden chair across the room from me and slowly stirred the apple tea she had been drinking before we arrived. The smell was intoxicating. She sat there perfectly calm and poised, with her legs crossed at the ankles. Her maroon vintage dress fit her figure so perfectly in that position that if she had paused for a single second she could have been a painting of a duchess or a queen. Her spoon clanged against the porcelain china that held her tea, and she still did not respond. Bill, Connor, and I were all on edge. She looked up at me innocently and grinned.

"You know, Ally, I always wondered where you got your pendant that you so gloriously draped around your neck when we were together. You always said it was a family heirloom, but you failed to mention that it was both charmed and ancient." Scarlett was smiling and stirring her tea as she spoke, but her tone was accusatory, like I had lied to her. She made me more than nervous.

"I didn't know what it was. My father gave it to me, and no one told me it was . . . charmed."

She put her tea on the end table next to her. As soon as she drew her hand away from the china teacup, the silver handle of the spoon inside swirled across the cup and pointed toward her. I almost missed the slight movement, and Scarlett didn't notice at all.

"Ah! I see. You were so naïve then; I forgot that about you." I think she was insulting me, but all I could think about was the tiny metal spoon. It was *attracted* to her.

"Well, anyway," she continued, "I do know where Cornelius is, but I can't possibly divulge that information to a Seeker and a"—she looked at Bill and waved her hand in a shooing fashion—"whatever *that* is. I'm guessing it's not mortal."

Bill scrunched his brow, like he took offense. As far as I knew, he was reeling with anger from the fact that Scarlett had lied to him back in Madrid—but as far as Scarlett knew, that had been Cayden, not Bill.

"Scarlett, please," I said, pushing my fear aside. "We are looking for the scroll. We need it."

"Just the scroll?" she asked, intrigued.

"Yes, the scroll." I stumbled on my own words. "No, I mean, the Book of Lazarus and the scroll . . . all of it."

"Where did you learn that name, Lazarus?" Scarlett asked.

I hesitated. I had read it inside the book -- which would have given away that I had seen it before -- but luckily I had another excuse.

"Bill told me." I responded. That seemed to satisfy her.

"Why do you need it?" she demanded. "Tell me why and I will help you find Cornelius."

I paused again out of fear. I did not want to tell Scarlett that I was no longer immortal. She thought so little of mortals that I was afraid she would want to help me even less than she already did. Plus, due to the position of the metal spoon, I was concerned that in the last hundred years, Scarlett had become much more powerful than I remembered. I froze with panic and couldn't speak.

"Ally is mortal now," Connor said. "We need the ancient Imati Book, or whatever you people call it, to help her regain her immortality. And for some reason, Bill here wants it too."

"Connor!" I said, suddenly embarrassed. My cheeks flushed red, I felt so exposed. I could tell Bill was not happy that Connor had added him into the equation. Scarlett took a one-eighty-degree survey of the room. She looked at me on the couch with sympathy, then she looked to Bill by the windowsill with curiosity, and lastly she looked to Connor, sitting next to her, with indignation.

"Connor," she inquired, "why are *you* here?" We were all confused by her question, which had almost nothing to do with anything Connor had just told her.

"Excuse me?" he replied.

"Well, you are a Seeker. Just a few months ago, you were tracking me, hunting me, and preparing to kill me. Now, here you are, with an ex-Imati, trying to help her. My only conclusion is that you love her. But, alas, that is why I am so confused, because if you love her, wouldn't *you* of all people wish her to remain mortal?"

Leave it to Scarlett to ask the hard questions, the questions that nobody wanted to be forced to answer. In the last few days, Connor had thought about or tried to kill me on two occasions, and now he was back in my life . . . who knew if he still loved me. While I was shocked that Scarlett had been so forward, my ears perked back and I realized that I, too, wanted to know his response.

Connor was still for a moment, and then he looked at me and not at Scarlett when he answered.

"I do love her, and I want to save her, even if that means giving up a life with her."

My eyes welled up and I quietly began to cry. Single tears streamed down my cheeks. Connor came over to the couch, sat down next to me, and took my hands in his. "Ally, I love you. This is going to sound strange, but even when I thought I had to kill you, I still loved you. I'm sorry I never told you that I was a Seeker, but I lied for the same reasons you didn't tell me you were an Imati. I was scared of what you would think of me and what might happen. But now, the thought of losing you scares me even more. I will do anything I have to in order to keep you safe . . . I need you."

I looked into his blue eyes, and I could tell he was telling me the truth. For the first time since all of our secrets had been shared, we kissed. Once again I was swept back up into the essence that was Connor, and I felt more powerful than I ever had before.

Our embrace was interrupted only by the sound of cheerful clapping. "Bravo! Bravo!" Scarlett shouted. She got up and kneeled in front of me. "Oh, Ally, you know I love you, and you know how much I enjoy tragic love stories. I feel just awful that you're a Lagga now, and I will do everything in my power to help you."

"I think I prefer *human*," I said, suddenly realizing how much it hurt to be called a Lagga.

"Of course, darling. You know I don't mean it like that; it's just habit and I adore you." She smiled as she hugged me.

I was so relieved by Scarlett's outpouring of generosity that I leaped off the couch mid-hug and practically tackled her, all the while giggling like a child. My life was starting to get back on track, and despite the fear of imminent death by beheading at any moment by Quinn or some other random Seeker assassin, I was surprisingly happy.

"What does Lagga mean?" Connor chimed in while Scarlett and I were mid-embrace.

Bill laughed. "It's what Imatis call humans, Connor."

Connor looked offended, as he should have. "So, what does it mean?" he asked.

"Technically, it comes from Old Scandinavian, but it's been around for a while. It's a way to say that humans are slow, backward, and struggling to keep up . . . it's their way of mocking you."

Connor looked at me as disappointment splashed across his face. "You don't think that, do you, Ally?"

"No!" I used the word all the time, yes, but it's just a word—or, I guess, it was until Scarlett used it on me.

Scarlett took over. "Connor, it's Imati slang, it means nothing. Besides, you're a Seeker, not a Lagga." Then she stood up. "Also, we don't have time for this little after-school special, so come now," she said. "We must get to Belfast before it's too late.",

"Belfast!" Connor, Bill, and I all said at the same time, leaving the lesson in name-calling for another day.

"You don't mean Maine . . . do you?" I asked.

"You know, I thought Ireland would have been your first guess, but yes, I actually do mean Maine. In America. How delightful, yes?"

Scarlett was, of course, completely unaware that we all lived in Belfast, that Quinn and Dawson, too, were in Belfast, and that pretty much all the danger we had been running from was in Belfast!

"What's wrong?" Scarlett asked. "You all look like you just saw a ghost . . . and not the nice kind."

"Scarlett," I began, "we just came from Belfast. That's where we live. People want to kill us there. Or they want to kill me, at least. Are you sure that is where Cornelius is?"

"I'm positive. And, might I add, what an extraordinary coincidence."

"Why is he in Belfast?" Bill said from the back of the room. I forgot he was even still listening, he had been so quiet.

"Wow, you people really don't know much about the contents of the Imati Book, considering you are risking life and limb for it." Scarlett seemed irritated that we were so ignorant of our own endeavor.

"Please . . . enlighten us," Connor said in a pompous, I-am-so-going-to-kill-you-later kind of way.

"Well, Mr. Seeker, you are correct that Lazarus has rituals which can create immortal life. But it also opens the Gate to the Immortal Realm, the realm in which the Sidhe and the Eternal Council reside. A realm that we mere Imati, stuck here, cannot enter."

"So the book *does* have a way to gain access to the Eternal Council without their consent?" Bill's voice was eager as he accidentally revealed his intentions. Connor, Scarlett, and I turned all at once to face him. He realized he had just shown his cards, and it seemed they spelled out revenge.

"I'm sorry," Scarlett inquired. "Who did you say you were again?"

"I didn't," Bill snarled back.

"He is a Souljumper," I said. Bill shot me a nasty look. "I'm sorry, Bill; she is going to help us, so we might as well be honest."

"Oh, my. A *Saturo* in our presence. I bow down to you, sir." Scarlett said sarcastically.

"Don't," Connor added. "He is still mortal . . . he is a *cursed Saturo*, or whatever you called him."

"How intriguing," Scarlett said in a whimsical fashion. "Have we met before, Souljumper?"

"I am afraid not," Bill said. "I would have remembered you."

"Charming," Scarlett replied. "Unfortunately, you could be lying, but we'll just leave it at that."

During the awkward exchange between Scarlett and Bill, I was still confused as to why everything was happening in Belfast. "Um, Scarlett, can you explain why we are going to Belfast, then?"

She glanced away from Bill, whom she had been studying intensely. "Oh, right, I forgot! The only Gate in North America is in Belfast. The ritual won't work anywhere else. The Imati discovered it centuries ago, but the book has been in hiding for quite some time, and only Cornelius has the knowledge and gumption to actually perform any of the ancient spells. He is quite extraordinary."

"He gave you that necklace, didn't he?" Connor asked her point-blank as he motioned to the sapphire jewel sitting around Scarlett's neck. She looked shocked at his astute observation. I wondered how he'd known that.

"Why yes, he did, Connor, thank you for noticing."

I had to admit, I was jealous; Scarlett, too, had an Imati pendant (and hers wasn't cracked), which made mine seem less powerful. Secondly, Cornelius wouldn't even acknowledge my presence in Paris, even when I tried to talk to him, yet he meets with Scarlett and gives her ancient charmed pendants. He obviously trusted her enough to respect her as a high-powered Imati. Maybe Connor and Bill were right to be scared of her.

Scarlett did not elaborate on how she knew Cornelius or why he gave her the necklace. She had a way of circumventing the truth and leading the converstion in the direction she wanted it to go. "Listen, team, like I said earlier, we should leave now because we don't have much time."

"Honestly, I'm not all that eager to get back to Belfast, Scarlett. I'm just a mortal now, and Connor's Seeker friends want to chop off my head . . . or simply shoot me, I guess."

"Sorry, Ally. Cornelius is trying to open the Gate. He wants to transcend from this world and join the Immortal Realm. He has lived too long in this earthly existence and hopes his time to depart has finally come. He is close to what he needs, and I fear that if we don't catch him in time, then your window to get the book and perform the ritual for immortality will have passed."

Bill jumped off his perch on the windowsill and grabbed the keys. "You heard the woman—let's go." Bill held the door while Connor and I walked past.

"I'll grab some apples for the car ride," Scarlett said as we were leaving.

"Seriously?" Connor said, annoyed. "What's with you two and all the apples?"

"What do you mean?" Scarlett asked innocently as she came back from the kitchen with a fresh bag of delicious, green apples.

"Yeah, what do you mean?" I added.

"Is this a weird Imati thing? I thought you guys didn't really need to eat." Connor looked irritated.

"Well, I technically need to eat *now*," I said as felt my stomach growl. I forgot how irritating it was to be hungry, and an apple sounded wonderful at the moment.

"Isn't it obvious?" Bill started. "The apple is temptation; it is the pure metaphysical representation of Imati life. They can't help but love them." Bill laughed as he spoke.

"Excuse me?" Scarlett said, offended. "Was that an insult, *Saturo*?"

"No," Bill rebutted, "but think about it: the original immortals used apples to escape their world, to live here on earth. It's practically in your DNA."

"Bill," I began, "the apple as a biblical metaphor for temptation is just that: a metaphor. It can't possibly manifest itself into our wants and desires," I said, half wondering if it actually could.

"Ally, all stories come from somewhere. Myths, legends, religion—they all started out as moments of truth. For all we know, you love apples because they are more than just a metaphor."

We continued to walk to my car, and I caught up with Connor. "Don't listen to Bill; he makes apples sound evil. Honest, I just like the way they taste."

Connor looked at me dubiously. "I believe you," he said, "but I also believe Bill. You may like them for reasons you don't even know . . . a subconscious love for—"

"For temptation?" I said as I looked up at him.

"Or knowledge," he said as he put his arm around me. "Or a slightly sweet and crunchy fruit." I smiled at his joke and realized that behind me, Scarlett and Bill had also dropped the apple talk. Scarlett was now busy interrogating him for answers.

"I'm curious, Bill, how did you all know to look for Cornelius?" she asked slyly.

"From a letter we procured from an old Imati who was recently killed. It was addressed to Cornelius." Bill was a quick liar.

"Ohhh," Scarlett said, with an air of intrigue. "A letter, you say? Hmm . . ." They walked across the street behind me and Connor.

As we all piled in the car, Scarlett addressed us as a group. "You know, I once possessed a letter to Cornelius regarding the Book. A friend of mine hid it in a Spanish church," she began. Then she sighed, as if remembering her dark past, and stopped herself from saying more. "Oh, never mind," she said. "It's a boring story."

Scarlett – New Orleans, Louisiana – Eight Months Ago

THE STREETS BUSTLED with partygoers, music blasted from every corner, and beads rained from the sky. The hubbub of Mardi Gras was in full swing. Scarlett was in her element, surrounded by people whose sole purpose was to experience all of life's vices in a single week. She had seen many of these festivals before in Brazil and Germany. In the time just before Lent, the world let loose and the party dresses came out.

Scarlett smiled. She was a little surprised that Cornelius had picked February of all times to meet her in New Orleans; he was a reserved fellow, not much for talking, and had more or less checked out of this world. Scarlett had not seen him in many years and was anxious for their reunion. He had taught her so much in their brief time in South America together, and if she had not been brutally kidnapped by the Seekers and sent back to dreaded Europe at the turn of the century she knew she would have gotten more out of it. She was certain, however, that Cornelius would later find her in Madrid, and he had. She owed him her life.

The fiery femme continued to walk through the colorful streets like a blaze of fire, warming everything she came in contact with. Passersby, in the midst of inebriation, still found a moment to admire her force and her beauty. Scarlett brushed past them, now oblivious to her own effect on her admirers, for by now it was a common experience. She arrived at a small Creole café, down a narrow side street, where she was to meet him.

Scarlett's blue satin heels clicked on the cobblestones beneath. A tiny bell chimed when she opened the café door. Sitting at a small table in the back corner of the restaurant, Cornelius stirred a cup of apple tea. He glanced up when she arrived. He did not stand to greet her, but he motioned for her to sit down.

"Scarlett, good to see you found the place," he said in a very cordial tone.

"It wasn't hard; I have passed by this street hundreds of times. I've never come into this establishment, but it's quite delightful." Scarlett waved the waitress over as she spoke, and without missing a beat, she said, "Apple tea with sugar, please." She looked back to Cornelius. "You look well, friend. You haven't aged a bit!" she said with a rambunctious laugh.

Cornelius did not smile. "You know I don't find you humorous, and yet you continue to jest. If this were Tudor England, I could just have you killed," he replied, completely serious.

"Oh, come now, Cornelius, stop being so boorish. You know you love visiting me, or else you wouldn't do it so much." She sipped her tea with complete confidence in her statement. His mouth didn't move, but his eyes smiled, and that was enough for Scarlett.

"Listen, Red," Cornelius began. He always called her Red when he felt at ease. When Cornelius first met Scarlett in Chile she had been wearing a red dress, with red-stained lips, and her hair was pinned up with a red ruby broach. The nickname was a bit obvious, but was a sentiment that Cornelius did not hand out to just anyone, and Scarlett thoroughly enjoyed it. He continued to speak in a matter-of-fact manner, "I have something for you." Cornelius handed her a small piece of paper with an address on it. "There is a hotel there, and in that room there is a package taped under the bed. Inside is a necklace. I want you to have it."

"What's it for?" she inquired, knowing all too well that Cornelius did not haphazardly hand out gifts, and the ones he did give were not usually simple trinkets.

"It's a sapphire Imati amulet. It has been charmed for protection. If you wear it, no Seeker can read you, no spell can harm you, and no curse can plague you. Not even a Sidhe can track you. It blocks out your energy and provides a mystical shield of sorts." Cornelius carried a nonchalant air as he spoke of what Scarlett believed to be a very powerful weapon. Taking into account Cornelius's disposition, she held back her excitement over her new possession.

"Thank you very much for thinking of me with such a treasure," she politely replied.

"It's for selfish reasons, Red. I need you to keep it safe. Also . . ." He hesitated. "There is more. I need you to do me a favor in return for the gift."

"Anything," Scarlett replied, and she meant it. She would sacrifice her own life for Cornelius, or at least give it her best effort.

"I need you to locate the Book of Lazarus for me."

As always, Cornelius was very direct in his request, and his face was stern as he awaited her response. The room was suddenly quiet, and Scarlett could swear she felt a wind blow through the restaurant. She knew what the book was, and she knew that the time had come for Cornelius to begin his departure from the Mortal Realm. He had spoken of his plans many times in the past few years, but Scarlett had always assumed that he had the book with him and that he was simply biding his time until he could find the Gate. It dawned on her that Cornelius, for all his planning and calculations, was missing a very important piece of the puzzle.

"You don't have it?" she asked, surprised. "I have seen you studying with the scroll. Cornelius, what happened?"

"Lazarus is missing. It always has been. I was hoping I could locate it over the years, but nothing panned out. Time is of the essence, and now I am desperate to leave. I seek your assistance in locating it."

"Why me?" Scarlett asked.

"For one, you are the only one I trust. Secondly, I have reason to believe that a friend of yours may be in possession of the Book, and I need you to locate her."

Scarlett looked confused. She racked her brain for who Cornelius might be speaking of, but nothing came to mind.

"Her name is Alastrina Byrne."

Scarlett laughed so hard her knees knocked into the table beneath her, causing it to rattle. "Ally . . . with the Book! Oh, my!" Scarlett took a breath. "This is highly unlikely, darling. She is barely an Imati, trust me. Besides, I haven't seen her for over a century."

Cornelius took Scarlett's hand from across the table. "Scarlett, this is very important to me. I have looked everywhere for it. Everywhere. Then, I remembered my time in Paris many years ago; I was taking refuge with a Guide friend of mine, a powerful Sidhe named Tegan. His newest Imati was a girl—your friend, Alastrina. I didn't pay attention to her. She was very young, and I could care less for her survival. She seemed more like a human pest than an immortal. Tegan, however, took quite the liking to her and stayed with her for several years, well beyond his call of duty. Before I left, I asked him why he would care so much about her. He told me that he could not find her for over a decade, that she simply wandered around undetected by anyone. He was bothered by it because it is completely impossible for a newborn immortal to yield such power as to hide from a Sidhe Guide."

Scarlett was intrigued by Cornelius's story. She had never imagined that her beloved Ally would be so integral to the Imati world or could possibly harness such power.

"I'm shocked, Cornelius . . . and confused. What is she?"

Cornelius continued his story. "She is not anything. At the time, since I didn't think much of her, I barely listened to Tegan's intrigue of her. I dismissed his words as quickly as I had dismissed her. It did not dawn on me until recently that the only way a newborn Imati could have done what she did . . . is if it had an amulet."

Scarlett continued to ask questions, excited about the idea of reuniting with Ally. She never knew what happened to her. She came back one day and Ally was simply gone. All she had left was a good-bye note that barely said anything at all. Scarlett was glad to know that she was still alive. "What does that mean, Cornelius? How did *she* get the amulet?"

"It means she's royalty, and if she has a necklace, she probably has the missing book. The necklace works as a key to the chest which at one time held the two together, as well as a protection shield. Ergo, whoever gave it to her had access to the Book. You're the only one who spent a significant amount of time with her, so I need you to find her."

"And do what, exactly? Take the Book?" Scarlett asked, slightly frightened that Cornelius was asking for more of an assassination than a robbery.

"Do whatever you have to, Scarlett. Everything is ready, but without that Book, I can't open the Gate. I am sorry to ask this of you, but I know that of all people, you can do it."

Scarlett's stomach knotted up. If it came to it, could she kill Ally for Cornelius? She knew she couldn't say no.

"Of course I'll do it . . . anything for you, darling," she said with a confident smile. "Where shall I meet you once I have it?"

"Unfortunately, I can't say . . . when the time is right, I'll let you know where I am."

Cornelius still distrusted her, despite the fact that he was putting his fate into Scarlett's hands. Inside, Scarlett was nervous, and the knots in her stomach kept paining her. She felt a sadness and a guilt that she had been able to suppress for almost her entire immortal life. The bright light that was her essence was being suffocated by Cornelius' request. She truly loved and missed Ally, and the relief at hearing of her survival was quickly replaced by the fear of imagining her demise.

Scarlett, ever the charmer, could not and did not let any of this show. She held it in, packaged it down, and wrapped it ever so tightly with a red little bow, never to think of these feelings again. She looked at Cornelius, smiled, and said, "Well, then. I sure do feel like some apple pie. Let's order, shall we?"

Belfast, Maine – October – Present Day

Death's Door

THE RIDE BACK to Belfast was laden with tension. Scarlett rambled on about trivial subjects, crunched on an apple, and seemed not to notice everyone else's somber mood. I was lost in thought as I drove. The road was winding in front of me, and the night sky blanketed the highway. The blackness of the road created a trance-like state, in which I existed for a large portion of the drive. Completely tuning out Scarlett's stories, Bill's complaints, and Connor's scowls toward the company in the back seat, I lost myself to feelings of fear and isolation.

I was wracked with guilt because the book, which I hid in my upstairs bedroom, was probably—definitely—the same book that everyone was looking for. They would all think I was lying to them and that I had something to hide (which I did). I hadn't meant to keep it a secret, there just never seemed a good moment to say, *By the way, I have the book, please don't kill me.* The truth was that I was scared. A few days ago I didn't know whom I could trust; besides Connor, I was not convinced that the two characters in the back of the car were entirely on my side or looking out for my best interests. Every half hour or so, Connor would notice my dazing off and reach over to touch my hand on the steering wheel. While his touch was comforting, it made me feel even guiltier about the secret I held. I decided that as soon as we got back to Belfast I would go home, get the Book, and bring it back to Bill's house. I hoped they wouldn't all hate me.

Once we arrived, Bill shot out of the car like it was about to explode. I could tell he wanted to get as far away from Scarlett as possible. Unfortunately, he was stuck with her, as we needed her to find Cornelius.

I waited until everyone was at the front door before I made my move.

"Hey, everyone" I began. "I'm going to run home real quick and grab some clothes. I'll be back in twenty minutes." They all turned to look at me, and distrust permeated through their eyes.

"You're leaving?" Scarlett asked, as she cocked her head to the side.

"Just for a bit," I assured her. "I'll be back, I promise." Connor ran up to me, panicked.

"Ally, you can't go anywhere by yourself. You're too vulnerable." He grabbed my shoulders and leaned over me as if I were a child.

"Connor, I think I can manage driving the few miles to my house and coming back on my own. I've survived for over two centuries." I pushed past him to my car.

"You survived as an Imati, not as human. It's different now." His face was full of concern, but it still felt irritating.

"May I remind you that I *was* human, and eighteenth-century Ireland was a lot worse than this."

He held his tongue to that statement. It was like he was forgetting I was older than him and I could take care of myself. I could see his jaw clenching. He clearly wanted to protest, but he knew I would do what I wanted to and this was only wasting time.

"Fine, go," he said. "But be careful."

I got in my car and drove away. Five minutes later, I was at my house on Bayview Drive, looking over the Atlantic. The bay of water was relatively calm tonight. The eerie black surface floated like satin and for the first time the vastness of the ocean made me a little uncomfortable. Usually, the dark water and immeasurable depths made me think of endless opportunities reaching out over the horizon, but now it just made me feel insignificant. Fatalistic images entered my mind, and I thought about falling off the rocks and landing in the water. The waves would crush me and take the air from my lungs until I could no longer breathe, and I would cease to exist. All it would take to kill me now was a few moments without oxygen. The ocean, which was once my comforting companion, was now my enemy. Everything was now, because, as a human, everything could kill me. These thoughts, with the realization that I had opted out of protection from Connor, made me nervous to enter my own home. I decided I would be quick about it, like a burglar, and no one would know I was there. Through the door, up the stairs, to the bedroom and back out . . . easy as pie.

I opened the front door and all the lights were off. I thought it would be better to keep them that way, just in case someone was inside waiting for me.

The flash of all the lights coming on would obviously give me away. I climbed up my wooden staircase and it creaked with every step I took. *Not so stealthy*, I thought to myself. At that point, I wished I had a dog to greet me and tell me everything was okay in the house and that there were no monsters hiding in any closets. Cat was no good at sounding the alarm, mainly because he spent most of his time sleeping.

I clumsily found the door to my bedroom; I walked in and turned on the light. Empty and safe. I felt relieved. I went to my bedside nightstand, where I kept the book under all my socks and journals. I never stashed it in one of my PO boxes or safes because it was almost all I had from my real life, and I needed it close to me. I laughed a little on the inside as soon as I saw it piled under a bunch of nothing. It's funny how something can be hidden so long simply because no one ever thought to look there.

As soon as I grabbed it I turned to leave, but just as I was about the reach the door, a body jumped out at me and pinned me to the floor. It happened so fast that I only barely felt the pain as my body smashed against the hardwood. I screamed, but the sound was muffled by the figure's glove-covered hand. The size, strength, and stature told me the figure was a man. I struggled beneath him, wriggling like a worm, but it made no difference; he barely had to move to keep me pinned. I was completely helpless. Ordinarily, by this time I would have thrown him off of me, and quite possibly through the glass window. However, the new me, the seventeen-year-old girl version, could do nothing. I was already fatigued, and my puny strength was no match against his. Despite the fear rolling inside of me, I stopped struggling.

"Wow, this one is not very strong, Quinn. She's already giving up," a male voice said from on top of me.

"Bring her up so she can talk," his counterpart replied. Even without the name reference I could tell from the sound of his voice that it was Connor's so-called dad. The man on my back lifted me up so that I was standing and held my hands behind my back. I was out of breath and could barely speak. Quinn went first.

"Ally, so good to see you again," he began in a calm and sophisticated manner. I wished I had my strength so I could punch him in the face.

"You know, a funny thing happened: a little bird told me that you were an Imati. What do you say to this?"

In my shortness of breath I didn't say anything, but rather mustered the courage to spit across the room at him instead. It fell short of hitting him, but I think he got the message. I might have lost my strength, but I certainly hadn't lost any gumption. Hatred was seething from inside me, and Quinn clearly felt the same way. He stared at me with anger; he was a man who did not care to be insulted, especially by a girl. He walked up to me and slapped me across the face.

Holy crap, it burns! was my first and only thought. I could tell he had held back, but even with half his strength his slap made my cheek sting, and I could feel it begin to swell. Then he reached up and grabbed me by the chin. "Listen to me, you little Imati. I know your secret, I know that right now you are just a weak little mortal, but in this world, that doesn't just happen. You have power you're hiding from me, and I hate being lied to, so give me what you took from your nightstand and we can put this all behind us."

I was officially scared. So scared I could feel my body begin to tremble from within. His hand was forcing me to look him in the eye, and I knew he was serious. I also knew that whether or not I gave him the Book, he was going to kill me. I knew that the last person on this earth I would see would be Quinn, and that made me mad. I was out of options, out of super powers, and almost out of time.

I pointed over my shoulder with my head and my eyes, since his friend was still holding my arms, to motion toward the Book. I had no other choice but to give him what he wanted, bank on the fact that he couldn't read the contents, and hope for the best.

"Over there, the little book," I said, desperately trying to hide the fear in my voice. Quinn walked over to pick up the small book, which had fallen out of my hands when I was attacked. He tried to open it, but the covers wouldn't budge. From my view, it suddenly looked like it was made of stone.

Quinn became angry. "This! This is what you give me? A book that won't open!" He paced back and forth in front of me and then shoved the book into my chest. The solid nature of it hurt when it hit the bone of my sternum.

"Dawson, let her go." Dawson—I now knew his name—let go of my wrists. They felt bruised and strained. Then Quinn continued, "Ally, open this book . . . or I'll kill you. Slowly."

I was nervous and took his threat very seriously, especially since he'd added the "slowly" part. That was just mean. What he didn't know is that I was actually as confused as he was; I had never seen the book do that before. As soon as I grabbed it from Quinn as he held it against me, it was paper and leather again. It opened immediately. I stuttered as I began to speak. "Um . . . I think it might be charmed."

Quinn glared back at me. "Oh, really—you think?" he said sarcastically. He was not amused by the Book's defense mechanism. I was baffled; no one had mentioned this to me before or even spoken about the book being unable to open. *Am I the only one who can see inside it?*

I opened the book as Quinn looked at its contents over my shoulder. "Stop," he demanded, and made me pause on page one. "What does Lazarus mean?" He asked.

"I don't know." I said and quickly flipped the page to avoid discussing it further.

"What is all this, what does it say?" Quinn asked, obviously confused by the coded language of the book.

I looked up at him, scared to respond. "I don't know, I can't read it."

I could tell he didn't believe me. Why would he? In one swift move, his hand was around my throat and he had pinned me up against the wall. My feet were slowly coming up from the ground as he raised me higher and higher. I flashed back to when I had done the same thing to Amelia. Now I understood why her arms had flailed about helplessly and why her eyes had watered in desperation. I was exhibiting the same actions. I struggled, I threw my arms about, I kicked . . . I did everything my body would allow me to do, but it was no match for his strength. Internally, I began to panic. I was unable to breathe, and I could feel the life literally being drained from me. Karma was playing a cruel joke.

"Ally, remember what I said about lying. I *hate* liars. Tell me what is in this book!"

I tried to speak but I couldn't. His hand was wrapped so tightly around my throat that it felt like my head was going to pop off. My eyelids felt heavy as they drooped further down and the room began to spin. The images in front of me, which were once bright with light, were now blurry and dark. I blacked out.

When I came to, I was on the ground with Quinn standing over me. Oxygen rushed back into my brain and I could see again.

I heard him speak. "Sorry, doll, I forget you're human now. That was a close call . . . can't have you dying on us before we know how to read this Book." He kicked me a little, like I was a dead dog, as he spoke. "Wake up now," he added.

I choked on the air rushing into my lungs and coughed out, "I can't read it. I wish I could."

Quinn was about to kick me harder when I put my hand up. "Wait," I said. Guilt began to build in my stomach because I knew I shouldn't divulge any more information to him, but I was in so much pain I had no choice. "It's written in code. You need the scroll to translate it. But I don't have it."

Quinn took a breath and pondered whether I was telling the truth. "Fine," he said. "Say I do believe you, even though you are an Imati and prone to lying. Tell me what exactly is in the book."

I hesitated. I decided that half-truths were good enough. "Rituals . . . ancient Imati power. They can grant immortality to mortals and do charm spells . . . like the one on the book itself." I felt that Quinn didn't need to know about the Gate to the Immortal Realm. Who knows what he was planning?

"So the only obstacle left, then, is finding the scroll," he said to himself, half under his breath. "Dawson, tie her up; she is coming with us."

Dawson reached for my hands again, but in a rush of adrenaline I quickly rolled away from him. Under my bed I kept a dagger (always be prepared), and I reached for it once I got to that side of the room. I stood up, knife in hand.

"I'm not going anywhere with you. I told you what you wanted to know. Now, either you will let me go or kill me. Either way, you'll never read that book—you can't even open it."

I was shocked at my own courage. I was still acting like an Imati, which was problematic, since I was human. The situation in front of me seemed dire, but I no longer cared. Quinn and Dawson would surely kill me sooner or later, so I might as well die fighting. My mother would surely be proud.

"Alastrina, do you really think you can get past us with a sad dagger?" He obviously thought I looked ridiculous.

I did not hesitate in my response. "No, but if I can stab you just one time and make you bleed even a little, it's enough for me."

Quinn and Dawson laughed at me. "Well, dear, you have given us an ultimatum. It looks like we have no choice but to kill you."

Then, in a samurai-like move, Dawson drew his Seeker sword and held it out for me to see. The blade glistened under the lamplight, and I swear I could see my own fearful reflection. Unexpectedly, Quinn placed his hand in front of it to stop him from moving forward. "Dawson, please—we don't need a Seeker sword to kill a small girl. We can use our hands."

I stood my ground as Quinn approached me. The closer he got, the more I wanted to kill him. I lunged at him with my dagger, and to his surprise (and mine), I sliced his arm.

"You bitch!" he said. Then he grabbed my arm and forced the dagger from my hand. It fell to the floor with a thud. It appeared that the moment had come for my life to end. I continued to fight him, the urge to survive taking over. I elbowed him in the stomach, kicked, and screamed, but he merely lifted me and threw me back onto the bed. The force was so great that I rolled off and hit the floor beneath me. *Ouch.* Pain was not a pleasant human experience. Quinn walked over, picked me up, and threw me across the room. I hit the wall, and it cracked from the force of my body. Once again I fell to the floor like a piece of lead in water. I felt my necklace chain break and slide to the floor beneath me. My back and ribs throbbed from the blow. Quinn walked across the room, and just as he was about to grab me again, someone threw my bedroom door open and pushed him back.

Connor, making a well-timed entrance, rushed over to me. He touched the warm, red blood, which trickled down my face. He brushed my hair away, which was stuck to my cheeks from blood and sweat. My face was still swollen from Quinn's slap earlier.

"Ally," he whispered, "now that you are mortal, you have to try not to bleed so much." I laughed at his joke, and it made my side hurt.

Connor got up quickly, remembering his surroundings. He drew his sword.

"Quinn, back off," he said sternly.

Quinn looked betrayed. "Connor, she is a corrupt Imati with information that *we* need. She brought this on herself. We weren't actually going to kill her."

"Oh, really. That's why she is bleeding to death on the floor, beaten to a pulp." Connor was fierce when he was mad.

"Enough of this," Dawson yelled. "We don't have to explain ourselves. She has information that is valuable to the Brotherhood, and we have the right to do anything within our power to get it." I could hear Dawson's boots move as he marched toward me.

"Dawson, stay back," Connor warned.

"I don't listen to you, boy. Remember your place." He continued to approach.

Connor, sword already drawn, made a sudden, swift move from right to left. From the floor I could see the shadow stretch across the room, and I could hear the blade slice through the air. I knew the exact moment when it hit Dawson's neck and cut through his bone, because it made a cracking sound. As soon as I looked in front of me, I could see Dawson's head eye-level with my own as it hit the ground. Battle lines were now drawn in blood, and Dawson was dead.

Quinn jumped to his feet. "Connor!" he yelled, shocked by the events of the moment. "How could you do that?"

"He was going to kill her, Quinn, and I will do anything to keep her alive." As terrible as it was to see a person decapitated, Connor's words and actions were comforting.

Quinn stood there frozen. "He was your Brother," he said, and his tone showed his disappointment in Connor's kill. "Gregory Dawson was a powerful member of Lux et Veritas, Connor, and you have now unleashed a wave of fury you do not want to meet." His disappointment quickly turned to anger and threats. "They will come for you."

Connor put his sword down to his side, removed a small ring from his left hand, and threw it forcefully to the ground. "Let them come." The ring made a pinging noise as the metal hit the floor, and it disappeared from sight.

He said it with such strength and determination that Quinn had to realize he'd officially lost Connor. Looking for an escape, he opened my bedroom window, trying to determine if he could make the jump. When he was half out, he looked back in, and his eyes met Connor's before he gave his final warning: "I hope you know who you are risking your life for, Connor. This is not over." Then, with a single leap, he was gone.

Connor knelt down to help me up. In my delirium, my first thought was to find the book.

"Connor, over there, the little leather book." I pointed with my arm for him to get it.

He brought it back and handed it to me. "It's made of stone, Ally. What is it?"

As soon as I touched it, it turned back to paper. "It's not," I said. "It's just charmed." Connor's shock was written all over his face. He was amazed by the transformation of the book in front of his eyes and confused as to why I, of all people, had it.

"Is that it?" he asked. "Is that what everyone is looking for?"

I nodded yes, as it was still difficult to speak and pure guilt was making it hard to use words. Connor's mood quickly changed from relief to betrayal. "Ally, you lied to me. You lied to everyone. You had the book this entire time." I could tell he was disappointed by my actions.

I tried to explain myself. "No, Connor," I began, but I could barely get the words out because I was in so much pain. "I didn't know—when to tell you—I was coming here to get it and bring it back." My words were interrupted every few seconds by heavy gasps for air.

Connor was silent, but the silence was loud. He picked me up and carried me out the door to my car. We stood there in my driveway, a newly built wall between us. Apparently, he felt like he could no longer trust me. After every-thing we had gone through, we were once again back at square one. My knees wobbled, and I had to lean on my car for support, my body still recovering from battle. The man who had saved me was no longer feeling chivalrous enough to hold me up.

"Connor," I began, "I swear I was going to tell you. I wanted to wait until we were alone, because I didn't know who else I could trust."

He was still angry. "Yeah, Ally, that is really convenient to say *now*, isn't it . . . now that you have been caught red-handed."

His arms were moving as he spoke, and the volume of his voice increased the more momentum he gained. "Jeez, Ally, I just risked my life for you. I just decapitated my childhood teacher for you. Sure, he was an ass, but he was part of my Brotherhood, part of my society. I just gave up everything for you—including Quinn, who was like a father for me. And what have you done? You lied to me . . . again. How am I supposed to trust you?" His anger and frustration was causing him to pace in front of me, kicking the gravel of my driveway as he moved.

"I'm sorry! What can I say? I told you the truth, and if you can't believe me I don't know what else to do!"

This moment felt like déjà-vu. Connor and I had already had this argument, and it was quickly becoming a theme in our relationship. Maybe our worlds were so different that we would never be able to blend them together. His people did kill my family, after all.

He stared at me intensely for a second and then shook his head. "I don't know. I don't know what to do anymore." Then he took a few steps backward and started to walk away.

I screamed after him, "You're leaving again? That's how you solve everything—you just leave. Don't be such a coward!" My stomach and my ribs stabbed me with pain as I spoke. My entire body was swelling and I couldn't feel my left eye. This was not the time to be having an argument with Connor. Emotional and physical pain should never be in the same room at the same time.

"I'm not leaving, Ally. I just need time to cool off and think, okay? I'll meet you at Bill's house."

"How are you getting there?" I asked.

"I'll walk. I like walking alone . . . I learned that from you, remember?" he said.

Salt in the wound. He turned and slowly disappeared down the road out of sight. I got in my car, sat still for a second, and just held the book in between my hands. For two centuries it had been with me and never caused any problems. Now, it was costing me my life and my happiness. I suddenly hated the book. I wanted to rip it up and destroy it. I frantically opened it and began to rip the pages, but they wouldn't move. The harder I tried the sturdier they became, until in a split second they turned to stone.

"Stupid charmed defense mechanism!" I screamed out loud as I threw the book to the passenger's side seat. It hit the window and made a small crack. I let out all my anger and frustration by banging on the steering wheel, accidentally hitting the horn a few times, which let out a blaring honking noise. After a few minutes, and total exhaustion from crying and screaming, I took a deep breath and told myself to gain control. I would drive back to Bill's, give up the book, make up with Connor, and make everything right. My wounds would heal and everything would be okay.

Ophelia Winfield – Paris, France – Eighteen Months Ago

OPHELIA ARRIVED IN Paris at the Gare du Nord, unsure of why she was there. Originally, their plan had been to destroy the secret sect of the Brotherhood, Lux et Veritas, for what they had done to her father. She had hoped her own brother would come back to them, but he was far too indoctrinated in the Seeker ways for that to happen. Her mother had warned her of that, but she'd been too naïve and optimistic to listen. Now, she was in Paris, awaiting news from her mother about something she knew nothing about. This was a new twist in the plan, and part of her was scared of what she would find.

Ophelia's mother had told her to meet her in the neighborhood of the 10th arrondissement near the Canal Saint-Martin. It was evening when she arrived, and the spring Parisian air warmed her fears. The canal was lined with bohemian youth drinking wine, eating, and laughing jubilantly as only a young person can. The entire canal was lit from the twinkling yellow café lights surrounding the area. Ophelia grazed through the crowd looking for her mother. She spotted her on a bridge in the center, leaning against a rail, gazing north toward the night sky.

"*Bonjour, Mama,*" Ophelia said with her impeccable French accent.

"Hello, darling. I've missed you greatly!" Her mother embraced her whole-heartedly, for their love was strong.

"What are we doing here?" Ophelia asked.

"Well, my dear, we are drinking wine and gorging on delicious French cheese, the kind we can never get in dreary London." Her mother revealed a bottle of French wine and a large bag filled with baguettes and *fromage*.

"Where did that come from?" Ophelia laughed, knowing her mother had simply conjured it up in that moment.

"Magic, darling . . . it makes the world go 'round." Her mother was in good spirits today. In fact, she was in a better mood than Ophelia had seen her since her father was killed.

They found a seat on the side of the canal and opened the wine with a corkscrew, so as not to draw any more attention to themselves. As Ophelia ate, her mother began to speak. "I have something to show you, and it is very good news." She pulled out a piece of paper that had been photocopied. "Obviously, this is not the original," she said as she handed Ophelia the sheet.

Ophelia began to read the words, but was not entirely sure of their meaning; it looked to her more like a poem.

Only the past these eyes can see; a warrior lost in bravery
His destiny a path, laid with light,
shines to a girl who never sees night.
Her blood comes forth both silver and red;
its river reaching the Gate to the Dead

She straddles the worlds both mortal and not
She can open the portal, but her life will be lost
In her death lies her fortune, but let it be shown
Be warned of the Gate, for this realm is unknown

Unleashing a smoke, an air of fire and bite
All Magics be damned, their power gone white
When the seal is broken, spare the rod
For the Gate only closes by the hand of a—

Ophelia stopped reading and turned the page over as she noticed its unconcluded end. "Where is the rest of the poem?" she asked.

Her mother grabbed it back. "It's not a *poem*, Ophelia—it is a prophecy. Well, it's a fifteenth-century scribe's translation of a prophecy. The end on the original has been torn off, and it's still lost."

"Prophecy of what?" Ophelia said, still confused.

"To open the Gate to Lost Souls, silly. With this, I will be able to find your father and bring him back." Her mother folded the paper and returned it carefully to her sack.

"How can you be so sure it will take you to the Realm of Lost Souls? It speaks of fire and bite, not—"

Her mother cut her off. "Because it mentions the Gate to the *dead*, and that's where your father is, I know it. It's the same thing; it has to be."

Ever since the Seekers had brutally killed Ophelia's father Dannon when she was little, her mother's life goal had been to destroy Lux et Veritas and every Seeker she could find. As a Sorceress, she had the power to do this. However, if she wrongfully murdered mortals, her magic would be stripped from her, so she always had to be careful of the ways in which she used it.

A few years ago, she had discovered Blue Magic: not quite evil like the black arts, but not quite in balance with the universe, either. It was a loophole she was using to her advantage, and one she had passed down to Ophelia. Through Blue Magic she began to discover the other realms, the worlds of immortals, and how many layers of the universe there really were. It became her mission to once again find Dannon and bring him back from the Realm of Lost Souls, where she was certain he had gone. Once she brought him back, she would take on the Brotherhood and retake Connor from their indoctrinated grasp.

"How are we to find the girl?" Ophelia inquired. "Or do you already know who it is through Magic?"

"Not through Magic, darling, we will find her through Connor." Ophelia's expression told her mother to elaborate on that statement.

"Connor is a great warrior; he is the son of a Seeker and a Sorceress. There are none like him. He will show us this young girl without even realizing it."

"How can you be so sure?"

"Because, Ophelia, he and Quinn are moving to America: Maine, to be exact. They are on to something big—why else would they be going? Secondly, I read the stars to be sure, and they tell me that a great power is aligning there. I can only assume that when Connor gets to Maine he will run into this power and, luckily for us, it will change the scope of everything."

Ophelia, knowing her mother, knew she was never wrong when it came to reading the stars. If she said a great power was aligning, then it was. After all these years of looking for other realms, their hard work was paying off, and they had finally found the key they had always needed. Unfortunately, it meant that some girl she had never met would have to die. As bad as she felt about that, she wanted more than anything to have her father back and avenge his brutal murder. She felt in her heart that if her mother was successful, Connor would surely come back to them and join them as a family, rejoicing in their conquest and thanking them for saving his life.

Belfast, Maine – October – Present Day

Off The Beaten Path

AS I DROVE back to Bill's house, the road was blurry from the tears that were still falling as a result of my most recent fight with Connor. I knew that I was in the wrong—I should have trusted him with the book—but part of me was still confused. It was only recently that I'd become mortal again, for reasons unbeknownst to me, and I was not quite sure about the new direction my life was headed. Suddenly, the knowledge of this book and the prospect of eternal life and ancient Imati rituals had everyone suckling at the tit of power. Was all of this worth losing my life over? Now that my existence finally had an expiration date, I felt more fragile than ever, and I wasn't sure who truly wanted to protect me. Looking back at Connor's actions against Quinn and his violent killing of Dawson, another member of the Brotherhood, I realized that he could be trusted. Unfortunately, it was too late, and he felt betrayed by me, of all people.

I continued to drive through the mist-soaked air. The fog had continued to grow thicker the more I drove, and now I could barely see ten feet in front of my car. I slowed down to make sure I didn't hit a deer or something when suddenly, a figure appeared in front of me.

My headlights beamed straight ahead and lit up a figure draped in white cloth. I swerved my car to the right, but I couldn't see anything. The mist was heavier now, and I continued to hold the steering wheel as it gyrated beneath my hands, shaking back and forth. I realized I was no longer on the road, but travelling upon rocky ground as the car shook beneath me. It continued to propel itself forward until it ran into something with a thud. My neck thrashed forward. The crash deployed the driver's airbag, and pine needles fell onto my windshield, covering it with dirt and branches. I could see smoke elevate from my crashed hood as it traveled upward, climbing its way out of the fog. The airbag hit my chest and face, which felt more like being punched than having my life saved from wreckage. After a few seconds, I regained my composure and realized I had just been in a car accident. I remembered the flash of a figure in white and wondered what or who had run me off of the road.

I climbed out of the car, making sure to grab the book, and measured the damage; I could barely see anything except for my smashed headlights against a pine tree. I must have driven straight off the road into the outlying forest. I checked my cell service . . . nothing. With no idea where I was and no means of communication, I concluded that I was in a sticky situation, to say the least. I checked my jeans pocket for my necklace with its broken chain, which I had shoved inside; it was thankfully still there. My body was still intact and the only blood on me was dried, a departing gift from Quinn when he tried to beat me to death. There was some broken glass layered throughout my hair from the smashed window, but none of it cut-worthy. I walked in the direction the car had skidded from, but the more I journeyed, the darker it became.

Something was off; the forest around me felt—alive. Rather than the trees thinning out as I got closer to the road, they became thicker and thicker. The forest cover enveloped my surroundings and a morsel of fear camped out in my stomach.

From behind me, I heard a voice. "Hello there," it said in a calming, motherly tone. I turned around and came face to face with the white figure—only it wasn't just a figure, it was a woman with lustrous, dark, curly hair, which stretched down to her lower back. She floated toward me like an angel, illuminated only by her own regality. She stopped a few feet in front of me.

"Who are you?" I asked, knowing full well that this woman had not only run me off the road, but had followed me into the woods. If I was paranoid about trusting people before, I sure as heck did not trust her. Goose bumps rose from my forearms and practically screamed *danger*.

"I am Carinthia. What is your name?" Her voice was like a song, perfectly pitched and soothing to the soul.

"I don't have a name," I replied coyly. I began to back away, debating whether or not I should just run. *But where to? And how?* I felt like a bear cub, trapped by the evil hunter, and lost from my family and protection.

She kept her response lighthearted. "Oh, come now, I don't believe that." She laughed as she spoke. "Everyone has a name, and I am sure yours is extraordinary." She inched forward the more I stepped back. My steps made the forest floor crunch beneath me as I moved. "Don't be scared," she said as she realized I was about to run, "and don't try and scamper away. It only means I will have to chase you, and I think we both know you won't be fast enough with your mere mortal legs."

Her use of the word *mortal* made the hair stand up on the back of my neck. She obviously knew who I was.

"What do you want?" I said angrily, completely fed up with people trying to kill me. I raised the tone of my voice and began to scream. "Is this it?" I pulled out the book to show her. "Is this what you want?" I threw it at her chest, where it simply hit with a thud and fell to the forest floor. "Take it! I don't care, I don't even want it!" I was in hysterics. My body ached, still bruised from Quinn and Dawson's beating and now even stiffer from the accident. I was a little surprised I was holding up as well as I was. My emotions and adrenaline were carrying me, but I felt that the moment I sat down, all my organs would fill with blood and my heart would finally give out. I had to have been critically injured, and the woman in white could probably tell I was weak. She glanced at the book I had just thrown at her and simply stepped over it, barely giving it a second look.

"Little girl, I don't want the book. I am beyond that." She walked up to me and stroked the hair out of my face. I stared at her in fear, barely able to hold up the weight of my legs.

"Then what do you want?" I sniffled out.

"I want you," she said simply and nonchalantly as she continued to stroke my face. "I need you and only you." Just then, another, smaller girl emerged from the shadows.

"Ophelia, is everything ready?" the woman asked without leaving my gaze.

"Yes, Mother," she spoke softly and obediently.

"Perfect. Come, child." She was addressing me. "You must come with us."

She turned to walk toward her daughter, and I furrowed my brow as she moved away. "I am not coming with you," I said sternly.

"Yes, you are," she replied definitively with a mischievous grin.

Then, without consciously doing so, my feet began to move, and I started to follow them deeper into the woods. As my body was pulled forward, I tripped over roots and stones that protruded from the ground. It was impossible to keep my balance without control over my body, and the ground was nowhere near level. I fell and hit the floor; dirt, leaves, and rocks smashed against my face and palms. My body continued to crawl. At the last minute I saw my book on the ground, and while my knees shuffled me forward I reached over with my arm to retrieve it. I managed to get back up to save myself from remaining in the dirt any longer and continued to struggle against the forward movement of my legs. I tried to stop, I tried to turn around, to run away . . . but I finally gave in. I was no longer in control of my own body—somebody else was.

"Stop it!" I screamed at Carinthia. "Let me go! You can't do this to people, you witch!"

She stopped abruptly and turned around me. "I am *not* a witch!" she said, obviously offended. "They are cruel, evil creatures who garner their power from Black Magic." She continued to explain herself, "I am a Sorceress, I garner my magic from nature, in balance at all times with the elements of the universe. There is a difference, and I would appreciate your respect."

My mouth dropped open. She wanted me to respect her as she kidnapped me and dragged me through the forest? This lady was nuts.

We continued to move forward, until we hit a small clearing in the woods. I couldn't tell if it was a real clearing or if Ophelia, the young girl, had made the trees part, for we stood in a perfect circle in the middle of the forest with not a stump in sight. The tops of birch trees and pines were silhouetted against the night sky and a full moon shone in the background. In the center of the circular clearing was a stone slab illuminated by several strategically placed candles, which, as I approached, I noticed were floating in the air.

My body, still under Carinthia's control, had me lie down on the slab. Once there, roots rose up from the ground and bound my arms and legs. They tightened their grip, and I could not move even an inch. At this point, I realized there was no escape plan. I had no magical powers, no super Imati strength, and no ability to jump out of my body. I was trapped, a mere mortal, tied to a stone slab. In the scheme of things, I was pretty much as powerless as the world can make a person.

Around me, Carinthia and Ophelia released elements into the air with various fragrances. I thought I smelled sage and lavender, but I wasn't sure if that was them or the Maine forest air. I could barely see my captors, since my vision was involuntarily directed upwards toward the sky. I felt like a doll that had come to life internally but could not move my own porcelain body. It was both frustrating and terrifying at the same time. I stared at the stars above me; they were completely visible, since we were in the middle of nowhere, devoid of any city lights to obstruct their glow. They twinkled sporadically, and I imagined the grand scope of the universe. What else was out there? There were clearly other worlds and other realms, as I had recently discovered, and I wondered if I was staring at them right now.

My existential thoughts were broken as I suddenly felt the cold steel of a knife slice into my left wrist. I screamed and writhed in pain, but I was held down by my shackles made of roots. They were still alive, because they tightened as I struggled against them. The more they tightened, the more the stinging sensation in my wrist worsened. It was like rubbing salt in a wound. My mortal flesh was weak, and the stinging cut caused silent tears to drip from my eyes. Just as the pain was becoming constant, my right wrist was sliced open as well. More pain. I tried to focus on anything else except for my arms, which I wished I could separate from my body. I closed my eyes and concentrated. Still in pain. I opened them and took a deep breath. I calmed my breathing, made it strategic. I matched my breathing with the pain. I tried to gain control of my surroundings. It felt hopeless. I could feel the warm blood drain down my arm. I turned from left to right to see the wounds, but all I could see was a red pool of blood collecting beneath my elbow. For someone who rarely bled, I sure was making up for that tonight.

Carinthia began to chant, and as far as I could tell, her daughter was out of sight. "White Doves, I beseech thy power, thy grace, and thy light . . . find what has now been lost, but will be again." As she spoke, I could feel a surge of energy wash over me. Her voice stopped, and I felt a trickle of cold water hit my arm. When I looked over, I discovered it was my own blood. A small stream of thick silver flowed out of my wrist, striping the pool of blood, creating a swirling effect like a small peppermint candy. The mercury-like substance had returned to my body. *This is weird.* After this fleeting moment of confusion over why my blood was changing elementally, I was once again surged into a state of extreme pain as the wounds grew deeper. I started to feel dizzy and lightheaded. I was losing too much blood. The world felt like it was spinning. I could hear Carinthia clap as she called over Ophelia to take a look at her accomplishment.

"Look at this, look at this—the Imati blood is still there. It glows. I knew she was the one!" she said happily, and then added, "You see, the Imati aren't the only ones with great power!"

I could see their faces above me now. They were slightly blurred and wobbly, but I could feel the look in their eyes. They both stared at me like I was the freak show at a carnival, basking in my obvious suffering. The pain was worsening, and I could once again feel my life draining away. I closed my eyes and focused on something happy, something less painful than my piercing wounds.

Connor's face was the first happy thing to come to mind: his dark hair, his blue eyes, and his cute British accent. Everything about him was magnificent, and his image brought a comforting feeling to me. I could almost feel the fire between us; the unnerving feeling that comes with being around someone who is so perfect for you, the serene bliss that blankets your soul when you are in their presence. I needed that blanket now. I remembered our evening walks through town, the summer bonfire, our first paintball date, school, the coffee shop. Our relationship played in my mind like a home movie. I remembered how nervous and excited I had been when he was coming over to my house. How he held my hand on the couch as we watched movies. I had felt safe then. To think that was less than a week ago was mind-boggling. I let the images and comfort of Connor take me into a deep sleep. I felt sorry that I would never see him again and that I would die without telling him one last time that I loved him. The more I faded away, the harder it became to concentrate. I wondered where he was, and if by some miracle he could come save me.

My eyes opened suddenly from their deep sleep as a bright light flashed across the sky and lit up the night. It was so fleeting that I was not sure if it had really happened, or if I was merely going mad on the brink of death. A wave of heat rolled across my body. The hairs on my arms and legs stood up again. A new presence had entered the circle, and I could feel it. A black shadow flew in front of me. I heard Ophelia scream in the distance; she made a long, wailing sound, like her heart had been manually ripped from her chest. Instantly, the floating candles went out. I blinked and tried to keep my eyes open. My wrists were still bleeding, and my arms felt like lead weights that could not be lifted from the stone slab. I tried to move and the roots loosened. I sat up, dizzy and confused. I swayed back and forth, unable to find my equilibrium. I could barely see, and my body was failing me. I looked straight ahead and saw a cloud of dust in the night air. As it settled, I noticed it form a blanket over a lump on the ground. I squinted my eyes to make out the shape and I saw Carinthia's body lying on the floor, perfectly still, covered in debris. She was dead. I was alone in the forest. Too weak to continue to keep my head up and revel in my captor's death, I let gravity pull me back toward the stone, which was stained with my own blood. I lay back down and waited for the cold to overtake me.

An arm began to shake me. "Alastrina! Alastrina! Wake up . . . wake up!" I could hear the voice, but I couldn't move. I tried to open my eyes but I couldn't. "Dammit, Alastrina, wake up! Don't let me be too late. Please, after all these years, don't die on me. I need you, Alastrina." I almost didn't recognize the voice it was so out of place, but the more he spoke, the more I knew who it was. Tegan had come back for me. The warm feeling of joy and elation blocked out the excruciating pain in my wrists, and for a brief second I felt safe. I slowly lifted my eyelids and saw above me his beautiful, blond, glowing face.

"Tegan . . ." I whispered.

"Yes, I am here. You are safe now." He stroked my cheek and hugged me, a rarity for him. He lifted me up and carried me like a child. As we walked, I could only muster a few words. "What happened?" I asked. "Where is Carinthia?"

Tegan continued to walk forward, without breaking his stride for even a second. "I killed the Sorceress, Alastrina, but the small girl got away. I chased her and she disappeared. I felt that saving your life was more important."

"She's dead," I said, more to myself than to him. Something about her death pained me. She was so freely powerful, and even though she had tried to kill me, I felt oddly connected to her. The thought of her death was disconcerting.

"Tegan . . ." I began.

"Yes, Alastrina," he replied.

"I knew you would come back for me." With those last words, I passed out, unsure of where we were going or how Tegan was able to find me.

Tegan – The Immortal Realm – Present Day

TEGAN STOOD BEFORE the Council, exhausted. He had been arguing with them for hours, and the more time that passed, the closer Alastrina came to death. He reiterated the statement he had said a thousand times: "The Sorceress is opening the Gate and we *must* stop her." Tegan pleaded his case, but felt he was getting nowhere. It seemed once the Council's mind was made up, there was no changing it.

"It is not our place to meddle in the lives of mortals, Tegan. There is nothing we can do." The Council all nodded in agreement, putting forth their standard argument of noninterference.

"This is absurd. She is opening the Gate to the Damned! She does not know of these powers, and once opened it will be impossible to close. Mortals and non-mortals alike will die!" Tegan felt like he was speaking to brick walls and no amount of words could break them down.

"Tegan, we understand your concern, but it is not our world, and if they choose to rupture the very fabrics which protect them, that is their own path to follow." The Eternal Council stared him down and continued to chastise him. "Plus, your judgment is clouded by your love for the girl."

A muttering of disapproval erupted from the room. Tegan's attachment to Alastrina had always been a sore subject in his dealings with the Council.

Tegan, while unable to muster a large amount of emotion, became as furious as a Sidhe could be. "She will die, and the opening of the Gate will unleash a war in the Mortal Realm that could otherwise be avoided."

"It is not our place" was their only response.

"It is your place!" Tegan said firmly. "You intervene all the time when it suits you. You send Seekers and Souljumpers to do your dirty work. Why not now? A war in the Mortal Realm cannot possibly be in our best interests. Besides, if they can open that Gate, others will follow, and soon they will open *this* Gate and be able to stand before you, jaded and angry at your refusal to help them."

The Council slammed their fists. "They will never find this Gate; our universe is too far for them to reach. You know this, so do not threaten us with impossible situations." The Council was growing impatient with Tegan's request to enter the Mortal Realm and dangerously alter the future, just to save the life of a mere mortal.

Tegan did not want to threaten the Council, but he saw no other way to get through to them. Their complete lack of compromise made him more resolute to leave, with or without their permission. "I will go, and I will save her. You cannot stop me, for I am free to leave of my choosing." Tegan firmly stood his ground, never before having challenged the Council in such a manner.

They met his gaze and stared Tegan down. If their eyes had been swords, they would have sliced right through Tegan's skull. He would not flinch. The Council gathered for a brief moment, and then unexpectedly resigned their refusal on the matter.

"Fine. You may go, but be warned, Tegan: you can never come back. It is your choice. You are free to leave, but we are free to close the Gate to your soul. Take a moment to contemplate this, and choose wisely, son."

Tegan was shocked at their decision. To ban him from the Immortal World was a cruel punishment indeed. He had never lived in the Mortal Realm for a permanent period of time before—well, his version of permanent—and he was not sure Alastrina's life was worth sacrificing his relationship with the Eternal Council. He took a moment to think about his decision. He pictured Alastrina, and how completely alone and helpless he had left her. It was painful to think of her dying, bleeding to death and with no one even trying to save her. In a hundred years, would he be able to forgive himself for her death, or would he constantly carry the guilt of a murderer?

He decided he could not stand by and let her die. "Have it your way," he said. The Council looked confused by his statement, unsure if he was staying, as they wanted, or leaving forever.

They must have assumed he was bluffing, because they did not open the portal for him, so instead he would have to use another method. He took out his dagger and held it high in the air for all to see. The Council gasped as they realized what he was doing. In one swift slice, Tegan brought down the dagger with a violent force and ripped a hole through the fabric of his universe and shot down to earth as a bolt of lightning, forever changing the future of the Mortal Realm—and his very own existence.

Belfast, Maine – October – Present Day

Revelations

WHEN I AWOKE, I was in Bill's living room. A crowd of people stood around me, concerned looks splashed across their faces, and worry laced their questions. All of the noise was jumbled and I couldn't make out the separate voices. *Is she okay? What happened? There is so much blood. She looks dead. How did this happen? Wait, she is moving.*

"Everyone calm down. Alastrina, are you awake?" Tegan's voice was finally distinct among the murmurs of death.

"Yeah," I said, weak and groggy.

Too much had happened in the last few hours, and my body was beginning to crash on me. I looked around the room. Everyone was there: Scarlett, Bill, and Tegan all stood around me, forming a half circle. My eyes surveyed the room for Connor, but I did not see him.

"Where is Connor?" I asked instinctively, momentarily forgetting our fight and how he'd abandoned me after my attack from Quinn. I guess he'd technically saved me also. *Ugh—now my head hurts as much as my body.*

"I'm here," his voice came from the back of the room.

When I looked through the crowd I could see him sitting in the corner, sulking. He got up to come talk to me. "I'm right here, Ally." I could see the guilt on his face. He probably felt like my near-death experience was his fault. He knelt down beside me. "I'm sorry I left you," he said, his eyes starting to well up. "When Tegan brought you through the door, I thought"—he paused, trying to compose himself—"I thought he was carrying a corpse."

Connor grabbed me and pulled me into him, his strength wrapped around me so tightly that my bruised body stabbed with pain. I didn't care; it was worth it to have his arms comforting me once again.

Bill interrupted our moment. "Well, now that she is awake, maybe we can figure out what happened—and why this Sidhe is here." Bill pointed to Tegan like he was a rat that needed to be destroyed.

"Yes," Scarlett agreed. "Ally . . . are you okay to speak?" I looked at all of their faces. They were all apprehensive and confused. Connor must have told them about our run-in with Quinn, and how I had hid the book from all of them, and then Tegan must have filled in what happened in the forest. What else did they need to know?

"You can start from where I left you, Ally," Connor said. "They already know about Quinn, but Tegan, or whoever he is, said he wouldn't speak until you woke up."

I looked at Tegan, wondering why he had kept so mum, and he looked away. I began to tell my story about the woman, the car accident, and the ritual. "She said she wanted *me*," I said as I wrapped up the night's events. "Not the book, just me."

"You have the Book of Lazarus?" Scarlett and Bill gasped at the same time. Connor, in an attempt to protect me, had not told them that valuable piece of information yet. I instantly regretted mentioning it. "Yes," I admitted. "I have had it since I was in Ireland. I never knew what it was."

I brought out the book from under my shirt and put it on the floor next to me. All of them eyed it like hungry vultures circling their prey. Tegan stayed quiet. No doubt he, too, was shocked it was in my possession; however, he made no indication and his face remained still as stone. I didn't know exactly how much he knew of Imati power. He never recognized my necklace, so I reasoned he was more or less in the dark on the matter. The book, sitting out in the open, suddenly became like an elephant in the room, so I slid it back behind me as not to distract everyone. Their trances broke and they went straight back to interviewing me.

"What I don't understand," Connor began, "is why some witch with magical powers would be trying to kill Ally."

"She's a Sorceress, not a witch." Tegan finally broke his silence. "And I killed her. So it's done. The bigger problem is that Alastrina is in too fragile of a state right now. We need to make her immortal again."

Connor grimaced at Tegan's dismissal of his question. I could tell from Tegan's response that he didn't trust anyone in the room enough to tell them what was really happening. They all looked to me to clarify what he had just said. I shook my head. "I am just as confused as all of you," I responded. Then I grabbed Tegan's hand. "Tegan, please tell us what is going on. You can trust us."

Tegan hesitated. He was kneeling on the floor beside me, and then stood up to address the room like a teacher in a classroom full of kindergarteners. He spilled everything he knew in one solid breath: "According to an ancient prophecy, Alastrina's blood has the ability to open Gates to other realms, because her life currently straddles this world and the next. As long as she is mortal, her blood can act as a key using Blue Magic."

Everyone was silent, and still confused. Scarlett held her stoic gaze, but I doubted she was well-versed in the art of Magic. Tegan took their blank expressions as motive to further explain. "The Sorceress thought she was opening the Gate to Lost Souls, in order to find her fallen husband. Unfortunately, the opening of the Gates is random, and the closest realm to your own—the Gate which is most likely to open—is that of the Damned." He paused as he awaited our reaction, as if we were supposed to be well-versed in the different realms. He sighed and continued, "It's like opening Pandora's box. It will unleash demons and damned souls that will enter and wreak havoc on your world."

We all stared at him in shock and disbelief. Connor was the first to speak. "So this Sorceress was trying to unleash Hell, basically?" he said while simultaneously laughing. "That's the most ridiculous thing I have ever heard!" Tegan did not find Connor's mocking amusing. I, too, however, was skeptical.

Scarlett furiously turned toward Connor. "You're daft, boy; it's not ridiculous. Haven't you been paying attention? We all wanted that book in order to find the portal to the Immortal Realm. Now a Sidhe tells you it's possible, and you laugh?" Her tone was brutal as she chastised Connor like a misbehaved schoolboy. "Cornelius, as we speak, is waiting to transcend. Now, I don't know why you think this is all so funny, but in my opinion, this puts us closer to the Gate than ever!"

Tegan quickly shot a worried look toward Scarlett. "*That's* why you all want that book . . . to find the portal?" Tegan demanded. He looked so angry and his voice was so fierce that Scarlett actually took a seat and looked to Bill to respond.

Bill stuttered, and then composed his words carefully. "Well, technically, it's to get Alastrina's immortality back, but the ritual to open the Gate is in there as well . . . a ritual that does not involve Ally's blood, of course." Bill, obviously nervous speaking to Tegan, also took a seat.

Tegan growled, "Yes, I know of the ritual. I have heard of the ancient Imati powers, but I didn't realize this"—he pointed toward the book that was behind me—"was *that* collection of power. I have never seen it before." Tegan paced the room, and then he suddenly knocked all the books from the shelf to the floor in one swoop of his arm. Everyone froze.

"You idiots! This book was hidden for a reason. The ancient Imatis knew this power was too much for even them, so they ceased their ignorant practices—and here you all are, trying to conjure up lost magic."

The room fell silent. Tegan sat on the green suede couch in the middle of Bill's living room and contemplated his next move. The cushions sank beneath his weight, and he looked awkward in his position. I remained on the floor, still broken and weak from Carinthia's knife.

Connor came over to sit next to me and whispered in my ear, "I'm glad you're okay, Ally. If Tegan hadn't killed that Sorceress, I would have hunted her down if it was the last thing I ever did."

I looked up at Connor and whispered back, "I love you and I never want you to leave ever again," and I rested my head in his lap.

He brushed my face with his hand and then leaned in to kiss me on the cheek. "Promise?" he said.

I turned to look up at him. "It's you and me now, forever."

Asher Lamont – Dublin, Ireland – 1726

ASHER ANXIOUSLY PACED back and forth across the tiny room of the Black Roof Inn. He had spent most of the evening downstairs in the drinking hall guzzling pint after pint of ale, trying desperately to pass the time. After hours of failing to drown his feelings in drunkenness, he finally told the innkeep to send any messengers up to his room. His apprentice, Maxwell, was already a day late, and Asher felt in his bones that something had gone awry. If Maxwell couldn't find the package, all would be lost. Growing more and more impatient, he kicked the small wooden table resting against the eastern wall. It flew upward and crashed down with a bang. Splices of wood now littered the floor. "Dammit, Maxwell!" Asher cursed his dear friend for making him wait so long.

The silence of the room was broken by the sound of heavy riding boots running up the stairs. Asher ran to the door and peered down the short hallway. He saw the black, tussled mane of his apprentice, out of breath and looking confused. "Oy, Max," he said, motioning for Max to enter. "In here, quickly!"

In between deep breaths, Maxwell began to apologize for his tardiness. "Sorry, Asher, God knows I tried to get back as quickly as possible."

"Were there problems? Do the Seekers know?" Asher was more than concerned that the Seekers knew of ancient Imati power and that they, too, were in search of the Book of Lazarus and it's scroll, which Asher had valiantly protected for the last thirty years. Due to this paranoia, he had asked his most trusted friend to use his key and retrieve Lazarus from its secret hiding place.

"No, not those problems. I think the Seekers are in the dark. Lux et Veritas is on the trail, but even they aren't sure exactly why. However . . ." Maxwell paused.

"What, Maxwell? You look ill." Asher could see the pain in Maxwell's face.

"I ran into a mystic, from the Order of Ajna."

"Did she try to kill you?"

"No, she said she came as a warning. She prophesied that they were coming for us. All of them, and in full force."

Asher took this grave news with a heavy heart. He knew that when the Seekers were sending Lux et Veritas to do their dirty work, it was a dire situation. Asher had felt for some time that he was being hunted. He could feel the shadows lurking, and the ghosts on his back. He knew that soon he would die. That was the real reason behind sending Maxwell to retrieve the package, only he had not admitted it to himself until now.

"Max. I need to ask a favor." Asher looked at his friend with pleading eyes.

"Anything—you know I would die for you." He truly meant it.

"You're a good man, Max, but I need you to stay alive. They will come for me first; they know of me more. We must separate for a few years, so they cannot track us. Also . . ." Asher paused. He wasn't quite sure how to ask Max the favor he was about to propose. "In case I die, I need you to send that package to someone. It's pertinent that she have it."

Max took a moment to think about Asher's request. If Asher died, he would want to keep the package himself, but he knew this would be wrong. His friend trusted him with sacred power, and he vowed to himself to fulfill a dying man's wish.

"Of course, Asher. I hate to think of such comings, but I will deliver this wherever you choose. But I must ask: will you not put this person in danger with such a gift?"

Asher had already thought of this. "No," he replied. "No one will know her. It will be safer in *her* hands than any other."

Maxwell nodded with comprehension, but a flicker in his eyes gave away his lack of comfort in their situation.

"What is it, Max?" Asher asked.

"You know it is *just* the Book of Lazarus, correct?" He cleared his throat. "There was no scroll."

"I know," Asher replied confidently. "They were separated. In these times, it is too dangerous to keep them together."

The two men stared at each other for a moment, each knowing that the other, within mere years, would be dead. The Seekers had discovered them, and it was now only a matter of time. While a few years in a human life would be treasured as a gift, for two Imati they felt like fleeting seconds. Asher had been on this earth for over two hundred years, and now his life was coming to an end. His last moments would be spent running, fighting, and desperately trying to stay alive.

He walked over to Max and gave him a hug. "Good to see you again, friend. And thank you."

"Asher, you were the greatest mentor I could have asked for. Hopefully, the fates that have been cast are wrong and we will meet again soon." He said the words, but knew they held no weight. "Where will you go?"

"I might make my way to France. Better you not know. But first, I must stop in Cork." Asher assumed that Maxwell already knew this.

"I see." Maxwell knew all too well why Asher would go to Cork, and now was the time to ask the question he had been avoiding. "Asher, why not use the power in the book? Give her eternal life!"

Asher had contemplated this for many years, but he knew he could never do it. "I can't," he said. "I am not God, and I do not wish to be."

"Well then, tell her I say hello, and best of luck, dear friend." Maxwell placed a friendly hand on his shoulder. If it were him, he would choose to play God.

"I will," he replied. As Asher left the Black Roof Inn and readied his horse for the journey to Cork, he glanced up at the tiny window where Maxwell peered down. There was a soft glow of candlelight illuminating from the room. It was the last time the two men would ever see each other.

The journey to Cork was a three-day ride. Asher pushed his horse harder and harder to the point of exhaustion. He was in a rush to reach the village just beyond the city walls and see the woman he knew he loved. Falling in love with a mortal was never part of the plan, especially not Asher's plan. However, he knew from the moment he saw her that she was his. In life, complications always arise, but in this case there was no solution, no pragmatic way to look at things. Logic was useless. Asher would never age, and the love of his life would someday die. It was one of God's cruel tricks, and there was no way to fight it.

As Asher came closer and closer to the small village, he put his worrying thoughts aside. He had not seen her in several months, and was afraid her love for him would have faded like a burned-down candle, and all that would be left was a waxy stub unable to light for even a second.

It was nighttime when he arrived at the small peasant hut. He hated that she lived like this, but knew it was not his place to change her circumstances; it would only make things harder than they needed to be. In fact, Asher knew that he had already plunged too deep and there was no way out of it; he was trying his best to make sure she still had a normal semblance of a life. He knocked on the door. He heard voices inside, and the small scuttling of feet could be heard from just beyond the door. A very petite young woman opened the door. She must have been no older than twenty years of age. She stared at Asher in disbelief. She knew he was coming, but the sight of him still took her breath away. Instantly she was in his arms. He breathed in the scent of her. Her hair, her neck, her clothes; all of it was intoxicating. Asher did not want to break away, for the words to be spoken would be those of good-bye.

"I'm so glad you're here," she said. Her thick Irish accent gave away her low-class status immediately.

"I rode as fast as I could," Asher said as he desperately clung to her.

"Come, let us go fer a walk." She grabbed his hand and motioned for him to follow her.

"Wait," Asher paused. "Is *he* here?"

"No. He has been away a few weeks now." Asher's heart almost jumped out of his chest at the realization that her husband was away from Cork for the time being. This was his chance.

"Can I see her?" he asked timidly. In the three years that his daughter had been alive, Asher had only seen her a few times, and each fleeting moment was more special than the last. He never planned on having a child, especially not with a mortal, but it was fate, and thus out of his control.

"She is inside, playing with Cordelia." The young woman pointed to the back corner of the room, and Asher peered inside. Sitting next to a dark-haired child Asher knew was Cordelia was a radiant, golden girl, glowing from within. He walked up to her and sat beside her. The child looked up at him curiously with big green eyes, which mimicked those of a cat. Her hair fell down her tiny back and shone brightly next to the fire.

"Hello there, Alastrina, my name is Asher," Asher said with trepidation in his voice. The child looked from the man in front of her to the reassuring face of her mother. She said nothing.

"She's a bit shy," her mother said.

"Well, she doesn't know me. Not yet." Asher looked to his lover; from the look on her face, he knew that he would never get the chance to know Alastrina. Not in this lifetime. He grabbed a small object wrapped in paper from his sack and handed it to the small girl.

"What's that?" the mother asked.

"An apple," he said. "For Alastrina."

"As-sher," the child spoke suddenly and grasped the shiny apple in her hand. Her happiness broke the blanket of sadness, which had covered the room just a moment before. Asher beamed with pride at the mention of his name. He stared at the beauty of her, and the pit in his stomach told him she was different. She would inherit his life and there was nothing he could do to stop it.

"Let us go," the young woman said. "We'll talk out back."

They left the room of innocence for the dark night of Ireland and cold reality. Asher stared at her and she began to silently sob.

"I have to go away for a little while," he began. "Some terrible things are happening, and I need to disappear."

"Take me with you." She whispered it knowing that they were the four words she shouldn't say.

"I can't. You have a family, and a husband, and a life. All I can offer you is death."

"Without you I want to die." She squeezed his hand and brought her mouth up to kiss his cheek. "You are everything to me."

"I wish I were different. I wish it wasn't like this. If I stay, I will die. If I take you with me, you will die. I love you too much to be responsible for that."

Asher so badly wanted to grab his love and her children and run away, but at some point the same problem would occur, over and over again, like a never-ending plague, taking as many souls along the way as it could capture. She would age, her children would age, and someday he would helplessly stand by and watch them as the life was slowly sucked out of them and the light no longer shone behind their eyes. In two hundred years, Asher had seen too many people he loved die and was no longer willing to partake in their demise.

"I love you so much, Asher. Alastrina loves you too, but I worry about her. She is different, I know it. You saw her, she is . . . glowing." She stopped and took a deep breath. "I think my husband knows. He doesn't like her, won't even look at her sometimes. She is too beautiful, just like you."

Asher smiled. "No, she takes after her mother." He kissed her forehead. "I do believe that she is different, but there is no way to be certain. Thus I have something important to tell you, and you must remember this carefully." She looked at him, her eyes wide and eager to receive whatever he was about to tell her.

"In the event that I die, I am sending you a package. It is for Alastrina, and only her. You must remember to tell her that she is special, and that the necklace will protect her."

"What necklace?" she asked, suddenly fearful of the harsh reality that Asher was bringing into her life.

"It will be in the package. Without it, she will be lost. All will be lost, do you understand? It is a key, and it is charmed to protect her from all the evils that come with being of our kind."

"I will tell her. When she is older, I will explain everything to her. She will know her real father, and love him as much as I did." She hugged him and began to stroke the hair on the back of his head. "Stay with me tonight." It was both a question and a command.

Asher smiled. "Always."

"I love you, Asher, for tonight, for tomorrow, and forever."

"My Fia, my beautiful little Fia, forever is a long time."

Belfast, Maine – October – Present Day

Goodbye

ON THE OTHER side of the room were Bill and Scarlett, still somber from Tegan's lashing. Both of them sulked in their separate chairs, thinking about this new information. It seemed like neither one believed Tegan, and they had come so far in their quest for the book that there was no turning back.

Bill got up first and addressed the room. "This is absurd. *He* is a Sidhe. He is practically an envoy to the Eternal Council; whatever he tells us is just an attempt to protect their interests."

Tegan glared at Bill's remark. "That's not true; I am here of my own volition. They did not send me, nor did they want me to come."

Bill made a *humph* sound. "You expect us to believe you went against the Council? I don't think so, compadre. That's impossible . . . I know from experience."

Tegan looked away, no longer wishing to engage in a confrontation with Bill. Scarlett, listening to their argument, jumped up from her chair and straightened out her dress. She looked fabulous compared to me and my swollen body. "Souljumper here is right: a Sidhe can't be trusted. He would lie to keep us from reaching the Immortal Realm." Bill nodded in agreement, but Scarlett didn't notice or care. Instead, she walked over to Connor and me, and while I thought she was coming to hug me, she reached around my back and grabbed the book. "Sorry, Ally, Cornelius is waiting for this." To my surprise, it did not turn to stone as it had all the other times.

I was so surprised that the book remained leather and paper that I couldn't speak. Scarlett continued to walk away, back toward the door.

"You are a fool if you use that to open the portal," Tegan said from the couch. The tension in the room was building, like a slow-heating oven.

"Then I am a fool," Scarlett said.

She grabbed her bag and marched for the door. Right then, Bill jumped in front of her. "Where do you think you are going with that?" he demanded as he reached for the book.

Scarlett quickly moved it away so he could not grab it. "Now, now, Bill, don't be hasty. This is my book and I am leaving with it."

She turned around to address the rest of us. "It really has been a pleasure seeing you all again; Tegan, wonderful to see you are still Ally's white knight. Unfortunately, I must bid you all farewell—toodles."

She went to exit, but Bill would not move from her path. "Scarlett, give me the book," he demanded.

She leaned in closer to his ear. "I don't think so, *Saturo*," she said, and then she pulled out a small knife and stabbed him in the gut. Blood poured out of Bill's stomach and stained his shirt red. He gaped at her, shocked by what she had just done. Scarlett, as always, was unfazed. "Don't think I forgot Madrid, Cayden. Have fun dying; see you in another life." She chuckled, and then stepped over Bill's dying body and walked out the door with the book we all needed.

Connor and Tegan ran to Bill, also in utter shock. Scarlett had stabbed him so quickly that no one had time to react. I crawled over to catch up to them.

"Bill! Oh my gosh! Bill, are you okay?" I said frantically. Connor was trying to cover his wound to stop the bleeding. Bill coughed up a large amount of blood. We all knew in our hearts that he wouldn't make it. My heart pounded against my chest in fear, but I was helpless to save him.

"Ally," he choked on his words, "I will find you."

With those last words, Bill's eyes rolled to the back of his head, and his body sank into the floor like a pile of rocks. Blood gathered all around him, still flowing from his wound.

I looked at my dead friend on the floor and began to cry. This was an example of mortality staring me straight in the face. Bill Barnes lay dead in front of me, unable to speak or breathe, foreshadowing my own future. I knew his soul would jump, but who knows when or where I would see him again. Bill was gone.

"I knew she was evil," Tegan said.

Connor and I were silent for a minute. Then, after the silence became unbearable, I decided to ask what everyone else was thinking. "What do we do now?"

Tegan stood up. "We have to stop Cornelius from using that book to open the Gate; he doesn't understand what he will unleash."

Connor agreed with Tegan. "Great, we stop Cornelius and save the world. Sounds like a plan." He obviously wasn't as devastated by Bill's death as I was.

"It's not that simple," Tegan said. "We also need to make sure these Seekers don't find Ally, and more than likely the girl from the woods will come back to look for her mother and see if she is still alive."

I remembered Ophelia's scream; she must have seen her mother being killed by Tegan, which prompted her to disappear.

"You think Ophelia will try and finish what her mother started?" I asked Tegan.

Connor suddenly looked up, a pained expression on his face. "Who?" he asked.

"Ophelia," I responded. "Her mother Carinthia was there, too . . . why?"

Connor's face went white and his eyes froze, looking straight ahead, lost in thought.

"Connor, are you okay?" I asked him as I got up and placed a hand on his shoulder.

He stepped back. "What?" He looked confused. "Yeah, I'm fine . . . it's nothing." Tegan dubiously measured his reaction, unsure of what was happening in Connor's mind. I, too, was perplexed.

"Yes, I think Ophelia could come back." Tegan continued the conversation where we had left off before Connor's interruption. "That being said, Alastrina, I need to speak with you . . . alone." Connor shot an angry look toward Tegan. He still did not fully understand who Tegan was or what my relationship with him had been. I wasn't sure why, but Connor never saw even a glimpse of Tegan when he read my memories that fateful night at my house.

I motioned for him to go to the other side of the room. He reluctantly left us, allowing Tegan and I to speak in private.

Tegan stepped in front of me, partially blocking my view of Connor. I looked up at him anxiously, waiting for him to speak. "First of all," he began, "are you okay? Your wounds are bad, but the wrapping should hold for now."

I swallowed hard. "I know," I said. "I think I will be fine in a day or two, just mainly sore." Really, though, I had no idea how long it took a mortal's body to heal.

He nodded, glad to know I wasn't quite dead yet. He looked around to make sure Connor was completely on the other side of the room. "In that case, I have something important to tell you," he began once Connor was out of earshot. "I believe we will be able to successfully perform whatever ritual is in the book to give you back your immortality." He placed his hand on my shoulder like he was asking me a great favor. "I trust that is what you want, correct?"

Before I could answer, I looked past him and saw Connor on the opposite side of the room, staring out the window toward the night sky. He looked sadder than he did before, like he had just lost something. He looked back at me as I spoke to Tegan, and I could see tears welling up in his eyes. He mouthed the words *I love you* and then looked away. Now I understood why Tegan had wanted to speak to me alone. I turned my attention back to Tegan, who was still waiting for me to respond. I didn't speak. I didn't entirely know what to say.

"Alastrina, I know you love Connor, but in this body you will surely die if you remain a mortal—and if Cornelius does open the Gate, you will not last more than five seconds against the demons that will pour out of it. You must be strong enough to fight."

Tegan was right; I needed to be an Imati for my own protection. I had two options: live as an immortal and someday watch Connor die, or remain mortal and possibly die myself. I looked at Connor from afar one more time.

"Yes," I said, "I want to be an Imati again."

I think.

The End

About the Author

C.T. Hillin graduated from Yale University in 2007 with a degree in Political Science. As a screenwriter from Los Angeles, she has had several movies produced including "A Stranger in Paradise" and "Pernicious" -- a horror flick directed by James Cullen Bressack, which just wrapped production in Bangkok, Thailand. She previously wrote for the entertainment news website TMZ and is currently writing for *The Huffington Post*.

Her love for history—a major inspiration for The Imati—is due to her own world travels, from studying abroad in Paris, filming in Thailand, and many trips around the world. She also loves dogs and popcorn.

Made in the USA
Middletown, DE
30 June 2021